# There is Always One

Margaret Alty

Published 2025 by arima publishing

www.arimapublishing.com

ISBN 978 1 84549 846 7
© Margaret Alty 2025

Typeset in Garamond

Swirl is an imprint of arima publishing.

arima publishing
Eagle House, Sudbury Road,
Great Whelnetham, Bury St Edmunds,
Suffolk IP0 0UN
t: (+44) 01284 717884

www.arimapublishing.com

# Prologue

## Ekabe, Zambia : Friday 20th October

It had rained heavily during the night. A torrential storm, unexpected and weeks before the end of the dry season. Pools of rainwater had collected in front of the smashed door of the bungalow; shards of glass had scattered across the tiled floor, some of them embedded in the hand-woven rug in the centre of the room. Footprints, muddied and indistinct, led the way across to the hall and the open door to the kitchen to where they had abruptly ended in a pool of blood already congealed and staining the tiles a dark ugly rust colour.

The bungalow was one of twenty, equidistant from its neighbours, and forming a section of the semi-circle backing on to the college building and playing fields; the whole area fending off the encroaching bush by shoulder-height wire fencing, culminating at either end by round-the-clock security guards.

When the police arrived shortly before dawn and began their questioning no-one professed to hearing any disturbance during the night, and even if they had, it's debatable whether they would have taken any notice, having grown more than a little complacent relying on such fort-like protection.

A thorough search in and around the vicinity of the bungalow was made as soon as it was light the only evidence the forensic team came up with was a trail of blood leading out to the car park at the side of the building, but no sign of any vehicle.

It was virtually impossible to know the time of the break-in, only that it must have been between the hours of seven the previous evening and shortly before sunrise at five-thirty on the Friday morning with the start of domestic activity around the campus.

At four-thirty in the afternoon two school children on their walk back to their village spotted a pick-up truck among a mass of undergrowth, its front wheels balanced at the lip of the gorge, below which the river roared its way down to join the Zambezi. They'd had the presence of mind to memorize the registration number and ran back to Ekabe to report their find to the police. The college were quick to confirm that it matched the missing vehicle allocated to Alan Lorimer, one of their lecturers.

In the absence of a body, although with strong evidence that a murder if not committed had been intended, the case was passed to the coroner to reach a decision The investigation carried out met with the legal criteria and his verdict was duly issued, stating that in the absence of a body, he had to rely on circumstantial evidence; namely, a presumption of death verdict.

Theoretically, the case still remained open although the police appeared to be taking no further action with their enquiries, the consensus of opinion, certainly among fellow expatriates, that it had been a rare break-in, a random and un-premeditated act by out of town thugs who, when disturbed, had panicked, over-powering their victim, forcing him to drive away from the bungalow and finishing off their assault at the edge of the ravine.

A brief mention of the incident was made in the English-speaking newspaper with an added piece from the college, albeit of few words, suffice to say that they had lost a fine and much respected lecturer and that he would be sorely missed by his colleagues and students.

# Chapter One

'It's from Alan.'

'I thought I recognized his writing; what does he have to say?'

'Read it for yourself, Myra; he's truly surpassed himself this time.' Callum said, passing his brother's letter across the breakfast table to her and, not wanting to see how her expression would change when she reached the last paragraph, he stood up. and taking his half-drunk coffee with him walked over to the French windows, turning the key and pushing the door open.

The early morning mist was clearing; a light gauze-like silvery screen drifting slowly over the stream at the far end of the lawn. No signs yet of an end to the Indian summer he thought, stepping out on to the terrace. noticing how the heavy downpour of the night before had left patches on the terracotta tiles. Even the roses bordering the gravel pathway had not escaped; droplets of moisture balancing delicately on their silky petals. The rattan chairs were still damp and would need to be wiped before anyone could use them. Random observations, barely skimming his consciousness and entirely at odds with what he was really thinking.

Alan's letter. It had been entirely unexpected, and he needed these few moments to himself; to try and fathom out why his brother had felt the need to contact him in such a way when an email would have been immediate. Surely, he must be aware of the vagaries of the postal service between here and that god-forsaken place where he'd decided to hide himself away for the past eighteen months. Or, he thought bitterly, what was wrong with the phone.

The news of Alan's impending divorce hadn't been all that surprising, but learning there was another woman in his life certainly had been. Cora she was called. Cora Hamilton. Sounds Scottish, not that he'd bothered to elaborate. He couldn't have known her for long, but then as they had scarcely communicated over the past eighteen months, that was no surprise either. But what did any of that matter – Alan's private life was hardly relevant: this news that he would soon be home was.

'Well,' Myra said coming up from behind him, Alan's letter in her hand, 'he's a dark horse, isn't he? Pity he couldn't have been more informative, but at least he's doing something positive about his disastrous marriage and we're unlikely to see Valerie again. Thank God.'

'Is that all you can say?' turning to face her and practically snatching the letter from her.

'Good Lord, Callum, why on earth are you getting so agitated? Your normally level-headed brother has finally decided to make what I suppose, for him that is, a much overdue change to his otherwise predictable life.'

'More to the point, Myra, he's neglected to explain why he's cut short his contract out there; he's still another six months to go. This unpremeditated return is not going to help the smooth-running of the business; I'm now going to have to spend time re-organizing everything. And what about John Milne? Once Alan is back, his services will no longer be required, which means I'm going to have the unpleasant task of telling the man we're going to have to sever *his* contract! More bloody expense!'

'You're over-reacting. As usual. It's quite obvious to me that you're only thinking about yourself. The business is thriving and will continue to do so with or without John Milne's input. It has nothing to do with cash flow either and you know it! It's time you learned to bury that chip you've being carrying around for goodness knows how long. Give Alan some slack, Callum! He deserves happiness after years of putting up with a woman who only married him for his money - .'

'- that's a bit harsh, isn't it?'

'I don't think so, but of course, I was forgetting.' a tiny smile hovering on her lips.

'What do you mean?' but as soon as the words were out of his mouth, he regretted them. He knew exactly what she was getting at, and he was in no mood for an argument.

'You've always liked Valerie, haven't you, Callum?' taunting him.

'I felt sorry for her, Myra.'

'You what!'

'I felt sorry for her because she made the grave error of marrying my brother. That's why.'

'My God, that remark is really pushing your paranoia to the limit, Callum.' and turning away from him, went back inside.

She just did not understand. No-one did. For over forty years, ever since his brother was born in fact, he had suffered from being the oldest: *You're the oldest, Callum, you should know better*, being one of his mother's favourite forms of appointing blame. In rare moments he had allowed himself to question why both his parents made no attempt to disguise their favouritism, but it was quite simply that Alan could do no wrong and when five years later Bruce came along it made no difference; even being the youngest, Bruce was treated with a detached disinterest. Not that being virtually ignored appeared to affect him, but then that was Bruce: resilient and seemingly impervious to any insult, veiled or otherwise.

Myra had accused him of over-reacting, but Alan's letter had done more than re-ignite the old embers of his resentment towards his brother, much more, and the very thought of her finding out was too dire to even consider. Alan hadn't given an actual date for his return, only to expect him by the end of the month. It was now the seventeenth which at the very most only gave him fourteen days. Fourteen days to remove any shred of evidence for him to pick up on as soon as he was back working, but first there was a phone call he had to make and for that he needed privacy, a near impossibility in a house which was also used as a business when, during working hours, there was always someone around. He could, he supposed, send Ben a text instead and, dialling his number, keyed in the message:

Ben, something's cropped up. Important we talk. Sometime today? Suggest the "Royal". Callum

He didn't have long to wait:

Okay. Midday.

A man of few words, but that was Ben: not much to give and a great deal to hide, and deleting the texts, he went back into the house. Myra had gone and he had the dining room to himself. He poured out the remainder of the coffee from the cafetière and sitting down, smoothed out Alan's letter and read it once more. He'd taken his first sip when his mobile rang, frowning when he saw Bruce's name come up on the display.

'Have you forgotten the board meeting, Callum; we're just about to start?'

'Hell! I'll be with you in five minutes.' scrambling to his feet and cursing under his breath: he'd allowed Alan to get to him. Again. Even thousands of miles away he had this crippling effect on him, and finishing off his coffee, he made his way along the hall to the meeting.

\*\*\*

The hall of Ashburn House formed part of the annexe to the administrative hub of their family's soft fruit business. It had been their grandfather who'd first recognized the potential of the twenty acres of land adjoining the property with its rich soil and south-facing aspect into growing fruit for the wholesale market, although it wasn't until his death some years later with the ownership passing to his only son, Graham, that the business began to flourish with investment in machinery and state of the art polytunnels, enabling them to expand competitively into the overseas market and Graham, now well on in his seventies, had made it clear to his three sons he had no intention of relinquishing his controlling interest in the business.

The door to the board room was closed, but his father's voice reached him clearly before he had even reached it, reminding him of being called to the headmaster's office as a ten year-old over some misdemeanour, so long ago he couldn't remember what it might have been, but it must have been pretty harrowing at the time if the memory was still there, and taking a deep breath, he opened the door.

'Ah, Callum, there you are. At last. Now, perhaps we can make a start.'

He made no apology for being late, knowing his father would be instantly dismissive.

*Very often, Callum, an apology is an excuse, and as you well know, I have no wish to hear one.*

Silent words, but another unwanted echo from the past.

Kirstie, his father's secretary, who'd been working for him for years, handed him a copy of the minutes of their last meeting and of that day's agenda, at the same time giving him a sympathetic smile.

Like, the rest of the family, Kirstie understood him although why she put up with him, he would never know, but then they all knew she idolized him for some unfathomable reason, so much so it was doubtful whether she even noticed how unreasonable he could be. He made no excuses for his father. How could he? Graham Lorimer, a larger-than-life character, impervious to anyone's sensitivities, low on tolerance, was totally unapproachable.

Bruce, sitting across from him, raised his eyes in the way he would often do at these meetings; meetings which their father always insisted were conducted along conventional boardroom procedures for a full complement of shareholders and directors filling the space around the twenty-foot conference table, and not merely with a handful of family members seated sparingly at one end.

Myra, still tight-lipped from earlier, hadn't looked his way once. He knew she didn't particularly enjoy these meetings, but as their Company Secretary, she had little choice but to attend them. In all the eighteen years they'd been married, he had never heard her utter one word of criticism of his father; their relationship seemed to him an amicable one. He had never asked her what she thought of him, it hadn't occurred to him, but no doubt in Graham's view, she fulfilled what he expected in a daughter-in-law: respectful: compliant and non-argumentative. His wife was smart, but then he'd always known that. She was one of those women, Callum had realised right from the early days as newly-weds when he had brought her to Ashburn House, who was quick at adapting and although it must have been something of an eye-opener to be transported from her one-bedroom flat in Edinburgh to living *en famille*, she had never complained. Theirs was a sound marriage, and he could understand her dislike for Valerie; the two women were polar opposites, regretting now for being short with her.

The meeting dragged on, his attention wavering more than once, but eventually around eleven-thirty all the points on the agenda had been covered satisfactorily, except for the request by Bruce for an increase in the travel allowance for their two sales reps which predictably had been rejected, his father agreeing with obvious reluctance that the matter would be raised for further discussion at their next board meeting, and as there had been no other business issues, Callum made to get to his feet when his father tapped his pen against the edge of the table.

'You haven't thought to mention Alan's decision to return home earlier than we expected, Callum.'

It would seem Myra had beaten him to it.

'I intended to, Father, but his letter only arrived this morning.' the best he could do, waiting for the inevitable.

'Good news should be shared, Callum, especially when it concerns the business.'

'Of course, although this sudden change in Alan's plans means we will have to make adjustments.'

'Such as?'

'John Milne's contract with us, father; once Alan is back we can't justify keeping him on therefore we will need to compensate for the shortfall in severing his two-year contract with us.'

'We're satisfied with his work?'

'Very. He's well qualified; we were lucky to get him.'

'Quite. We won't make any decisions yet, Callum, but instead we'll wait until Alan is here. Agreed?'

What could he say? *Yes, sir, yes, sir, three bags full, sir!*

'I heard that.' Bruce said, walking along beside him as they left the boardroom.

'Well, it's the case of the prodigal son, isn't it?'

'Hardly, but you should be used to the old man by now, Cal; he'll never change.'

'Don't I know it.'

'Anyway,' nudging him in the ribs, 'wonder what the girlfriend's like, eh.

7

Alan's sprung that piece of news on us, wouldn't you say?'

'Do you think she's the reason he's broken his contract?'

'It's certainly out of character, but I dare say we'll find out soon enough.'

'What did father have to say about it all; I presume Myra enlightened him.'

'Oddly, very little.'

'Hmmph, not like him, probably can't think beyond the fact that Alan's on his way home. Any idea why he's so keen to keep John on?'

'Not really; some new ideas mulling through his brain which he's not ready to tell us about until he's good and ready? You know what he's like?'

'I don't think you expect me to answer that one, but I think you could be right; about him holding back on some new plan he's been hatching.'

'Possible, I suppose.'

'Hence his objection for taking John off the payroll.'

'You've just reminded me; I've been meaning to mention it actually, but it slipped my mind.'

'About John?'

'Yes, the other evening; everyone else had left but I noticed there was a light on in your office – '

' – there shouldn't have been.'

'That's what I thought; I knew it wasn't you because I'd just seen you and Myra drive off, so I walked across the yard to check it out.'

'And it was him?'

'Yes, he was on the computer.'

'And?'

'Nothing else; I didn't go in, just watched him for a few minutes. He didn't see me; too engrossed in what he was doing I expect.'

'Perhaps you should have.'

'I know, but he didn't seem furtive or anything, and I reckoned that you would have known about him being in there.'

'This must have been after seven; Myra and I arrived at "The Shipwreck" around half-past.'

'About then, I reckon. Are you going to mention it to him?'

'I'll have a word with him later. Odd though.'

'What?'

'He's already got the code for the buying of stock on his own computer in the main office and the code for the distribution of all our products is only accessible from the hard drive in my office.'

\*\*\*

The lounge bar was filling up with the usual lunchtime crowd when he arrived shortly after twelve. Ben was already there, at one of the tables at the far end of the room and gave a brief nod of recognition when he spotted him, and ordering a beer from Andy, he walked over to join him.

'Hi, Ben.'

'Hi. So, what's the panic, Callum?'

'Not panic exactly,' pulling out the chair opposite, 'but we could have a problem.'

'We?'

'Yes, Ben. We are in this together, remember.'

'Keep your voice down.'

'Nobody can hear us.'

'Don't be so sure. Anyway, get to the point. What's up?'

'We'll have to make some radical changes to our schedule.'

'Why?' his eyes narrowing as he glared across the table at him, 'Explain.'

'Alan's on his way back.'

'What do you mean; you told me his contract was for two years and that it was more than likely he would renew it. There is a hell of a lot pending on this arrangement and one you assured me was rock solid.'

'I know, but I had a letter from him this morning. He didn't give any reason for cutting it short, only that –'

'– when, Callum?'

'The end of the month.'

'Christ! That's only a couple of weeks away!'

'We'll have to put a stop on the next deliveries.'

'For Christ's sake, Callum, get real. Apart from that being virtually impossible, I have no intention of losing out on this deal. They'll have to go ahead as planned and you will just have to make damn sure that brother of yours doesn't find out what's going on.'

'That's out of the question. Don't underestimate him, Ben, within twenty-four hours of his return he will be fully hands-on. We've no choice. We must stop them and then I'll crash the system.'

'And you believe by doing that, crashing your computer system, will solve what is far more than a problem. It's not just a glitch, Callum; it is a potential disaster!'

'What's your solution then?'

'Stop him.'

'What do you mean – stop him?'

'Exactly that. Prevent him from coming back.'

'I don't think I like the way you're thinking, Ben.'

'Tough. You know the rules.'

He knew exactly what he meant. There was no need for him to put the implication into words. He had always recognized Ben Maitland's ruthlessness, but this was the first time he had felt the full brunt of it. He may have harboured a deep-rooted dislike for Alan, but for God's sake, he was his brother. He could feel a trickle of sweat between his shoulder blades as the enormity of such an act hit him. What had he got himself into here?

'We have no choice, Callum.'

'There is always a choice.' he protested but recognizing the hopelessness in his voice.

'In this particular instance, there is no choice.'

'This has gone far enough, Ben. I'm pulling out of the syndicate, and you'll have to find someone else to handle the distributions.'

'Chickening-out, eh. Afraid it's too late in the day to do that, my friend.'

'That sounds like a threat.'

A shrug was his only answer, but one look into those ice-blue eyes, unblinking in their intensity, told him what he didn't want to know. Ben would go ahead regardless, and he was powerless to stop him. There was not one ounce of regret, compassion, or even fellow feeling in his expression.

'This could be the time to take stock, you know.' Callum said, breaking the uncomfortable silence, 'We have had a good run these past eighteen months, Ben. Perhaps it's time to cut our losses – '

' – and run, Callum, is that what you're trying to say?'

'I have a reason.'

'Christ! Will you stop talking in bloody riddles! Say what you mean or just shut up!'

'I believe that John Milne has his suspicions.'

'Who the hell is he?'

'Sorry, I was forgetting, you wouldn't know. He's our works manager on a temporary contract with us while Alan's away.'

'Go on then. What about him?'

He watched Ben closely as he repeated what Bruce had told him, but apart from a slight tightening around his jaw, he showed no other reaction.

'Why the silence,' he couldn't resist asking him, 'doesn't this – er – development worry you?'

'Worry me, Callum; not particularly, should it?'

And with that, he had to be satisfied. Ben didn't have another drink, making the excuse he had people he needed to see that afternoon, and saying he would be in touch he pushed his chair back and left..

## Chapter Two

Valerie furiously tossed her tennis racquet on to the back seat of her car. Wednesday mornings. Repetitive and predictable, when an unwritten club rule among expatriate wives, with nothing more pressing to occupy their time, were expected to meet and participate in mindless games of tennis. And why a Wednesday? Why not a Monday, Thursday, or any damn day of the long monotonous week which comprised her life. It was a miracle she had lasted this long, jabbing the key into the ignition with such force she nicked the side of her thumb, tiny spots of blood sliding across the nail. For a year and a half she had put up with this existence, she muttered, wiping away the blood with a crumpled tissue.

It had been January. The fifth. England, in post-seasonal doldrums with hung-over folk shivering in sub-zero temperatures and dire forecasts of snowstorms, as she and Alan had boarded their British Airways flight to Lusaka. Ten and a half hours later they had arrived in Zambia's capital, blasts of tropical heat enveloping them as soon as they stepped down from the plane, and it had only been seven in the morning.

"Good God, Alan!" she'd gasped, remembering how she had struggled to catch her breath, "I'll never get used to this!"

"You will." he had laughed, "you will soon become acclimatized, Valerie, you'll see."

He'd been right: it hadn't taken her long to take the climate for granted; to wake up each morning and feel warm, but he had been wrong in so many other ways. The sheer boredom for instance. He had neglected to warn her about that.

Their marriage was far from ideal, even back then, but at least she could work, that is if she'd actually wanted to. She had her own bank account. Her own independence. There were only another six months of Alan's contract left before they could leave; a fact, which as the time grew nearer, had been a slight incentive to try and act as she was expected to in such a tight-knit community. She had given little thought beyond the day when she would be in the departure lounge of Lusaka airport waiting to board their flight, but now after Alan's bombshell last night, she was not so certain about a future she had always taken for granted.

In all the years they'd been married, she had never imagined that he would be the one to want a divorce. Any such idea would have been unthinkable given his temperament: conservative, reluctant to change which she had to admit proved to be something of a misnomer when he had insisted in that dogmatic way of his, in taking two years away from the family business to follow some idealistic dream in a third world country.

He had given no real explanation why he wanted to end their marriage and, naturally, she immediately assumed meant there must be another woman.

"Who is she, Alan?" she had challenged him, "You may as well tell me; I will find out you know – "

" – don't kid yourself, Valerie," he had interrupted, "we both realise we've been unhappy together for a long time. I should never have brought you out here. I realise how much you hate it all: a completely different culture and one you've made no attempt to understand, or even tried to adapt to. It's also quite obvious you blame me, but when I say I no longer wish to be married to you, I mean it."

"And you expect me to believe that! Why wait so long, Alan, why now? It's Cora Hamilton, isn't it? Is she the new woman in your life?" but apart from a slight tightening of a muscle at the side of his neck above the collar of his shirt, she couldn't tell whether it was a reaction on hearing her name mentioned or to the effort of remaining silent.

"I'm right, aren't I?" she had persisted, "I would have thought she was rather young for you, but perhaps she's looking for maturity, or – " pausing for a fraction of a second, determined to make maximum impact, to dent that solid barrier of indifference of his, " – it could be she's looking for a man of property." goading him, but it wasn't working; without looking at her, he had turned away and picked up the book he had been reading earlier.

She was married to a stranger. That was how it felt lying next to him later; a huge space in the bed between them. Fifteen years reduced to this: a cool dismissal, no regrets for closing those years so finally and without any show of emotion. She had taken a couple of paracetamols hoping they would help her to sleep, but their affect had taken a long time to kick in. It must have been almost dawn when she felt herself drifting off, her last conscious thought that she would deal with the problem tomorrow.

She knew she was driving too fast, finding it difficult to concentrate, to ignore the anger, instead of trying to reach the club in one piece, but it wasn't until she almost mounted the pavement at the roundabout into town, she managed to ease her foot from the accelerator. One thing was certain, she would do anything to prevent Alan from divorcing her. Absolutely anything. But what? Plead with him to relent, to change his mind, to remind him of their marriage vows? But, remembering how he'd looked at her, the shut-down expression and the way he'd avoided any eye contact, made her realise she would be wasting her breath. Besides, she was damned if she was going to plead for him to think again, to assure her they would stay married. She could, she supposed, merely ignore him, refuse to agree to any divorce, but just as quickly dismissed the idea. If Alan was determined, and she had no doubt that he was, he could easily provide evidence which would give her no option. Her relationship with Steve for a start, not that he was the only male in Ekabe she'd had an affair with, a couple of them pretty intense. There had been nothing intense or even remotely romantic between her and Steve although they hadn't been exactly discreet, but then she had believed that if Alan found out it wouldn't have mattered all that much to him. How wrong she had been. And how stupid.

Thinking of Steve, a germ of an idea began to take shape. Perhaps there was a way to prevent Alan going ahead with any divorce proceedings. It wouldn't be easy, but if it worked, and it just might, the rewards would far outweigh the risks. She had to be clever though; no falling apart and allowing her nerves to take over as they'd been threatening to do and, above all, Steve must never know. He was going to be her alibi.

Five minutes later and she was pulling up outside the club and, collecting her bag and tennis racquet from the back seat, walked up the steps to the main entrance. There was no-one around in the foyer and it looked as if she had the place to herself which was good as she needed to ring Steve. He wouldn't be too pleased for her calling him at work, but it couldn't be helped: this was an emergency, and scrabbling around in her bag finally found her mobile. She didn't keep his number on her contact list, but knew it off by heart anyway, and quickly dialled.

'Valerie; this is not a good time.'

'And good morning to you too, darling.'

'Sorry, but I'm about to go into a meeting – '

' – Steve! I need to talk to you!'

'Oh, okay, but not now; where are you?'

'At the club for the bloody Wednesday morning tennis, where else!'

'Providing the meeting doesn't run over, I could be with you around midday. Alright?'

'I suppose so. We do need to talk, Steve. It's important.'

'We will, and Valerie?'

'Yes?'

'Try to calm down; act as you would normally, you don't want any of the busy bodies asking what's wrong, do you?' and he'd rung off before she had a chance to say anything further.

She could hear voices outside, realising she only had minutes to make an effort to release the build-up of tension. Act normally, he'd said. Prance about the bloody tennis court as if she didn't have a care in the world and pretend to be interested in what a bunch of feather-brained women had to talk about? When what she wanted to do right now, was to think. Ideally, she needed to be on her own, but that wasn't going to be possible. Later. She knew one thing: she would have to rely on her own ingenuity, more importantly, her own judgement. How well did she know Steve? Of course, she was aware of the obvious: he was married, but apparently not in love with his wife, otherwise why was he so keen to jump into bed with her? He was ambitious; disillusioned with his career, suffered from an inferiority complex in the way he would avoid even the mildest of debates and non-confrontational at the slightest sign of an argument, or even a difference in opinion. And the less obvious? These weren't so easy to define, but she would find out. How far, she wondered, would he go to achieve what he'd always believed were beyond his reach. *Everyone has his price, Valerie*, she murmured, pushing open the glass door out to the tennis courts.

*** 

'Sorry about earlier, Valerie, but it was a bit awkward – '

'Not your fault, I shouldn't have phoned you at work, but as I said it is important.'

'What's happened?'

'It's Alan.'

'Thought it might be. I suppose he's found out about us?'

'It's not quite that simple.' selecting just how much he needed to know, she went on to tell him about Alan's plans to divorce her but decided not to mention Cora Hamilton's name.

'All of what you've just said – well, it strikes me as somewhat out of character.'

'What, that there's another woman, you mean?'

'Well, yes; quite frankly I wouldn't have said he was the type.'

'And is there a specific type, Steve? How intriguing; do tell me.'

'Come on, sweetheart, there's no need to take your anger out on me, you know.'

'You're right and I'm sorry; it's just that it's a hell of a lot more complicated than the classic triangle: the appearance of *the other woman*, tears, recriminations, etc., etc., and then the divorce and everyone lives happily ever after!'

'Look, Valerie, let's discuss this rationally - and quietly.' he added, glancing over towards the open door. They had been fortunate so far, no-one else had come into the bar, not unusual during weekdays, but there was no guarantee they could remain uninterrupted, also he would soon have to return to work.

'Okay, you're right of course, but he must be stopped.'

'Stopped?'

'From going ahead with the divorce, Steve.' trying not to show her exasperation.

'But isn't this what you want? I know it's all rather sudden, but if you are right about there being another woman involved, well you and I have nothing to worry about – '

' - you don't get it, do you?'

'Sorry?'

'You really have no idea why I've stuck with him all these years, have you, so I'll tell you; I married into one of Scotland's wealthiest families and if I agree to a divorce I will not only be homeless, but without any financial support. No, hear me out, Steve,' forestalling him, sensing he was about to interrupt, no doubt to accuse her of over-dramatizing. Acutely aware she was at the point when she had to manipulate the conversation in such a way that the embryo of her plan, fragile though it was, was his idea and not hers, she continued to explain the inevitable outcome of severing her ties with the Lorimer family. Although she had never heard any of them say as much, she instinctively knew that once the divorce was *un fait accompli*, she would be socially excluded from the life she had enjoyed, so much so she would have to move away from Calder Bay, and it was for those reasons she was prepared to risk one hell of a lot.

'Valerie.' he said, taking so long to say anything, she didn't think he was going to.

'Yes?'

'You love me, don't you?'

'You know I do.'

'And you want us to be together.'

'Why all these questions; you know the answer, Steve, but honestly, any future we could have hoped for seems impossible, especially now.'

'What you've told me about Alan and his family, well it's made me realise exactly how much you'd be losing if this divorce goes through. Oh, I know we could then be together, openly I mean. I don't envisage any problems with

Kate; we haven't been close for a while, but it's not that: I don't believe either of us would be content with what could be called a compromise.'

'What are you trying to say?'

'I'm not sure, actually, but first I need to establish a couple of points.'

'Go on.'

'Am I right in saying that you are Alan's beneficiary?'

'Yes, that's right, I am.'

'The only one, you've already told me that you've no children.'

'I'm the only one, Steve and in case I hadn't made it clear when I was telling you about the family business, if anything happened to Alan, his shareholding would pass to me, but of course that will all become null and void now.'

'He's made a will?'

'Yes, this was drawn up when we got married, but even if it hadn't been, the family would never renege on what they would consider their moral obligation towards me. Tradition, and what most people would consider to be quite archaic values, mean a lot to the family, Steve.'

'And this will is still valid; I mean you've been married for what - ?'

'Fifteen years, but to answer your question, yes, it is, also we lodged a copy with a firm of lawyers in Ndola not long after we arrived here, in the event of anything happening to him during his contract with the company.'

'I see.'

'You mentioned you had a couple of points.'

'I did, yes.' lowering his voice to no more than a whisper, you've never asked me about my past, have you?'

'No, I suppose not, but it's hardly relevant surely.'

'It could be, or I should say that you might think so.'

'Go on.'

'I've not lived an exactly blameless life, Valerie.'

'You have a criminal record?'

'Not exactly; I've been lucky. This was all years ago, but I took some risks.'

'And you didn't get caught.' finishing for him.

'I didn't get caught.'

'I understand.'

'Do you? It's important that you do, sweetheart.' taking both of her hands in his.

'We need to talk some more.'

'I think we do.' an inscrutable expression on his almost handsome face and one she found impossible to read.

'This evening?'

'It will have to be after the rehearsal.'

'Of course, I was forgetting about the play.'

She had allowed herself to become so distracted she hadn't given a thought to the club's production later in the week, even to the part Steve was playing. She had agreed to help with front of house duties, but not with any great enthusiasm. Accepting reluctantly that at least for three evenings she would be occupied, even if it would only be handing out programmes and showing people to their seats.

'I'll have to get back.' he said, giving her hands a final squeeze, 'but don't worry, sweetheart, everything will work out.'

'I hope so.'

'It will.'

She allowed him several minutes to reach his car before leaving, wanting to get away unnoticed, but such hope was quickly dashed by the plump figure of Peggy Bovington walking across the foyer towards her.

'Valerie, you're still here.'

'Yes, Peggy; I was thirsty after our tennis.'

'You could have joined the rest of us ladies out on the terrace for coffee or soft drinks if you'd wanted to, but it would appear you had other plans.'

'Sorry?' playing for time and not fooled by the ambiguity of her comment.

'I think you know what I mean, my dear.'

'I don't actually.'

'I've been an expatriate wife for many years and sadly I've witnessed many women living in the tropics with too much time on their hands behave in such a way that invariably caused them tremendous unhappiness.'

'Interesting, Peggy,' controlling her rising temper with difficulty, 'but I find what you're implying quite insulting.'

'You are a very attractive young woman, Valerie and certain men are drawn to you for that reason. Naturally you find life boring here; of course, if you had a couple of youngsters demanding your attention you wouldn't have time to look beyond your marriage.'

'Have you quite finished?' moving to one side of her in an effort to reach the main door before she said something she knew she would regret.

'Not quite. Steve Burrows is a married man, my dear as I'm sure you are well aware, and as Kate's friend, I don't like to think of her being hurt as she certainly would be were she to learn of these little *tête-à-têtes* you've been having with her husband.'

She managed at last to extricate herself although it was a while before she felt calm enough to switch on the engine and drive back to the bungalow. Her whole body was shaking with impotent rage, each word of Peggy Bovington's narrow-minded bigotry literally ringing in her ears. The more she thought about what the woman had said, the more she realised the injustice of such a verbal attack. *She had absolutely no grounds for her accusations, none whatsoever,* she muttered and for the second time that day rammed the key into the ignition.

# Chapter Three

The desk sergeant at Calder Bay police station took an agitated telephone call from Harry Myers, the owner of the newsagents in the High Street, at five minutes to nine on Wednesday morning and, after listening to what he had to say, buzzed through to DCI Alistair Dale's office on the first floor.

'My wife found him, Chief Inspector, but she's in a dreadful state so that's why I'm phoning you –'

'It's alright, Mr Myers, you did the right thing; I can well imagine how distressing this must be for you both, but I can assure you there will be an officer with you in a matter of minutes. His first duty will be to secure the crime scene prior to the arrival of the forensic team –'

'– oh, dear, this is going to cause a great deal of disruption; does it mean we'll have to close?'

'I can't say for sure until we have assessed the situation, but I wouldn't have thought that will be necessary. If I remember correctly, the door to your tenant's flat is at the far end of your building and as long as the incident doesn't attract too many spectators, your business should continue much as usual.'

Before phoning the forensics department at Dundee police headquarters, Alistair had a brief word with Dan Aitken, giving him the scant information he had so far in as much that Harry Myers' wife had had the misfortune to find the mutilated body of their tenant in the flat he had been renting from them.

'Right, sir; I'm on my way.' Dan said, straightening his tie and striding towards the stairs. DI Aitken had only been with them for six months; with the escalating crime rate in the area over the last couple of years, Calder Bay had qualified for additional resources, hence Dan's transfer from Aberdeen. During this time, he had adapted well, not only to the slower tempo of a seaside town such as Calder Bay with its fluctuating seasonal community, but towards the locals. He was a likeable character, unflappable; it would be interesting Alistair thought dialling the Dundee number, to see how he tackles what will be his first murder enquiry since his arrival.

Less than thirty minutes later, Dan phoned through to say that the police surgeon had been. He'd verified the death and would be sending his report on to the procurator fiscal's office later in the morning.

'And the victim, Dan?'

'A Mr John Milne, sir. He'd taken out a two-year lease on the flat eighteen months ago. The Myers don't seem to know much about him; apparently, he leased though the local estate agents in the High Street, although he did mention to the Myers that he was working for "Lorimer Fruits".'

'Right; it looks as though you're going to have your hands full for a good part of the day, so I'll leave you to get on with the preliminary enquiries, house-to-house, you know the drill, Dan. Incidentally, any sign of this news having leaked out yet?'

'Surprisingly, not so far; I'm doing my best to keep it all as low key as possible and,' he added, 'for as long as possible.'

'It's all we can do, but if past experiences are anything to go by, it will only be a matter of time before the media get to hear. Meanwhile, I'll make my way up to the Lorimers' place and break the news to them. Hopefully, someone there will be able to tell me more about him.'

'It was a pretty vicious attack, and it appears he must have put up quite a struggle if the state of the flat is anything to go by.'

'Hmmph. What are your first impressions, Dan,' he asked, 'random or premeditated?'

'Hard to say. There are no signs of a forced entry, but whoever it was made a neat job of picking the lock. Either that, or he had been known by the victim. However, he'd neglected to close the door when he left; in fact, that was what caught Joyce Myers' attention when she was opening up the newsagents.'

'Could indicate he was disturbed, but the picked lock; that sounds professional.'

'It does, sir.'

'We'll have to wait and see what forensics come up with.'

Early days, he thought, taking his jacket from the back of the chair, but the more ground they could cover before the arrival of the media, the better. Regrettably, the body would have to remain where it was until the pathologist had completed his initial examination which meant it would be impossible not to attract the attention of anyone who happened to be walking past at the time. But then, he sighed, in a town the size of Calder Bay where in recent months had had more than its fair share of drama, it was to be expected.

*** 

The olive green wrought-iron gates leading into the Lorimers' property were wide open, the heavily embossed sign making it impossible to miss: "Lorimer Fruits: est. 1900" and, changing gear, he turned into the tree-lined drive. Another notice, less ornate, directed him to the administration offices: a one-storey stone built extension leading off from the main building. He parked between a dark blue BMW and a silver-grey Porsche with a personalized number plate, unclipped his seatbelt and walked up the shallow steps to the sliding glass doors.

He hadn't known what to expect but had to admit he was surprised at the elegance of the reception area: stripped oak flooring, concealed ceiling lights, cream-painted walls, with enlarged black and white prints of then and now images of how the Lorimers' family business had evolved over the years. Prospered too, Alistair murmured under his breath as he approached the girl behind the desk and, taking out his warrant card, introduced himself.

'Detective Chief Inspector Alistair Dale,' she read out loud, a questioning expression on her face as she glanced up at him, 'how can I help you, Detective Chief Inspector?'

'I'd like to speak to Mr Graham Lorimer, please.'

'I'm sorry, but he's on a long-distance call at the moment, but I'll ask one of his sons to see you.' and gesturing over towards a leather armchair by the open window, she pressed a button on a state-of-the-art telephone console, all the time her eyes remaining fixed on him. It would appear, the cynical thought slipping into his mind, visits from the local constabulary were rare events in the daily lives of the employees of this prestigious family business.

Having grown up in Calder Bay, he knew the town and the surrounding area well: mostly farmland away from the coast. He had fond memories of cycling up to what was then known locally as Lorimers' fruit farm with one of his school friends during the summer holidays to help out with the fruit picking. It had all been so casual; they would lean their bikes against the hedge bordering the start of the long lines of raspberry bushes, collect a small wicker box from the make-shift table at the end, and once they'd picked enough raspberries to fill it, returned to the starting point where it was weighed, the pair of them eagerly waiting to receive their payment which, once back in the town, they spent on packets of crisps and coca cola. Thirty years ago. Certainly, Lorimer fruits had come a long way since then if their 'front of house' was any indication.

'Good morning, Chief Inspector, I'm Callum Lorimer.'

He had been so engrossed in his boyhood reminiscences he hadn't heard him approach.

'Good morning, sir. I'm afraid I am the bearer of distressing news.' coming straight to the point.

'Not one of my family?'

'No, no; one of your employees, Mr Lorimer: John Milne.'

'John! Our works manager: what's happened to him? Has he had an accident; he's alright I hope.'

'His body was discovered a short while ago –'

'He's dead! Is that what you're saying: the man is dead!'

'He has not been formally identified, although the couple he was renting his flat from have assured us that he was John Milne, also that he was working for your company.'

'And did they – what I mean is, did they actually see his – body?'

'Yes.'

All the colour had drained from his face; there was no doubt the man was shocked, but there was something about his manner which struck Alistair as being at odds with the way he would have expected an employer to react on hearing of the death of one of his members of staff, albeit a violent one, although Callum Lorimer wasn't yet to know that.

'Do you have any idea who is responsible, Chief Inspector?'

*He's assuming the man was murdered.*

'No, not yet, but we will. I have a good team, Mr Lorimer; they're thorough and even if we do live in a small town, in the last year or two they have had considerable experience in conducting such an investigation. With positive results, I might add.'

'Oh. Well, that's good to know. And,' hesitating for a fraction of a second, 'how did he die; you haven't said?'

*And you haven't asked.*

'He sustained a number of savage blows to his head and shoulders. We are waiting for the pathologist's report, but it's clear they could not have been self-inflicted, therefore we're treating his death as murder.'

'Murder.' the word scarcely audible, 'How horrible.'

'Indeed, sir. However, there are questions I need to ask you about the deceased, routine you understand.'

'Of course, but there really isn't much I can tell you, Chief Inspector. His contract was a short-term one, only for two years to cover the period while my brother is working overseas, Zambia actually. John wasn't in the habit of socializing with us, the odd beer or two in the office after work on a Friday, that sort of thing.'

'I see. One of my officers will be talking to the estate agents who handled the lease, but I'm fairly sure they will only be able to provide what information would have been necessary for them to carry out the normal check when someone's renting one of their properties. I'm more interested in the personal side of his life.'

'Well, as I've –'

'- for instance, any friends he may have had, any he'd made perhaps since coming to Calder Bay.'

'I honestly wouldn't know. He probably had made friends: he was young, single and I can't see him sitting alone in his flat when he finished work here; I expect he went along to one of the pubs in the town.'

'It's possible. I understand he took up the lease of the flat a year and a half ago, would this have been the same time as he started working for you, Mr Lorimer?'

'Yes, it was.'

'And this was for two years?'

'A two-year contract, yes.'

'Presumably, you'll now be looking for a replacement.'

'As it happens, Chief Inspector, that isn't going to be necessary.'

'Really?'

'I had word from my brother yesterday to say he was returning earlier than we expected.'

'A change of plan; did he tell you why?'

'Not really, but I got the impression it was personal.'

'He didn't elaborate?' Alistair pressed him. *Like getting blood from the proverbial stone.*

'No, he didn't, but then Alan is like that, sparing with any details which he no doubt considers unnecessary.'

*Must run in the family.*

'I see, well I don't have any more questions to ask you for the present, except would you mind telling me where you were last night?'

'What!' the first spark of emotion emerging, colour instantly returning to his face, 'You suspect that I could have had something to do with this – this business!'

'Not at all, sir; at this early stage of our enquiry, we don't suspect anyone. The questions I'm asking you are all routine and in line with standard police procedure. Therefore,' Alistair repeated, 'where were you last night?'

'I was at home with my wife, Chief Inspector; in our apartment in Ashburn House.'

'Thank you, sir. Incidentally, do other members of your family live here?'

'My father of course and my two brothers, Alan and Bruce.'

'And your brothers, are they married?'

'Only Alan.'

'His wife, sir; is she with him in Zambia?'

'Of course.'

'Does your father live alone?'

'My father is a widower – ' his tone bridling with indignation.

'Yes, sir, I come from Calder Bay, and I already knew that.'

'Ah, well,' looking slightly embarrassed, 'that's alright then.'

'Right. There will be an officer with you later today to take statements from your family, including those of your staff.'

'Good God! Is this necessary, Chief Inspector? The news about John will be disruptive enough when I inform them, never mind having them subjected to a barrage of questions. I shouldn't have to remind you, but I have a business to run: delivery targets to meet, incoming orders to be checked and recorded –'

'– Mr Lorimer, if I may stop you there; while I appreciate the points you've raised, in any murder investigation there is bound to be a certain amount of inconvenience, but unavoidable I'm afraid. I would, therefore, ask for your co-operation.'

\*\*\*

Driving back to Calder Bay, a distance of no more than three miles, Alistair mulled over exactly what was concerning him so much about Callum Lorimer. He was an average sort of guy: early to mid-forties, but with the mannerisms of someone years older. Fairly average in fact. Medium height and build; mid-brown hair, not exactly a short back and sides, but not far removed. He had been reasonably friendly, but it had been hard to know whether it was a polite pretence of tolerance. There had been nothing to dislike about the man, or like either, recalling his earlier feelings of disquiet. His reaction to John Milne's death, for instance: the way he had assumed it hadn't been a natural one by straight away asking who had been responsible. Callum Lorimer had expected to hear that John Milne had been murdered. So, did that make him a suspect or not? Either way, there was some undercurrent there which needed clarifying. Could have something to do with the brother, the one in Zambia, Alistair thought; he'd got the vibes there was no love lost between them. Could merely be sibling rivalry, of course, especially as living – and working – under the same roof when it must be practically impossible to avoid each other. Very claustrophobic, and reminiscent of "Downton Abbey" in the twentieth century, smiling as he made the bizarre comparison and pulling in next to Dan's Peugeot in front of the main entrance to the station.

'You've just missed a call from DCI Prentice at headquarters, sir.' the desk sergeant told him as soon as he walked into reception.

'Thanks, Sergeant, I'll call back shortly.' continuing along the corridor to his office.

Dan had left a brief note on his desk detailing his visit to the estate agents, together with a copy of the lease application form signed by John Milne, quickly scanning it before returning Craig Prentice's call. As he had expected, a standard format incorporating the personal details required to obtain permission to lease a property which, although helpful, didn't provide much of an insight into the actual background of the deceased. He had only been thirty-two, unmarried, his previous address being Rose Cottage, Mill Lane, Perth and his bank, The Royal Bank of Scotland, where he had held an account since 1983. He'd had a healthy balance and with the salary, confirmed by the letter of appointment from "Lorimer Fruits", more than adequate income to cover the rent on the furnished flat owned by Mr & Mrs Harold Myers. No surprises there he thought, dialling the number of Craig's direct line.

'Morning, Alistair,' Craig greeted him, answering on the first ring, 'thanks for getting back to me.'

'That's okay, no doubt you've heard about our latest murder.'

'You can't say it isn't keeping Calder Bay on the map; in a manner of speaking that is.' followed by his dry chuckle.

'One way of putting it, I suppose.'

'I won't keep you, Alistair,' he went on, 'I can imagine what it must be like with you, at the start of a murder enquiry and the scurrying about that involves, but this one has caught the attention of Interpol.'

'Really?'

'Thought that would surprise you.'

'It does, yes; it shouldn't though when I think about the last couple of murder investigations we've had in Calder Bay and not all that long ago either.'

'Quite. Well, apparently this one triggered off alarm bells with them.'

'The victim was known to Interpol you mean?'

'Not necessarily, Alistair, it was the fact that he was employed by the company, "Lorimer Fruits".'

'I'm intrigued.'

'Of course you are and I'm only sorry I can't tell you more, but due to the sensitive nature of Interpol's investigation, I've been advised that any further discussion will have to be carried out face-to-face.'

'Right.'

'My contact with them is a guy called Adrian Roberts and he's requested a meeting with you as soon as possible.'

'Where is he based; at their main offices in Manchester?'

'No, London; he has offices in Camden, but someone will pick you up at Heathrow, so you won't have to concern yourself with taxis.'

'I could make it tomorrow, Craig. I will have had a full briefing with my team by the end of today, which will give me time to prepare my initial progress report; better than arriving empty-handed.'

'That's fine, I'll give Adrian Roberts a call; he's already told me that they'll make the travel arrangements, so all you have to do is make your way to the airport.'

Replacing the receiver, he buzzed through to Dan and asked him to arrange a team meeting for five-thirty. Before then, he had to report to his superintendent, something he wasn't exactly relishing.

Bob Cunningham, or "Breezy Bob" as he was uncharitably nicknamed around the station, was not the easiest of bosses, but Alistair had learned that murder cases made him more than usually short-tempered; how he was going to react when he heard that a highly regarded organization such as Interpol were apparently showing a keen interest in this new investigation, didn't bear contemplating. Less than twelve months off retirement, his tolerance would be paper-thin; the last he would want is any discordant note at this late stage in his career. Better get it over with he decided, walking further along the corridor to the superintendent's domain.

'Interpol!" a predicted explosion, but then not all that surprising, 'And you're saying that Craig Prentice couldn't enlighten you any further?' disbelief written quite plainly across his broad features.

'Only that their interest wasn't primarily focused on the murder victim, but with the fact he was employed by "Lorimer Fruits".

'"Lorimer Fruits" eh?'

'Yes, sir.'

'This is not good, Alistair, not good at all;' tapping his fingers impatiently on the desk in front of him, 'Graham Lorimer, as I'm sure you know, is one of Calder Bay's most influential residents: a councillor, justice of the peace and a tireless patron for our cottage hospital. In other words, Alistair, not a man to upset, if you understand what I'm saying.'

'I certainly do, but until I've met up with Mr Roberts tomorrow, I'm not in a position to make any useful comment.'

'Of course you're not. All I'm asking is that you make certain this case is handled meticulously; there will be no room for any slip-ups; every move must be carefully considered. At all times.'

'I assure you they will be, sir I'm holding a briefing this afternoon to collate our findings to-date, and there will be a report on your desk first thing tomorrow morning.'

'And Alistair.'

'Sir?'

'I want to be kept informed at every step you understand, at every step and I'll expect a further report from you giving me full details of your meeting in London immediately upon your return.'

\*\*\*

'There's been a development since the discovery of John Milne's body,' Alistair said, standing in front of his team in their hastily prepared incident room where a whiteboard had been erected with black and white prints of the victim and the beginnings of a diagram highlighting those who were known to him, 'and one from the least expected quarter.'

'Not another body I hope, sir.'

'Don't tempt providence, Sergeant.' Alistair responded, trying to keep his face straight; at times Colin's attempts at jollity could irritate the more sensitive, but he was a damn good police officer, 'It appears that this murder has attracted the attention of Interpol; I'm unable to give you much in the way of an explanation at this stage, but I've been asked to meet with one of their officers tomorrow.'

'Do you have any idea what has triggered their interest, sir?' Dan asked.

'Only that it is connected in some way to the company who was employing John Milne.'

'"Lorimer Fruits"?' Sergeant Lilian Wood asked, frowning.

'It sounds so – so, vague.'

'I couldn't agree more, Dan,' Alistair nodded, shuffling the few papers he'd pulled from the newly created file, 'however, I suggest we don't engage in any guessing game; that would be non-productive and a total waste of police time and energy, 'However, we must bear in mind that this particular development will require more sensitive handling; no word should leak out beyond those persons immediately involved with the investigation, especially in respect to the press.' he added.

'That's going to be a nightmare.'

'Couldn't agree more, Colin, but we must be extra vigilant.'

'They can be so devious.' Lilian grumbled.

'And we know who you mean.'

'Beverly Grant.' she sighed.

'Right,' Alistair said quickly, 'let's go over what we've covered so far today. I've read your notes on your visit to the estate agents, Dan, but for the others present, John Milne was thirty-two, single, took out the lease for the flat in the High Street eighteen months ago and a customer with the Royal Bank with sufficient income to support the rent.'

'I have a copy of the signed agreement, sir.'

'That's fine, so no surprises there. Anything from the house-to-house enquiries?'

'All negative I'm afraid; the usual response, nobody saw or heard anything untoward last night.'

'Disappointing, but not unexpected. As a rule, people don't. Are there any cctv cameras covering the newsagents, Dan?'

'Only one but it's positioned facing their front door only and doesn't look as if it stretches even as far as the door to the flat.'

'Does the camera belong to the Myers?'

'No, the council; I've requested footage for last night through to the early hours and they've promised to deliver by ten tomorrow morning.'

'Good.'

'I spoke to Ken Morris at "The Shipwreck", sir,' Colin said, 'John Milne was a regular customer there and it seems he had a girlfriend.'

'Go on.'

'Ken didn't know her, but he reckoned she could have moved here fairly recently; she started coming in about six months ago and she was always with him.'

'What about last evening?'

'I asked Ken that; they came in as usual he said, had a few drinks and then left about ten.'

'Together?'

'Yes.'

'Right, Colin; try and find out who she is. Suggest you go along there again, talk to the regulars, someone's bound to know something about her, her name if nothing else. She may not live in Calder Bay, but she might work here.'

'Will do, sir.'

'How did your visit to "Lorimer Fruits" go, Lilian?' he asked her.

'I wasn't able to speak to Graham Lorimer unfortunately, the receptionist told me he was out of the office, but I've made out my report of the other family members and employees I spoke to,' she said, passing him a printed sheet of A4, 'including statements covering their movements for last night.'

'Thanks,' taking it from her and tucking it in beside the other papers in his file, 'I'll go through it later, but any salient points we should be following up on?'

'Only on a couple of the alibis, sir.'

'Yes?'

'Bruce Lorimer and Kirstie McKenzie; she's Graham Lorimer's P.A.'

'Let's take Bruce Lorimer first then.' pulling his pad towards him and writing Bruce Lorimer's name at the top of the page.

'He and his girlfriend, Sara Anderson, met up in the lounge bar of "The Royal" with their friends, Peter Small and Amanda Russell, at eight. They had a meal in the restaurant at eight-thirty and returned to the bar after they had eaten, finally leaving the hotel at eleven-fifteen. This was all confirmed by the head waiter, also by one of the bar staff.'

'They all left at the same time?'

'Yes, Bruce Lorimer told me that he went back to his girlfriend's place and spent the night there, returning home at around six this morning.'

'Did you get her address?'

'Yes, sir; she has one of the apartments in Carlogie House.'

'Pricey.' Colin murmured under his breath.

'And the two friends, Lilian?' Alistair asked, choosing to ignore him. Colin was quite right though, remembering when he'd gone there to interview a witness the year before, who not only lived in one of the apartments, but had been the architect for the renovation of Carlogie House, all of which only went to prove how small-town Calder Bay really was.

'Peter and Amanda.' Lilian answered, appearing not to have heard Colin, 'They followed them out of "The Royal's" car park and Bruce assumed they would be going straight home. Sorry, sir, but I didn't get their address.'

'Not to worry, Lilian. Dan,' he said, turning to him, 'I would like you to try and get hold of Graham Lorimer; I can't help but get the impression he's avoiding us.'

'I'll go up there first thing, sir.'

'That's fine; perhaps when you're there you could ask Bruce Lorimer for his friends' addresses.'

'Of course.'

'Right; there is a fair bit of checking up to be done and I'm hoping we'll have the pathologist's report by the time we finish today; it's important to get a closer fix for the time of death from the one we were given earlier.'

'Especially if it falls in around closing time when you consider that the "The Royal" is practically next door to the newsagents.'

'Exactly, Dan.' sighing in frustration and not for the first time speculating on why members of the public are keen enough to see what they can when disaster strikes, but when it comes to admitting they have seen or heard anything out of the ordinary, they become silent. 'Anyway, Lilian, Kirstie McKenzie's alibi?'

'Apparently she spent the evening with her friend, Mary Struthers who lives in Green Lane, next door to the ice cream parlour '

'Not Hawthorn Cottage?' Colin interrupted.

'Yes, that's right. So?'

'I'm surprised the name didn't jump out at you straight away, but then I don't think you were up there last year on the Henderson drug case – '

'– Oh, of course; I guess I just didn't make the connection. Sorry, sir, the name should have rung a bell.' she added, turning back to Alistair.

'Not to worry, Lilian; we have all had a busy twelve months or so since that business. I hadn't realised Hawthorn Cottage had sold though.' going on to explain the complexities of their last murder investigation to Dan.

'I knew about the case, sir and remember how it didn't take long to hit the headlines.'

'Too true; let's hope this one doesn't go the same way. However Lilian, you were saying that Kirstie McKenzie was with her friend on Tuesday evening. Did she tell you anymore; when she arrived there and how long she stayed, perhaps?'

'She got there around seven Kirstie said and left at ten.'

'And her address, Lilian?'

'The flat above the greengrocers in the high Street.'

'Right. It would only have taken her about five minutes or so, if she was driving that is, to get home. Mind you,' he went on, 'she wouldn't have been able to park there, so she must have a regular place. Her friend may know; you will need to talk to her in any case, Lilian to establish her alibi, but if she doesn't know, give Kirstie a call. So, if what we are saying is right and she had to walk back to her flat from where she parked her car, it would have been closer to eleven by then.'

'I'll try and see her friend in the morning, sir; apparently she's retired so she there's a good chance she'll be at home.'

'That's fine. Provided I am back from London at a reasonable time tomorrow, we'll have a further briefing then.'

# Chapter Four

<u>Wednesday 18th October : Ekabe</u>

Cora wasn't certain it was such a good idea to go along to the club that evening, but Kate, the friend she'd made during her three months secondment from the LSE in London, had been insistent and she'd finally agreed. It was her last night before returning to London the next day, and the chances of her ever being in Ekabe again were unlikely, but that didn't alter her trepidation as she walked up the steps and pushed open the main door, neither did it diminish her rising anxiety in the event that Alan's wife would be in there. She hadn't been entirely convinced by his reassurances of the unlikelihood of any unpleasantness from her, but cowardly, she wished he had waited until she'd left the country before confronting her about the divorce. Although she and Alan had been discreet, nothing altered the unsavoury fact that she was the *other woman*, and she was fairly certain that Valerie Lorimer would literally milk that for all it was worth.

'Cora, come and join us!' Kate waved over from the far end of the bar.

'We're going to miss you, my dear; you've been like a breath of fresh air to us all.'

'That's kind of you, Peggy.' and it was kind of her; Peggy Bovington was one of the few remaining colonials, having spent over thirty years in the country and possessed a somewhat unnerving ability to read into a person's innermost thoughts; at least that was how Peggy made her feel, but then, stifling a sigh, she did have a guilty conscience.

'I don't believe you've met Sheila, have you,' she asked, giving the woman standing slightly behind her a gentle nudge, 'Sheila, this is Cora Hamilton; Cora, Sheila Campbell.' formally making the introductions.

'Hello, Cora; Peggy has been telling me that you've been here on a secondment posting from London.'

'Yes, that's right; I'm with the London School of Economics.'

'I actually studied there,' she said, her soft Scottish accent immediately taking her back to her childhood; summer holidays spent with her grandparents on the east coast of Scotland when the days had been long and the sun always seemed to be shining, 'some years ago, I might add!'

'We were just talking about the club's next production before you arrived, Cora.' Kate said.

'Such a pity you're going to miss it.' Peggy's husband put in, 'One of Alan Ayckbourn's plays, damn clever playwright; I'm looking forward to seeing how our very own thespians tackle it.'

'Don't sound so caustic, Derek; you know very well we have considerable acting talent here.'

'Of course we do, my dear. Steve has a part in this one, doesn't he, Kate?'

'Yes, he does. Cora, you haven't a drink; what would you like – a G&T?'

Cora didn't think the others noticed the abrupt way Kate changed the subject. She had looked positively uncomfortable when Derek mentioned Steve's name; why was it, Cora wondered watching her closely as she moved nearer to the bar to catch the steward's attention; there was an awkwardness in her manner, almost as if she didn't want to hear her husband mentioned. It could be that her own heightened sense of awareness was making her super-sensitive to the point of imagining problems in a relationship when they didn't exist. She hardly knew Steve; he seldom came into the club's bar and, according to Kate, preferred to do his socializing next door at the rugby club. It had therefore come as something of a surprise to learn that he was keen on amateur dramatics which had seemed, given his outward appearance of being one of the boys and liking nothing better than a few beers, as out of character.

'So, Cora,' Peggy broke into her thoughts, 'have you enjoyed your time here?'

'I have, yes.'

'I'm sure you'll be happy to return to the *real* world though.'

'Honestly, Derek,' Peggy protested, but only mildly, the banter between them reminding her again of her grandparents although not realising back then that what appeared to be their constant bickering hadn't been serious; it had taken a chance remark by a shop assistant to convince her. It had been her Gran's wedding anniversary that day and she'd told the woman behind the counter she'd been married for fifty-eight years. Congratulating her, the woman asked whether she regretted marrying so young, her Gran unhesitatingly replying: "I don't regret one single day", that simple sentence echoing now in Cora's sub-conscience and one that never failed to enthral her.

'I only speak the truth.' Derek said.

'You're such an old cynic!'

'If you say so, dear.'

*The real world*. He was quite right, Cora thought, only half aware of the easy exchange between a group of people who spent most of their leisure hours together. To them, with presumably the exception of Derek, this was their real world. It would be unfair of her to label them as insular, but she seriously wondered if they appreciated just how privileged they were, especially the wives: spared from the everyday challenges of balancing a demanding job with running a home, in many instances single-handedly, and at the same time juggling with other demands. Most of their husbands were on a contract; a transient situation and as Alan had said to her the other evening, they were only passing through; some stayed longer than others, but eventually would leave and return home, reluctantly or otherwise, to what Derek had described the real world.

'So, what do you think, Cora?'

'Sorry, Kate, I was miles away.'

'Well,' she laughed, 'you soon will be!'

'That's true; anyway, what were you saying?'

'Only about Halloween, whether it should be celebrated in the over-the-top way which seems to be the norm these days.'

'Well, it used to be just for children, but for some peculiar reason we adults have become more involved.'

'A good excuse for a party though.' Sheila said.

She wasn't too concerned about the merits of the ancient rites of saints and sinners, but felt she should make a show of interest in what they were all talking about. She couldn't recall ever feeling as much at odds with her surroundings which had, over the weeks, become so familiar: the bleached wood-panelled bar, fronted by the row of high stools; framed black and white prints of actors and musicians covering the walls; one of them, pride of place, of Louis Armstrong taken during his second African tour over thirty years ago. Ekabe's social club, funded by Southern Mining Limited, commonly referred to as SML, for their staff, but with the membership extended to other expatriates living and working in and around the town, the social hub in fact and she knew she was going to miss the easy camaraderie, but that evening she felt in a kind of limbo where she had already mentally switched off from where she was at that precise moment: having a few drinks with a group of people, with the exception of Peggy's friend, Sheila, she had known since she arrived in Ekabe three months earlier. For the first time she felt homesick, wearying to be back in her own habitat and wishing she could fast forward to the moment when the London taxi would drop her off outside her flat in Bloomsbury. Lost in her imaginings she could almost feel the cold metal of the key in her hand as she slipped it into the lock of her front door.

'Sorry, everyone,' she said, pulling herself back from wherever she'd been, I'm afraid I'm not much company this evening.'

'Journey proud.'

'Sorry?'

'My mother used to say that,' Sheila explained, 'difficult to describe; it's quite an old saying apparently, but it was used to describe that unique feeling between nervousness and excitement before a trip; you know, when you can't sleep the night before you go away.'

'Is it a Scottish expression?' Peggy asked her.

'I don't know; could be I suppose.'

'It's American I believe.' Derek put in.

So, Cora smiled to herself, that's what is wrong with me, I'm journey proud, deciding she must remember to tell Alan when she saw him again which would only be in a couple of weeks. She would need this time to herself to slow down; their relationship had developed so quickly, as though subconsciously they were trying to make up for lost time: Alan, in a fifteen-year old marriage which had brought him much unhappiness and, having met his wife, she didn't doubt his sincerity for one minute. As for herself, without the commitment of ever marrying Mark, the man she'd lived with for six years and had once believed the love they had for each other was something special, when they'd separated, the raw emotions she'd gone through had remained with her for a while and the last she expected when she agreed to the offer of the secondment from the LSE was to become romantically involved again, certainly not so soon.

'It's only natural, dear,' Peggy was saying, 'to feel a little apprehensive, I mean about uprooting yourself again when you've not been here for all that long, but Africa, you know, does have a way of endearing itself to you.'

'And there speaks the real colonial.' Kate laughed.

'Sounds as if the dress rehearsal has finished,' Derek interrupted, 'we'd better get another round in before they all barge in demanding to be served!'

As he spoke the double doors to the auditorium opened and the hub of voices grew louder as they were immediately outnumbered. Cora recognized most of them: Jack Simpson and his pretty wife, Christine, the acknowledged leading lights in their theatre group; Phillip Edwards, manager of the branch of Barclays Bank in Ekabe; Harry Ford and his girlfriend, Sally, a nurse at the hospital and many of the others, except she couldn't recall all their names.

One of them, Cora thought it could have been Jack, put a tape on and the sweet voice of Celine Dion's "Think Twice" poured into the room. Most apt, she thought, warding off another twinge of guilt.

'How did the dress rehearsal go?' she asked Christine.

'Don't ask!'

'Bloody disastrous!' Harry chipped in, pulling a face.

'Well, you know what they say?'

'And what do they say, Derek?'

'A bad dress rehearsal, a great opening night.'

'Where's Steve,' Kate asked, 'is he still in the theatre?'

'Probably nipped next door to the rugby club, Kate,' Jack said.

There was something in the way he said that which caught Cora's attention; it wasn't so much the words, but the slight intonation in Jack's voice which she couldn't quite understand. But before she could read anything meaningful into what was no more than an impression, Kate quickly dispelled this by a shrug of her shoulders with the comment that Steve always did say the beer tasted better in there.

The general conversation around the bar focused on the following evening's first night of the play and the plans most of them were making for Saturday night which only succeeded in making her feel more of an outsider than ever and after she'd finished her drink, once all the farewell wishes had been made, and Kate saying they must keep in touch, she left, with Celine's last words: "Baby, think twice". Don't remind me. Cora sighed, closing the doors behind her and walking down the steps to the car.

She was about to put the key in the lock when she heard voices; not exactly whispering but spoken softly: a man and a woman. It was quite dark out there with the only light coming from the club windows behind her and the single lamp outside the restaurant across the square; difficult to work out where they were coming from, although she thought she recognized them, the woman's voice anyway. Valerie Lorimer had a distinctive Essex accent which she had gone to some lengths to disguise, but to Cora, having spent several years in London, easily picked up the odd cockney twang when, presumably, she forgot to use her 'posh' voice, this being one of those moments Cora reckoned as her eyes, becoming adjusted to the darkness, she was now able to see the outline of two figures standing next to the wall of the rugby club. Only a few metres away, but she was unable to hear what they were saying, although she detected a sense of urgency in the man's voice and then when he raised it slightly she realised who he was. Kate's husband. Her first instinct was to leave, get in her car and drive back to the sanctuary of her room at Ekabe Lodge, but she held back; why, she didn't know. Whatever the relationship between these two, it was no concern of hers. She hardly knew Steve, nor Valerie: the wife Alan was in the process of divorcing, but over the weeks and months she would need to have been deaf not to have heard the various rumours circulating around the club about her indiscriminative behaviour. There had never actually been any proof there was any substance to what was little more than gossip, but that hadn't altered the fact that Valerie was not liked, and definitely not to be trusted by the wives in the close-knit expat community.

Poor Kate, she thought, turning away from the two shadowy figures, how was she going to react when she learned that her husband's eagerness to frequent the other club wasn't only for their beer. But then, it was always possible it would come as no surprise, remembering how uncomfortable she had seemed when Steve's name was mentioned earlier.

# Chapter Five

D I Daniel Aitken pulled on to the forecourt of the main entrance to "Lorimer Fruits"' administration offices, but before going into the building, he walked along the length of the annexe looking for any evidence of security cameras. Finding it difficult to accept there would be no electronic equipment installed to ensure the family's privacy and safety he took his time, unconcerned that he may be attracting attention, although so far he hadn't seen anyone, pausing now and again to scrutinize the lintels surrounding the upstairs' windows, even across to the line of poplars bordering the driveway, in the off chance of spotting any cameras concealed within their foliage, but couldn't find anything. Pretty well hidden if there is, he thought, making his way back to the entrance.

Although Alistair had told him what to expect about the money-no-spared affluence of the reception area, he had to admit he hadn't been prepared for the sheer elegance the Lorimer family had gone to convey just how wealthy, and presumably how successful their business was. He hadn't realised how much money there was in fruit growing.

The receptionist made a poor effort to disguise her alarm when he'd introduced himself, more so when he asked to see Mr Lorimer, senior.

'I'm sorry, Inspector, but he's attending a conference for most of today and won't be available.'

'Miss – ' trying to read the name printed on the tiny badge pinned on to the lapel of her jacket.

' – Alison.'

'Alison,' regretting the need to add to her unease, but he had a job to do, 'it's important I speak to him, but I do understand your reluctance to interrupt him, however, I understand he has a personal assistant?'

'Yes, he has; Miss McKenzie, but,' floundering now and he knew exactly what she was going to say next, 'she will be in the conference room as well, Inspector.'

'And you are not prepared to call her?'

'I have been told they are not to be disturbed.'

'Well, that's unfortunate, Alison because I will have to find your conference room and make myself known to Mr Lorimer.'

'No, no, Inspector, you mustn't. I'll – I'll buzz through to Bruce; he can explain the situation to you.' pressing some buttons on the console alongside her computer before she had even stopped speaking.

Interesting, Dan thought, obviously the youngest son didn't warrant a title and making a silent bet with himself that the other senior members of this extraordinary family would expect no less when referred to by members of staff. Of course he was only surmising. Up to now, he hadn't met any of them, but what he'd seen so far had gone a long way to paint the picture of a family who continued to cling on to the rigid standards set up by generations of Lorimers. Fanciful and he could be way off beam.

He didn't have long to wait until a door in the wall panelling to the left of the desk, one he'd failed to notice, burst open and a man with a mop of dark hair flopping on to his forehead strode into reception, his hand stretched out in greeting.

'Many apologies, Inspector Aitken, God knows what you must think about us. I'm Bruce Lorimer, by the way.' he added, impatiently pushing back the wayward hair.

'Your receptionist has told me I won't be able to see your father today, but I don't have to remind you Mr Lorimer how crucial it is to interview everyone who was close to the victim; all part of police procedure.'

'Of course. Of course. This was already explained to me yesterday when your sergeant was here interviewing us all.'

'Except your father.'

'Except him, yes. Look, would you like some coffee? I know I would.'

'Thank you.'

'Alison, sweetheart,' he called over to her, 'do you think you could rustle up some coffee for us.'

Without waiting for an answer, he steered him away from the desk towards a spiral staircase.

'You may well look surprised, Inspector; I admit they look a bit awkward and not for the faint-heated, but we have a small guest area upstairs, on the mezzanine floor, which will give us some privacy.'

'Very futuristic.' Dan commented, wondering whether the irony would be lost on the man, and placing his hand on the curved steel handrail, followed him upstairs.

'I suppose you could say that,' he laughed looking back over his shoulder at him, 'but it looks pretty impressive on our publicity bumph, although I might add most people prefer to use the lift.'

*Window dressing. What you see therefore is not necessarily what you get.*

Bruce Lorimer's modest description was something of an understatement: L-shaped, the space immediately at the top of the stairs furnished with comfort in mind; dove-grey leather sofas and glass-topped coffee tables, ceiling-high windows looking out on to Ashburn House's manicured lawns and, in the distance, the rooftops of the town with glimpses of the sea in the distance.

'Great view.' Dan said, anxious now to progress; already too much time had been lost in exchanging words which had no relevance to the reason why he was there.

'It is, isn't it;' gesturing to one of the sofas, 'coffee won't be long, Inspector.'

'Apart from interviewing your father, Mr Lorimer – '

' – Bruce, please,' interrupting him, impatiently pushing away the offending lock of hair, 'I'm not in favour of too much formality; mind you, the old man's a stickler for it!'

'Quite. As I was saying,' realising if he wasn't careful, he was in danger of losing the thread of what he wanted to say, 'there are a few points I'm hoping you will be able to clarify.'

'Of course, Inspector; if I can.'

'I could see no obvious signs outside the property of any security cameras.'

'No, you wouldn't; our system, recently installed I might add, operates on sensors to detect movement once it's dark by external lights coming on, or in the event some unauthorized person attempts to enter the property, will trigger off an alarm to a central point in the main building. All very high tech and fortunately has so far not been required.'

'I see, fairly comprehensive, then.'

'Very.'

'Therefore,' Alistair asked, 'when any member of the household returns at night, the surrounding area will immediately be floodlit?'

'Yes, that's right.'

'And this is fully operational?'

'Of course.'

'Presumably, you will all have passes for the main gate.'

'We don't use cards, merely key in the code.'

'Right.'

'I honestly don't see how this can be relevant, Inspector. The guy wasn't murdered here; apart from the fact that he worked for the company, as far as I can see that is the only connection.'

'At this stage in our investigation, we don't have enough evidence to indicate there is any connection, unlikely though it may appear. And,' he added, 'this is why we have to be so meticulous in asking what may seem unnecessary questions which does include knowing the movements of the family and any members of staff on Tuesday night.'

'And this was achieved yesterday by your sergeant.'

'Yes, but with one exception.'

'Ah, of course, my father.'

'Exactly.'

'Point taken, Inspector and I'll make sure that as soon as he's free I'll ask him to get in touch with you.'

'Good, I trust you will. Before I leave, I would be grateful if you could give me the addresses of the two friends you were with on Tuesday.'

'You're not going to bother them, are you?'

'I merely want to establish your alibi that evening, that's all.'

'Pete's going to be really pissed off, you know, Inspector, but,' shrugging, 'I suppose it's necessary. He and Amanda live together; they'll both be at work, but I'll give you Pete's mobile number, if that's okay?'

'That's fine.' and thanking him for the coffee stood up and, as he walked over towards the stairs, he noticed a dozen or so glossy posters along the wall behind where he'd been sitting. The images were all of fruit, not those familiar to the average British person, but of the exotic variety, colourful arrangements of the tropical variety: kiwis, avocados, dates, mangoes, papayas, lychees and many more he didn't even recognize, far less know their names.

'They're not called exotic fruits for nothing, are they?' Bruce said standing next to him.

'Obviously you don't grow them here.'

'More's the pity. No, we import them from our Amsterdam supplier, re-pack and distribute them to hotels and restaurants throughout Europe, even as far afield as the States. It has become very big business these last few years and we are very much aware of the changes towards more adventurous menus, no doubt thanks to the plethora of the television cookery programmes.'

'I'm impressed.' and he meant it. 'And your role in the business, sir?'

'Marketing, as no doubt you've already guessed.'

*Smug bastard.*

Not a productive meeting Alistair decided, also leaving in its wake a disturbing feeling of disquiet which he was trying to fathom out. Could it be that he found Bruce Lorimer just a tad bit too smart. Or the impression, unpleasant though it was, of being played. Not manipulated exactly; that was too strong a word. Bruce Lorimer had been reluctant to talk about John Milne, hadn't even mentioned his name, far less shown any concern over his death. Why? But, more importantly, the real burning question was the reason for

Interpol's interest in this seemingly high-profile fruit business. As Alistair had stressed at the meeting yesterday, it would be pointless to speculate, but not so easy to ignore ideas beginning to form in his head. Amsterdam. The company's main supplier, according to Bruce Lorimer, were based in Amsterdam. Why, allowing his thoughts free rein for a second, did that trigger off notions of illicit trading. He had absolutely no grounds for such suspicions, except, as he pulled away from Ashburn House, a niggling, but persistent doubt that he could be right.

\*\*\*

Hawthorn Cottage was next to Mario's ice cream parlour in Green Lane and seeing the fringed blue and white striped awning above the doorway immediately reminded Lilian of Saturday mornings spent there with school friends indulging in his delicious strawberry milk shakes. The little café didn't look much different she thought: the bistro-style tables and chairs on the paved terrace set back from the kerb and even with summer long over, a small group of unmistakable looking tourists were seated outside. Enticing though it was, she had to resist the temptation to stop for a coffee, but she had work to do.

She parked the car on the other side of Mario's and walked back to Hawthorn Cottage wondering what sort of person the new owner was like and whether she had known about the gruesome events surrounding the property. One thing was for sure, Lilian decided, unlatching the gate and walking up the short path to the front door, if the woman hadn't, there were more than a few locals only too ready to supply her with all the unpleasant details, liberally embellished with the rumours, this cynical thought accompanying her as she knocked on the door.

Mary Struthers was a neat grey-haired woman, the loosely tied ponytail and the faded jeans giving her a youthful appearance. Also, she displayed no sign of nervousness at finding a police officer on her doorstep, a reaction Lilian was all too familiar with although she'd come to realise it didn't really indicate guilt, quite the contrary she'd often found.

'I can't say I'm all that surprised to receive a visit from you, Sergeant Woods,' she said, handing her back the warrant card, 'won't you come in; I've just made some fresh coffee.'

'Thank you, that would be lovely;' stepping into the hall and following her into the kitchen at the rear of the cottage; sliding glass doors opened out on to a wood-deck terrace with a table and chairs, late-flowering chrysanthemums in glazed ceramic pots adding a riot of colour, 'I only have a couple of routine questions I need to ask you Miss Struthers.' turning away from the window and watching her as she poured coffee into two mugs and placed a plate of chocolate digestives on the table.

'Kirstie phoned me yesterday to tell me you'd been up to Ashburn House to interview everyone there and,' she added, 'to tell me the shocking news about that poor man. I do hope you find who is responsible, Sergeant. I really do.'

'We will, Miss Struthers and this is why we need the help of those people who knew him, also from anyone who may have seen or heard anything unusual on Tuesday night if they happened to have been anywhere near where he lived.'

'I understand. Of course, I was here at home as Kirstie would have told you.'

'Yes, she did, also that she left here at ten.'

'Oh, I thought it was a bit later, nearer to half-past, but I'm sure she's right. I must admit I wasn't looking at the clock.'

'I assume she would have been driving.'

'Oh, yes. I know it isn't so far from where she lives, Sergeant, but except in the middle of summer, it's always dark when she goes home.'

'Of course. I neglected to ask her yesterday where she usually parks her car as I realise the High Street is a no-parking area.'

'She always uses the council car park beside the library; not ideal, especially if the weather is bad, but it's the nearest to her flat.'

Thanking her for her time and refusing another coffee, she managed to take her leave, only too aware of her disappointment. Probably lonely now she's no longer working, Lilian thought returning to her car. As witnesses went, Mary Struthers certainly fell into the vague, 'if you say so' category, and whether she should put any importance on her uncertainty over the time Kirstie left on Tuesday night, was going to be practically impossible to check.

\*\*\*

Beverly Grant was in the Hertz queue at Edinburgh airport when her sub-editor called her. She had only just turned on her mobile after her flight from Heathrow, wishing now she had waited until she had at least picked up her hire car.

'Where the hell are you, Beverly?'

'Edinburgh airport, Andy.'

'What!'

'Edinburgh airport.' she repeated, taking a step closer to the desk and balancing her mobile in one hand at the same time as trying to extract her driving licence from its wallet with the other.

'You're joking!'

'Andy, listen to me. Please. I arrived here about fifteen minutes ago and I'm waiting my turn at the Hertz desk and once I've collected my hire car I am going to drive to Calder Bay- '

'- I knew it – ' his patience, always on the slenderest of threads, had obviously expired, ' – I presume this is because of – of some whim of yours. For God's sake, Beverly, get real! Because a guy, nobody has ever heard of before, gets himself killed in that nineteen-sixties' seaside resort, you feel in your infinite wisdom you're going to get another scoop. Life isn't like that, Beverly. You're an investigative journalist – remember? Based in England's capital!'

'I'll ignore your comment about Calder Bay where, as I remember you once telling me, you had never visited. But, yes, I am an investigative journalist, Andy – a freelance investigative journalist.'

'Okay, okay, calm down, but don't you think, even for you, this immediate response to Calder Bay's recent drama is OTT and could be a waste of time?'

'It could be, Andy, but then it's my time, isn't it, not yours?'

'You don't produce newspapers, Beverly.' *Therefore, you need an editor. You also need someone to approve legitimate expenses and any copy you turn out. And, Beverly Grant, as far as your freelance contacts are concerned, up to now, I am your bread and butter.*

He didn't need to spell it out and didn't he damn well know it. It wasn't the first time he'd reminded her, no matter how obliquely, but each time it rankled, especially when she knew his high handedness wasn't justified. She'd never failed to come up with genuinely resourced content in her written copy; she didn't fabricate and although her methods of obtaining information may not be entirely orthodox, she managed to stay well ahead of her fellow journalists. The trouble with Andy Walters was that she was no longer on the staff and hadn't been for the last seven years. a fact he appeared to have some difficulty in remembering, far less acknowledging.

'I'll have to go, Andy; it's almost my turn now. I'll get in touch when I have something positive to tell you.'

'Be careful, Beverly; don't do anything rash.'

Smiling as she slipped the mobile back into her bag; true to form, Andy always backed down in the end.

It didn't take long to complete the paperwork and within fifteen minutes she was on the M90 heading north.

The clock above the town hall in Calder Bay's High Street was chiming midday as she pulled into a parking space in front of "The Shipwreck Hotel". *Déjà vu.* Less than a year since she'd last been here and, as then, she felt drawn to the town: the long main street where gift shops and cafés sat quite comfortably between the traditional high street shops; the wide pavements with sufficient space to display newspapers and post cards, fruit and vegetables and further along from the hotel, flowers and plants outside the florists. There was a general busyness about the place, but where people had the time to stop and chat. She had no idea where Andy got his nineteen-sixties image from, but then, he was a Londoner and held strong north of the border prejudices.

The same young woman was on duty in reception, and smiled warmly and for a brief indulgent moment Beverly felt she was here, in one of Scotland's prettiest seaside towns, at the start of a holiday with nothing more demanding than deciding what she would choose from that evening's menu, and not as someone hell-bent in finding the story behind a crime, someone who was not averse to using questionable methods to reach that goal. The scoop!

*Okay, so it's personal. And why not? And this is no whim, Andy Walters. A murder has been committed in this town and Beverly Grant was going to be on the spot when he – or she – was found.*

She unpacked the few things she'd brought with her; ran a comb through her hair, added more lip gloss, a quick spray of *Nina Ricci* and picking up her shoulder bag, went back downstairs. She almost collided with a customer in the doorway to the bar and it wasn't until, after a hasty apology, and he'd walked away that she recognized him. D S Colin Fielding. She had hoped to have been in Calder Bay somewhat longer before seeing one of their officers. It could have been worse though; it could have been their arrogant inspector, Alistair Dale, remembering only too well how condescending he'd been towards her at the press conference last year. Beverly wasn't entirely immune to how a good section of the general public viewed members of the press and had learned over the years not to take the name-calling personally, but there had been something about Alistair Dale which, if she was being entirely honest with herself, had unnerved her. Could it be that he had what the Scottish called the second sight? *Very whimsical, Beverly. You'll be seeing wee ghosties next!*

She ordered a white wine from Ken Morris, appreciating that first reviving sip. More customers were coming in; she recognized the woman from the estate agents and a few other familiar faces from the last time she was here, in particular, the old boys in a huddle at the corner of the bar; they were the same three, she could even remember their names: Bill, the one with the drooping white moustache, Ed, the bookish old guy, and Jack; he was the quietest, although today must be the exception because he seemed to have plenty to say, his voice reaching her quite clearly over the chatter around the bar.

'I still say you shouldn't have told Colin Fielding where that lassie worked, Bill. It wasn't right.'

'Don't go on, Jack; Colin is only doing his job.'

'Bill's right you know,' the one called Ed chipped in, 'what you don't seem to realise he's got to speak to everybody who knew that poor man; to eliminate them from their enquiries.'

'I'm not saying you're wrong, but just think for a minute what she's going to be thinking: she'll be trying to come to terms with what happened to her boyfriend and then the police turn up at the bank. I feel sorry for her.'

'Ah, well,' Ed replied, on the point of draining his glass, 'it is a murder enquiry after all, Jack and it's the police you should be feeling sorry for; they have a heck of a job finding who 's responsible.'

'How is it, Bill,' Jack asked him, obviously choosing to ignore his friend's words of wisdom, 'you were able to tell Colin that John's girlfriend was called Laura Thomson?'

'Anyone who's a customer at the bank will know her name.'

'There is more than one bank in Calder Bay, in case you didn't know.'

'Of course there is, Jack, but as far as I'm concerned, there is only one bank and that's the Royal *Bank of Scotland*.' he emphasized.

Beverly took a sip of her wine which she'd almost forgotten about so intent on what the "Shipwreck's" regulars had to say and as on a couple of occasions before the gist of it was most enlightening: relevant information literally handed to her and all she had to do was listen and extract what she needed. So, in a record-breaking time of arriving in the town, she had learned that Calder Bay's recent murder victim had had a girlfriend called Laura Thomson and that she worked at the Royal Bank. She now had to think how best she could make use of this. Presumably, when she'd seen Sergeant Fielding, he would have been on his way to talk to her. She had to exercise a degree of subtlety here; the last she wanted was any complaint of harassment. Although he had appeared not to have recognized her, she was pretty certain he had. *He was a police officer after all, and weren't they trained to remember people especially those who had caused them aggro.*

Deciding she was unlikely to learn anymore, she ordered another wine and took it over to a table by the window overlooking the High Street, less busy now it was lunchtime; with the holiday season over, most of the smaller shops would be closed until the afternoon. She wanted to recap, put together the few notes she'd made since she'd heard of the murder. She didn't have much as undoubtedly Andy would have enjoyed pointing out to her, but it was a start.

The news report had only given the salient points, but it had been enough to spark her interest, also her insatiable curiosity, the most significant being that Calder Bay, once a fishing village, but for several years a popular seaside town, was in the national news for the third time in less than three years. She was not connecting the murders, if anything, it was the statistics of the whole business which intrigued her, not that she had any intention of actually working out the figures, but neither was she going to justify her quick decision to re-visit the town. Not even to herself. She was here, and as far as she was concerned a man had been murdered and therefore, it was a mystery. And mysteries made stories.

John Milne, according to the information released by a Police Scotland press officer, had been on a two-year contract with "Lorimer Fruits", a fruit growing and distribution company owned by an old Calder Bay family and had been renting a flat in the town's centre where his body was discovered early yesterday morning by the owner, a Mrs Joyce Myers. His death was being treated as murder, the investigation being led by D C I Alistair Dale, who it would seem had now been promoted. Learning that the victim had a girlfriend gave her a little bit more to go on; she now had to decide how to make the most of what were really the basics, at the same time avoiding Calder Bay's police force.

She took out her notebook from her bag and began to formulate her thoughts, jotting down the facts as she knew them and arranging and re-arranging them in order of importance; some she put to one side to be considered later, others she examined more closely, trying to decide what could be ignored. When it came down to it, she had to admit, albeit reluctantly, she had one heck of a lot of filling in to be done. She read again the newspaper clipping she'd brought with her, the paper somewhat crumpled now, and for the first time wondered why John Milne had been on such a short contract. Suddenly, it seemed odd, certainly required an explanation. Presumably the girlfriend would know. There had been no mention of how he'd been murdered, whether it had been a violent death. And what about motive? There had to be one. He'd been renting a flat in the centre of the town; that meant the High Street. As far as she could recall, the whole length of the street was taken up by commercial properties; there were no houses, only flats and they were on the first floors, above the shops. It shouldn't be too difficult to find where Joyce Myers had her business. All of which ruled out a random attack. John Milne must have been the target, meaning his murder had been premeditated. By progression, she came full circle back to motive. Why would anyone want to break into his flat, situated as it is in the centre of the town with a constant flow of people walking along the pavement, not necessarily so many during the night it was true, but in close proximity to two hotels when there was always the risk of someone being around? Beverly knew it wasn't her job to conduct a full-scale investigation; that was for the police, but she needed to know as much as she could about the background of the victim and the people with whom he associated. How else would she be able to put together a credible newsworthy piece for her newspaper?

***

Alistair arrived back in Calder Bay shortly after six having made good time from the airport despite the usual after-work exodus from the city as he'd joined the motorway. As always, when he'd been away, even for such a short time, that feeling of sheer happiness, contentment even, never failed to surprise him. *No longer that ambitious aiming-for-the-stars young man, eh.* Smiling to himself, and taking two steps at a time, he reached the main doors to the station and pushed them open. All appeared quiet: too early in the weekend for the customary round-up of the beer-happy, caught up in drunken brawls and, sadly, all too often resulting in domestic incidents inundating the duty sergeant with the inevitable fall-out from the rabble and sorting out all the paperwork police procedure demanded.

There was considerably more activity in the area, space being at a premium in Calder Bay's old police station, they had in recent years converted into their incident room; the atmosphere this afternoon felt as though charged, immediately reminding Alistair what it had been like during last year's murder investigation, particularly in the early days with those involved concentrating their efforts on any fresh lead they could find before they grew cold and were lost for ever.

Dan was waiting for him, a manila folder under one arm and trying to juggle two mugs of coffee at the same time: 'They told me at the desk that you'd arrived, sir. Thought you might appreciate a pick-me-up.' he added, passing one of the mugs to him.

'Thanks, Dan; you're not wrong, this is exactly what I need.'

'Exhausting, was it?'

'In many respects, yes, but productive.' taking a long and satisfying gulp of his coffee waiting for the caffeine to work its magic.

He opened the briefing by giving them the gist of his meeting with Adrian

Roberts, allowing them a few moments to assimilate how the complexities of what they had considered was a relatively straightforward murder investigation had significantly altered, not least how it would impact on each of them over the coming days.

'Drugs – again.' Colin was the first to break the silence, his lips formed in a silent whistle.

'Although on a much larger scale it would seem from our last case, Colin.'

'I know, sir, but I was just thinking that, as then, it looks as if our small seaside town has become embroiled right in the middle of it all.'

'Always the cynic, Colin.' Lilian said giving him one of her exasperated smiles, but it couldn't hide the real concern in her expression. Lilian Wood was a good officer, a credit in fact to their team and Alistair didn't need any proof to convince him that she would work uncomplainingly to the long hours which were going to be inevitable.

'As I've said,' he went on, 'Interpol have been working on this investigation for well over a year and while they've been successful in locating the man they're calling the key operator in the syndicate for the source of the drugs following their route into this country, from thereon they appear to have become stymied.'

'Until John Milne's murder.' Dan put in; his voice thoughtful as no doubt he was trying to work out the logistics of the whole operation.

'That's right and then I suppose you could say if they hadn't had this man Maitland under surveillance, they wouldn't have known about his friendship with Callum Lorimer.'

'This chap, Maitland,' Colin asked, 'where is he based; I was wondering how he communicated with Callum Lorimer.'

'He has a base in Amsterdam, also offices in London, but for the last eighteen months he's held a long-term lease at Arbroath harbour for an ocean-going motor cruiser, licenced under his name I might add.'

'Sounds a flamboyant type of character, not exactly in hiding.'

'That may be so, Colin, but it gives him the flexibility of making a quick getaway.'

'Tricky.'

'Very.'

'What do you think, sir;' Lilian asked, tapping her biro on her note pad and probably unaware she was doing it, 'about the other brother severing his contract out in Zambia and returning home, I mean. Do you think this could have acted as some sort of trigger to what happened to John Milne?'

'It does seem a reasonable assumption and, if it is, I think we can expect some further developments, but we must do our utmost to ensure this does not result in further loss of life.'

'Are Interpol ruling out John Milne as having any part in the smuggling, sir?' Dan asked.

'Yes, they are. They ran a background check on him immediately: he attended Glasgow University and after graduating worked for one of the major horticultural firms in Perthshire, during which time he went on a two-year work-based horticulturist course, becoming fully qualified prior to starting with "Lorimers' Fruits" eighteen months ago; lived with his parents before coming here.'

'I've been able to find out the name of John Milne's girlfriend, sir.'

'That's good, Colin; have you spoken to her yet?'

'I'm afraid not, sorry. According to one of the regulars at "The Shipwreck", she works at the Royal National Bank in the town, but as luck would have it, by the time I went along there they were closed, this being the first week of their winter timetable. She's called Laura Thomson,' he added, 'she's not in the phone book unfortunately, so it looks as if I'm going to have to wait until tomorrow morning when the bank re-opens.'

'Sounds as if she might be a relative newcomer to Calder Bay, but make it your top priority for tomorrow, Colin; there's always the chance she might be able to tell us something useful. If we are all thinking along the same lines that his death is somehow linked to his employers, always assuming he was innocent of any involvement, he may have sussed something out and shared whatever it was with her.'

'It would give us a motive.' Dan suggested.

'It would, wouldn't it?' Alistair said, his voice thoughtful as he mentally followed through the likelihood of such a hypothesis. 'You were up at Ashburn House today, weren't you,' he asked him, 'were you able to see Graham Lorimer.'

'No, I wasn't; he's so obviously trying to avoid any meeting and as much as I would have liked to insist, I decided not to, bearing in mind the Superintendent's concerns about his status.'

'I'm sure you're right, although we can't allow his reluctance to speak to us to continue, especially now since my talk with Adrian Roberts.'

'I was able to interview Bruce Lorimer though.' and going on to tell him about the company's security system.

'And what did you make of the man; I'm just wondering whether he's anything like his brother?'

'Well, the way you described Callum Lorimer, sir, I would say, the opposite.

He's something of a pompous character: completely lacking in any sympathy towards the murder of one of their employees, more concerned in promoting the success of the business. From what he was saying it seems they import vast quantities of exotic fruits which they distribute throughout Europe, their main supplier being an Amsterdam firm.'

'Interesting and it ties in with what Adrian was saying about Amsterdam playing a major part in the drug smuggling.'

'So, who is the 'mole' in this set-up I wonder.' Colin commented, 'Are we saying it's one of the Lorimer family?'

'Could be, Colin, but going down that road is, I'm sure you will agree, pure conjecture. We need to know more about the background of not only family members, but those employed by them, even their close friends and associates. Each alibi for Tuesday night to be checked and double-checked. If, and when, the time comes when an examination of the company's records is considered necessary, that directive will come from Interpol. Given the scale of the case, that will not be our decision. Have any of you any questions before we finish for the day, anything you may want to add.'

'There is one thing, sir which is slightly concerning me.'

'Yes, Lilian?'

'I saw Mary Struthers this morning to confirm Kirstie McKenzie's alibi. She was a bit vague as to when Kirstie left her house on Tuesday night. Kirstie had told me she left at ten o'clock, but Mary thought it had been later, nearer to ten-thirty, but it's not only the timing which is puzzling. According to her friend, Kirstie always uses the council's car park next to the library and would have had to walk back along the High Street to her flat, but she wasn't on the cctv footage which was dropped into the office this afternoon.'

'Are you sure?'

'As sure as I can be, sir. I've double-checked, also there's a streetlamp immediately outside the newsagents and she didn't walk along that stretch of pavement during the times we're talking about.'

'Strange, especially as the car park and her flat are on the same side of the street, unless for some reason she'd decided to cross to the other side of the road, but then why would she have done that?'

'Saw someone she knew.' Colin suggested.

'Possibly.'

'To avoid the camera.'

'Again possible, Dan. Whether there is anything significant or not, we should find out more about Kirstie McKenzie. How long she's worked for the company. Her relationship with any member of the family, socially or otherwise. In fact, anything about her. I'll leave that with you, Lilian. Dan,' he said, turning back to him, 'I'd like you to have another go at contacting Graham Lorimer tomorrow. There must be a reason for him avoiding us and that bothers me. Is he merely demonstrating his immunity of being questioned by the police, or is there another reason?.

# Chapter Six

<u>Friday 20th October: Ekabe</u>

Kate must have been in a deep sleep because she didn't hear Steve leaving for work; she hadn't heard him come in last night either, wondering as she idly watched the sunlight filtering through the thin cotton of the curtains how the first night of the play had gone. No doubt the club bar would have been packed; the atmosphere euphoric after the build-up of nervous tension these past few days. Would Steve have been among them, or would he have made his escape, unpleasantly remembering the other night the way Jack had sounded after their dress rehearsal when he'd said Steve had probably gone to the rugby club, as though his frequent forays there were common knowledge. The thought that her friends more than suspected the growing rift between her and Steve was an uncomfortable one and something she knew would have to be resolved before it reached that unthinkable point of no return and their relationship would end up like many others here in Ekabe, but not yet, and not today. Also, there was the play; it still had two more nights to run and it wouldn't be fair to distract him. She'd try and find a suitable moment next week.

It wasn't until she came back into the bedroom after her shower, that she became aware of how quiet it was; there was something different, some element at odds with how it usually felt at this time of the morning. It wasn't until she was getting dressed, her mind moving away elsewhere, that she realised what it was: she couldn't hear the rhythmic slashing of the machete, a sound so familiar it had scarcely registered before. Silas's grass cutting of the large expanse of grass around the bungalow was one of the houseboy's daily tasks, and one he always tackled first thing in the morning before starting on the housework, but for some reason this morning there had been a change in his routine. Although curious to know what it must have been, by the time she was dressed she had forgotten, but after drawing back the curtains, and seeing his abandoned machete lying on the grass, realised that as far as Silas was concerned, it must be something serious.

'Madam, something very bad has happened!' his first words to her as she walked into the kitchen, 'Madam!' he repeated, his eyes wide, either in fear or excitement, it was hard to tell.

'What's wrong, Silas?' deliberating keeping her voice level not wanting to make him even more agitated.

'It's Mr Lorimer, Madam.'

'Yes?'

'A bad man broke into his bungalow last night – ' struggling to go on, but she didn't prompt him, feeling it best to give him time to tell her at his own pace, '- there was much blood, Madam – and Mr Lorimer – he has gone now, Madam – '

'Alright, Silas,' not sure who she was trying to calm; what he'd just said sounded so extreme, so unbelievable, but one look at him, his forehead glistening with beads of perspiration, convinced her, 'how did you hear about this?'

'Noel. He told me.'

'Noel?'

'The houseboy of Mr Lorimer, Madam. I was outside - cutting the grass. He came and he told me.'

'What about the police, Silas?' she asked, trying to make some sense of what he was trying to say, his words now becoming more jumbled and incoherent, 'do they know?'

'They know. Madam Lorimer - she phoned the police when she saw –'

'Alright, Silas,' not wanting him to start all over again, 'this is very, very sad news, but there is nothing we can do. It will be up to the police; they know best.'

'Yes, madam,' he muttered, and although obviously still distressed, he picked up the sweeping brush and went through to the lounge to make a start on his chores.

She made herself a pot of coffee and took it outside on to the terrace. It was a lovely morning; the heavy rain of the night before had cleared the air which for days had been overbearingly humid; their garden, a riot of colour: the bougainvillea's scarlet blossom; the vivid purple, yellow and green of the frangipani and the deep burgundy of the aptly named African violets. Normally, she would have found solace merely by just sitting there, but not this morning. The imagery of what had happened was too much, dulling her senses with the awfulness of it all.

Alan had been an unassuming sort of guy, quiet, easy-going which he'd had to be, poor man, being married to a woman like Valerie. The Lorimers had only been in Ekabe for about eighteen months and it had been obvious right from when they first arrived that Valerie had no intention of adapting to what she must have realised would be a totally different kind of life. She was bored, restless and it didn't take long until she earned herself the reputation of being a potential marriage breaker with the inevitable result that among the wives she was treated with extreme caution. Whether Valerie had loved her husband or not shouldn't make any difference; she would be alone, in a foreign country, and presumably still suffering from shock, especially if she had been the one to discover his body.

Shouldn't she be doing something, Kate thought, feeling guilty. It didn't seem right that she, a fellow compatriot, should be sitting here in this glorious sunshine with nothing more taxing than to refill her coffee mug while a woman only three bungalows away was struggling to understand why her husband had been killed. She was still battling with her conscience when the crunch of gravel on the driveway prevented her making that decision. She couldn't see the vehicle from where she was sitting, but she recognised the grinding of the brakes as it came to a sudden standstill under the carport and wasn't surprised to see the portly figure of Derek Bovington come striding round the side of the bungalow.

'Morning, Kate,' he called out, 'you've heard the news I expect.'

'I have yes, Derek, so shocking, I still can't believe it.'

'Don't suppose you can, my dear.' plonking himself down on one of the rattan chairs and taking out a large, checked handkerchief, mopped his brow, 'damned humid today, that storm didn't do much to clear the air.'

'Let me get you a cold beer, and then perhaps you can tell me what you know about what's happened to Alan.'

'Thanks, Kate, that's exactly what I need. Ah, here he is!' he said, a delighted smile on his florid features. Silas, having seen Derek's jeep pulling up outside the kitchen window, had instinctively known he would welcome a cold drink.

'Thank you, Silas,' she said, 'that was thoughtful of you.'

'Good man.' taking the glass from him.

'Have the police any idea who's responsible?' Kate asked him after Silas had gone back inside the bungalow.

'Early days, Kate,' he answered, taking a deep gulp from his glass, 'it has all the appearance of a random break-in, although it would seem that, apart from leaving the lounge in a bit of a mess: no real damage: chairs overturned, books hauled out of the bookcase, cushions on the floor, that sort of thing and according to Valerie nothing has been stolen.'

'Were they disturbed do you think?'

'Could have been.'

'But surely, isn't it more usual if that happens, they immediately run off?'

'They probably did, my dear.'

'But they attacked him, Derek; they killed him - '

'Hold on there, Kate,' he interrupted, 'we don't know that.'

'But – honestly, Derek, this is a ridiculous conversation we're having! Alan *is* dead, isn't he?'

'As to that,' he answered slowly, 'we don't know.'

'What are you saying, there was no body? But, Silas said there'd been a lot of blood - '

'There was, Kate, but Alan was not in that bungalow.'

'I don't understand.' and she couldn't, trying to remember Silas's exact words - there was much blood he'd said, and then – Mr Lorimer, he has gone.

'I've spoken to the inspector in charge,' Derek explained, 'Christopher Musenge he's called, seems a capable chap. They can't say for sure whether it's Alan's blood or not, but we should know by the end of the day once they get the pathologist's report. Alan's pick-up wasn't there although there were traces of blood close to where he parked it, therefore it appears likely that he must have managed to get away, but that is the gist of it all so far, Kate.'

'My God, I don't know what to think now. Where can he be, Derek? Surely, if he'd been able to drive he would have gone to someone he knew or the hospital perhaps.'

'I'm afraid it's another, I don't know.'

'It doesn't sound good, does it?'

'No, it doesn't, Kate.' he agreed, levering himself out of the chair, 'And on a less serious note, we'll see you this evening.'

'The play, yes; I'd almost forgotten.'

*** 

News of the break-in and the whereabouts of Alan Lorimer was the main topic of conversation around the expatriate community for the remainder of the day accompanied by wild speculation as to what really had happened, some of the suggestions of his disappearance becoming more outrageous as the hours passed and there was still no sign of either him or his pick-up.

It was much later in the afternoon before they learned how a couple of schoolboys, walking back to their village, came across a dark grey pick-up truck, the driver's door hanging wide open and the front of the vehicle overhanging the edge of what was known locally as Ekabe Ravine: a deep rocky gorge through which one of the Zambezi's tributaries swept, and reputed to be crocodile infested. The boys had retraced their steps back into town and presented themselves at the police station, full of excitement over their find; one of them, the oldest, proudly handing over a scrap of paper on which he'd written the registration number. It didn't take long for the vehicle to be traced to the Ekabe Technical College, and was allocated to Alan Lorimer, one of the college's lecturers.

Inspector Christopher Musenge had been at his desk in his newly renovated glass-fronted office when the blood test result came through and, having already obtained Alan Lorimer's blood group from the college's staff records, he was able to confirm that it matched those prints taken at the bungalow. It had been a long and harrowing day with numerous telephone calls from headquarters demanding a progress report. Apart from now establishing that Alan Lorimer had been physically attacked following a break-in at his bungalow the night before, he had nothing of a more positive note to add to his initial report; the victim, whether still alive or not, had not been found and, apart from the fact his pick-up truck had been located at the ravine was no proof that he had actually driven it there. As no prints had been detected, it immediately suggested someone had taken the precaution of removing them, whether by Alan Lorimer himself or his attacker, was one more problem for the inspector to solve.

The forensic team had worked for hours scouring the area; as the light had begun to fade, flood lamps had been brought to the site, but the density of the scrubland defeated their efforts and it was decided they would have to wait until the following morning before continuing.

Christopher Musenge was on the point of calling it a day, looking forward to a couple of beers in the police club before heading off home, when there was a light tap on the door and Sergeant Brian Phiri came into the office.

'Sorry to interrupt, sir, but just checking with you before I finish.'

'That's alright, Brian,' turning off his computer, 'I think we've done all we can today. Would you like to join me for a beer; I think we deserve one?'

Five minutes later and they were comfortably seated in a corner of the police club's bar; apart from four officers playing pool at the far end of the room and a couple more having a chat with Edward, retired from the force, but now managing food and beverages for the club, they had the place to themselves.

'No sign of the press yet, sir.' Brian commented, a wry expression on his face and taking a sip of his beer.

'Not sensational enough for them, Brian.'

'You mean no body?'

'Exactly. Also,' he added, 'as they're probably not classing it as a local crime, the victim being a foreigner, I mean.'

'Even although it has all the hallmarks of a local crime?'

'I agree that it does appear like that, but quite frankly, I'm inclined for the moment to keep an open mind about the whole business.'

'Because of the missing victim?'

'Yes,' Christopher Musenge nodded, 'that's puzzling. Why attempt to kill him? There should have been no need for that, Brian; they'd broken in, presumably to steal what they could get their hands on and then they were disturbed, perhaps they thought the bungalow was empty. I believe their natural instincts would have been to run off, get as far away from the place as possible.'

'Which I suppose they did.'

'True and that is what's worrying me, Brian. They didn't steal anything and, apart from the general disorder, there was no damage done and perhaps more importantly, it didn't seem like a normal break-in, not like the ones we're used to, I mean.'

'You mean it looked contrived?'

'Yes, in some respects it did. We need to know more: about Alan Lorimer, also his wife, their marriage, we need to build a credible picture of, not only who was responsible, but why whoever it was chose the Lorimers' bungalow to break into last night. Their immediate neighbours were questioned this morning but none of them are saying they saw or heard anything untoward. I realise we can't pin the time down to when it happened, but at a rough estimate, between seven and eleven.'

'Odd no-one heard those terrace doors being smashed.'

'True, but I suppose that could have been muffled in some way.'

'As some of his neighbours were at home, sir, I wonder why he didn't call on them for help, instead of driving off.'

'That's if he did, Brian. But if he didn't, it does raise the question of why would his attacker take such a risk.'

'It's a puzzle, sir.'

'You're not wrong, and it's one we have to solve, preferably without the intervention of Lusaka's big boys.'

\*\*\*

The bell rang at ten minutes to seven in the club bar to summon members of the audience to their seats which immediately put an end to the speculative exchanges between many of them. Kate couldn't be certain who had put forward the theory that Alan must have been thrown clear of the vehicle when it had crashed through the bush, even going so far as to suggest that his body had fallen down the steep bank of the ravine to be swept away in the fast-flowing river below. She supposed it was as credible as anything else she'd heard that day.

She quickly finished her drink and followed Derek and Peggy through to the auditorium, Peggy having told her when she'd arrived at the club that Sheila had phoned to say she wouldn't be able to be with them.

"That's a shame," she had said, "she was so looking forward to seeing the play. She's not ill, I hope."

"Oh, no, she sounded fine; anyway, she would have said if that was the reason. I expect it's something to do with her riding stables; it is inclined to take up a great deal of her time. So much for her being retired." Peggy had laughed.

"What sort of work did she do before she came here?"

"She always described herself as a civil servant; in London, I think."

"She was with the Home Office, Peggy my dear."

"Oh, was she really, Derek, but then Sheila is a very modest woman; she would never brag."

"Hmmph. Well, if you want – "

Somewhat fortuitously, they were spared from having to listen while he expounded on what she guessed was one of his favourite topics, by the bell ringing and was still smiling when they finally found their seats. Derek was so predictable. At least she thought as the lights dimmed, he wouldn't be able to spout forth whatever views he had on British politics.

It seemed strange to see Steve on the stage; somehow, although some distance away from where she was seated, he appeared larger than life. He was playing the part of Bob, one of the three adulterous husbands in the play, and was portraying the character very well. He was something of an chameleon this husband of hers; anti-social almost to the point of rudeness, yet on stage he had morphed into an entirely different being: expansively gregarious. Which one was the real Steve? She didn't think she knew anymore.

There was one final curtain call, an enthusiastic applause from the audience of well over a hundred, before everyone filed out of the auditorium, many of them making a beeline for the bar where the more experienced, or extra thirsty, collected their pre-ordered drinks.

'Very pro-active of you, Derek.'

'Well, Kate, one has to be.' passing a gin and tonic to her, 'Did you enjoy this evening's performance, or did you find it difficult to switch off from what has been happening among this expatriate community of ours.'

'It has been rather dreadful though, not knowing whether Alan's still alive.'

'Oh, he can't be, Kate,' Peggy protested, her glass poised to take a sip of her whisky, 'he couldn't have survived such an awful fall. No-one could.'

'We're assuming that's what happened?' a voice behind Kate's right shoulder piping up.

'Ah, Harry,' swivelling round to face him, 'didn't see you come in.'

'Sorry, didn't mean to eavesdrop, but let's face it, this awful business is all we've talked about today. But,' he continued quickly, 'what I meant was that none of us know whether he was even in the car when it ended up where it did. That's all.'

'A good point though, and you're right, somebody else could have been driving and – ' pausing, Derek, for once, stuck for words, ' – dragged him from the bungalow, I suppose. There was a fair bit of blood in there which could indicate he was in no fit state to drive.'

'But,' Sally said, coming up beside her boyfriend and putting her arms around his waist, 'where is Alan? He certainly didn't turn up at the hospital, I would have heard first thing this morning when I arrived there, even although I hadn't been on night duty.'

'I would have thought, if he was able to drive, that's where he would have gone.'

'But he didn't, Peggy.' Kate reminded her.

'I know.'

By the time the cast had joined them five or ten minutes later, their mood of despondency had lifted and they were good-naturedly arguing over the open morality of Aykbourn's plays. Steve surprised her by turning up, pausing now and again on his way over to them, to accept praise for his performance.

'Hi.'

'Hi, stranger.'

'What's that supposed to mean?'

'Just that,' Kate said, keeping her voice down, 'I've hardly seen you all day; in fact, Steve, apart from fleetingly when you came home to change after work, we've scarcely exchanged a word with one another.'

'Well, we're exchanging a few now, aren't we?'

'Smart arse.' she muttered under her breath, and not wanting to start an argument, moved away to talk to Philip Edwards who had just come in.

More rounds of drinks were ordered, voices grew louder, interspersed with the occasional burst of laughter and she did her best to relax, but this evening she was finding it difficult. It wasn't only the growing tension between her and Steve, it was something else; elusive and intangible, but lodged in her brain, in some corner impatiently waiting to be recognized. What she needed was someone to talk to, suddenly missing Cora. She had been a good listener, also she hadn't been in Ekabe long enough to become entrenched in the insular way of the rest of them, but she wasn't here, a situation she would have to accept. Their friendship of only three months, the length of Cora's secondment, aptly described the transient nature of their lives out here; there was no real stability, no point in settling down to the expectancy of years of friendship with people in the comfortable knowledge they would all be around for some time. The downside of living the expatriate life. Mostly it didn't bother her, but recently, and especially now with all this mystery surrounding Alan, she wished Cora was still here. Thinking of her, Kate realised she ought to let her know about Alan, certain she would want to know, deciding to give her a call in the morning.

She had another drink with Peggy and Derek and the others before heading off for home, not too surprised to find that Steve was no longer in the bar, but this time she wouldn't embarrass herself by asking if anyone had seen him. She knew where her husband was; at least she thought she did, for the first time a tiny flutter of suspicion made its unwelcome appearance. She had never had any grounds for believing he was unfaithful; it just hadn't occurred to her. Perhaps it should have done, finishing the last of her gin and tonic and, calling goodnight to everyone, left the club.

She had to drive past the Lorimers' bungalow before she reached their own. There was nothing to show that the property, identical to all the others on the campus, had been the scene of such a violence to cause harm to someone, especially as the police tape had been removed from the front of the gate, but Kate could not envisage a time in the weeks and months ahead when she wouldn't be reminded each time she drove past.

She was turning into their driveway when she caught a flicker of light in the rear view mirror against the dense blackness of the night. At first, she thought she'd caught the reflection from her own car's headlamps, but when a couple of seconds later, it was repeated she realised she'd been mistaken. It was torchlight. Somebody was out there, walking along the front of Alan's bungalow, the light appearing more often now, wavering slightly as it neared one of the boarded-up patio doors, obviously too soon for the glass to have been replaced. Parking the car just short of the carport, she cut the engine and stepped out on to the gravel drive and. continuing to keep an eye on the other bungalow, walked across the grass towards bougainvillea bushes which would shield her from whoever was over there. She didn't know how long she stood there, five, perhaps ten minutes, and was on the point of giving up and going inside when she heard the distinctive engine of a pick-up truck. It could be Steve, but unlikely; it was too early for him to come home. She remained where she was, more out of curiosity than anything else. The vehicle was now in view, the headlamps illuminating the stretch of laterite road in front of the bungalows, but instead of continuing it stopped outside the Lorimers'. She continued to watch as the driver emerged, the click as he closed the door sounding excessively loud. The gate must have been open because he appeared to only give it a nudge before he was walking up the drive to the bungalow. He had almost reached the building when the figure with the torch came running towards him, arms outstretched to embrace him. It was too dark to make out whether she recognized them, but the woman must be Valerie; as to the man, she could only guess and not wanting to catch their attention, she turned away.

*In any case, Kate, it doesn't concern you.*

Or did it?

It wasn't until she was inside that it occurred to her that it might have been Alan she'd seen, but that hope was instantly dashed when she remembered that his pick-up truck had been involved in the collision and presumably would be out of action, at least until it had been repaired, although more likely the police had impounded it as being part of their evidence.

If it hadn't been Alan, she reasoned, filling the kettle to make a coffee, not bothering with the cafetière, whoever it was not only knew Valerie, but was no mere acquaintance calling to find out how she was coping, because of course the person with the torch was her. Who else?

She took her mug into the lounge, switched on a table lamp and, slipping a disc into the CD player, allowed the sweet voice of Whitney Houston to engulf her. She needed to still her troubled mind; nothing was to be achieved by all this introspection, suspicions with no grounds, no substance at all, unless she was to include a persistent gut feeling. *The wife is always the last to know, Kate.*

# Chapter Seven

Friday 20th October: Calder Bay

Although it was only the third day since the body of John Milne had been found, there was no police tape outside any of the shops or offices in the High Street to indicate there had been a murder, equally Beverly cynically reasoned as she slowly walked along the pavement looking up at each doorway for the proprietors' names, no visual reminder to either the curious or otherwise that once again Calder Bay was in the media spotlight.

It didn't take her long to find the Myers' name on a small brass plaque above the doorway of the newsagents, and without hesitating she went inside. The woman, plump with short curly grey hair, looked up and smiled at her.

'Good morning.' Beverly said, but with no real plan of how she was going to conduct the conversation she hadn't prepared a script in readiness. Not that she worked like that. Spontaneous in action and spontaneous in speech, that had always been her motto and so far, hadn't let her down, much to the detriment of Andy's nerves.

'Good morning; it's Miss Grant, isn't it, the journalist from London.'

'You remember me?'

'Of course I do.'

'You surprise me; I don't think I've been in here before.'

'Perhaps not, but I remember seeing you in the "Shipwreck" the last time you were here. In fact,' she went on, obviously not in the least concerned that she was a member of the dreaded press, 'I always read your column in "The Times".'

'Well, thank you.'

*So, Andy Walters, not everyone in Calder Bay runs a mile when they see me coming!*

'I expect you're here because of this dreadful business.'

'I am, yes, Mrs Myers. I understand the victim was renting your flat.'

'That's right, he was. Such a terrible shock it was – seeing the poor man lying there.'

'It must have been.'

'It doesn't bear thinking about; what it must have been like for him, I mean. The flat's in a terrible state, even the furniture has been moved about.'

'Oh, dear, and I expect you've had the added stress of the police being there.'

'Yes, but I can't complain; they've been very considerate. My husband and I thought they would have been all over the place with their vans and all that blue and white tape, but by yesterday afternoon nobody would have known that anything so awful had ever happened. It would have been so bad for our business.'

'Of course it would. And you've lost a tenant.'

'And a very good one he was too; very quiet and considerate and although he had a girlfriend, he never took her up to the flat.'

'Yes, I heard he had a girlfriend.'

'Poor lassie, I feel so sorry for her.'

'She works at the Royal Bank I believe.'

'That's right; she'd only be with them a few months, I think that's when she moved here.'

'She's not local then?'

'No, dear, she isn't, came from down south somewhere.'

'Perhaps she'll go back there after what's happened.'

'She might, but then she'd only known John for a very short time.'

'I suppose it depends how close they were, and how much she likes Calder Bay, that is if she lives locally.' wondering for a moment whether she had overdone her interest, but she seemed to have forgotten she was talking to a journalist.

'She lives in one of those houses along the front, near the tennis courts and the putting green. Very nice they are, but I expect she's only renting."

With more information than she had hoped for, and within such a short time, she managed to make her exit. There had been no stopping the woman and she seemed reluctant to see her go. Joyce Myers was indeed a rarity among the many she'd ever interviewed. Beverly had initially planned to try and speak to John Milne's girlfriend at the bank or, if she could be persuaded, to meet when she'd finished work, but knowing now where she lived, although she didn't have the girl's exact address, might be better.

First of all, she decided, walking away from the newsagents, a coffee. She was spoilt for choice, counting at least half a dozen coffee shops before she was even halfway along the street, finally deciding on one across the road and next door to a florists: red and white gingham curtains at the bow windows and small tables and chairs outside on the cobbled pavement with matching tablecloths and cushions. Obviously, she reckoned, a popular venue for locals and holidaymakers alike as there was only one free table. She ordered a cappuccino, taking out her notebook to jot down the progress she had made so far.

By the time the young waitress reappeared with her coffee, including a complimentary biscuit, no ordinary biscuit, but an Abernethy; a traditional Scottish accompaniment and mouth-watering, she had worked out her next plan of action although realising it may not achieve anything worthwhile and that she could be placing her head in the proverbial noose, but convincing herself that she had a story she wanted to write and for it to have any substance, there were certain risks she had to be prepared to take.

The double gates to the Lorimers' estate were wide open and Beverly dutifully followed the signs to the visitors' parking area at the side of a rather attractive annexe. A massive lawn, chevron-striped, faced the property and sloped down towards a line of willow trees, their branches trailing over and across a narrow stream at the bottom of the garden. Quite a setting, Beverly thought, not without a touch of cynicism, but that was her first impression as she stepped out on to the white gravel drive and looked around; even the annexe, which had presumably been added to accommodate the staff employed by the company, didn't look out of place: the golden limestone matching so well with that of the main house, there was no way of knowing when it was built. She could hear voices in the distance as she walked up the few steps to the main entrance, the glass doors sliding open as she approached.

There was no-one around in the reception area: ultra-modern and a complete contrast to what she was expecting. Windows along the length of one of the walls faced out to where she'd parked the car and further to the left beyond a waist-high beech hedge, row upon row of fruit trees. Obviously, a highly organized business and, having read up what she could find on Google about "Lorimer Fruits", was not all that surprised. A number of framed black and white prints caught her eye, wandering over to have a closer look; they dated back to the early nineteen-hundreds, most of them photographs of members of the Lorimer family down the years, the more recent at the end. One of them, again in black and white, must have been taken on a special occasion: a birthday perhaps of the older man with a thick head of hair and a Hercule Poirot moustache seated in the centre flanked presumably by his three sons and two women, one of them with a mass of dark hair smiling directly into the camera.

'Quite the rogues' gallery.' a voice said close behind her startling her; she hadn't heard him approach.

'Very impressive.' she said, turning round to face him, 'Your family, I presume?'

'You presume right.' a quirky smile hovering as he slowly appraised her. 'Bruce Lorimer and I apologise if you've had to wait for someone to see you.'

'No, that's alright. I didn't make an appointment which I should have done, but I'm only in Calder Bay for a couple of days. Beverly Grant,' she introduced herself, 'I'm a journalist, Mr Lorimer; freelance I might add and –'

' – Oh, dear; why do I find that somewhat – disturbing?'

'I fully appreciate that our profession is not the most popular, but I can assure you that there is nothing underhand in the way I work; I don't belong to what is known as the media pack. I'm selective in the topics I choose and I never fabricate to woo my reader, Mr Lorimer.'

'I see. So, Miss Grant, why are you here?'

'I'm doing some research for an article I intend writing in respect to the recent murder in Calder Bay and I was hoping that as the victim was employed by your firm, I may be able to get some background material on him.'

'I would say straight away that there is nothing we can tell you about John that you probably don't know already; namely, that he was on a two-year contract with us – '

' – he was a qualified horticulturist?'

'Correct.'

'Therefore, Mr Lorimer, why was he not employed on a more permanent basis?'

'Because he was here merely to cover for my brother while he was working overseas, in Zambia actually.'

'Zambia? He would have been on the Copperbelt out there I expect.'

'That's right. You've been there?'

'No, but I had a boyfriend who did; he was in Kitwe.' plucking the name from her meagre knowledge of the country.'

'Really, Alan's in Ekabe.'

'Oh, I see. You mentioned he's on a two-year contract, does that mean that was the same length as John Milne's?'

'Yes, that's right.'

'How long then had he been working for your company?'

'Eighteen months actually.'

'So, he still had another six months left on his contract.'

'He would have yes, but as Alan is returning sooner than we had expected, regrettably we were having to sever his contract.'

'He probably wasn't too happy about that.'

'As it was, we had yet to speak to him, but then all of this has nothing to do with what happened.'

'No, of course not.'

'Now, enjoyable though it has been talking to you, Miss Grant, 'I'm afraid you will have to excuse me; I have a number of overseas calls to make before midday.' his dismissal, smoothly delivered, left her in no doubt she had outstayed her welcome. Once again, her journalist status had rendered her *persona non grata*. Although she had found his patronizing manner slightly off-putting, her thick skin prevented her being offended, quite the reverse. In his arrogance he probably hadn't realised he had supplied her with far more than he intended. He hadn't even seemed phased by her barrage of questions. Bruce Lorimer, she decided, thanking him for sparing the time and walking away, was not as smart as he obviously thought he was.

During the short time they'd been talking, a young woman, presumably their receptionist, was now behind the desk, making a pretence of busying herself while doing her best to hear what they'd been saying. Wrong timing, Beverly regretted; she might have been more forthcoming than her smooth-talking boss. Interesting though how he remained at the window watching her as she drove back down the drive. Not an entirely wasted visit, wondering whether he realised by now that he'd given her a piece of extremely useful information. The other brother. Why was he coming back early? Working overseas he'd told her. Could be a simple explanation, but with only six months to the end of his contract and with the inconvenience such a decision would no doubt cause to whoever was employing him, it didn't sound right. Perhaps she was being too suspicious, looking for anomalies that weren't there. Or, perhaps she wasn't.

*** 

There was a time, Colin Fielding grumbled under his breath, when a request to speak to the bank manager was met with a positive response: provided he was free, you would have been ushered into his office, courteously offered refreshment, before stating your business. Not now. For a start, banks didn't have managers *per se:* they had consultants and they didn't have their own office: they had a desk, surrounded by other desks, the distance between them obviously calculated with precision to comply with banking standards, with the result other customers, unless they were hard of hearing, could follow what was being discussed. Colin's visit on Friday morning to Calder Bay's branch office of the Royal Bank was one of routine which meant there was no way he could pull rank and expect preferential treatment. All he wanted, for pity's sake, was to speak to one of their employees. After what seemed an interminable wait, he was waved over to one of the desks by a young man who looked as if he should still be at school, although he was quick enough to tell him that Laura

Thomson hadn't turned up for work yet.

'She could have slept in, Sergeant Fielding.'

'It is eleven o'clock,' Colin reminded him unnecessarily, 'do you know whether she's phoned in to say why she's late.'

'I'll have to check with our personnel officer.' a frown furrowing his pale brow as, with obvious reluctance, he pressed a button on his mobile.

'No,' he said, continuing to look worried, 'she hasn't phoned.'

'While you're still on the phone,' Colin asked him, 'it is important we contact her as soon as possible, therefore would you ask for Miss Thomson's address, please.'

'I don't think they'll be able to give you that information, Sergeant; for confidentiality reasons.'

'I can understand that, but I'm involved in a police enquiry and Laura Thomson is one of the people we would like to talk to. Therefore,' Colin continued, his tolerance starting to wane, 'would you please ask your personnel officer to provide me with her home address?'

With Laura Thomson's address finally obtained from a much-relieved bank clerk, Colin emerged from the bank. Number thirteen Beach Road was one of four villas facing the tennis courts, the one he wanted at the end. His first impression as he approached was that they had seen better days; it wasn't as if they weren't being maintained, paintwork on each of them looked recent and there were no bedraggled hedges or gates hanging on their hinges, it was the sort of melancholy, bygone appearance which he found slightly depressing. He rang the bell twice and when there was still no answer, walked round the side of the building to the back door; a plain glass panel down the centre gave him a clear view of most of the kitchen: cream-painted wall cabinets, enamel sink unit, an eye-level fridge/freezer and in the centre of the room, a wooden table and a couple of matching chairs. All the curtains were drawn back, even the ones at the front when he went back to ring the bell again, but still no response. He had no option but to give up and come back later. Also, he'd call the bank before they closed to find out whether she'd been in touch with them. It was too early to seriously consider anything significant in not being able to contact her, although as he made to turn away, he couldn't prevent his brain telling him differently.

'Excuse me!' a disembodied voice called out to him, immediately followed by a woman's head peering over the top of the dividing hedge, 'I don't think she can be in.'

'You've seen her go out this morning, madam?' he asked her, moving closer to the hedge; she must be eighty if she's a day he thought, taking in what he could see of her features between branches of hawthorn: a round smiley face, but heavily wrinkled, the bright red lipstick adding a startling dash of colour against her pale cheeks.

'Who are you anyway, young man; I don't believe I've seen you here before.' her voice loud, the Edinburgh vowels accentuated as she peered at him, her manner changing significantly when he showed her his warrant card. 'Oh, dear me; you're police. Is there something wrong? I do hope not; we've never had any trouble in this road in all the years my family have lived here and I can tell you that is a very long time indeed.'

'There's nothing to worry about, madam, but we're currently conducting an enquiry and Miss Thomson is one of the people we would like to talk to.'

'I see. What sort of enquiry?'

'It's regarding an incident which occurred the other night in the town – '

' – I suppose you mean the murder of that young man.'

It wasn't a question. She might be elderly, but there was nothing debilitating about her intelligence, realising it would be pointless to fob her off with some tame explanation, besides he reckoned, there wouldn't be many of the town's residents who hadn't heard about the murder.

'We understand that your neighbour was a friend of his and as with anyone who knew the victim, we have to interview them.'

'To eliminate them from your enquiries. That's what you say, isn't it, Sergeant?'

'It is a crucial part of our preliminary enquiries, you're quite right, madam, therefore, if you could tell me, for instance, when you last saw your neighbour, it would be helpful.'

'Well, the last time I saw her, Sergeant was yesterday around half-past one. I must admit I was somewhat surprised to see her returning home from work so early in the afternoon, but then it was none of my business. I'm not one to pry.'

'I see, but you don't think she's at home this morning; did you perhaps hear her leave the house?'

'Well, to be honest, I didn't, but then her car's not outside. She always parks it as close to the house as she can and it was definitely there when I went shopping yesterday afternoon.'

'Would you happen to know the make of her car, madam?'

'Of course; I will have you know that I was a professional rally driver in the nineteen-seventies and I have retained my interest in the motor car and I can tell you that Miss Thomson drives a bright yellow Ford Focus – '

71

'Thank you, that's extremely helpful – '

' – just a moment, young man; you'll want the registration number, won't you?'

Duly chastened, and thanking her again, he managed to make his escape.

\*\*\*

Beverly drove along Beach Road and once she spotted the green mesh bordering the tennis courts, she slowed down and pulled into the side. There were only a few houses at this end of the road, a good stretch of it taken up by two golf clubs and a small sports shop, the four villas reminding her of the old seaside properties on the south coast with their wooden verandas on the first floor and facing out to sea. These were little different, the front gardens were also similar: clumps of pampas grass and shrubs of rosemary, even the grey concrete sun dials. One of those must be Laura Thomson's she decided, and unfastening her seat belt, made to go over and have a closer look. She had opened the door when she saw the same police officer she bumped into the day before. Colin Fielding. He was coming away from the end villa; he didn't look across the road, and she watched him as he walked away, back in the direction of the town.

She waited until he was out of sight before leaving the car and going across the road, taking her time until she reached the end of the row of villas, stopping when she came to the gate. She didn't think she was wrong in assuming that this was where Laura Thomson lived. Why else had he been here. If it was true she had been John Milne's girlfriend, it was only logical that the police would want to speak to her, but surely, she'd be at work, so why had he been to the house? Why hadn't he called at the bank to see her? Unless, the explanation suddenly blindingly obvious: she wasn't there. Her journalistic instinct was too strong to dismiss, possible reasons running through her brain.

*And what makes you so certain, Beverly, he hadn't been able to speak to her? Eh?*

There was only one way to find out, one way to dispel that gut feeling she recognized as instinct, and lifting the latch of the gate, walked up the gravel path to the front door. There was no response to her repeated knocking which only went to prove she had been right: Laura Thomson wasn't in, but if she was, she didn't want to see anyone. Everyone is entitled to their privacy, Beverly thought as she turned away and retraced her steps to the gate, halting half-way at the sound of rustling. It was coming from the hedge at her left-hand side, but the foliage was too thick to see clearly, and deciding it was probably a neighbour's cat, she carried on. She would come back later in the afternoon, but already she had the beginnings of the article she would be writing, not dissatisfied with her first morning's work.

The same pensioners were in their usual corner of the bar when she went in there just after midday, amused at the way they made a point of ignoring her, but then not all that surprised. By now, they would know why she was in Calder Bay and no doubt would be labelled 'press' – to be avoided. She was used to being treated as some sort of undesirable and it didn't bother her, the barrier she'd developed over the years in the rough and tumble of the newspaper world had made sure of that, although very occasionally, as with the woman at the newsagents earlier, she would meet someone who treated her as if they actually *liked* her.

There were no available tables by the window and as she'd done the day before, remained at the bar although making a point of not standing too close to the three regulars; she just didn't want to make her interest in what they were saying too obvious to them, not that it mattered where she was, she would still have no problem in hearing them.

She'd ordered a glass of the house white and had taken her first sip when she heard Laura Thomson's name mentioned. She turned her head slightly in the direction from where the voice was coming. It took her a couple of seconds to separate it from the rise and fall of all the other voices, in particular the two guys standing next to her, loudly voluble in their impatience to be served.

'Don't you think it strange then, Patsy?' managing to block out their voices and to pick up on the thread of what the two girls further along were saying.

'She has just lost her boyfriend in the most awful circumstances; she just probably couldn't face coming in today.'

'Look, I'm not disagreeing with you, but the point I'm trying to make is this; if she felt like that, she would have phoned in, but she hasn't.'

'Are you sure about that, Jenny?'

'I am actually; I heard them talking about her in Personnel as I was leaving. They've been trying to phone her all morning, but without any luck. Also,' she went on, Jeremy told me that Sergeant Fielding had been into the bank earlier asking for her and insisting on being given Laura's address.'

'Oh, dear, I don't like the sound of that.'

'Could be just police procedure in a murder enquiry; you know how they have to question everyone who knew the victim.'

'Put like that, it sounds – well, frightening.'

'You have to admit though,' the one called Jenny said, 'it's all quite exciting.'

Beverly missed the other girl's reply by the arrival of more customers pushing forward, eager to reach the head of the queue which had been forming, but she'd heard enough, and much more than she had expected. She had seen Sergeant Fielding leave what must be Laura Thomson's house, after presumably learning she hadn't turned up for work. Also, from what she'd just overheard, the bank had been unable to get hold of her, which in itself as far as her journalistic antennae went, was more than interesting.

\*\*\*

Callum's nerves were at breaking point. He had scarcely slept for the last two nights and even Bruce, who was not the most observant of people, had commented on his haggard appearance at breakfast that morning, followed by Myra's insistence that he should be delegating more, a constant theme of hers, especially since Alan had been away. *As if he bloody could!* The mere thought of her finding out the real reason for the way he was acting didn't bear thinking about. Those hours he'd been lying tense, eyes wide open in the darkness of their bedroom, were self-destructive; he found himself going over and over the last meeting he had with Ben, picking out every word he'd said, analysing it, enlarging it, until it grew out of all proportion and lost any meaning. Certainly, his reaction on learning of Alan's imminent return had been extreme. Was he a cold-blooded murderer? Or capable of ordering such an act? And then, to add to the confusion in his middled brain, was the way he'd practically dismissed what he'd said about Bruce seeing John in the office after work. He had been totally concerned about Alan coming back and remembering the clear meaning behind what he'd said brought him out in a cold sweat. There was a dreadful inevitability about everything and for the first time in his life Callum was afraid.

By the afternoon he felt no better, if anything he felt worse. He'd tried a number of times to call Ben, but each time was put through to voicemail. He hadn't left any message. Ben would be able to tell it was him, therefore it was obvious. He was avoiding him.

He felt trapped, realising now when in all probability he had left it too late, that there was nothing he could do about the whole ghastly business, not only his own personal situation, but the reputation of the business. The fact that he only had himself to blame merely added to his anguish. He had allowed his own dissatisfactions and desire to escape to motivate him, to disregard the consequences if anything should go wrong with what Ben had convinced him was a foolproof plan. He had been so confident. 'You play your part, Callum,' he'd said when they'd formally shaken hands on the deal, 'and I will play mine.'

Well, he had, and to be reasonable, so had Ben, but like a house of cards, once Alan had made the decision to come home early, they were faced with a major problem.

The receptionist buzzing through came as a welcome release and he leaned forward across the desk to press the switch.

'Yes, Alison?'

'It's Mrs Lorimer, sir – '

' – my wife?' frowning.

'No, sir, Mrs Valerie Lorimer.'

'Oh, right,' the breath catching at the back of his throat making him cough. As he waited for the girl to put the call through an overwhelming sense of unease settled in the pit of his stomach and remained there long after Valerie had finished telling him about what had happened to Alan.

'Callum. Callum, are you still there?'

'Yes, I'm here. I'm just trying to take it all in, Valerie. You say, he's disappeared. After the break-in at your bungalow.'

'It's believed that whoever broke in last night attacked him – '

' – why do they think that?' interrupting her, impatient to hear more.

'Because of the blood, Callum.'

'God!'

'Yes, there was quite a lot of it on the hall floor, the police reckon he must have disturbed them, also there was more outside, where he parks the pick-up truck.'

'But you said the truck wasn't there, so he must have been fit enough to drive.'

'To a point, yes, but we don't know how injured he might have been. However, a couple of schoolboys found the pick-up this afternoon; it was off the main road, in the bush and overhanging a ravine. They reckon Alan must have been flung from the vehicle and rolled down the bank. It's very steep and the river, well, it's known to have crocodiles.'

'Oh, my God, Valerie.'

'I know, Callum, it's awful, isn't it, but I thought the family should know.'

'Of course, but is it possible – could he have survived.'

'The police think it's extremely unlikely. They're searching the area, but they're not holding out much hope. There's a native village nearby, the one the boys were heading for, and they've spoken to the village headman, but nobody has seen him, so I'm afraid it doesn't look good.'

'No, - no, it doesn't. So, what are the next steps, Valerie?'

'There's going to be an inquest on Monday – '

' – but there's – there's no – '

' – I know, but apparently from what the police have told me that doesn't prevent them holding one.'

'I see.' but he didn't see, he didn't see at all.

They didn't spend much longer on the phone, Valerie saying she would call again after the inquest, and as he replaced the receiver, he was shocked to see how is hand was trembling, so much so, he made two attempts to get it back in its cradle. The shock was intense. Waves of dizziness made him sway slightly as he stood up but, taking a firm grip on the edge of the desk and breathing deeply, succeeded in gaining control of both his limbs and his troubled mind. He had to see his father, and Bruce of course. They needed to be told as soon as possible, in the event that the news, although thousands of miles away in Central Africa, should reach Britain before he had the chance to prepare the family.

The dread he was feeling as he walked along to Graham's office was nothing to what he had ever experienced before. Callum was only too aware that his father wasn't the most sympathetic of men; he could have asked Myra or even Kirstie to break the news to him, but it was his duty. He was no coward and he was the oldest son.

# Chapter Eight

Alan didn't know how long he'd been lying there, drifting in and out of consciousness; it may have only been minutes or even longer, but somehow he didn't think so. He tried to work out what had happened, but the effort proved too much; each time, just as he was on the point of remembering, a wave of dizziness would drag him back again. Memories. Images. A kaleidoscope of moving patterns floated behind his closed eyelids. There was a moment when he'd sensed rather than heard, a movement near him, sufficient to force him to open his eyes. His vision had been so blurred it had been almost impossible to focus, also to ignore the throbbing pain at his right temple, but through sheer determination he'd managed to make out the hazy outline of a man's head and shoulders stooping over him, but it wasn't until he stepped back that he recognized him.

He must have drifted off again because when he next came to, the pain had eased off slightly and by the complete silence he knew there was no-one else in the bungalow. This time, he found the strength to pull himself upright and, using the wall for support, walked the short distance into the kitchen towards the back door; opening it, he stumbled across the square of concrete to the pick-up. It took him several attempts to unlock the door and he had to use both hands to manoeuvre the key into the keyhole. He knew he was in no fit state to drive, but he felt compelled by the fear that whoever had attacked him would return.

He didn't know how badly he'd been hurt. It had been too dark inside the bungalow and in his haste to leave he hadn't taken time to check just how serious his injuries were, but he couldn't fail to see by the dark stain on the floor once he was on his feet that he had lost a fair amount of blood and should do the sensible thing and go to the hospital, but he was reluctant, although for some inexplicable reason he didn't know why this was. There was one thing he was sure of and that was he needed time to think. Seeing Steve Burrows had been no illusion, no delirious hallucination. It had been him alright, staring down at him as he had been lying semi-conscious on the hall floor.

Steve Burrows. The man he'd suspected for some months of having an affair with Valerie, but in the beginning had chosen to ignore the signs. It wouldn't have been the first time she'd been unfaithful; she had just become more adept at hiding them from him. He'd often been close to confronting her, but each time changed his mind, deciding she would never have admitted it any way and, ostrich-like, had continued to kid himself there was nothing wrong with his marriage; that was until he met Cora. He had not enjoyed telling Valerie he was filing for a divorce; her reaction had been predictable, but the overwhelming feeling of relief afterwards convinced him he'd been right. Cora had shown him in such a short time that he could be happy.

He was driving erratically, but the road leading away from the campus was deserted. He reached the junction where, if he took the road to the right it would lead to the hospital, but instead, he went the other way out of Ekabe towards the Ndola and Kitwe highway.

Once he'd turned off the main road the surface rapidly deteriorated, the pick-up juddering as he manoeuvred around the potholes in the hard-packed laterite. Ekabe Lodge was about ten kilometres along what was now little more than a track, but by the time he was only about half-way, the constant jerking and swerving brought the return of the light-headedness, causing him to repeatedly tighten his grip on the steering wheel.

Without warning, the glare of headlamps of a vehicle fast approaching from behind dazzled him, obscuring the road ahead. As the light grew closer he made to accelerate, remembering that the entrance to the lodge could only be metres away but, panicking, his foot slipped off the pedal at the same time as his truck hit the edge of a pothole. The engine stalled, throwing him forward in his seat, and for the second time that night as his forehead thumped hard against the dashboard, he felt himself slipping into oblivion.

This time when he woke he wasn't lying in a heap on the hall floor, neither was he crumpled up at the side of the road. He was in a bed, a single one, a light cotton sheet covering him, a soft pillow beneath his head and surrounded by a swathe of mosquito netting with a woman he had never seen before sitting on a bamboo chair next to him.

'Oh, good,' she said, leaning forward and peering closely at him, 'you're awake. How are you feeling?'

'Confused,' he managed, but his throat felt so dry he had difficulty in forming the words, 'where am I?'

'First of all, have some water. Here you are,' she said lifting the edge of the mosquito net and handing him a tumbler of ice cold water. It was delicious.

'Better?'

'Yes, thank you; I can talk now. I crashed the pick-up, didn't I?'

'You did, that's true. You've also a rather nasty gash at the side of your head; it isn't a deep wound so there shouldn't be any need for stitches. I expect you'll have a few headaches though, but not so bad that a couple of pain killers won't remedy.'

'I don't remember much, only that someone broke into my bungalow. I must have disturbed them because the next thing I knew I was lying on the hall floor.'

'You were rambling a bit, but I gathered something like that must have happened.'

'Oh, God, was I?' concerned over what he might have said.

'I shouldn't worry. I'm Sheila Campbell by the way and you're at my farmhouse, no longer a farm but stables now, just outside the town, and I must apologise but I took the liberty of looking in your wallet, so I know you're Alan Lorimer and you're a lecturer at the Technical College in Ekabe.'

'That's right. We haven't met before, have we?' concerned whether they had and he was suffering from memory loss.

'No, we haven't. We've probably got mutual friends though. I'm kept pretty busy with the horses, but I usually manage to get to the club fairly often to meet up with friends for a drink.'

'Last night was the first night of their play; were you there?'

'I was in the club, yes and I was driving back here when I saw you in front of me. I don't know where you were coming from, but it's a wonder you got anywhere considering the way you were driving.'

'I know; I was stupid, I should have gone to the hospital, but well – ' faltering, not sure how to explain, or how much he wanted to say.

'I expect you had your reasons; I suppose you were making for Ekabe Lodge.'

'You're right, I was. I thought I would spend the rest of the night there, but, well I didn't quite make it though.' pushing himself upright, wincing at the sudden movement, 'How long have I been here; I really must get back - '

' – to answer your question,' she said, placing a steadying hand on his shoulder, 'quite a while; you've been asleep for a good part of the day, but I thought it best not to disturb you.'

'I appreciate that and I can't tell you how grateful I am to you for rescuing me; God knows what would have happened to me if you hadn't, but there's a lot I have to do and there's the pick-up, that's if it's still there.' swinging his legs down from the bed and using the edge of the small bedside cabinet, pulled himself upright.

'I can guess how you must be feeling, but there have been certain developments since last night which mean you may have to stay here for a while.'

'What! I know I've had a bang on the head, plus a further shake-up when I ditched the pick-up, but – '

'I'm sorry, Alan; the last I want to do is to add to your confusion, but I hope once you've heard and considered what I have to say you will agree to my proposal.'

\*\*\*

It had been no easy task to haul the semi-conscious man from the driver's side of the pick-up, the effort made even more strenuous by having to drag him clear of the truck and into the passenger's seat of her own vehicle with only the meagre light from a cloud-shrouded moon for guidance. Out of breath, she'd waited a few moments before driving away, and wondering, as she looked across at the slumped figure next to her, how on earth she had managed.

No doubt, she decided, switching on the ignition, years of training in the service had a lot to do with the way her well-honed muscles had responded, also the last five years spent running the stables with only a couple of native lads to help her with the heavy stuff. She couldn't help feeling more than a little pleased with herself, taking another look at him. She didn't believe he was in any danger; although still unconscious, his breathing was steady and the gash at the side of his head, although fairly recent hadn't been caused by him driving into the ditch. It must have bled quite profusely at some point judging by the deep stain on his shirt collar and streaks of dried blood down the side of his face, but as she was closer to the farmhouse than the local hospital decided what he needed right now was probably rest, rather than a load of medics making him feel a whole lot worse.

Ten minutes later she was home and her night watchman was quick to rouse himself from where he'd been huddled inside the fence to unlock the double gates for her. She thought it unlikely in his half-awake state he would have noticed she had anyone with her, not that it mattered; the locals who worked for her had all been with her since she bought the property and over the years had proved their loyalty. She was aware they gossiped, but it would only be amongst themselves. Pulling up as near to the front door as she could, she cut the engine. She had been dreading this last manoeuvre but by then he was more or less conscious and, with her help, was able to walk, albeit slowly, the short distance from the car to the inside of the farmhouse although she wasn't sure just how aware he was and once they'd reached the room to the left of the hall, the one she used for guests, he collapsed on to the bed, his legs becoming tangled up in the edge of the mosquito net. He'd had his eyes closed, whether through exhaustion or he was choosing not to communicate, she wasn't sure. Deciding there was no point in trying to rouse him, she pulled off his shoes and, covering him with the sheet, left him there.

Although it was late, almost midnight, she knew she wouldn't be able to sleep, besides she felt she ought to keep checking on him, beginning to wonder whether she had done the right thing in not taking him back into Ekabe to the hospital, but it was too late now. She'd see how he was in the morning and feeling she deserved a whisky, poured herself a generous measure from the old crystal decanter she kept on the sideboard along with an eclectic collection of glasses.

The next time she looked in on him about an hour later, he was sound asleep although he'd moved over on to his side, presumably to avoid the light from the hall, and his wallet which must have been in the back pocket of his jeans, had fallen out. She picked it up and flicked it open, feeling only slightly guilty, but just as quickly dismissed this with the excuse that she should try to find out who he was. There had to be a reason to explain the condition he was in. He'd mentioned a break-in and although he hadn't said anything about being attacked she reckoned that was what must have happened.

There wasn't much in the wallet: a few Kwacha notes, a couple of credit cards for Barclays and Citibank and a security pass in the name of Alan Lorimer which stated in smaller print that he was a senior horticultural lecturer at Ekabe College. So Adrian Roberts had been right, Sheila sighed, slipping the card back inside the wallet.

Adrian had made his first contact with her on Wednesday via a secure text, giving her a briefing of their ongoing investigation, "Operation Gemma", explaining that with the recent murder of an employee of "Lorimer Fruits", they were expecting a possible follow-up in Ekabe where the syndicate could be targeting one of the directors, namely Alan Lorimer, currently on contract with Ekabe College. Adrian's instructions had only been for her to be on alert, and unless unavoidable, not to become involved He'd also said that if there were signs of any significant occurrences developing , he would immediately arrange for the deployment of one of their officers to join her, but meanwhile, she was very much on her own. It was imperative therefore, late though it was, that she should call him. Adrian would expect nothing less and as she looked down at the unsuspecting sleeping form of one of the Lorimer brothers, was beginning to speculate on the complexities that lay ahead and the involvement she would be expected to take. *You've been out of the field for five years, Sheila. Do you think you can cope? But then, do you really have any choice?'*

Returning to the lounge, this time closing the door behind her, she dialled Adrian's mobile number. It took three rings before he answered, and although it was apparent by the slight croakiness in his voice she'd woken him, it didn't take him long to recover, dismissing her apologies.

'No problem, Sheila; it must be important.'

'I believe it is, sir.' going on to tell him as much as she knew about the attack made on Alan Lorimer.'

'They haven't wasted much time, have they? Sounds as though whoever they hired, which they must have done I suppose, were in too much of a hurry. However, Sheila, this botch-up job could act in our favour.'

'Yes?'

'You're one hour ahead aren't you - hold on a minute while I switch on a light.'

'It's almost two o'clock here, sir.'

'Good, still a few hours until dawn. This pick-up truck of his, Sheila, how badly damaged is it?'

'I couldn't see property, but I would say it's drivable.'

'Let's hope you're right then and if you are, this could give us the chance we need to fool them into believing they've been successful, that the accident last night had been fatal and there would therefore be no risk of him returning here; it would give us time to set something up at this end to intercept the syndicate's next assignment which, although scheduled for Sunday is, given the inevitable police activity surrounding the Lorimer family, likely to be aborted. However, they'll not want to hold on to their precious cargo any longer than they have to which means we will have to keep them under close surveillance over the next few days and it's important they believe their plan to dispose of your man there has succeeded.'

'That's if his attack is connected, sir.'

'You're absolutely right of course, Sheila and I don't like to assume, but in these somewhat convoluted circumstances, feel we should make an exception. We'll need his agreement of course,' he added, 'so what do you think; any ideas?'

'It depends on how amenable his is, sir, hopefully he's going to remember what happened before the crash when he finally wakes up.'

'Well, do your best to persuade him, and if he isn't, call me and I'll have a word with him.'

'Do you think I should mention the suspicions we have about his brother?'

'I think you have to; he's not going to like it, but I guess a lot depends on how close the pair are.'

'About the pick-up, sir.' she prompted.

'Ah yes, I haven't forgotten. You've said it's at the side of the road, not the main road admittedly, but someone is going to spot it and when that happens the police will be quick to organize a search for him; we want to avoid that if we can.'

'There could be a way, sir.'

'Yes?'

'It's right what you say, someone will be bound to notice it, and most likely sometime today. It's a relatively quiet road and apart from my property, there's only Ekabe Lodge but it's a fairly popular place, not only for the toing and froing of guests at odd hours of the day and night, and with their restaurant has become quite popular, also there's a number of delivery trucks for the lodge.

'Where does the road lead?'

'I was just coming to that,' she said, 'it's actually a dead end coming to what's known locally as Ekabe Ravine; a tributary of the river Zambezi flows through, extremely rapidly I might add; not exactly a tourist attraction although it is quite spectacular. The last few yards of the road are no more than a track. What I was thinking was if I could drive the truck as far as I can towards the edge, that when it was eventually found, they would all reach the same conclusion - '

' - that he really had perished;' finishing for her, 'it would certainly give us the breathing space we need. We would need to clear this with the Zambian authorities in Lusaka of course, not me, personally, but my superior will handle that side of things. Not yet, though. There are too many imponderables. It isn't as if we can give the Zambian people any assurances. I'd be in favour of waiting a few more days to see what transpires.'

'This will depend on Alan remaining incognito.'

'Oh, yes. The problem is, Sheila,' he went on, 'at the moment we don't know when the next assignment will take place, but if everything goes according to our plans, we will certainly be ready for them.'

'Do you anticipate any difficulties with the authorities here, sir?'

'No, I don't. Given the worldwide concern with the smuggling of illicit drugs, Zambia can ill afford not to comply. No, I don't see any problems. Britain has always maintained a good relationship with the country which of course does over-ride a number of political barriers. Once we've set this up, Sheila, I have every confidence this syndicate lot will be lulled into a false sense of security which should be to their downfall.'

'It could work then.'

'It should, but my only real concern is that we're placing considerable responsibility onto you and that worries me slightly. Take this damned vehicle for instance, do you honestly believe you can manage to move it to this ravine on your own?'

'I think so. I've been thinking the best way I could do this and, rather than driving back to where we left his truck, it makes more sense if I were to walk – '

' – walk! Do you think that's wise, Sheila; that doesn't sound a good idea.'

'Actually,' stretching the truth slightly, 'it isn't all that far away; it wouldn't take long and at least there would only be the sound of one vehicle. Even at this time of night, there is always the possibility of someone being awake and it would mean I'd be less likely to be noticed.'

'If you're sure?' although he sounded doubtful, but after a couple more minutes of reassuring him and promising to give him a call when she had returned to the farmhouse, he had reluctantly agreed.

***

Over-riding the initial shock of hearing how the family business had become embroiled in what he understood to be international drug smuggling with his older brother playing such an integral part in the whole god-awful set-up, was the proposition Sheila Campbell was now putting to him.

'You are asking me to feign my death, to cruelly deceive my family!'

'Worded like that, Alan,' she said, 'yes, that is what we're asking you to do, but it would only be for a short period.'

'And if I refuse?'

'We hope, once you've had time to consider, that this won't happen.'

'Well, I've considered. I am totally opposed.'

'Perhaps you're being too hasty – '

' – no, I don't believe I am, Miss Campbell. There is something you and – your colleagues? -don't seem to have taken into consideration and that is the impact such a plan would have on, not only my family, but my own life. I have started divorce proceedings and I have no intention of delaying these, also and most importantly, the hurt and confusion which this would cause the woman in my life. That would be considerable.'

'You don't accept that the smuggling of drugs is a national problem and is a potential killer? However,' she went on, moving away from where she'd been standing by the side of the bed and over towards the open door, 'I don't expect an answer straight away, affirmative or otherwise; as much as I dislike saying this, Alan, but if you continue in your refusal, I have to stress that to do so is a civil offence –'

'- this is absolutely ridiculous! You have no right, no right whatsoever!'

'I may not, but I can assure that the people I work for have full authority to implement this ruling.'

There was silence in the room, seconds passed as he appraised the woman who was effectively holding him prisoner. She looked so *ordinary:* mid-fifties, perhaps more, but then he'd never been any good at guessing a woman's age. Who was she anyway? Presumably, if what she'd told him was true, she must be attached to MI6, but surely retired, especially as she was living what seemed a fairly reclusive kind of life. He'd read somewhere that their officers could be recalled out of retirement, but his knowledge was sketchy. He knew one thing though; she had been right about the civil offence, therefore, giving an involuntary shrug to his shoulders, he didn't have much of a choice. In fact he didn't have any choice, he would have to go along with it all, but with one exception; there was no way he was going to subject Cora to the stress of believing their relationship was over before it had really begun. Somehow, he would think of a way to contact her.

'I don't see how you, or whoever is behind you, can bring this plan of yours off, but it appears I'll have to go along with what you want me to do.' he said to her at last.

'So you agree?'

'Reluctantly, yes.'

'Good.'

'What about my pick-up; although I can't remember exactly where I crashed it, it's bound to be spotted.'

'It's been taken care of.'

'Presumably to set the scene for my untimely demise.' unable to keep the sarcasm from his voice.

'Exactly.'

# Chapter Nine

'Why the hell did Valerie phone you, Callum?'

'I don't know, father; I expect she was concerned about breaking the news to you.'

'Tell me *exactly* what she said again.'

'That there was a break-in at their bungalow last night sometime, but there was no sign of Alan, also that his pick-up truck had gone.'

'And that's it?' Graham Lorimer demanded, his knuckles white as he grasped the arms of his chair, 'Everyone assumed the worst!'

'Probably because of where the truck was found this afternoon.'

'Assuming, Callum! Assuming! I refuse to believe that my son is dead!'

'Perhaps we'll learn more by tomorrow.' realising as soon as the words were out of his mouth how dismissively inept he must sound.

'Callum.'

'Yes?'

'I'm not a fool you know.' the way he had lowered his voice should have been a warning, but his brain was refusing to accept what he most dreaded to hear. His father knew! Intuitively, the way he had always done, he had sussed him out. His father had interpreted his reaction to the news about Alan.

'Are you deaf, Callum?' each word calculated to remind him of his controlling dominance as the patriarch of the family, a dominance which demanded total compliance. His father's strength of character had not diminished over the years, and somehow, he had to find a way to deflect the route his mind was taking.

'I do understand how you must be feeling;' Callum said to him, only too aware he was probably wasting his breath and making matters worse, 'hearing about Alan the way we have has been a dreadful shock, but perhaps he has been able to survive. We shouldn't lose hope, father.'

'Do you realise how bloody patronising you sound? Do you, Callum? As I've said, I'm no fool and I don't believe in coincidences either.'

'Sorry?'

'News of two sudden and unexplained deaths within a matter of days of each other! Are you going to stand there with that mealy-mouthed expression and tell me they are not connected? Of course they are! What the hell is going on, Callum? Eh?'

'How can they be connected; both incidents are thousands of miles apart.'

'Do you know,' his voice moving up a notch, 'I cannot make up my mind whether you are just plain dumb or – or,' he repeated, not taking his eyes from Callum's face, 'you are deliberately, for reasons of your own, attempting to conceal something.'

'You're quite wrong, father.' *You can't even lie convincingly, Callum.*

'I don't think so. Why else are we being inundated by visits from the local constabulary? No, Callum – ' holding up his hand, 'allow me to speak, if you don't mind. I am sure it will not have escaped your notice, but we have had three police officers here since Wednesday morning: a sergeant, an inspector and their chief inspector no less. I would say that that is something of a stretch on police budgets, wouldn't you? And, don't insult my intelligence by saying they are only doing their job.'

'I would say the reason for so many visits was partly an attempt to speak to you, father.'

'Hmmph. Well, for your information they did. This morning. I happened to be available when their Inspector Aitken called and was able to provide him with my alibi for Tuesday night.'

'Well, that should satisfy them; they've now got alibis from all of us.'

'I doubt that very much, you know, Callum. The inspector gave me the very strong impression he was more interested in a motive for John's murder, the implication being it was premeditated.'

'I would be interested to know why they should be thinking along those lines.'

'I would say the answer is fairly obvious; John met an untimely end to his life and on the same day his body was discovered, the police were informed that Alan was cutting short his contract and returning home and a day later he is subjected to a physical attack. And you, Callum, are trying to convince me that the two crimes are not connected!'

'I – '

' – just go, Callum, just go.'

He couldn't remember his father ever being so furious before, seriously concerned about him; his blood pressure must have risen to an alarming level, but knew if he'd stayed with him any longer, it would only make him in an even worse state. Walking back along the hallway to his own office, he tried calling Ben again, but this time instead of being put through to voicemail, there was only silence. He'd blocked his calls. So, he thought, slamming his office door behind him, what the hell was he to make of that. *You've well and truly landed yourself in the mire now, haven't you, Callum?*

He'd have to tell Myra about Valerie's call, already anticipating her reaction, knowing he couldn't expect any sympathy, or support either from her. As for Bruce, well, inwardly shrugging, of course he was going to be shocked. Perhaps his reaction would be the same as his father's, but did it really matter? He was on his own. His father already had suspicions about him; the fact that he couldn't be held personally responsible for whatever happened to Alan, it didn't prevent him feeling responsible. As for Ben Maitland? What about him? He could come and go as he wished. Even if the authorities had their suspicions, as far as he knew, Ben was a free agent; he had his cruiser and could leave at any time. May have already gone. Leaving him to – to what?

There was no way he could concentrate and that included facing Myra. She would have to hear about Alan from his father, taking his jacket from the back of his chair and picking up his keys from the desk, made his way through to reception and out to where he'd parked the car. Fortunately, Alison was on the phone, sparing him any awkwardness of concocting a reason for leaving the office; he'd almost reached his car when his mobile bleeped. His first instinct was to ignore it, but force of habit prevented him. He should have been relieved when he saw Ben's name flashing up on the tiny screen, but instead he was filled with a terrible foreboding as he clicked to access the text message: *consignment eta 2100 hrs Sunday 22nd*

*\*\*\**

Beverly was on her way downstairs to the bar much later that afternoon when Andy called. Somewhat surprised as she was usually the one to contact him, the only exception being if there was some point with any copy she'd sent through to which he objected, therefore it was with a sense of anticipation as she pressed the green button on her mobile.

'Hi, Andy.'

'An interesting piece of news has just come through on Reuters.' characteristically launching in without any social nicety.

'Yes?'

'Should whet that insatiable appetite of yours.'

'Andy, please! You're doing this deliberately, aren't you?'

'Sorry, couldn't resist. There's been an incident in Zambia, in a small copper mining town to be exact, involving a member of the Lorimer family; namely Alan Lorimer.'

'What do you mean by incident?'

'Just that, Beverly; nobody really knows exactly what happened yet, but apparently he was the subject of an attack last night; his bungalow was broken into, left in something of a mess by all accounts although nothing was stolen. There was no sign of him though, or his pick-up truck.'

'So, he managed to escape?'

'It would seem so, yes, but a further piece came in about thirty minutes ago to report that the truck had been found at the edge of some ravine a few miles out of Ekabe, that's the town by the way, and the general consensus of opinion being that he must have lost control of the vehicle, crashed into a thick belt of trees and with the impact been thrown clear - . '

'- and did he survive the crash?' interrupting him when he hesitated.

'It doesn't look like it, Beverly. They're continuing their search, but up to the time the report came through, they hadn't found him, therefore it looks as though they're coming to the conclusion he must have landed up in the river which we've since learned is crocodile infested.'

'Ouch!'

'Quite.'

'The press out there have been pretty quick off the mark, haven't they?'

'I would say so, and whoever it was, sufficiently motivated to notify the Reuters office in Lusaka. Anyway, not much more to add, Beverly, except to say the inquest is on Monday.'

'In Lusaka?' she asked, not that it really mattered, but any information helped to give her a better picture.

'No, in Ndola which is thirty-odd miles from Ekabe.'

'Ekabe.' she repeated, 'that must be where Alan Lorimer was working.'

'You knew he was there?'

'I did actually.'

'How the hell did you find that out?'

'I'm an investigative journalist, Andy. Remember?'

'Okay. Okay, I hold my hands up, but if this business has anything to do with the murder of the guy from "Lorimer Fruits", be careful.'

'Of course.' relieved to end the call; she had a great deal to think about and didn't need Andy to interrupt her thought process. With this latest development, she would have no trouble in writing up a two-to-three column piece, but her conscience wouldn't let her: what she had gleaned so far was not enough; it lacked substance, hard facts to support her growing suspicions. A man had been brutally murdered with no apparent reason, and now thousands of miles away, another man had supposedly met an untimely end, both incidents occurring within a couple of days of each other and with "Lorimer Fruits" being the likely connection. What was that connection? Who, she wondered, stood to gain. Somebody did, that was for sure and, deciding to give her brain a rest, did what she had intended to do before Andy's phone call: relax over a large glass of chilled Chardonnay in the "Shipwreck's" bar. Who knows, Beverly thought, picking up her bag and checking that her notebook was in there, she might get lucky and find a little bit more to feed what Andy had described as her insatiable appetite, not for the first time regretting her inability to access the resources which were so freely available to the police but, she shrugged, closing her room door behind her and going downstairs to the bar, she'd always managed to pull the rabbit from the hat and saw no reason why she couldn't do the same again.

The place was buzzing, not so different from Fridays in London when office workers converged on to the pavements and making a beeline for the nearest pub as a prelude to their weekends. She recognized the same two girls from the bank over by the window and as she waited to be served they were joined by a blonde-haired girl, and a tall thin guy with Hugh Grant spectacles. Royal Bank employees she reckoned, but when she looked closer at the blonde one, realised she was the receptionist at "Lorimer Fruits". It was definitely her and so far she hadn't seen her.

Beverly ordered a Chardonnay from Ken Morris, at the same time wondering how she was going to manoeuvre her way across to where they were, when the couple who'd been at the table next to them got up from their seats to join a group further along the bar. *Now Beverly, here's a fine chance to find out anything you can about the set-up of blondie's employers.*

None of them appeared to notice when she came over, not even when she pulled one of the chairs nearer to their table from where she hoped it would make it easier to attract the receptionist's attention. She'd taken a couple of sips of her wine before an opportunity arose and as it happened, quite a natural one: the scarf, a long silky one, had fallen on to the floor from the back of her seat. They both noticed it at exactly the same time, but Beverly was quicker than her, bending down to pick it up.

'Thanks,' she smiled, 'should have known better than to leave it there, I've lost count of the number of scarves I've left behind in pubs!'

'Dreadful, isn't it; I have the same problem.'

'Oh - I've just realised,' she said as she took the scarf from her, 'I saw you this morning talking to Bruce Lorimer, didn't I; my boss.' she added unnecessarily and with more than normal curiosity, remembering how she couldn't keep her eyes off them earlier.

'I really would have liked to have had a word with you actually, but somehow the timing wasn't right.' Beverly said.

'He wouldn't have approved of the staff being over familiar with the customers; the company have rather strict policies.'

'Not surprised;' the Hugh Grant look-alike butted in, 'you're a journalist, aren't you?'

'How did you know that, Jeremy?' she asked him.

'Sorry,' he said, ignoring her and focusing on Beverly, 'that was rude of me, but you are, aren't you?'

'I am, yes.' Beverly answered not offended; the tough skin she'd developed over the years had inured her to far worse.

'But, Jeremy,' one of the other girls asked him, sliding her chair nearer to Beverly's, 'how did you know?'

'Well – ' beginning to look uncomfortable, no doubt embarrassed by his crassness, ' – I remember seeing you in here last year at the time of the murders and John Henderson's arrest. This is a very small town,' he explained, 'and people are inclined to revel in anything out of the ordinary happening in their midst and of course the press had a field day, well more than a day actually, and since then, I've often read your column in "The Times". I suppose you're here to cover John Milne's murder.' he added.

It wasn't really a question; it was obvious he had worked that out for himself and he wouldn't be the only one, therefore she didn't think it warranted any confirmation; she hadn't travelled five hundred miles up to Scotland to be quizzed by the local populace.

'Did you know John Milne?' she asked him.

'Er – not as such,' the direct question obviously unsettling him further, 'he was just one of the regulars in here, that's all.'

'John was a nice guy.' the same girl from the bank said, Beverly remembering now that she was called Jenny, 'Laura thought so anyway,' she added for Beverly's benefit, 'they'd been an item for about three months.'

'I heard he had a girlfriend; what a dreadful shock for her.'

'It was, especially the way she found out.'

'Yes?'

'You've probably learned Laura is one of our colleagues at the Royal Bank.'

'Ye – es.'

'It must have been not long after we opened on Wednesday morning,' starting to explain, 'Laura had quite a few customers waiting to be served and she overheard a couple of them discussing the murder; how the police had been outside the newsagents earlier, then how the ambulance turned up to take the body away. And, as it was clear that the victim had been living in the flat above was John. Well –'

'How awful, poor girl.'

'I know, but she was very professional; she must have been in shock of course, but she was terribly upset.'

'Especially as we knew there was nothing we could do to help her.' the other girl put in, 'She was determined to act as if nothing had happened, she didn't even mention how she was feeling to anyone in personnel.'

'A pity she hadn't though, Patsy.'

'What do you mean?'

'Well, if she had, at least personnel would have been prepared for her not coming in today, and I might have been spared the third degree from a certain Sergeant Fielding; talk about throwing your weight about!'

'Oh, Jeremy, surely he wasn't as bad as all that.'

'Hmmph.'

'I expect you've had the police up at Ashburn House, Alison?' Jenny asked her.

'That's an understatement; we've been inundated since first thing on Wednesday morning and they still keep coming.'

'Why do you think that is?'

'Not sure, but I think it's mostly to do with alibis for everyone and of course our M.D. hasn't exactly made himself amenable to being interviewed, but one of their officers finally caught up with him this morning.'

'That should put an end to their visits then.'

'Don't you believe it; their Chief Inspector turned up just as I was leaving the office and he did not look happy.'

'Perhaps something else has happened.'

It was as if they had forgotten she was there, their whole attention was focused on this new piece of information, something more to titillate them. She was probably being unreasonable; there was no question of their concern for their colleague, but her inbuilt cynicism of human nature told her otherwise: someone they had known, albeit not well, had been murdered and immediately their everyday lives had become, not to put too fine a point on it, decidedly more interesting. She had deliberately not contributed to their conversation, not that she had anything to add. The combined knowledge of the four of them probably didn't amount to much when most of it sounded more like guesswork, although hearing that her arch enemy, DCI Alistair Dale, had made a late afternoon visit to the offices of "Lorimer Fruits", must surely concern the disappearance of Alan Lorimer.

How long would it be Beverly wondered before Fleet Street would be alerted of a possible international connection between the murder of a young man in northern Scotland to the mysterious incident in Central Africa. Not long, she was certain, meaning she only had a matter of hours until the media pack descended on Calder Bay making it more difficult for her to achieve that front page scoop.

*\*\*\**

'The lady is very persistent, sir; she says she will only talk to you.'

'Alright, Sergeant,' Alistair sighed; he had been on the point of finishing for the day and looking forward to opening a bottle of Merlot and sampling a couple of slices of the slab of camembert he'd bought earlier at the new delicatessen in the high street, 'put her through.'

'Miss McFarlane, how can I help you?'

'You *are* the Chief Inspector?'

'Yes, I am – '

' – good. I'm phoning in connection to the murder of that unfortunate young man, Chief Inspector.'

'Yes?'

'I live next door to his girlfriend, Laura Thomson and I believe something very serious may have happened to her.'

'You say you believe something may have happened to her, does this mean you're not sure?'

'Well, I suppose if you put it like that, I have to admit I cannot be positive.'

'Miss McFarlane, perhaps if you tell me what's concerning you, we can take it from there.'

'Very well. Let me explain then; earlier this afternoon, I took in a parcel on her behalf from one of the courier firms. I must admit I was somewhat reluctant because I wasn't sure when she would be home, especially as I'm going away for the weekend and my nephew would be picking me up at six this evening. Anyway, I agreed to take the parcel from the driver, but then as she hadn't returned I decided to find a secure place in her back garden and drop a note through her letterbox to tell her what I'd done.'

She stopped abruptly at that point and for a moment Alistair thought they'd been cut off, but then she continued, sounding less assertive and slightly out of breath.

'Take your time, Miss McFarlane.' realising how useless that must sound, although accepting it was one of those stock phrases in the faint hope that it might help.

'I do apologise, Chief Inspector; I must be more affected by what I've seen that I realised.'

'Would you prefer if I were to call and talk to you; perhaps less stressful than trying to explain over the phone?'

'No, no, I'm fine now and besides Johnnie will be here very soon for me.'

'If you're sure – '

'Oh, I am. However, as I was saying, I went into Laura's back garden and then it occurred to me that perhaps she had returned and I'd missed her, so I knocked on the door, but there was no answer and, I don't know what made me do it, but I tried the handle and found that the door was open. I called out naturally, but there was no reply although I noticed her handbag on the kitchen table, the one she always uses.'

'So, was she in?' anxious for her to reach the end of what she trying to tell him, but realising nothing would be gained by trying to rush her.

'No, she wasn't. I went into the lounge, calling out to her as I crossed the hall, and then I saw that the room was in utter chaos, Chief Inspector; cushions had been thrown on the door, books dragged off the shelves, papers scattered everywhere, such a mess. I couldn't even imagine what could have happened.'

'Alright, Miss McFarlane, if you would wait until I arrive; it will only take me about ten minutes to reach you. Can you do that?'

'Of course.'

'Just one question before I ring off, did you venture upstairs?'

'I did go up to check and I can tell you my heart was in my mouth, but she wasn't in any of the rooms. What do you think has happened to her, Chief Inspector?'

# Chapter Ten

Cora was woken shortly before nine on Saturday morning by the persistent ringing of the telephone. It would be Alan she thought, throwing back the duvet, annoyed for allowing herself the indulgence of drifting back to sleep after the alarm had gone off earlier, but she'd been late home last night, staying longer in the pub than she had intended catching up with all the gossip since she'd been away.

She had been so certain it would be him that it took several disappointed seconds before she recognized Kate's voice.

'Kate? '

'I'm sorry, Cora, have I woken you?'

'No – well, yes, but it doesn't matter; it was time I was up anyway. How are you?'

'I'm fine - '

' –is something wrong? Is it Steve?'

'No, not Steve; it's Alan; I thought you would want to know, Cora, but there was a break-in at his bungalow on Thursday night and – well it seems he was attacked – '

'Oh, no! Is he alright?'

'I'm afraid not. This is so awful having to break the news to you like this, over the phone.'

'Is he – ' struggling to find words she was afraid to utter.

'They've not been able to find him, Cora -,'

' – I don't understand - ' her desperate concern turning to impatience.

' – nobody knows what really happened, except that it looks as though he managed to drive away from the bungalow – there were traces of blood – on the hall floor and outside by the carport.'

'But – but, Kate, surely if he'd been injured he would have driven straight to the hospital.'

'He didn't though because his pick-up was discovered yesterday afternoon outside the town: at Ekabe Ravine, you probably know where I mean?'

'Yes; just off the road before you come to the Lodge, I used to pass quite close to it every day when I drove into town. This is so – so unbelievable, Kate; what are the police saying?'

'There's been no official report yet – '

' - they will continue to look for him, won't they?' her words sharper than she intended.

'I'm not sure, but I don't believe they will give up altogether, not until after the inquest on Monday anyway.'

'Inquest! Oh, my God, they're assuming the worse then.'

'I'm so sorry, Cora.'

'I take it Valerie wasn't at home when it happened.'

'No, she was at the club, as we all were.' she added. 'I don't know what time she got back to the bungalow, but it must have been in the early hours of the morning; according to Derek who spoke to her later yesterday, she'd called the police immediately.'

'I see.' she said quietly, 'Whoever it was then, the person who broke into the bungalow, didn't – didn't kill him.'

'There's no way of knowing; not yet.' Kate's response barely audible.

'You believe he's dead, don't you?'

'I – I'm not sure; honestly, I really don't know what to believe, but from how they've described the way the pick-up was positioned; the front end right on the edge, also the driver's door had been wrenched open, probably that happened when he crashed through the undergrowth.'

'So, is that what the police are saying – that he was flung from the truck and – ' finding it impossible to continue.

'I don't really know, but it does seem that's the way they're thinking. I'm so sorry, Cora,' she went on, her voice full of sympathy, 'I realise how close Alan and you were.'

Kate's use of the past tense didn't escape her; intentional or otherwise, but it still hurt.

'I'm sorry,' Kate repeated, as though reading her mind, 'that was tactless of me.'

'I hadn't realised it was so obvious; about Alan and me, I mean.' feeling the need to qualify.

'To me, it was. I've known Alan since he and Valerie first arrived in Ekabe. They weren't happy together, that was obvious to us all and, of course, Valerie didn't make life any easier for him.'

'I know.' embarrassed now, anxious to bring the call to an end, but at the same time reluctant to sever this link with her; to not knowing what was happening. She wanted to learn more, to hold on to the hope that he may have survived. 'Kate?'

'Yes.'

'You will keep in touch won't you? There has to be a chance that he'll be found; there's a native village near there, I remember hearing children's voices; someone could be looking after him, if he's injured that is. Oh, God, I don't know what I'm saying. I just can't believe he's gone, that I'll never see him again – '

'Cora. Please. I wish I'd waited now before I told you.'

'No, I had to know.' Poor Alan.'

'I know. I know. It's all so unfair; he didn't deserve this. We're all in a state of shock here, but listen, Cora, I've told you all we know so far and I'll call you as soon as there is any further news, that's a promise, but meanwhile, I don't think you should be on your own. You need someone you can talk to, to confide in perhaps.'

'I'll be alright. Don't worry about me; I only wish I was there, I feel so useless.'

'There's nothing any of us can do, Cora.'

Her hand was shaking as she finally replaced the receiver, Kate's voice echoing back to her - " – it seems he was attacked .... his pick-up truck was discovered..... Ekabe Ravine ..... right on the edge .... the driver's door had been wrenched open .... "

She found it hard to accept the police had already given up on their search, but it sounded as though they may have done. And what about Alan's wife? Valerie. In spite of their estrangement and the impending divorce, surely she had some feelings, a natural concern for the man she had been married to for a number of years. Had she, as apparently everyone else had, accepted that Alan had lost his life in such horrendous circumstances. A strangled sob caught at the back of her throat as she tried to ignore the images which flashed through her brain, but the tears which had been threatening from the moment she'd finished talking to Kate now fell unchecked, blurring her vision and causing her to stumble as she made her way through to the kitchen and reaching out blindly for the kitchen towel roll. She didn't know how long she remained there, leaning heavily against the worktop, a wodge of sodden paper towel clutched in her hand, but at last, her breathing slowly returning to normal, she found the strength to make some coffee; only instant, but she needed an immediate infusion of caffeine.

The simple task of spooning coffee into a mug and waiting for the kettle to boil helped a little; after taking her first sip she felt calmer and able to think rationally about what may or may not have happened to the man she had fallen in love with, never expecting for one single moment that their relationship would be cut short in such a cruel way.

Mentally, she was back in Ekabe: the long straight laterite road branching off from the main Ndola/Kitwe highway, passing beneath the avenue of full-bloom poinsettia and on into the town: single-storey buildings with wooden overhangs and verandas, still with the old hitching posts, remembering how she'd described her first impressions of Ekabe to Alan: "it's so like a scene from a wild-west town in the States where you could expect Clint Eastwood to come riding in at any moment," she'd said laughing, "with the soundtrack of "A Fistful of Dollars" playing in the background." Side-tracked by the memory, she had to make a conscious effort to rein in her emotions, emotions which would only further muddle what her troubled brain was trying to work out.

She was on her second coffee when more words floated into her consciousness. It was something Kate had said, a remark , spontaneously made and one often uttered following a sudden and entirely unexpected tragedy. "It's all so unfair," she'd said, "he didn't deserve this". Of course, it went without saying that Alan didn't deserve to be attacked in his own home, but now that the initial shock was beginning to dissipate, she was starting to try and make some sense of it all.

Why, of all the bungalows on the campus should the intruder choose Alan's? Had it been picked at random? They had been taking a risk. They must have known that the whole campus was protected by security guards at either end. Kate had said that nothing had been stolen, but if Alan had been disturbed by them it was possible they didn't have time. Had it been a bungled robbery attempt which had gone drastically wrong, or – and here she paused to take a deep breath, realising with a sinking feeling she was about to consider other, more sinister reasons. What if the break-in had been a calculated act, not to steal but for an entirely different intention. To harm Alan. To go even further, to committing the ultimate act. Once her brain had accepted that possibility, she found it impossible to dislodge it, to ignore it, no matter how bizarre it sounded. He had been injured, evidence of the trail of blood outside substantiated that but, from what Kate had been saying, there was no proof of Alan actually driving the pick-up away from the bungalow. But if he hadn't, and this sounded even more unlikely, his assailant would have taken the added risk of removing him from the bungalow and somehow forcing him into the vehicle. But why would he have done that? She should have asked Kate whether the police had said anything about Alan's prints being discovered, but then she didn't suppose they would divulge that sort of information. The more she tried to make sense of the way her thoughts were going, the more confused she became. And afraid.

She was in the shower, hoping there would be some therapeutic relief from the cascade of warm water on her skin which, in spite of the flat's central heating, felt cold and clammy, when another question occurred to her. If Alan had been driving, why had he gone to the ravine? Why hadn't he gone for help; to the hospital, not in the other direction away from the town? The ravine was at least a couple of miles from the road which as far as she knew ended in a dead-end at Ekabe Lodge. Perhaps that had been his intention, to spend what remained of the night, but the question still remained: why had he branched off halfway along, why hadn't he just kept driving until he reached the lodge where he would be safe from any further attacks and ask for help if he felt he needed any.

None of it made any sense. She had to find out more and deciding, as she pulled on jeans and a navy-blue polo-neck sweater, that until she did she refused to believe that the man she had fallen in love with was dead. How she was going to do that she had no idea, but nothing was going to be resolved by remaining here. She'd walk along to "Gino's" for breakfast. That would be a start she told herself and picking up her bag and keys she let herself out of the flat.

It was a bright, sunny morning and reasonably warm for the end of October; the plane trees lining the street outside the building had already started to shed their leaves, her feet crunching over those scattered on the pavement. Normally, she would have enjoyed the short walk to "Gino's", may have even taken a detour through Tavistock gardens to absorb the sense of tranquillity which living in the city never failed to surprise and delight her, but not this morning: Alan occupied her mind so completely there was no room for anyone or anything else.

"Gino's" was on the corner near the traffic lights and before the road joined busy Woburn Place and where the pavement was wide enough for his half dozen tables and chairs with their pretty blue and white checked cloths, flapping gently in the breeze.

'Buongiorno, Cora;' Gino called out to her from the open doorway as soon as he saw her, 'Bentonado!'

'Buongiorno, Gino. Grazi.' and suddenly it felt good to be back and for a few moments savoured his warm welcome. She had been a regular customer for the last five years, from the very first day she arrived in London from her native Scotland and moved into her flat, and seeing him again, went along way to calming her and, hopefully once she'd had one of his famous home-made brioches and his equally famous cappuccinos, liberally sprinkled with grated chocolate, she could come up with some sort of plan and think of someone who could help her, to stop her groping around in this awful fog of hopelessness.

She followed Gino inside the café and across to her favourite table by the window overlooking the Gardens. As she waited for her coffee and brioche, the lilting refrains from Gino's medley of his country's best known music playing softly in the background, it wasn't too difficult to imagine herself transported, if only for a short time, to the tranquil beauty of Naples where she knew from an idyllic holiday there a couple of years earlier, that the highlight of each day was deciding which restaurant to choose for lunch.

Someone had left a copy of that morning's "Times" on the table next to her and when it looked as if it wasn't going to be reclaimed, she reached over to it. The news was depressingly predictable: a jewellery robbery in Old Bond Street; an aborted terrorist attack in Whitehall and a warehouse fire in Camden. Same old stuff, she sighed, turning over to the next page. The two-column piece was one of many, but it was the mention of the town which instantly caught and held her attention:

"DOES THE CALDER BAY MURDER HAVE INTERNATIONAL CONNECTIONS?

"Murder is no stranger to Calder Bay, a small seaside town snuggled as it is in a natural cove on Scotland's north-east coast, but the discovery of John Milne's body early on Wednesday morning was no less shocking to its residents. John Milne, a horticulturist, had been employed by "Lorimer Fruits", an old-established family fruit growing business, on a two-year contract. Mystery surrounds what has every appearance of an unjustifiable attack: there was no evidence of a forced entry into the first floor flat occupied by the victim and while it cannot be ruled out at this stage that he knew the assassin, consideration will no doubt be given to other possible explanations: the assailant had a key to the premises, or he had the expertise to unlock the main door without leaving any sign, the latter suggesting the murder of John Milne could have been professionally carried out.

"However, by an ironic twist of fate, news was received yesterday of a suspected fatal attack carried out on Alan Lorimer, one of the directors of "Lorimer Fruits", who is currently working as a lecturer at one of Zambia's technical colleges. News continues to come through from the Zambia News Agency, but it would appear that the incident occurred on Thursday night when Alan Lorimer's bungalow was broken into and it was during this disturbance when the physical attack on him was carried out. When the police arrived at the scene, there was no sign of Alan Lorimer or of his pick-up truck, the latter being discovered hours later at the edge of a ravine on the outskirts of the town. Regrettably, the authorities are holding out little hope for his survival, although the search for him continues.

"Surely it is stretching credibility too far to discount there is no link between the murder of John Milne and the attack on Alan Lorimer, however implausible this may appear. If one is officially established, the enquiry will undoubtedly fall under the jurisdiction of the international authorities, but it is hoped that the fate of John Milne will continue to be at the forefront of Calder Bay's police investigations. The people of the town deserve a thorough investigation to enable them to return to normality.

Beverly Grant

Investigative Journalist"

'My God!' Cora breathed, dragging her eyes away from the print, which was starting to blur, but more disturbing, not to say embarrassing, were the waves of dizziness. *For Christ's sake, Cora, don't faint. Take deep breaths. You know how to do it. Get a grip.* It worked; gradually she felt her heart-beat steadying and she was able to look around, but nobody appeared to have noticed her, presumably unaware of how close she had been to passing out and making a spectacle of herself.

'I am sorry, Cora, for taking so long,' Gino was saying, 'the telephone; always it rings at an inconvenient moment.'

'That's alright,' she actually managed to smile up at him, 'it's the weekend and I'm in no rush.'

He may have noticed the change in her, but more customers were arriving and he hurried over to serve them. She ate the brioche while it was still warm, but with none of her usual enjoyment, barely aware of the aromatic sweetness; there was no space in any of her senses except for the underlying implication behind the words in the news article, words she was certain had been selected judicially, and wiping the crumbs of the pastry from her fingers with a tissue, pulled the newspaper towards her and read the article again, this time more slowly, memorising certain parts; she would return to them later.

There was one word which disturbed her in particular. International. What had the journalist meant? Had it been because both incidents had occurred continents apart, or for a more specific reason? The overall impression she was getting was one of constraint: Beverly Grant had been sparing in what she'd written and to Cora's reasoning that implied she had been deliberately holding back. But why; the woman was a professional and would be well versed in the laws of libel. Could that be the reason, she wondered.

The inference made by the journalist to an international connection could be implying something of a more sinister nature, but Cora had no doubt that, however obscure, they were connected. For them not to be was too bizarre to even contemplate. Moving her focus for a second away from what had been written about Alan, she considered the man who had been murdered. She remembered Alan telling her about the young man who would be covering for him while he was away, he hadn't mentioned his name, but the article had said he was on a two-year contract, therefore it had to be the same person. And there was another indication of the way the journalist was leading: "*suggesting the murder of John Milne had been professionally carried out*". That's what she'd written. Did she have some grounds for that comment: provocative and so very chilling. If, as was being suggested, there was a connection, struggling to formulate her hazy reasoning and absently taking a sip of her coffee which was now cold; something other than the link with "Lorimer Fruits". Alan had told her that he'd written to his brother telling him he was returning before he'd completed his contract, but she didn't think he would have explained in any detail, probably preferring to wait until he was back and they could talk face to face. No doubt the letter would have arrived by now, wondering what his family's reaction had been. Strange though, that the two incidents had happened so closely together: John Milne's body discovered on Wednesday morning, presumably he was murdered the night before, and Alan's break-in happening only two nights later. A coincidence? Instinct was telling her this was no coincidence. *Alright, Cora,* giving her inner voice full rein, *why not expand on your theory – someone wanted to silence John Milne for some reason and that same someone wanted to harm Alan. Why? To prevent him returning to Calder Bay?*

Was that it, gasping at the possibility. Had her sub-conscious offered up a possible answer? She had no illusions that given the same information, the police would have already reached the same conclusion, but if didn't prevent her trying, however wrong she may be, to make some sort of rational deduction to disprove to those who were assuming the worse. The fact that there had been no sign of Alan when the police arrived at the bungalow, also that his pick-up had gone, must mean that he'd been able to drive away, therefore, logically he had survived the attack. The assailant may have thought he'd succeeded and Alan's first thought must have been to get as far away as he could.

At first, when Kate had said where the truck had been found, she couldn't understand why, but then, having had some time to think, he could have been heading for the Lodge, but it would seem he didn't get that far. If she was right and that had been his intention, something had happened to prevent him, but what?

Kate had been right in saying she should have someone she could talk to, someone who could share her concern, to prevent it turning into despair, but who? She had friends, close friends even, but none of them had known Alan; the ones who did were in Ekabe. She could, the idea suddenly coming to her, give his family a ring, his brother perhaps. She had nothing to lose; they would either refuse to speak to her, considering she was intruding on their grief, or they just might welcome a call from the woman their son had planned to introduce to his family. She had no number for "Lorimer Fruits", but it only took minutes before Directory of Enquiries supplied her with what she needed and, not giving herself time to reconsider, she began to dial.

*** 

Myra took the call from Cora in Callum's office; his door had been open when she passed on her way along to her own office and she'd known he wasn't in the building, not that she had any idea where he might be. He had been more withdrawn than usual lately; not only since the distressing news about Alan. but before then, to Tuesday when Alan's letter arrived. And now, she sighed, as Alison put the call through, here was this woman calling to speak to him.

'Hello,.' she said, 'I'm afraid Callum isn't here at the moment, but perhaps I can help you.' realising how bland and formal she must sound, but her feeling of awkwardness was making it impossible to act normally, silently blaming Callum although admitting she was being unreasonable.

'I'm Cora Hamilton, Alan's friend,' she was introducing herself, 'and I apologise for phoning you at this dreadful time. I know now it was a mistake, but I felt the need to speak to his family and as he'd often mentioned your husband's name, well – '

' – you don't have to apologise,' suddenly feeling sorry for her, and if she had been really close to Alan she could understand; her action had probably been a spur of the moment one, 'we are in a state of – of suspended shock I suppose you might say.'

'You don't believe what the police are claiming.'

It wasn't a question. Myra had always thought of herself as a fairly perceptive person and the vibes she was getting from Cora Hamilton were that here was a woman deeply troubled, so much so that she had risked being snubbed by phoning a family she had only learned about second-hand.

'We have been told so little,' she said, 'only from a very brief telephone call from Valerie yesterday, and then later in the day my father-in-law had a visit from the local police.'

'Have you read the article in today's "Times"?'

'I have, yes, but you can't still be in Zambia?'

'No, I was only there on a three-month secondment from the LSE and arrived back on Thursday. I live in London,' she added, 'and I only heard about Alan this morning when Kate, a friend I made out there, phoned me and then a short while ago I read that piece in the paper.'

'How shocked you must have been.'

'I was, terribly, and still am, but I simply cannot believe – that I'll never see him again.' her voice breaking, 'I'm sorry.'

'Don't be, Cora,' using her name for the first time, and wishing she could say something, anything, to ease what she was obviously going through, 'if it's any comfort, there appears to be no evidence to support what actually happened that night and until there is, I guess there is always hope.'

'Yes, you're right.' her voice barely audible.

'I've known Alan for years and he's an extremely resilient person and I am certain he wouldn't have given up without a fight.'

'Are you hopeful that he survived then?'

'Yes, I am and I know his father feels the same way. He was adamant after the officer's visit yesterday, in fact, he kept on insisting that he intended to go out there and find out for himself what happened.'

'He must feel very strongly.'

'Oh, he does, but he's well on in his seventies and although extremely fit going out to Ekabe would I'm afraid prove all too much for him.'

'I wonder though whether it would be any good to go there, but I suppose we have to have confidence in their police force. Also, the country is very protective of their tourist industry which makes me think they will go all out to find him, and Alan being a foreigner will I'm sure make them even more determined.'

'You have a point, Cora. But, you've been there, three months you said, what do you really think about his chances?'

'Oh, dear, what a question, but there is something puzzling me.'

'Yes?'

'It's where his pick-up truck was found; it is really off the beaten track you know, Myra.'

'Perhaps whoever attacked him took him there.'

'But why? Why would they?'

'You mean they would have been too eager to get away from the bungalow.'

'If they were local thugs, I'm pretty sure they would be.'

'I don't understand; do you think there was something else behind what appeared to be a burglary which had gone drastically wrong?'

'I don't know how the investigations are going, but if the suggestions in that article this morning are anything to go by, it does make me wonder. Perhaps we'll know a little more after Monday.'

'Why, what happens then?'

'According to Kate, there's to be an inquest.'

'Oh, dear.'

'I know; it sounds so terribly final, doesn't it?'

'There was no mention in that article but could be the journalist didn't know. I have to say I didn't put too much credence to the inferences she was making; if anything, I probably thought they were too incredible to be true. I should have done I suppose, but we've all been so immersed in our own family's concern for John Milne we've been ignoring what happened to Alan, which is awful and so very insular of us.'

They didn't stay on the line for much longer, both acknowledging that they had nothing to add to what they'd already talked about, and ringing off, they promised to keep in touch.

Myra was thoughtful as she replaced the receiver. Cora's deep and much troubled concern for Alan had reached out to her; she could well understand her impulse to empathise with someone from his family. She hadn't liked mentioning Valerie's name to her, but it didn't stop her wondering about the sister-in-law she had learned to barely tolerate over the years, which with them all living at Ashworth House, had not been easy. There had been no mention of her in the article, whether she had been the one who had called the police or even if she'd been in the bungalow at the time of the break-in. Had she and Alan still been living together, but knowing little of expatriate life, only from what she'd read, somehow she reckoned they would have to be fairly circumspect.

She recognized Callum's footsteps in the hall and moved away from the desk; not knowing why exactly, except for some odd reason she felt guilty. It was true that he valued his own space which she'd always respected, all the same she couldn't help twinges of unease as he approached the office.

'Why are you in here, Myra.' his first words, but avoiding looking at her directly.

'Your phone was ringing, so as you weren't around, I answered it.'

'And who was it?'

'Cora Hamilton.'

'Cora Hamilto,' he repeated, 'what the hell did she want?'

'Callum!'

'What?'

'Why are you being so – so unkind?'

'I'm not; I'm being realistic. I cannot think of any reason why a woman we don't know should take it upon herself to phone us.'

'She only heard about Alan this morning and I think she just needed to talk to one of us, his family I mean. Surely you can understand.'

'Not really, Myra.'

'She sounded a nice woman.'

'Did she?'

His complete lack of empathy shocked and saddened her. Was this the same man she'd married? She couldn't recall a single moment these last few months when he'd looked up from what he was doing to give her a quick smile, a silent reminder that she still mattered to him. She had given up making excuses for him, always understanding his deep resentment towards a father who made no attempt to disguise his favouritism for his middle son, more especially now with him so volubly refusing to accept that Alan may be dead. She supposed, that contrarily, Callum had gone on the obverse: he was refusing to accept that Alan may just have survived. But instinctively she felt there was something else causing the gradual change in him and whatever it was she didn't think it was directly connected to either Alan or their father.

'Yes, Callum,' she said at last, trying to hold his attention, 'I liked her and like us all she's hoping Alan is safe.'

'Do you honestly believe,' frowning, 'there is anything to be gained by *hoping*. We're not talking about normal countryside here: this is tropical, Myra: forests, wild animals, primitive natives, not forgetting that ravine, which by all accounts is shark infested!'

'Cora did mention where Alan's truck was found.'

'By the ravine, yes.' his voice edged with irritation.

'That's the point she was making, Callum.'

'What point?' his voice sharp and she recognized the signs: he would soon lose patience with her and refuse to discuss the matter, probably walk away.

'All she was saying,' choosing her words carefully, 'was that she couldn't understand why Alan had driven there; apparently, it's some distance away and off the road leading out of Ekabe.'

'That's obvious I would say: he probably wasn't driving the damn thing, somebody else was, his attacker, and they wanted to dispose of his body.'

'You think that makes sense?'

'To me it does.'

'Somebody broke into the bungalow Callum, and whoever it was attacked Alan and you think it's quite feasible that rather than make a run for it, they would drag him out to his truck and drive out of town to fake an accident.'

'It's possible.'

'There's to be an inquest; on Monday.'

''Quite normal I would say under the circumstances.' he shrugged and made to turn away.

'I wish you wouldn't do that.'

'What?'

'Walk away when I'm talking to you.'

'Because, Myra, nothing can be achieved by continuing this conversation.'

'You think there is no hope that he may still be alive; is that what you mean?'

'Exactly.'

'Your father doesn't share your view, Callum.'

'No, I don't suppose he does; he's in denial, but eventually he'll have to accept what the authorities are telling him.

***

It was late on Saturday afternoon when Alistair, groaning out loud when he saw the light flashing on his internal phone, received an immediate summons to his superintendent's office. The last he wanted at the end of an unproductive week was a third degree from "Breezy Bob". He had virtually nothing to report and spent the few minutes it took to reach his superintendent's office to conjure up some shred of relevant findings which just might pacify him.

'I've had a call from Graham Lorimer, Alistair;' no preamble, straight to the point, not that he expected anything else, 'he's accusing us of not following up on the disappearance of his son. I know, I know,' he went on quickly, pre-empting any objection, 'until it is officially established as a crime, Alan as a British subject qualifies for protection, but once it is, will come under the jurisdiction of the Zambian authorities.'

'He has a valid point, sir.'

'Theoretically, yes. The crime has yet to be quantified which will presumably be established on Monday after the inquest, but whatever the outcome, the fact remains that it took place in their country which of course has its own laws, procedures and standards and any hint that they should liaise with us would be interpreted as interference.'

'And the strong implication there is a connection between whatever has happened to Alan Lorimer and the murder of John Milne wouldn't make any difference.'

'None, Alistair and it would be naïve of us to think otherwise. There's a very thin line here,' he went on in his pedantic way, 'and one which we have no authority to cross; that will be the part Interpol will presumably be playing as the investigation progresses. I take it you haven't heard from Adrian Roberts?'

'No, sir, not yet.'

'Hmmph. Right, tell me, have you made any progress on the Calder Bay murder?'

'We're no nearer to finding the person responsible, although there has been a slight development.'

'Yes.'

'John Milne's girlfriend, Laura Thomson she's called, didn't report for work yesterday and nobody's seen her today. We had a telephone call from her neighbour yesterday afternoon to say that her house appeared to have been broken into –'

' – and had it?'

'Sorry, sir.' not sure where he was coming from; there were times when it was almost impossible to define the meaning behind his words, whether he was genuinely asking for an explanation or whether he was being downright awkward.

'You said the woman's house *appeared* to have been broken into.'

'That's how it seemed to the neighbour, but there had been no visible signs of any actual break-in. Inspector Aitken went along there as soon as we'd received the woman's call and right enough it was obvious someone had been in there by the state of the place, both upstairs and downstairs: mattress overturned, clothes from the wardrobe strewn about, books hauled out from the bookshelves in the lounge; that sort of thing, sir, indicative of a fairly frenzied search having been carried out, although no sign of any forced entry.' and going on to tell him exactly what Dan had reported when he came back to the station.

'And the girlfriend; nobody's seen her?'

'Not since she left the bank on Thursday around midday.'

'Her car; you're saying there were car keys in her handbag?'

'We haven't located it yet; it isn't where she usually parks it apparently.'

'And how, Alistair, do we know where she usually parks the damn thing?'

'Again, the neighbour, sir.'

'Obviously got nothing better to do.'

'She is quite elderly, but having spoken to her, I found her extremely level-headed.'

'Good.'

'She gave us the make and the registration number of the car, sir and a search has already been put out; whether it will be helpful remains to be seen, but we're doing all we can to trace her.'

'Normally, I would say it was too soon to treat Laura Thomson as a missing person, but given the circumstances, the obvious search of her property and her connection with the murdered man, I believe we should reconsider.'

'And Adrian Roberts, sir?'

'He should be informed, Alistair – as a matter of urgency in my opinion.'

\*\*\*

It was well on into the afternoon before Callum heard from Ben Maitland. He had been loath to make the first move since Valerie's call earlier, but hearing what Myra had been saying about that damn truck being found miles away from the bungalow was worrying. He had no illusions of Ben's ruthlessness, but his brain was refusing to accept that he was involved in whatever had happened to Alan. It just seemed too extreme. While he realised that Alan's plan to return home earlier meant Ben having to find another outlet once the drugs hit the British shores, it didn't alter the unpalatable fact that he had quite willingly agreed to be part of the syndicate and any backlash couldn't fail to affect him personally, but that was a road he didn't want to even think about, not yet anyway, not until he had to.

'There's been a change of plan, Callum.' Ben said as soon as they'd ordered their beers and found a quiet corner in "The Shipwreck" bar.

'Yes?'

'The drop won't be on Sunday as planned.'

'Thank God for that!'

'We'll make an attempt next Thursday instead, *things*,' he emphasized, taking a sip of his beer, 'should have quietened down by them.'

'You think so?'

'Listen, Callum, we haven't much choice here; there is no way I'm going to stockpile that stuff until such time as you get a control of your collywobbles. If I'd had my way, I would have gone ahead with our original plan, but I knew you'd probably crack up.'

'I don't think you realise what it's been like since Wednesday; the place is crawling with police. I've lost track of the number of times they've been up at Ashburn House. They don't seem to be any closer to solving John's murder – '

' – hopefully, they won't.'

'That remains to be seen, but what I'm trying to say is until they do, they're going to continue being in evidence and now, of course, with this business with Alan, even more so. You read that article in the "Times" this morning, I suppose.'

'Of course. Okay, so what? They're making suggestions that the two crimes are connected. Let them. Where's their proof? Eh?

# Chapter Eleven

<u>Monday 23rd October: Ekabe</u>

'I was surprised to see you at the Inquest this morning, Mr Irvine.'

'In spite of these regrettable circumstances, Mrs Lorimer, your husband remains a client of ours which means we have to keep abreast of any developments.'

'Surely,' Valerie said, doing her utmost to remain calm, but she was finding his pompous manner insufferable; he really was the epitome of a dried-up old crone, 'the open verdict was a mere formality. There is no way that Alan could have survived.'

'There is insufficient evidence as indeed explained by the coroner, which must indicate there remains hope that Mr Lorimer is still alive. May I say, it is early days,' pausing for a fraction of a second, unpleasantly reminding her of one of her least popular schoolteachers, 'less than a week in fact, and I believe the police are continuing with their search.'

'And meanwhile, Mr Irvine, I am in limbo. I very much want to return home, but my financial status is unclear.'

'I can assure you my firm will keep in touch with you, Mrs Lorimer, also we will continue to liaise with the authorities and inform you of any progress which will affect today's verdict.'

'Thank you. Now,' taking a deep breath, not sure of the best way of approaching a subject which continued to infuriate her, 'the main reason for seeing you today, Mr Irvine is concerning my husband's decision to file for a divorce.'

'Ah, yes.'

*Good, he actually looks uncomfortable; he wasn't expecting that.*

'And now, in view of what's happened, there will be no need for that.'

'Er – no, theoretically of course you're correct, although your husband's request for us to prepare the necessary documents does still stand which we have done, but of course without signatures they will be classed as pending until such time – erm – as the present situation changes.'

'That's fine, Mr Irvine, especially as I had intended to prevent him going ahead. I'm quite sure that with a little persuasion he would have agreed he'd been a trifle impetuous, but then we'll never know, will we?'

'That does remain to be seen, Mrs Lorimer. Was there anything else you wished to discuss; time is running a little short; I have another client waiting.'

'Only about my husband's will.'

'Yes?'

'I will need a copy when I meet with my own lawyer in Scotland, Mr Irvine.'

'Of course, I'll ask my secretary to print out a copy for you.'

Jonathan Irvine, of Irvine, Cameron & Mulenga, Legal Practitioners, made a pathetic attempt to conceal his relief when their meeting came to an end and she rose up from the extremely uncomfortable high-backed chair which must have been in existence for years, but nothing compared to how she felt when she finally left the building after waiting for an inordinate length of time until a prim-faced woman emerged from one of the doors in the reception area and silently handed her a slim white envelope clearly marked in gothic script: *Last Will & Testament of Alan Lorimer*.

Valerie had taken an instant dislike to Jonathon Irvine, not only for his patronising manner, but she had the distinct impression he was keeping something from her; it was the way she'd caught him a couple of times, the pale eyes unblinking behind rimless glasses, looking at her with an expression she was finding it impossible to read, but once outside in the stifling afternoon heat and walking across to where she'd parked the car, she'd dismissed him from her mind only thankful she wouldn't be seeing him again. *Not long to go now, Valerie; you'll soon be on that flight back home and these months spent in this alien country will be a distant memory.*

She crawled through the traffic-jammed centre of Ndola and joined the long straight road back to Ekabe, the heat haze shimmering ahead, when her mobile pinged with a text message. Unable to see who was trying to contact her and hoping it wasn't Steve, she had no choice but to ignore it.

Steve was becoming a problem and one she could well do without. She had enough to worry about, wondering now in hindsight what she'd ever seen in him. Well, she thought, pressing her foot down on the accelerator to overtake a ramshackle lorry belching out clouds of dirty grey smoke, he had helped to ease the sheer bloody boredom over the months and she supposed she should be grateful to him for Thursday night's efforts, although a pity he'd taken it upon himself to deviate from what they had agreed.

She really did not know where he'd been coming from when he arrived completely unexpectedly at the bungalow on Friday night. She had only gone there to pack a few clothes in a bag and some toiletries to take with her to Ekabe Lodge – there was no way she was going to spend any more time there after what had happened – when the headlights of his pick-up shone through what glass remained of the patio doors and hadn't been boarded up by the police. She'd rushed outside and practically dragged him round to the side of the building out of sight of any neighbour who might be up at that time of the night. He had been shaking, his hair ruffled where he'd obviously been raking his fingers through it.

"What are you doing here, Steve;" she'd asked him, keeping her voice down, "I thought we said – "

" – I know what we said," as he'd roughly pulled her towards him, "you have no idea what I've been going through today, waiting for the opportunity to tell you that I didn't do it, Val, I didn't kill him."

"You're not making sense, Steve; why don't you just calm down."

"I didn't kill him; he was already dead when I got here."

"Just a minute! What you're saying is just crazy, absolutely crazy."

"You don't believe me, do you?"

"I'm finding it damn difficult. What you're saying is that *someone else,* someone out of the blue, decided to conveniently do the job for us! No, Steve, I do not believe you. You're panicking, that's what you're doing. But what I can't understand is why the hell you moved him out of the bungalow? Doing that was so – so stupid! There was no body, Steve for the police to find and I don't need a crystal ball to tell me what the outcome will be at the inquest on Monday. Thanks a lot!"

"I'm telling you he was dead! His body was just lying there, on the hall floor."

"Did you feel his pulse to make sure?" not even bothering to keep the cynicism from her voice.

"No. there was no point, Val; it was obvious."

"This is your way of wriggling out of all this, isn't it, well for your sake, Steve, let's hope you didn't leave any fingerprints because the police will be bound to have taken them if you did."

She hadn't been able to get away from him quickly enough; she had been dreading the inquest, already having a pretty good idea what the outcome would be and she hadn't been wrong. The sooner she severed her ties with Steve, the better; it was the way he'd reacted when she'd mentioned him leaving any prints in the bungalow which she'd found disturbing.

"Valerie," he'd said, taking a firm grip of her shoulders and giving her a slight shake, 'the police won't find any evidence of me being here and in case you've forgotten, I have an alibi, but do you?"

"Of course I do!"

"But, my sweet, you seem to have overlooked the fact that when the police arrived there was no body, therefore how do they know when the – the incident happened. Think about it."

The significance of what he'd said had suddenly hit her then: that was why he'd moved Alan! Of course. No body. No murder. And, as she had been the one to call the police she had been the only one there when they arrived. This meant they only had her word for it. Worse still, if they started thinking along those lines, she would become a suspect. There was no way Steve would admit he'd ever been there that night and if she told them, would they believe her?

Those had been the troubled thoughts which had accompanied her throughout the long weekend, followed by the ordeal this morning at the inquest and then that ghastly meeting with the lawyers. The only thing on her mind now as she pulled off the Ekabe road to bump on to what was little more than a pot-holed track to the Lodge, passing bedraggled police tape tied to the trees on either side of the opening where Alan's pick-up had been discovered, was to make her arrangements for the flight back to the UK and to sanity, but first a large glass of chilled wine in the lodge's lounge bar; anything to prolong the moment when she would have to call Steve.

It was dark by the time she pulled up outside the lodge, slotting in between a scraped and muddied land rover and a minibus, the brief sunset reminding her as often it had over the months of how, within minutes, the harsh and relentless light throughout the day could so rapidly be extinguished, replaced by a dense blackness she had never known anywhere else. At least, she admitted, walking into the wood-panelled reception area and on into the bar, Ekabe Lodge had a degree of sophistication, although a bit too rustic for her tastes: low glass-topped coffee tables, rattan chairs with blue and gold patterned cushions and matching floor-length curtains and the constant revolving of the ceiling fans, their answer to a cooling system, the movement of air so slight it was scarcely felt. Alan had never brought her here, their main entertainment, such as it was, being the club which to her, right from that very first day, had been the epitome of sheer boredom.

Although not long after six, the place was busy with many of the tables taken, but she found one, half concealed behind a huge tub of tall ferns, thick with foliage, which she hoped would give her some privacy, not wanting to be seen by anyone who knew her; she needed time to absorb the stressful events of a long day and to formulate her travel plans and, ordering a large glass of Sauvignon from Joseph, one of the lodge's older bar staff, opened her bag and took out the lawyer's envelope. It wasn't that she couldn't remember the various conditions and clauses, but she wanted to refresh her memory before she contacted her own lawyer once she was back in the UK.

Sliding the copy of the will from its envelope, fully expecting to see the name of Alan's lawyers in Edinburgh boldly printed in their familiar black and gold lettering in the centre of the facing page and not that of Irvine, Cameron & Mulenga, her first reaction was that the secretary had given her a copy of someone else's will, but as her eyes moved towards the top realised there was no mistake: Alan's full name, followed by the signature of Jonathan Irvine certifying it as being a true copy of his last will and testament and dated two weeks earlier, the 9th of October. With a growing dread, she turned to the first sheet, dizziness blurring her vision as she tried to focus, but there it was, in black and white, Alan's final bequest. He had left his entire estate to Cora Hamilton.

'He can't do this!' she gasped. *I'm his wife, this cannot be allowed to happen! How could he? How could he be so cruel? Of course I will contest it!*

'Are you alright, Madam?' Joseph asked, taking that moment when she was still reeling from the shock, to bring over her wine, his dark features creased with concern.

'I'm fine, Joseph,' forcing a smile from lips which were refusing to respond, 'just tired, that's all.' and waiting until he had gone before picking up her glass, aware of how her hand was shaking; the last she wanted was to draw attention to herself, although looking round the crowded bar, she was relieved to see that no-one appeared to be looking over in her direction and, reassured, took a long sip of her wine, relishing the calming effect of the chilled fruitiness.

The wine helped. With the easing of tension, she began to think more rationally without the debilitating waves of panic she'd been struggling with from the moment she started to read that damn will. She made the extreme effort of pushing her annoyance with Jonathan Irvine to the back of her mind, his furtive manner now obvious. So much for professionalism, she muttered angrily under her breath; the unlikelihood of him making any further financial gain from his client did give her satisfaction, small but gratifying.

Taking another sip of her wine, she concentrated on the main problem facing her; namely, Cora Hamilton. Whether she knew about the will or not didn't bother her one little bit, but the unpalatable fact that she was a threat and had to be dealt with. Valerie had to admit to herself, reluctantly, that the outcome of the inquest had done her a favour: it had given her time, but how much, that was anyone's guess. She wasn't so blind not to realise that whatever happened, whether Alan survived or not, she was in something of a cleft stick. If the former, he would go ahead with the divorce, with or without her agreement, and if his body wasn't found she would be in exactly the same position; either way was unacceptable.

'Why haven't you been back to me, Val?'

She hadn't noticed him approaching, his unexpected appearance causing her to jump; he had caught her unawares, annoyed in allowing a situation where she wasn't in control.

'Hi, Steve, I was about to call you actually.'

'Oh, yes?'

'I've had a dreadful day; I needed time to chill out.'

'You think my day has been any better?'

'It couldn't have been worse than mine; you didn't have to give evidence at the inquest this afternoon.'

'I suppose it must have been something of an ordeal.'

'You could say that.' wishing he would just go; she was in no mood to speak to him, knowing that when she did it wouldn't be what he was expecting.

'Look, Val, we have to talk and before you say anything,' pulling out the chair next to her and sitting down, 'I've been thinking, and feel it might be a good idea if we bring our plans forward.'

'I hadn't realised we had made any plans, not specific ones anyway, and now with the outcome of the verdict, quite frankly, Steve not a great deal has changed.'

'So what was the outcome, you haven't said.'

'An open verdict of course.'

'Shit.'

'Exactly, but inevitable.' she responded, tight-lipped.

'I suppose so, but that doesn't make any difference to us; even, if by some miracle, he's still alive, as his wife surely you're legally entitled to his estate.'

'That remains to be seen and that's why I'll have to return to the UK as soon as possible and take advice from my lawyer.' deciding to say nothing about her meeting with Jonathan Irvine. The least he knew about her present situation the better. She had no illusions about him: her appeal to him, aside from the physical, had been her financial status following her husband's swift demise.

'Of course you do and I'll make my own plans to finish up here and meet up with you back in the UK. Just as well,' he added, 'you didn't sign those divorce papers.'

'It is, isn't it?'

'Well, that's sorted then; we'll just have to make the most of things, Val. I'm going to get myself a beer,' he added, looking at her empty glass, 'Another Sauvignon?'

She watched him as he walked over to the bar, regretting now that she'd agreed to have another wine; it wasn't that she didn't want one because she did. She just didn't want to spend any more time with him; she felt emotionally drained and the thought of continuing a conversation which was bound to be unpleasant only added to an overwhelming sense of foreboding.

Steve was on his way back with the drinks when her attention was drawn to a familiar figure in the open doorway. He must have sensed her looking at him because he slowly turned round in her direction and began walking over, only a few steps behind Steve.

'Oh, no,' she murmured, 'this is not good.' but it was too late to warn Steve, therefore no way to prevent Inspector Musenge seeing them together and drawing the inevitable conclusions.

\*\*\*

Inspector Christopher Musenge had been thoughtful as he left the courthouse earlier that day. It hadn't been the coroner's verdict or even his detailed summing-up that was occupying his mind, which had been exactly as he had expected having attended numerous inquests in his twenty-five years of service; it was the irregularity of the case that disturbed him. Even to fully describe it as a crime didn't seem right somehow. Yes, a property had been broken into but apart from the smashed patio door there had been no other damage and apparently nothing had been stolen; traces of blood on the hall floor indicated that violence must have taken place, but there had been no body and the fact that the pick-up truck belonging to the victim, had been found abandoned at the edge of the ravine only suggested a fatality.

Something didn't gel. It wasn't as though a property break-in among the better-off people of Ekabe, including those in the expatriate community, was rare. It wasn't, but this was the first he had known where the intruder had forced an entry and fled empty-handed, the only evidence of them ever being there had been the broken glass scattered on the lounge floor, some slight disturbance to the furniture and the traces of blood. If they had disturbed Alan Lorimer with the smashing of the glass and attacked him, say rendering him unconscious, why had they not stolen whatever they could lay their hands on before making off? Christopher could not accept that Alan Lorimer could, or would, have been foolhardy enough to follow them. There was something of the drama about it all; staged, and reminding him of a west-end play he'd seen years ago during the time he was on a training course in London, where a murder took place in a faked robbery attempt accompanied by off-stage shouts, screams and the sound of running feet, but no sign of a body. Such unproductive meanderings weren't helping, although seeing Valerie Lorimer and the man she'd introduced as a friend enjoying a drink together in the lounge bar of the Lodge, could be blamed for the confusing way his mind was working.

There was no doubt that Steve Burrows had looked uncomfortable although he'd been quick enough to provide an alibi for Thursday night, perhaps a little bit too quick, eager to make it clear to him that any involvement he had with Alan Lorimer's wife was merely as a concerned neighbour. A neighbour who was conveniently having a drink after work, not in one of the two expatriate clubs in Ekabe, but conveniently, where Valerie Lorimer was staying? Christopher Musenge, in his habitual cynical way, didn't think so. Steve Burrows' alibi needed close scrutiny, recalling the precise way in which he'd presented it.

"I spent the whole of Thursday night and well into the early hours in our sports club, Inspector. Thursday was the first night of our theatre's production; one of Alan Aykbourn's plays, but I don't expect you will have heard of him, quite a prolific playwright, actually – "

"As it happens, Mr Burrows I have, but go on." unable to resist rising to his patronising barb.

"Really? Well, I had a part in the play which involved me being on stage in full view of a good-sized audience from when the curtain went up at seven-fifteen until the end of the play three hours later."

"And from then, sir?"

"I spent ten or fifteen minutes back-stage, removing my make-up and changing, during which time I might add, I was constantly surrounded by my *fellow actors*. I then went into the bar which was packed with enough witnesses, including our trusty bar steward, to verify I remained there until I left well after midnight."

"Thank you. Presumably there was an interval half-way through the production?"

"Of course: for twenty minutes." he'd answered unhesitatingly.

"Twenty minutes." Christopher had repeated, fully expecting him to display some kind of reaction to what could be construed as a loophole in his alibi, being mildly disappointed when he remained silent.

"When the play continued after the interval," Christopher had asked, deciding to give him a metaphorical push, anything to disturb his air of apparent impenetrability which didn't fool him for one single minute, "where were you?"

"What do you mean?"

"Exactly that, sir; were you on stage, or was your entrance some minutes later?"

"I cannot believe where you're coming from, Inspector!"

It had worked. He was rattled, and he'd permitted himself a brief moment of satisfaction. Steve Burrows, in his opinion, was not a likeable character, but aside from any personal prejudices, Christopher was certain he'd been lying.

"My line of questions are merely routine, sir; I am merely attempting to get a clear picture. However," continuing before he had the chance to make any further protests, "you said a few moments ago that you had left the club well after midnight, those were your actual words, I believe."

"They were."

"And you went home?"

"Of course."

"And can anyone vouch for that, sir?"

"My wife, Inspector, although as she was asleep, she won't be able to tell you exactly what time it was, but I suppose the break-in would have already taken place by then."

"Why should you think that; I've given you no timeframe."

"You didn't have to, Inspector," a smile had briefly occurred at that point, but one that failed to reach his eyes, ice-blue and hostile, "as I recall, you asked where I was on Thursday night, not in the early hours of Friday morning."

Touché. Tempting though it had been to retaliate, destroy his smugness, he resisted; Steve Burrow's disparaging attitude only further convinced him that he was right not to trust him.

"Mrs Lorimer," he'd said, turning his attention to her, "when you phoned to report the incident the time was noted by our desk sergeant as being ten minutes after four on Friday morning."

"If you say so, Inspector; I have to admit I had no idea what time it was. I was far to shocked."

"You were at the club on Thursday night; I recall you telling me this when I spoke to you?"

"Yes, that's right; I was helping with the production."

"Which involved what exactly?"

"Well, showing people to their seats and handing out programmes, that sort of thing."

"But, you would only have needed to do that prior to the play beginning, therefore how did you spend the rest of the evening?"

"If you don't mind me saying, Inspector, these are very strange questions; surely you don't suspect me for what has happened to my husband! I did attend the inquest this afternoon, you know!"

"I'm aware of that, Mrs Lorimer, but I like to make sure I have a full picture of people's movements, and that does include yours. Purely routine, you understand."

"If you insist, so for your information I spent the whole evening at the club, either backstage or after the show, in the bar. With friends." she added.

"Who left the club first, Mrs Lorimer, you or Mr Burrows?"

"Do you know, Inspector, I can't remember."

"Try, please."

"Steve wasn't in my group, but I think he must have left before me because he wasn't there when I finally left."

"You must have been amongst the last to leave."

"Oh, yes, I was. I usually am, Inspector."

"And did you go straight home when you left the club?"

"Of course I did; where else would I have gone?"

"How long was it once you reached home that you called the station?"

"Oh, for God's sake! Immediately, Inspector!"

"The drive from the club to your bungalow would have taken you ten minutes at the very most, wouldn't you say?"

"About that, yes. Does it really matter?"

"It could. However, I need to have the names of those people who were still there and who will be able to confirm when you left."

"I'll try and remember; I did have a few drinks, you know."

"I would appreciate it if you could. I won't detain either of you any longer, but I would like both of you to call into the station tomorrow, in the morning preferably, to sign your statements covering the points we've been talking about."

Neither of them, surprisingly, had demurred, but it had been quite apparent from their expressions they were relieved when he'd walked away. It had been a far from satisfactory interview, but he'd had to improvise, something he didn't like doing, especially as he would have questioned Valerie further, but on her own, without the belligerent presence of the man he was starting to have grave doubts about.

A light tap on the door interrupted the discordant way his thought process was going. He needed something definite to point him in a more credible direction; whether the Lorimer case turned out to be a random break-in that had misfired with the intruder making a run for it, or there was some other explanation and one which hadn't occurred to him when he'd called at the Lorimer's bungalow in the early hours of Friday morning and was now suggesting there could well be an unexpected twist to what at first had seemed like a straightforward investigation.

'Ah, Brian, come in; I was on the point of buzzing through to you, so is there anything new?'

'The final report from the forensic team has just come through, sir.'

'They took their time; as far as I was aware they'd finished at the ravine yesterday, so why the delay?'

'They've been waiting for the analysis on the prints they took from the area around the pick-up truck.'

'And?'

'They've been able to get a complete one, sir,' handing him a black and white print, 'which is clearly recognizable – '

' – recognizable as what, Sergeant?' his patience starting to fray.

'As not belonging to Alan Lorimer.'

'And how on earth can they know that?'

'Too small, sir; the senior forensic officer confirms it belongs to someone who takes a size five shoe.'

'A woman?'

'He believes so.'

'Well, this certainly puts a different light on the case, Brian and quite fortuitously as it happens.'

'Sir?'

'As you well know, we have to avoid assuming, but it doesn't rule out us seriously considering other possibilities.' going on to tell him about his meeting with Valerie Lorimer and the man she claimed to be her friend and neighbour. 'I'll be seeing her again tomorrow morning when she comes into the office to sign her statement and however unlikely it might appear that she is somehow involved in this business, we cannot afford to rule her out.'

'They could be in it together, sir.'

'Hmm, it is possible. Tell me, Brian,' he asked, 'you were with me when we arrived at the scene, what were your first impressions of her?'

'She didn't appear to be all that upset, sir.' his response given without any hesitation and matching his own exactly.

\*\*\*

Steve had never been so glad to see the back of anyone as he was when Christopher Musenge finally left. Apart from his inbuilt dislike for the police, there was something about Ekabe's chief inspector which unnerved him; not only the barrage of questions of his movements for Thursday night; they had been harrowing enough, but the intense way his eyes, an indeterminate muddy brown colour, remained focused on him. He knew he shouldn't read too much into his scrutiny, but he couldn't help himself: he had not reacted well, and this made him angry. Angry for being caught unaware and for allowing his nervousness to surface, but especially for submitting to the impulse of driving out to the lodge to see Valerie. Why the hell hadn't he waited until she had got in touch with him? What had been the rush; he had already worked out what the outcome of the inquest would be, and he'd been right, there had been no surprises there.

As much as he regretted the outcome, he was quickly coming to realise that he and Valerie could still go ahead with their plans and all the more reason for him to leave the next stage to her, hoping there wouldn't be any hitch when she met up with her lawyer. She seemed confident enough, therefore he had no option but to literally sit back and let her get on with the legalities. 'Wine alright?' he asked her casually, taking a sip of his own drink.

'Lovely, thanks. Look, Steve – '

' – I know what you're going to say, and – '

'Do you?'

'You're mad at me turning up here and I'm sorry, Val, it was damn stupid of me, but I had no idea that obnoxious character would take it into his head to pay you a visit.'

'You heard him,' she shrugged as if the last ten minutes were of no importance, 'his questions were mere routine.'

'Were they hell! He was trying to trip me up; that was obvious.'

'He was pretty close to the truth though, wasn't he, my darling.'

'The man was guessing, Val.'

'He may have been, but you'd be wise not to underestimate him.'

'Oh, don't you worry, I won't.'

'Good.'

'I interrupted you a minute ago,' he said, trying to work out the expression which for a fraction of a second had flickered across her features, 'what was it you wanted to say?'

'Only that we should try to avoid seeing each other for a while.'

'Well, yes, of course; we already agreed on that. Today, as I've already said, was a mistake, but I wanted to know about the inquest and there was nobody else I could ask. Anyway,' continuing awkwardly as she made no attempt to fill the silence which had fallen between them, 'as you'll be off soon that will narrow down the times we may be in the same place, therefore none of our so-called friends will be any the wiser.'

'I didn't only mean between now and when I leave, Steve.'

An alarm bell. It may as well have been one for the way her words reverberated in his head. For the first time since he'd arrived, he looked at her more closely. There was something odd about her and he didn't think it was anything to do with the inspector.

'I think you'd better explain.' unable to hide the coldness in his voice. He hoped he was wrong. They had spent many weeks, months even, talking about the time when they would be together and always, he had taken the lead in the various scenarios of what they called 'their escape', with Valerie going along with him. He had never questioned her acquiescence before and the fact she seldom contributed to any of his suggestions, but now in retrospect, watching her playing with the stem of her glass, he began to wonder.

He'd had no illusions about her, in fact how could he not be aware of her reputation among the expat crowd, but Valerie was a very attractive woman, she had no qualms of making the most of the sexy way she looked, and he had always reckoned that the rumours were grossly exaggerated. God knows, he was no saint and didn't go out of his way to conceal the fact that his marriage to Kate was a facade. Valerie, gregarious, vain to the point of narcissism, was the complete opposite to her, already having worked out that there lay the reason for his attraction for her. She'd often told him how much she loved him, how she longed to be free from what she had described as a loveless marriage. How genuine had that been? Had she changed her mind? Or, another explanation nudging its way into his brain, had he been a fool? Had she been stringing him along, meekly falling in with everything he'd suggested?

'Please don't look at me like that.'

'Like what?' playing for time, but he wanted her to spell it out. He wasn't going to help her. Thursday night, for all the detailed planning, hadn't worked out exactly the way he'd intended. It had started off alright: he'd left the stage at the interval, nipping behind a screen of props to avoid a couple of stagehands, then choosing the dimly lit passage to the back door of the building instead of the main entrance, sprinting across the tarmac to where he'd parked his pick-up. All the time he was increasingly aware of the situation he was in, the tightness in his chest as his pulse quickened, an unnecessary reminder.

There had been little traffic on the road, most of it going in the opposite direction towards the town and the drive to the college campus took exactly six minutes. The gates were open as he expected, the security guard giving him the briefest of nods as he drove through. The Lorimers' bungalow was the second one he came to; he'd pulled onto the verge and switched off the engine, allowing himself a couple of seconds for his eyes to adjust to the sudden darkness before climbing out of the vehicle. It wasn't an ideal situation, but there was nowhere else to park, the only advantage being that his pick-up was identical to all the other company vehicles in and around the college grounds. Lights were on in most of the other bungalows, including his own further along, but it wasn't likely there would be anyone outside at that time of the evening. Valerie had given him a key to the side door, assuring him that Alan would be in the room at the rear of the bungalow which he used as his study.

The feeling of vulnerability was strong as he walked up the driveway with no shrubs or bushes as there were in his own place to act as protection. It couldn't have taken him more than two or three minutes, but by the time he reached the door and inserted the key in the lock he could feel beads of sweat on the back of his neck and around the collar of his shirt. The key turned easily and the door opened smoothly except for the slight click the handle made when he released it before going inside.

He was halfway across the lounge, between the open door to the kitchen and the hallway leading to the other rooms, when he heard a scraping sound, as though a chair was being pushed or dragged along a wooden floor. *Shit! What now! This was not meant to bloody happen!*

'Is that you, Valerie; you're early?'

Instinctively, with a couple of strides, he stepped into the kitchen, pressing his body flat against the wall by the side of the door frame and from where he could see into the hall. He didn't have long to wait: seconds only, until he heard footsteps approaching, followed by the figure of Alan Lorimer. *Where the hell was he going? To the kitchen? There was no light on, so why should he. No, he was making for the side door. Now was his chance!*

With one movement, mindless of the noise he was making, he lunged forward and with his fist clenched struck out, sharp pain shooting up his forearm as his knuckles connected with the left-hand side of Alan Lorimer's forehead. The effect was instant: he had quite literally fallen at his feet, his head hitting the tiled floor with a resounding crack.

He hadn't hung about, just long enough to satisfy himself that he had achieved what he'd set out to do and, apart from an aching hand, felt he had emerged relatively unscathed with only the short drive back to the club to get through.

The security guard was asleep as he drove past which had worked in his favour, glancing at the clock on the dashboard; he had another ten minutes before the curtain would go up and, provided he managed to get back into the club without anyone noticing, he could afford to congratulate himself. It had all been so bloody easy. Or so he had thought. It wasn't until the end of the play, and he was standing in a straight line with the rest of the cast to take their final bow before the curtains drew to a close that the realisation hit him,

Such was the impact it felt physical; he could sense rather than feel the tingling sensation when bruised flesh was recovering from a sudden blow. For several seconds he felt disorientated, only vaguely aware of raised voices and the occasional burst of laughter as the others rushed past him on their way to the dressing-rooms. He held back, but only until everyone had gone and as he had done earlier retraced his steps outside to the car park, all the time cursing under his breath. He could not believe how stupid, how utterly mind-bogglingly remiss he'd been. He had been so damn smug: mission accomplished, carried out exactly as they had planned, so certain it had all been foolproof. What could go wrong they had agreed, exchanging smiles of complacency: the police will assume a local gang was responsible. Robberies, break-ins and killings were common occurrences in the country. But, in his mad rush to return to the club before he was missed, he had forgotten one very obvious part, and one he couldn't blame Valerie for. When the police finally arrived, all they would find would be Alan's dead body and the very obvious sign of entry, the side door which he had left open. He had no choice: he had to return to the bungalow.

This time, there had been no need for any subterfuge. He drove past Val and Alan's bungalow which, apart from the light in the back room, was still in darkness. Valerie would remain at the club for hours yet delaying her return for as long as possible, presumably hyping herself up for the part she would be playing in what they'd agreed was an infallible plan.

He unfastened the lock on the gates to his own bungalow but leaving it unlocked drove up to the side of the building and parked under the canopy outside the back door.

No light came from the space beneath the bedroom door when he reached the hall, but just to make sure the sound of the pick-up hadn't disturbed Kate, he stood outside the door for a couple of seconds to make sure, before returning to the kitchen.

The storm that had been threatening earlier in the day decided to break when he was half-way along the narrow path to the Lorimers' bungalow, rain falling in relentless sheets, the sheer force of it causing him to stumble a couple of times against the wire fencing. By the time he reached their side door, only seconds later, he was drenched, pools of rainwater following him as he stepped inside.

Suddenly, without any warning although he had been partially aware of thunder in the distance, white bursts of lightning, one, two, perhaps three, sliced through the darkness illuminating the lounge and the hall, but only a pool of blood staining the tiled floor revealed where Alan's body should have been lying. Up to that moment he had never understood when people described time as standing still, but as he stood there, between the kitchen and the lounge, he was totally incapable of moving, his brain also remained as though paralysed, with no recollection of how or why he was there in his neighbour's bungalow.

More lightning, staccato-like followed by deep rumblings of thunder as the storm moved overhead brought him back with a jolt, and taking advantage of the noise, he moved speedily to create what he should have done before.

He had hardly felt the rain pounding on his head and shoulders as he half-ran back along the lane, his feet sliding on the muddy grass verge. Once back in his own bungalow and starting to shiver, but unsure whether from the cold or the shock, he made straight for the bathroom and stripping off all his wet clothes, he shoved them into the laundry basket for Silas to deal with in the morning. The water from the shower was only lukewarm, but he didn't want to run it for long remembering the noise the boiler made, with the result he felt no warmer when he finally switched it off and emerged still shivering, grabbing one of their larger towels to wrap round his waist. All the time he was trying to stop his brain thinking, to question, to rationalize. He didn't know why Alan Lorimer hadn't been where he had left him. The man had been dead for God's sake. Dead men didn't just stand up and walk away. Did they?

'Steve?' Valerie's voice, impatient, and demanding his attention.

'Yes?'

'I don't believe you've heard a word I've been saying.'

'Sorry.'

'You sound it!'

'What do you expect, Val; you come out with a statement which has quite frankly given me a lot to think about.'

'You're over-reacting.'

'You have a very short memory.'

'What do you mean?'

'Have you any idea what I put myself through the other night; have you?'

'Of course I have, Steve; you shouldn't need to ask.'

'What's happening next, Val, eh. Are you planning to give me the big heave-ho?'

'You're being ridiculous – '

' – because if you are, Valerie, I suggest you think again!'

# Chapter Twelve

It was with some trepidation that DCI Alastair Dale had agreed to hold a press conference on Monday afternoon, but his superintendent, more than fulfilling his nickname of "Breezy Bob", had been insistent. There was nothing to be gained by making even the mildest of protests, however thinly disguised; he just would not be interested and would only make him more acerbic than ever. How he disliked these press conferences, especially when as in this case he had absolutely nothing to add to what the members of the press already knew and had literally milked dry from what they'd been reporting since the first news leaked out on Wednesday morning with the discovery of John Milne's body. It didn't help that he was restricted in what he could divulge, and which would dramatically affect the current murder enquiry, but Adrian Roberts' directives had been clear: as far as the general public was concerned "Operation Gemma" remained under-wraps. With a growing belief of a connection between the murder in Calder Bay of an employee of "Lorimer Fruits" and the mystery surrounding the disappearance of one of the company's directors in Central Africa, his task this afternoon was going to be more demanding than ever.

Their main meeting room, the one they used for press conferences, was already full, with all of the seats taken when Alistair, together with Dan Aitken, walked in. He recognized many of them, including Beverly Grant. *And why the hell is that woman still here? To squirrel out what was behind Laura Thomson's disappearance? He didn't think so.* Much to his annoyance he had permitted the journalist to rile him on more than one occasion. He couldn't remember ever having the misfortune of knowing anyone quite as ruthlessly ambitious; she was clever, not only with words, but in the way she always reached the crux of what she wanted to convey. The ways she veered so perilously close to the laws of libel were awesome, demonstrating to him at least, that she knew exactly how far to go.

'Good afternoon, ladies and gentlemen,' he opened up the meeting, giving them a few moments to settle down until ,with a shuffling of feet and scraping of chairs, he was confronted with the two dozen or so reporters and journalists momentarily silent as they waited to hear something new, 'the murder of John Milne is now almost a week old and, regrettably, although we are following a number of leads, we are not in a position to name the person responsible. However,' he continued, surprised not to have been interrupted. although, seeing Guy Browne from the "Courier" in the process of raising his hand, he moved on quickly, 'there has been a development which may very well be relevant to this enquiry. John Milne's girlfriend, Laura Thomson, has not been seen since she left work on Thursday afternoon. In itself, this would not raise any alarm, but we have subsequently learned that her house has been broken into, also there is evidence to suggest that she may have left the property in some haste.'

'Why do you suggest that Chief Inspector?' predictably, the man from the "Courier"

'Because the bag she normally has with her was on the kitchen table, together with a set of keys, one of them being for her car although so far we have not been successful in locating the vehicle.'

'You said her house had been broken into, Chief Inspector, was there any damage?' one of the reporters from the "Scotsman" asked.

'Only to the back door, but quite minimal.'

'Are you treating this as abduction, Chief Inspector?' Guy Browne again.

'At this stage we are keeping an open mind.'

'Have you declared Laura Thomson as a missing person?'

'Do you know whether she was in the house when the break-in occurred?'

'Who told you about the break-in, Chief Inspector?'

'One at a time, please. To answer your questions: yes, given the circumstances surrounding Laura, we are now treating her as a missing person. We have no evidence to indicate that she was actually in the property at the time of the incident which was reported to us by her neighbour late on Friday afternoon. This information gave us a timeframe of at least thirty hours from when she was last seen returning home from work on Thursday afternoon around one-thirty.'

'Did the neighbour have any idea of when the break-in was carried out?'

'No, she didn't.'

'There's a general opinion, Chief Inspector,' Beverly Grant spoke up for the first time and without waiting for him to acknowledge her raised hand, 'of there being a possible connection between John Milne's murder and the recent incident in Zambia involving a member of the Lorimer family. Can you corroborate this?'

'No, I cannot. I would remind you that this press conference has been called to update you on the current situation regarding our investigation into the murder of John Milne.'

'Does this mean you are discounting the possibility?' the "Daily Mail's" reporter coming in quickly, followed predictably by Guy Browne.

'Can we take it that you have no intention of keeping the residents of Calder Bay informed of the mystery surrounding this incident?'

'Until such time as there is anything positive to report you will be informed, but until then the enquiry is being handled by the Zambian authorities.'

'Even when an open verdict was declared at the inquest earlier today; doesn't that indicate, Chief Inspector, that the police are treating Alan Lorimer's *disappearance* as suspicious, hence an inquest in less than three days after *his* property was broken into?'

'I should not have to remind you, Miss Grant,' doing his utmost not to react to the woman's devious tactics, 'of the purpose for this press conference.'

'Does this mean, Chief Inspector, that you are not prepared to discuss what has happened to a member of a well-respected local family.'

'I have nothing further to say on that particular subject,' all too conscious of the challenging expression which briefly flitted across her features as he returned his focus on the rest of the room, 'unless there are any more *relevant* questions, I will now bring this meeting to a close and to thank you all for your attendance this afternoon.' swiftly collecting his notes together and stepping down from the raised platform, relieved, although somewhat surprised, at their collective acquiescence as they silently filed out of the room.

'She's certainly got her fingers on the pulse.' Dan Aitken commented drily as he followed him to the door.

'You can say that again, Dan. It comes to something when apparently, she gets her news ahead of everyone else.'

'Even the nationals; if they knew, they were keeping quiet.'

'No doubt she's puzzling over that as we speak, but one of these days she is going to outsmart herself.'

'You wish.'

'Yes, Dan, unprofessional as it may sound, I wish.'

\*\*\*

Graham Lorimer could not remember when he had felt so inadequate, coupled with the unpalatable fact, an admission which infuriated him even more, that he was too old to take any sort of physical action in finding out what had happened to his son. He had been totally opposed when Alan had told him his plans to take up a two-year contract in Central Africa and no attempts to dissuade him had any affect. He'd sensed for some time his growing frustrations; he'd felt stifled, no doubt unfulfilled within the confines of a business which, as far as he had been concerned, virtually ran itself. Alan had longed for new challenges and rather than discussing this with him he had instead made the decision to go to the extreme by spending two years among a bunch of foreigners! And, look what's happened?

'Have you got a minute, Graham?'

'Myra. Of course, come in.'

He turned round from where he'd been standing by the open window to face his daughter-in-law and, not for the first time, wished she'd married Alan instead of that disappointment of a son, Callum. She would have put a stop to Alan leaving them all in the lurch.

'I just wanted to know whether the police have been in touch with you today.' she said, coming into his office and closing the door behind her.

'No, they haven't, so I take it from their silence there is no further news.'

'Could be the Zambian authorities haven't been back to them yet, but perhaps it's too early; the inquest was only this morning – '

' – inquest, Myra? interrupting her, 'I didn't know anything about this.'

'Oh, I'm sorry, Graham, but I was sure Callum would have told you.'

'Callum, my dear, refuses to discuss Alan. In his opinion, his brother is dead.'

'I assume then that he wouldn't have mentioned the telephone call from Alan's friend, Cora Hamilton.'

'No, he did not.'

'It was me she spoke to actually; this was on Saturday and she'd only heard about Alan that morning and then she'd read the article in the "Times". I think she just wanted to talk to someone in the family; she was terribly upset.'

'I thought she was in Ekabe.'

'She's back in London now; she was only out there for three months, on secondment from the London School of Economics.'

'I see, and what did she have to say about this business?'

'She's finding it extremely difficult to believe the worse and from how she was speaking she really hopes he'll be found safe and well.'

'Hmmph. She couldn't have known him for long if she was only out there for three months.'

'She loves him, Graham; that was obvious to me.'

'It's not enough though, is it, Myra?'

'No, Graham, sadly I don't believe it is.'

'I wish to God I could go out there, find out for myself how, and why, this could have happened.'

'I am sure Cora thinks the same.'

'What makes you say that?'

'From something she said.'

'Yes?'

'About where Alan's truck was found; apparently it was well off the road beside the ravine and about a couple of miles out of town. Cora couldn't understand why it would have been driven there, whether by Alan himself or by his assailant.'

'And is this fact being looked into by their police, I wonder.'

'I don't know, Graham.'

'Which brings us back to the inquest. Presumably, and I use that word cautiously, Myra, the Zambian authorities will inform our people of the verdict, and if only as concern for Alan's family, they should let us know.'

'There's time yet, perhaps we should be more patient.'

'Patience, Myra, is something I am running out of, rapidly.'

'We haven't got much choice though.'

'I don't know about that, but it is quite clear we're getting precious little feedback from the local constabulary if their superintendent's attitude is anything to go by from when I spoke to him on Saturday. Incidentally,' he added, recalling with exasperation their telephone conversation, ' he said nothing about any inquest.'

'Could be he didn't know, Graham.'

'That's my whole point exactly; who the hell can we rely on?'

'We're going round in circles; it's time to call it a day. I'll go and mix us a drink, shall I.'

'Good idea; give me a few minutes and I'll be with you,' and adding as she reached the door: ''Did Cora Hamilton give you her telephone number, Myra?'

And his daughter-in-law being the discerning woman she was, didn't ask him why, although judging by her enigmatic expression he was left in no doubt she was well aware of the reason, grateful for her tact in the knowledge that she would keep her thoughts to herself.

\*\*\*

'We'll keep this de-briefing short; it has been a long day with unfortunately precious little to show for it.' Alistair told his team shortly after six when they had the main office to themselves, 'but if nothing else I'm sure you will all agree that this afternoon has shown up quite clearly that we can no longer ignore the growing belief there is a connection between the events here in Calder Bay and those in Zambia, with the undeniable link of "Lorimer Fruits". What I'd like to do is to run through the alibis we have to-date and perhaps discard any which may no longer be relevant.'

'Once the press conference goes live, we're not going to come out all that well, are we, sir?'

'Perhaps not, Colin. As we all know, the public is fickle, also their memories are short: our previous success in solving cases and bringing offenders to justice is all too quickly forgotten if we are considered too slow in showing positive progress in a current investigation, and for this reason we need to have a re-think. It's become obvious that we cannot continue to ignore the connection between John Milne's murder and the recent events in Zambia, but we're treading a very fine line here. Dan, what's your thinking?'

'I can't help feeling we've been placed in something of an awkward situation with Interpol literally breathing down our necks in the event we should exceed their no-go area.'

'You're right of course and if we continue to deny any connection, we're going to very quickly lose all credence if and when an over-zealous journalist of Beverly Grant's ilk should unearth the merest hint of any drug smuggling, well we can expect loud noises from above.'

'You're thinking of "Breezy Bob", sir.'

'Everyone has a boss, Colin,' Alistair smiled ruefully, 'even "Breezy Bob" as you so irreverently call him, but seriously, I think the time has come to be given if not a free rein exactly, but considerably more than we have at the moment, otherwise it will be tantamount to trying to function with one hand tied behind our backs. Therefore,' he added, 'it's time to put a call through to Adrian Roberts.'

'And if he doesn't agree, sir?' Colin asked.

'There's always that possibility,' Alistair answered, 'I'm sure he will appreciate how their restrictions are hindering our investigation, but there is the risk that by requesting more leeway we could be forced to hand the case over to London.'

'You mean the Met?' a look of genuine concern on Colin's face.

'That would hardly be an ideal situation, sir.' Dan added, looking equally dismayed.

'No, Dan, it wouldn't, but I'm looking at the worst-case scenario here, but there's nothing to be gained by negative speculation. Let's pick up from when we became sidetracked, otherwise we're going to be here all night. Alibis. By them, I mean the ones from those who were closest to John Milne.'

'When you whittle them down,' Dan said, 'there aren't many: members of the family mainly I would say,' turning over the pages of his notebook, 'as you know I've only interviewed Bruce Lorimer, and this was after Lilian had spoken to him on Wednesday – ',

' – I'll stop you there a minute, Dan, even although he's come up with an alibi for Tuesday night, what were your impressions of him?'

'Arrogant, super-confident but then I guess that's an asset for the position he holds in the company as their sales and marketing director but, that aside, he came over as slightly nervous, but could be that's normal with him, or as with many people, he felt uncomfortable being interviewed by a police officer. However, as to his alibi: up to the time he and his party left "The Royal" at eleven-fifteen, we only have Sara Anderson, his girlfriend, to vouch for him which she did, saying he'd left her apartment about a quarter to six the following morning.'

'That's if she's telling the truth.' Colin quickly put in.

'But, if she isn't, Colin, what possible motive would he have?'

'Don't know, Dan.'

'Whichever way you look at it,' Alistair suggested, 'another interview could throw up something we may have missed. I know I'm harping back to motive, but even if Bruce Lorimer isn't directly, or indirectly, involved, there is always the possibility, obscure though it may be, that he could be aware of what's going on.'

'Could account for his nervousness.'

'Good point, Lilian. So, Dan, I'll leave him to you.'

'Sir.'

'Lilian, anything further on the secretary's movements that night.'

'There is actually, sir. The council car park is only large enough for a dozen vehicles and I managed to speak to a man who uses it regularly. Apparently, he knows Kirstie and on Wednesday morning he had to leave early for the airport and told me her car wasn't there.'

'What time was this?'

'Six o'clock, sir.'

'And she starts work, when?'

'Eight-thirty, and I checked with the receptionist and Kirstie arrived at the same time as she said did on Wednesday.'

'So where did she spend the night then I wonder.'

'Could have a boyfriend?' Colin grinned.

'Colin,' Lilian frowned, 'be serious.'

'I am being.'

'She's nudging sixty.'

'So?'

'Alright, Colin,' Alistair intervened, but only half-heartedly, being frivolous for a few moments was a form of release and one from time to time they all needed. 'It doesn't sound as though she can be considered as a likely suspect, but don't let it go, Lilian.'

'What do you make of Callum Lorimer's alibi, sir?' Dan asked him.

'Ah, I was just coming to him. Given that I spoke to him before we learned about Interpol's findings in respect to his friendship with this Ben Maitland, his alibi justifies a closer look. In fact, I'm going to pull him into the station for further questioning.'

'That will put the wind up him.'

'That might not be a bad idea, Colin. Perhaps it is time to move this investigation forward, otherwise it is going to become stagnant. Let's consider him for a moment.' he suggested, using his team as a sounding board, but sometimes it was necessary if only to co-ordinate his half-formed thoughts and theories, 'He receives a letter from his brother the day before John Milne's murder informing him of his unexpected return home. If this sudden change in Alan Lorimer's plans would have had any impact on the syndicate's next consignment of drugs, we don't at this stage know, but for this exercise let's assume it did, and Callum passed on the information to Ben Maitland, this would have caused an element of alarm. While it may explain whatever has happened to the brother out in Zambia, it doesn't explain the fact that John Milne met his death that night. Therefore, the first question we must ask is why.'

'John Milne was an additional threat to them.'

'Yes, Dan, a valid and credible point, but how did it come about?'

'Do you think it's possible, sir,' Lilian asked tentatively, 'he knew about the syndicate.'

'I think he could have done, Lilian. If he wasn't involved along with Callum, we need to ask ourselves, how did he find out: did someone tell him, did he overhear someone or was there some other way?'

'We don't know much about John Milne's girlfriend.'

'Have you any particular reason for mentioning her, Colin?' Alistair asked, interested to hear the direction his sergeant's thought processing was going; he'd learned over the years they'd been working together not to underestimate his sergeant, what very often sounded no more than random comments turned out to be sharply relevant.

'It's just a thought, sir.'

'Go on.'

'Well, I've seen where she lives; it's not such an expensive area as Carlogie Road, but those properties in Beach Road don't come cheap.'

'She's probably only renting.'

'No doubt she is, Lilian, but all the same I bet the rent would be a bit of a stretch for a bank employee. Just a point, sir.'

'And a good one, Colin.' and he meant it; he had made a good point, and perhaps he was thinking along the right lines, ones which hadn't occurred to them. From what he'd seen of those houses along the front, there was no doubt they were in a prestigious position, and he reckoned the rents would be well in excess of five hundred pounds a month. He had no idea what her salary at the bank would be, but whatever it was, as Colin had said, a bit of a stretch.

'She might have private means.' Lilian suggested.

'Possibly.'

'Or someone else was paying the rent.' Dan put in, an awakening of interest in his expression.

'Could be this character, Ben Maitland.'

'Trust you, Colin.' Lilian smiled across at him, shaking her head, but only in mild exasperation.

'If we're going down that road,' Alistair suggested, picking up on the thread of their enthusiasm, 'Interpol may be responsible. Remember, they've been on the drug smuggling case for some time and with their suspicions concerning "Lorimer Fruits", they must know this town fairly well by now.'

'So, she could be working undercover then.'

'It's a consideration,' Alistair said nodding across at Colin, 'but it should go without saying that it wouldn't be a good thing to jump to conclusions; that would be too easy. If Laura Thomson has been put in place by Interpol, Adrian Roberts may well confirm this; I will certainly put it to him when I speak to him. Meanwhile, we should concentrate our efforts on finding her, including her car therefore let's check all exit routes: airports, ports, etc. Somewhat late in the day I admit, considering the last sighting of her was early Thursday afternoon, also if she is with Interpol it's going to be something of a waste of time, not to mention a substantial stretch to our budget.'

'And Laura Thomson may not even be her real name.' Dan said.

\*\*\*

Callum was on the way out to his car the following morning when his phone rang. He was already late for his appointment with the Chief Inspector and his first instincts were to ignore it; the last he wanted was any distraction, however slight, to heighten the nervous tension which had been gathering momentum ever since the call the evening before summoning him to the Calder Bay police station. Whoever it was, was using the direct house line, which more than likely ruled out a business call, but not wanting the search system to kick in and either Kirstie or Myra to answer, he picked up the receiver.

'Callum Lorimer.'

'Oh, Callum;' a woman's voice he didn't recognize, 'this is Cora Hamilton – '

' – Miss Hamilton,' he interrupted, instantly regretting the decision to take the call, 'I understand you've already spoken to my wife, and I wouldn't have thought there was anything to be gained by any further discussion about what's happened to Alan.'

'I'm actually returning your father's call – '

' – my father! You must be mistaken.'

'I don't think so; there was a message on my answering machine when I came home yesterday from a Graham Lorimer asking me to call him and this was the number he left for me.'

'I have no idea why he should have tried to get in touch with you, no idea at all.'

'Neither do I, therefore I'd be grateful if you could either transfer this call, if you can, or let him know I am returning his call.'

'I will let him know you phoned, Miss Hamilton and now I have to go.' and without any pretence at politeness, replaced the receiver.

*What the hell was his father playing at? Phoning that bloody woman! What in the world did he expect to achieve? Could the old fool not accept that Alan was dead?*

Apparently not, he thought bitterly, pulling his jacket from the back of his chair and storming out of the office, banging the door behind him. There was no way he was going to pass on Cora Hamilton's message. Bitter thoughts remained with him on the drive down into the town, taunting him in their familiarity, reminding him of how, for so long, he had been manipulated by his father into what now he recognized as a false sense of, not of security exactly, but of actually believing that as the eldest he would ultimately take over the company, that the position of managing director would belong to him. He had been fooling himself. His father had no bloody intention of retiring, of relinquishing his control of the business. Not to him certainly. Alan would be his first choice, the son he'd preferred, the son he had even agreed to taking a couple of years off before returning and slotting back into the business and nothing would have changed: he would remain in the background, his suggestions dismissed out of hand as unworthy of discussion while his father and Alan would sit for hours discussing the costs and viability of investing in new equipment. Was this why he stubbornly insisted that Alan was still alive? In his denial, he was refusing to accept that he and Alan would never be able to carry on as they had done before. It could explain his fury the other day and why he had had scarcely spoken to him since?

He pulled into an empty space in front of the police station and although by now more than fifteen minutes late, he remained in the car, his knuckles white from gripping too tightly on the steering wheel, while he struggled to control his emotions, to wait until his heartbeat returned to normal.

*For Christ's sake, calm down. The man you're going to see has no idea of what's going on inside your head. He only wants to ask you more questions about John Milne, someone you hardly knew.*

The sergeant on the desk led him along a carpeted corridor to a glass-panelled door marked 'Interview Room One'. This was the first time he had been in a police station and, apart from watching numerous police dramas on TV, had no idea what to expect. The chairs weren't plastic, the table had no scratch marks or rings left in the wood where countless cups and mugs had been and there were pictures on the wall: black and white prints of Calder Bay in years gone by. No, he decided, not what he expected at all, deciding this was what he had heard, again from television, described as the soft interview room, as the door opened, and DCI Dale walked in.

'Good morning, Mr Lorimer, thank you for coming in; would you like something to drink, tea or coffee.

'No, I'm fine, thank you.' Callum answered, wanting to make it plain right from the start he had no time for any pleasantries. As much as he wanted to complain for not only the interruption to his heavy workload, but for his objection of being treated like one of their suspects, he refrained, deciding there would be no point. He was here, he had suffered the embarrassment of being seen coming into a police station and all he wanted was to get through what he knew would be a total waste of everyone's time.

'If you're sure, then we'll begin. Take a seat, Mr Lorimer.' gesturing to one of the chairs and once he was seated, took the one across the table from him. 'First of all,' he said, 'I want to stress that this is an informal interview, and you are free to leave at any time you choose. Does that meet with your approval.'

'It will have to, Chief Inspector. I honestly can't think of anything else I can tell you about John Milne's death; I've already spoken to you and given a statement to Sergeant Wood.'

'Indeed, you have, but I'm hoping that this meeting with you will provide us with a clarity we've been lacking so far in respect to his murder.'

'Clarity?'

*Clarity? What the hell does he mean? This is a bloody trap, it must be!*

'Yes, clarity. I am sure I don't need to spell it out to you, but in any murder enquiry our main aim is to find out the person, or persons, responsible and to reach that conclusion it's imperative to find the motive. Up to now, this is something which has been continuing to elude us; here, was a young man, a virtual newcomer to Calder Bay who had recently been employed by your company on a two-year contract, and at the same time signing a lease on a flat in the town for a similar length of time, when with six months remaining on both contracts, was brutally murdered. His death was a violent one, Mr Lorimer; I will spare you the details, but suffice to say that whoever carried out the assault would have had a motive, whether personal or otherwise remains unknown, except it was no random act. There was no forced entry into the flat which could indicate he was known to the victim.'

'Why are you telling me all this?'

'You've no idea?'

'Of course I haven't! All this talk of motive! That's for you to find!'

'As I've said, you're free to leave whenever you wish, but you're not interested, intrigued even, to learn why I'm going to such lengths to describe the set-up to you of a recent murder which undoubtedly has a connection with your family –'

' – What!' jumping to his feet with such force that his chair slid across the polished floor, 'My family has got absolutely nothing to do with John's death!'

'Why don't you pick up the chair, bring it back to the table and sit down and try to calm down while I enlighten you.' and with shaking hands he found himself doing what he'd been asked when all he wanted was to walk away, exercise his prerogative, but realising he couldn't, and as he once again faced this smart arse of a chief inspector, began to wonder whether he needed to have a lawyer, but quickly dismissed the idea. Somehow, and at that precise moment he hadn't a clue how, only that he wasn't doing himself any favours by losing his temper.

'In view of your reaction, it would seem you strongly object to the suggestion of any connection, Mr Lorimer?'

'Of course I do; you have nothing to substantiate such claims.'

'You are dismissing them as coincidences?'

'What else? Could be that something in John's past had caught up with him.'

'And that sounds feasible to you?'

'More credible than using the good name of my family as a convenient scapegoat!'

'How did you feel when you learned your brother intended to return home before his overseas contract had expired?'

'What do you mean?' his rapid switch taking him completely off-guard, feeling trickles of sweat forming along his forehead.

'What was your reaction when you received a letter from him on Tuesday morning; were you surprised?'

'Of course.'

'Annoyed?'

'Not especially?'

*What the hell was he getting at. This is another of his bloody traps. He's trying his damnedest to corner me, force me into saying something – something incriminating and I don't know how to stop him!*

'Perhaps you viewed it as an inconvenience. Is that how you felt, Mr Lorimer?'

'Well, it was inconvenient; it meant I would have to let John go; the expense of severing his contract within the two-year period.'

'Ah, the expense. This was an immediate concern?'

'Of course it was.'

'You were satisfied with the work he was doing?'

'Yes, very.'

'You would agree perhaps he was an asset to your company.'

'Look, Chief Inspector, why are you asking me about John in this way; what has it got to do with his death?'

'It could be considerable, but if nothing else, it does give me some idea of how you viewed him.'

'Viewed him?'

'Yes, exactly that. You had no fault to find with his work, even going so far as to say he was an asset to your company and yet you were quick to accept that you would have to dispense with his services once you learned of your brother's unexpected return. Considering the size of "Lorimer Fruits", an internationally recognized company and prominently listed on the stock market, employing a large workforce, I would not have thought that continuing to pay the salary of a relatively newly-qualified young man for a further six months would have made much of an impact – financially.'

'What the hell are you getting at?'

'When I first spoke to you, Mr Lorimer to inform you of his death you asked me who had been responsible.'

'Quite natural to ask under the circumstances.'

'It would have been if I'd told you straightaway that he had been killed, but I was bringing you the news of his death, not of his murder.'

'You are twisting my words!'

'Why would you have made the assumption though? Did you have a reason to expect foul play, sir.'

'Of course not!'

'I would remind you that I'm conducting a murder enquiry. Someone wanted John Milne out of the way permanently and it is our task to find that person. All of which brings us full circle, back to motive.'

'And which has nothing to do with me, Chief Inspector, or any member of my family.'

'Who else would have known about your brother's return; I'm talking about a time frame here: from the moment you received his letter to a matter of hours before John Milne's murder?'

'This is outrageous – '

' – please, sir, if you could just answer the question.'

'My wife; I gave her the letter to read immediately after I'd read it.'

'And she would have passed the news on presumably.' it wasn't a question, but he was all too aware he was waiting for some sort of response, feeling the rising tension anticipating the inevitable way the questioning was going.

'We had a board meeting that morning and apparently she made the announcement then.'

'You were not there?'

'She went in before I did.'

'Why?'

'Sorry?' stalling, trying to pre-empt him.

'Why the delay.'

'I wouldn't call it a delay exactly; I was still in the dining-room, it was an early morning meeting: eight-thirty, shortly after breakfast.'

'And who was at your meeting?'

'Oh, my younger brother, Bruce, my father of course, his P.A Kirstie.'

'And what was their general reaction to this news?'

'My father was pleased.'

'The others?'

'I don't know, Chief Inspector; I didn't ask them.'

'Apart from those you've just mentioned, was there anyone else who would have been told.'

'At that stage, I doubt it.'

'What about yourself, Mr Lorimer; you were being *inconvenienced* from what you've been saying, did you pass this information on to anyone during the course of the day?'

'No, why should I have?'

'You tell me.'

'You know, Chief Inspector, I've had quite enough of your insinuations. I'm going – ' making to stand up.

'Before you leave there's a couple of questions I would like to ask you, purely routine, you understand.'

'I've nothing to add to what I've already told you and I've already wasted a good part of my morning.'

'It would appear you were late arriving at the board meeting, at least you were the last one to arrive, I was wondering why that was.'

'No reason except I wanted to finish my breakfast.'

Usually when a person is late turning up for meetings, especially anyone in a senior position of a thriving business, always at the beck and call of others, is held up by a last-minute phone call.'

'Well, that didn't happen.'

'It didn't?'

'I have already said so.'

'If we considered it necessary, we could always run a check on any incoming or outgoing calls, or texts, sir.'

'That sounds like a threat to me, Chief Inspector.'

'No threat, sir, merely stating a fact. So, what you're saying is you didn't discuss your brother's imminent return, vent your annoyance perhaps, wanting a sympathetic ear, with someone outside the confines of the business which must feel somewhat claustrophobic at times.'

'Well, I didn't.'

'You have friends presumably; outside the business I mean?'

'Acquaintances, rather than friends.'

'I see. No doubt meet up with them in one of the town's popular haunts.'

'Something like that.'

'Which is your favourite?'

'For God's sake, this is a total waste of my time!'

'What about last Tuesday, sir, did you go down into the town after work for a drink?'

'Not after work, no.'

*Damn! Damn!*

The palms of his hands felt unpleasantly moist as he clasped them tightly together, furious with himself for allowing his concentration to waver; it had only taken seconds once the words had left his mouth, but long enough to realise their impact.

'A lunchtime drink, perhaps, Mr Lorimer,' he asked, 'where did you go; the "Shipwreck", or somewhere less crowded at that time of day, like the "Royal" for instance?'

'I had a lager in the lounge bar at the "Royal".' determined now to keep his responses to the minimum.

'See anyone you knew?'

'One or two faces I recognized, Chief Inspector.'

# Chapter Thirteen

Steve woke early on Tuesday morning. He had not slept well, staring into the darkness and willing his mind to close, to leave him alone, but relentlessly a jumble of words and images vied for his attention, relentlessly persistent and accusatory. The double whiskies he'd had in the rugby club after he had left Valerie last night had been a mistake; they hadn't as he had hoped, brought oblivion. Quite the reverse. He realised now, in the harsh morning light, he had not handled the inspector's questions well. They may have been, as Val had said, purely routine, but she was wrong. Detective Inspector Christopher Musenge, it would seem, was a new breed of senior police officer, a product of one of the country's universities: super-confident, articulate with a diction devoid of any local dialect, he operated along less traditional ways, otherwise why ask him those questions in the first place when it was practically a foregone conclusion that the break-in had been carried out by a gang of local thugs?

The inspector with his probing wasn't the only person bothering him; there was the way Valerie had been behaving recently. She had seemed different somehow, offhand, distant; he couldn't quite pin it down, trying to remember when he had first noticed. It could have been on Friday when he'd called at the bungalow, arriving unannounced as he had last night at Ekabe Lodge. She hadn't been pleased to see him; she'd made that quite obvious, unwilling even to discuss Thursday night, but worse still had refused to believe him when he'd told her that Alan had been dead when he'd arrived at their bungalow the night before. The fact he had been stretching the truth didn't concern him unduly. She simply did not want to know. Val could be bloody hard work at times he decided, pushing away the crumpled sheet and climbing out of bed.

Kate was still asleep, in exactly the same position as she had been when he'd finally come to bed, one hand resting against her cheek and her dark hair fanning out on the pillow, reminding him for a moment as he crossed the room to the bathroom of how it used to be between them. He knew he should feel guilty about the way he was treating her, and had been for years, but his only emotion was one of frustration. Could be, their marriage had run its course; it was as simple as that. They barely functioned as a couple, seldom spending any time together. To no longer be married to him might even come as a relief, but how would he know? She had never given the slightest hint she was unhappy, therefore, it was up to him to make the first move. So, why was he hesitating? Could the fact that he would no longer benefit from Kate's growing success as a contemporary artist have anything to do with his reluctance? *Of course it does, Steve. Make sure of your options; you don't want to jump out of the frying pan into the fire, do you?*

He didn't need his conscience, that persistent little niggle inside his head, to warn him. Kate was no fool; if she were to learn of his relationship with Valerie or, God forbid, this business over the break-in, she wouldn't hesitate. She would be in touch with her lawyer before he had the chance to protest. He had therefore to be more circumspect and falling out with Valerie was not the way to go towards ending his marriage without ending up the loser. He would make it up to Val, unpleasantly reminded of how their evening had ended. He should not have threatened her the way he had; that had been a mistake. Another one.

He was spooning coffee into his mug, hoping an infusion of caffeine would give him the boost he needed to get through what he expected to be another stressful day, when he remembered about having to call into the police station. *Damn! Was there no let-up?*

Taking his coffee with him he went through to the lounge and opened the glass doors on to the patio. Silas was at the far end of the garden steadily working his way towards the bungalow, the scythe rhythmically slashing through the rough grass. A creature of habit their houseboy; he didn't need to check the time. It would be almost seven-thirty which meant soon Kate would be up and he would have to pretend: not the loving husband, that would be ridiculous, but at least a polite one which he realised with a sinking feeling at the pit of his stomach was going to prove well-nigh impossible the way he was feeling.

*Come on, Stevie boy. You can act, can't you? Just imagine you're on the stage performing in front of Ekabe's delightful expat community. Anyway, all this ducking and diving will soon be over.*

The visit to Ekabe's police station in the centre of town wasn't the ordeal he'd been dreading, mainly because there was no sign of the inspector. He had been shown into a small room by an officer who introduced himself as Sergeant Brian Phiri; a Christopher Musenge in the making, the cynical observation suggesting itself to him as he obediently took a seat. Two sheets of printed A4 paper were placed on the table in front of him, Sergeant Phiri painstakingly reading the contents out to him, pausing occasionally to look across at him, presumably to satisfy himself he had his full attention, until finally he came to an end and, handing him a blue biro asked him to acknowledge his agreement with his signature.

The sergeant then thanked him, and taking the signed sheets slipped them into a buff-coloured file with the embossed Zambian emblem prominently displayed along the top.

Steve had half-hoped he'd see Valerie while he was there but not wanting to draw attention to himself by hanging about, decided to give her a call in spite of her insistence not to contact her. It was suddenly important to know how she was feeling after the bitter way the evening had ended and, if necessary, to apologise; to assure her he hadn't meant his last words as he had walked out of the bar.

Reaching his pick-up and checking along the line of the other parked vehicles in case he'd missed her, he switched on the engine and pulled out into the main street, taking a left at the roundabout and heading back to the college. It was still early, not yet nine, but he should call in at the site office first before phoning Val. His work as senior building officer for the college's building and maintenance division had never seemed so pointless, wondering how he had tolerated the sheer tedium of ensuring Ekabe College was always ready for Lusaka's spot-check inspections. But then, he consoled himself, soon, very soon, these years will have faded into oblivion.

His mobile rang as he was walking across the parking area to the site hut. He almost didn't answer it and was on the point of switching over to voice mail when he saw Valerie's number on the display. Immediately he assumed she was phoning to apologise; to tell him she'd had second thoughts and wanted to see him: a multitude of explanations presenting themselves to him in the time it took him to tap on the green button.

'Hi, Val.'

'Steve, how busy are you?'

'Well,' wondering where she was coming from, her question catching him unawares, 'not especially, just about to start work.'

'I'm leaving today Steve – '

'– so soon?'

'I told you yesterday how important it was to get back to the UK and see my lawyer.'

'I know you did, but – '

' – I managed to get a seat on an Emirates flight leaving Lusaka at one o'clock.'

'That's a bit tight, isn't it?'

'Not really; it is doable; that is if I can get to Ndola airport in time to catch the ten-thirty domestic flight down to Lusaka. That's why I'm calling you actually,' she rushed on, not giving him a chance to speak, 'can you drive me there, Steve? Please.'

Her lack of tact was staggering, even for her. He didn't' believe for one single minute that there was no other male in Ekabe unable to come to her rescue and drive her the twenty-odd miles to Ndola airport; surely someone in authority at the college would have felt obliged to arrange transport for her.

'Well?' her voice impatient, giving him no chance to think straight, 'Can you, Steve?'

'Of course I can, Val.' his response automatic, choosing to dismiss the suspicion that she had probably had every intention of leaving without telling him if she hadn't been stuck for transport.

They said little during the forty minutes or so it took them to reach the airport; each time he made any attempt to start a conversation she made it abundantly clear she was in no mood to talk and certainly nothing personal. Even his attempt to apologise for last night was greeted with indifference and after a while he gave up. Only when they were approaching the airport. a murky grey flat-roofed single storey building which he always found infinitely depressing, and he was manoeuvring into the narrow space directly in front of the main entrance, did she turn to face him and leaning over, kissed him lightly on the cheek.

'Thanks for the lift, Steve. Sorry I'm such rotten company but I don't like flying; it always makes me edgy.'

'I understand; you'll phone me as soon as you arrive, won't you?'

'Of course.'

'You haven't said, but are you going straight home – '

' – home?'

'Yes, Scotland; Calder Bay, isn't it, that's where your family live?'

'That's right, Calder Bay.' catching the slight hesitation in her voice, 'But, no I'll be in London for a few days before going back to face them all, which I might add, I am not looking forward to.'

'I can imagine, from what you've told me about them I'm sure it's going to be something of an ordeal.' doing his best to sound sympathetic, but they didn't have much longer and then she would be gone, 'So, where will you be staying in London; which hotel, I mean?'

'I haven't decided yet, but I'll let you know as soon as I've booked in.'

'You must have some idea though.' inwardly cringing at how he must sound.

'At this precise moment, Steve, I have no idea. For Christ's sake, stop fussing!' unfastening her seat belt, the metal of the clasp clanging against the edge of the window.

'Okay. Okay.' holding up his hands in mock surrender, 'I'll get your bags. Don't forget the one in the back seat.' and stepping out on to the tarmac, walked round and lifted out her two travel bags, easily recognizable by their fancy gilt logo as top of the range Italian and for a moment, a fluttering of unease made him pause, *Let's face it, Stevie, you're not exactly in her class, are you? Posh Italian luggage, eh!* With an impatient shrug, he loaded the bags on to one of the trolleys lined up on the narrow pavement.

'Are you alright?' she asked him as she joined him, tossing the smaller bag on top of the trolley,

'I'm fine. Just thinking how much I'm going to miss you.'

'Me too, darling.' giving his arm a squeeze, 'Are you going to wait and see me off?'

'No, I'd better get back.' ignoring the impulse to remind her to call him, watching as she walked through the automatic glass doorway to join the other passengers in the queue for the flight to Lusaka.

***

By Tuesday Alan had reached his tolerance level, deeply regretting agreeing to what he was now seeing as a totally unacceptable proposal. He'd had plenty of time to think, to mull over what Sheila Campbell had told him on Friday morning when he was still suffering the effects of being knocked unconscious, followed by a further punishment when he'd pranged the truck. He had hardly been in a fit state to absorb what she'd been saying, physically or mentally. She must have realised this, using his weakness to her advantage, the belated realisation adding to the build-up of anger, and wanting to put an end to what felt more like being under house arrest as each hour passed; a house arrest without even the simplest of privileges: making a phone call to the woman he loved. He knew how futile it would be to make any attempt to prove to his captor that Cora could be trusted. *Get real, why should she believe you? This mess you've become embroiled in concerns drug smuggling on an international scale, in case you hadn't realised, Alan. The illegal distribution of drugs destroys. Your brother is involved. This is serious stuff!*

It wasn't working. He was incapable of any charitable thought for victims of drug crimes; his thoughts were completely focused on Cora, worrying and imagining how she must be feeling, whether she was believing that he was dead. He *had* to talk to her. It would only take minutes, long enough to reassure her that he was okay and to stress that she kept the knowledge to herself. They may not have known each other for long, but instinctively he trusted her. But how was he going to do it; Sheila or one of her stable-hands or house servants were always around. Even during the night when he was in his room, he could hear the padding footsteps of the night watchman. It was hopeless. But then, during the afternoon, an opportunity presented itself. There had been some sort of emergency in one of the top fields which needed Sheila to sort out, and for once he had the house to himself. The phone was in the kitchen and he didn't hesitate; quickly, and listening out for the slightest sound of anyone approaching, he moved away from where he'd been standing by the lounge window and crossed the hall to the kitchen.

Lifting the receiver, he dialled Cora's number and waited with increasing impatience for the connection to be made all the time expecting Sheila to appear in the open doorway. Finally, the ringing tone, only to be followed with a click as the answering machine kicked in.

*Of course! Cora wouldn't be home; she'd be at work!*

He had been so positive that all he had to do was call her and she would answer; the disappointment was devastating, far more than it should have been, reminding him how much he'd been depending on hearing her voice. He didn't leave a message as much as he wanted to but thought it wouldn't be the most sensible thing to do. If he knew how long he had before he was interrupted, he may have chanced it, but it was too risky. He had another reason, apart from word getting back to Sheila's people; he didn't want Cora caught up in any of what was going on.

'I hope you're not going to do what I think you are, Alan.'

He had been so engrossed in his troubled thoughts, standing by the phone with his hand on the receiver, he hadn't heard her coming into the kitchen.

'I'm getting more than a little fed up with all of this, you know.' for the first time his pent-up frustration turning to anger, 'How much longer do you intend to hold me here, a bloody prisoner?'

'That's a bit extreme.'

'Is it, Sheila? How else would you describe my current situation?'

'I did explain this to you, and you agreed'

'Under duress, yes.'

'Hardly duress.'

'The alternative was tantamount to a threat, so what kind of choice did I have?'

'You mean the civil offence I presume?'

'You presume right, Sheila, but this so-called conversation is getting us nowhere. And, yes, if we return to a few minutes ago, you were partly right. I was trying to phone someone, unfortunately I wasn't successful.'

'You left a message?'

'No, I did not.'

'Alan,' she said, even sounding sympathetic, 'I do regret this situation – '

' – do you?'

'Of course.'

'Do you know what I think, Sheila? God knows I've had plenty of time to do just that. I don't believe your lot, Interpol, MI5 or whoever, have a clue what's going on. Sunday was meant to be crunch-time, but the situation remains unchanged. It is now Tuesday, and I am still here – a bloody prisoner.'

'Alright, I hear what you say. And I admit it is very much a waiting game. And I'll try and put you in the picture; a shipment of drugs from Amsterdam was made at the weekend, scheduled to arrive in Arbroath on Sunday for the pick-up and distribution later that night. As I've mentioned, because of a heavy police presence in the area this couldn't go ahead. The drugs cannot remain where they are indefinitely, Alan. They will have to move them and that, in a nutshell, is what we're waiting for.'

'I see, well, I suppose I do.'

'It's important that you do; if the syndicate should learn that their attack on you was unsuccessful and that you could arrive back in Calder Bay, they would have to cut their ties with your brother instantly and we would lose them. But more importantly, we would also lose the ability to confront and arrest your brother for being in possession and personally receiving this current assignment of drugs. It would mean that almost two years of work, not to mention the expense, will have been in vain.'

'Why the hell didn't you pick them up before; you had names, you knew when the drugs left Amsterdam, you even knew when and where they arrived in Britain?'

'Because Alan, it would only be half a job done; we wouldn't have caught them in the act of handing the drugs over and following this up with how and when they were distributed and, more importantly perhaps, who else was involved.'

'Like Callum, you mean?'

'Of course, but remember, I'm very much on the periphery of the investigating drug team.'

He knew what she meant. If he hadn't landed up practically on her doorstep with obvious signs of assault, her people wouldn't have picked up on what they had been anticipating given the Lorimer connection. Their assumption, because that's what it was tantamount to, that this syndicate was hell bent on preventing his return to Calder Bay, could be wrong. In his mind's eye, he could see the tall figure of Steve Burrows bending over him as he lay on the hall floor. Up to now, with the hopeless situation he'd found himself in and his worry about Cora, he had almost forgotten, but seeing his neighbour had been no apparition brought on by a bang on the head. Steve had been there. He *had* been in his bungalow that night.

He had to say something. He couldn't, given the international scale of the drug smuggling, remain silent. Not to do so, would be to withhold evidence and if he was wrong and seeing him had been a delirious vision, well he could hardly be blamed. Someone had attacked him and he was convinced it had been Steve Burrows. *It does raise the question though, doesn't it, Alan? Why had Steve been in the bungalow? And how did he get in? Why had he just stood there? Why had he not helped him?* So many questions, but they would have to wait.

'There's something I haven't mentioned to you before.' he said to her, 'I don't know whether it's relevant, but it could be.'

'Go on.'

'It was after I'd been attacked and I was regaining consciousness when I saw someone, someone I knew.'

'Why didn't you say this before, Alan?'

'I suppose I forgot.'

'That's not much of an answer.'

'Sorry, but for – for personal reasons I think I must have mentally put it to the back of my mind.'

'Personal reasons?'

He could tell by the determined expression on her face, she wouldn't be content with any half-explanations starting to regret his decision, but there was no going back, already anticipating what her reaction was going to be.

'I've already told you I was in the process of a divorce. I've known for some weeks, months perhaps, that Valerie, my wife, had been having an affair with a fellow expat. I'd had my suspicions that it could have been Steve Burrows, but that's all they were, besides,' he went on, 'I didn't care; I had finally come to my senses if you like and started divorce proceedings, but when I saw him there on Thursday night, I reckoned I'd been right about the pair of them.'

'And you're sure it was him?'

'Yes.'

'You said you'd lost consciousness?' undiluted scepticism in her voice as she stood in front of him, arms folded, waiting for him to elaborate.

'That's true, but I'd just come to, and I'd remained where I was for a few minutes, in a crumpled heap on the floor afraid to get up, not knowing how much damage had been done, when I felt a sort of presence, you know, as if someone was watching me.'

'And then?' prompting him when he'd faltered slightly, trying to be accurate in what he could recall.

'I don't think I moved my head or anything, but I opened my eyes, and he was there, standing over me, only inches away and staring down at me.'

'It would have been dark?'

'Fairly yes, there had been a faint light from my study further along the hall. That's where I would have been when I was disturbed by the break-in – '

' – you don't remember whether you were then?' she interrupted him.

'Not exactly, but perhaps I heard something, and if I had I would have got up to investigate, how else did I end up where I did.'

'Alright, let's go back to this man. You don't think you could have been hallucinating. You've admitted that you'd been knocked unconscious, I would have thought you would have still been a bit woozy, even delirious.'

'I don't think so. My head ached, quite a bit I admit, and I could sense that I'd lost a fair amount of blood, but I didn't feel all that bad. It wasn't until I was driving, I reckon I was about halfway to Ekabe Lodge by then, when I started to feel a bit lightheaded. Delayed shock I expect. Well, you know the rest.'

'I don't know what to think Alan and I'm not convinced that you weren't hallucinating, but I can't ignore what you've just told me.'

'I did say I wondered whether it would be relevant or not.'

'I know, you did. Tell me, you mentioned the word break-in in relation to what happened at the bungalow. Did you see any evidence of this; a smashed door or window, broken glass, that sort of thing?'

'Why's that so important; naturally I assumed someone had broken into my bungalow. How else would they have got in?'

'When you regained consciousness, and I realise it was dark, but did you notice anything to show how they broke in?'

'Now you come to mention it, no, I didn't. I didn't put any lights on, I just wanted to leave in case they should return, but I'm sure I would have seen some signs, broken glass as you say.'

'Odd.'

'Yes?'

'Odd because most break-ins create a noise, usually by a window or glass doors, as they are the usual points of entry, but apparently that wasn't the case the other night.'

'Something disturbed me though.'

'Yes, but I think if it had been something like glass breaking for instance, you would have remembered. The noise wouldn't have been slight, like footsteps for example, a shuffling of any kind, but it would have been loud, quite piercing and it didn't register with your sub-conscience.'

'You could be right, but how did they gain entry?'

'The obvious way, I would say. They had a key.'

'Oh, God!' He had been right!

'Alan, I realise the way your mind is going and if we're right and this break-in turns out to not be one, what you've told me could certainly be relevant and needs to be reported to my people.'

'You believe that I wasn't imagining Steve being there?'

'Right now, I'm not sure, but he's certainly going to have some questions to answer.'

'Not too bright though, is he? He should have smashed a window or something, made it look like a forced entry.'

'My understanding is from what some quite reliable people I know in Ekabe have told me, that some damage had been carried out inside your bungalow that night; a smashed glass panel on one of the patio doors, general disruption in the lounge with the cushions, furniture, books, that sort of thing.'

'I don't know what to think now.' and he really didn't, but one thing was certain, Steve Burrows had been there that night and if he'd used a key it could only mean that Valerie was involved, shivering despite the afternoon heat.

'It will require some sorting out; whether the syndicate is responsible is now questionable. If they had been on the scene, they would have used force to make an entry and if they had then discovered that someone, namely Steve Burrows, had beaten them to it, made a hasty retreat. They certainly wouldn't have risked remaining there to ransack the place, and then to leave empty-handed. Alternatively, if Steve Burrows had arrived on the scene after they'd left and as you were regaining consciousness, and hadn't noticed any sign of a break-in, especially broken glass on the floor which would have been quite close to where you were lying, there's two questions you should be asking: why was he there in the first place, and why didn't he do something to help you.'

'Probably thought I was dead.'

'That's no answer.'

'What is the answer then?'

'From what you've told me, Alan, all you remember is him looking at you, he didn't make any attempt to find out whether you were still breathing or not.'

'You don't think I was attacked either by a gang of local thugs or some henchman from the syndicate?'

'Local thugs? Improbable I would say, but these people employed by the syndicate are professionals; they would have made a thorough job of it.'

\*\*\*

The accident happened on the Ndola/Kitwe highway, five miles from Ndola airport on a straight stretch of road notorious for speeding motorists recklessly overtaking lumbering air-polluting trucks and wagons. The mangled body of Steve Burrows had to be cut from the driver's seat, the resultant smashed up pick-up truck blocking the road in both directions until being hoisted on to a government's loading vehicle. It had been a further two hours before the body, having been officially declared dead at the scene had been taken to the mortuary in Ndola, before the road was re-opened and the traffic could resume.

Kate had been in her studio at the rear of their bungalow when Silas, nervously clutching a tea-towel, tapped on the door.

Seeing him there she was instantly reminded of Friday morning when he'd struggled to tell her about the break-in at the Lorimer's: *déjà vu*, she murmured under her breath and as then attempted to calm him, but the only recognizable word she could make out was 'policeman' and 'bad news, madam' and with an exasperated sigh, she followed him through to the front of the bungalow to find a uniformed police officer waiting for her. He moved towards her, gesturing for her to be seated as he introduced himself. She sensed what was coming; it wasn't only the solemn expression on his dark features and the way his voice faltered for a fraction of a second before telling her that Steve had been involved in a fatal road accident that caused her to gasp out loud and cover her mouth with her hand; it was more a sense of the inevitable, almost as though she had been waiting for just such a moment as this.

He was giving her time she supposed to absorb the news; at least he didn't bombard her with platitudes, and she was grateful for that.

'When did it happen, Chief Inspector?'

'Around ten-thirty, madam.'

'But you said it was a road accident?'

'I did, yes; up on the main road, five miles from Ndola airport.'

'The airport? I don't understand; are you sure?'

'At this stage we don't know whether he had actually been to the airport, but he had certainly been coming from that direction; we should know later today once the forensic team have some results for us.'

'My husband didn't mention he was going there, but it would have been unusual; if anything, he would have been coming from the Kitwe direction. I know there is some remedial work being done at the college there.'

Not that it mattered. Steve was dead. She wasn't sure she wanted to hear the details, wondering whether this not wanting to know was normal for a woman who had suddenly lost her husband. Probably not. It could be she was in shock, but then how would she know? No doubt DCI Musenge considered her reaction odd, but she had no intention of feigning a grief she didn't truly feel. For too long she had been pretending, ignoring the signs of Steve's indifference to her, his lack of interest in the hours she spent in the studio while he was at work and scathing comments when she started to make a breakthrough with her paintings. Those had hurt, but she hadn't responded, tried instead to understand why he should want to deflate her confidence. She realised that now wasn't the time to dwell on what had gone wrong between them, but what he'd said to her only a couple of days ago refused to be ignored, to wait until later when she was on her own and more able to think more clearly. "I trust you're not getting carried away, Kate;" he had said when she'd excitedly told him that she'd had two of her African landscapes accepted by one of London's art galleries, "this art gallery sounds pretty nondescript, it's not even in Bond Street!"

'Madame,' the chief inspector's voice bringing her back, 'you should not be on your own at a time like this; have you friends you could stay with perhaps.'

'I – I don't know. I have friends, yes, but I don't want to bother them.'

'If they are friends, I am sure they will be only too happy to help.'

He meant well, she was sure; he sounded sincere, and she had to admit he was right: she shouldn't be on her own. She would phone Peggy.

Before he left, appearing to be relieved by her decision, he tactfully mentioned how Steve's body would need to be formally identified. His words filled her with dread. He was asking too much; it was something she did not want to do. She didn't want to see him again: to look down at him on a mortuary slab, imagining how he would look. Her reluctance must have been obvious because he had been quick to suggest that one of their friends would be prepared to do it for her.

'No, Chief Inspector,' she said, 'I can't impose on anyone; I'll do it.'

\*\*\*

'No Peggy this evening, Derek?' Philip asked him.

'Er – no, Philip, she isn't.'

'Has something happened; you're looking a bit stressed out?'

'You obviously haven't heard about the accident earlier – '

' – been confined to the bank for most of the day.'

'It's about Kate's husband.'

'Steve?'

'Yes, he was involved in a pretty bad crash on the Ndola road this morning.'

'How bad?'

'It was fatal, I'm sorry to say; he was killed outright.'

'Good God! That's awful, absolutely awful. How did it happen and Kate, how is she; it must have been an almighty shock for her.'

'It was; she's staying with us for a few days, Peggy's keeping a careful eye on her.'

'Still in shock, I expect.'

'Probably; she hasn't said much, but then poor girl, what can she say. The chief inspector fellow broke the news to her, but he didn't elaborate; mind you,' he added, 'there wasn't a great deal he could tell her, merely that he'd crashed on that lethal strip of road about a couple of miles or so from the airport.'

'Speeding, do you think?'

'I don't know, Philip, but more than likely.'

'What was he doing over there, at the airport, I mean?'

'God knows.'

'Which way was he going?'

'Kate said that he must have been coming away from the airport.'

'Returning to Ekabe then.'

'Presumably. Why do you ask?'

'Oh, I'm probably wrong, I just wondered that's all.' his words tailing off, Derek watching him as he picked up his lager and took a long sip.

'It can't possibly be relevant of course but I've just realised who he may have been taking to the airport.'

'Who?' his own glass half-raised and momentarily forgotten.

'Valerie.'

'Alan's wife?'

'Who else, Derek. She was returning to the UK today after all.'

'Was she; she kept that quiet.'

'I wouldn't have known if Christine hadn't mentioned it when she called into the bank this lunchtime.'

'Christine?' frowning, sure he was missing something, 'Of course,' remembering, 'she works at the travel agency, doesn't she?'

'That's right and she managed to get a late booking for Valerie on an Emirates' flight to Heathrow this afternoon.'

'Oh, I see, and she'd need to get the domestic flight from Ndola. Odd though; I would have thought the college would have made arrangements for her. Why Steve?'

'You must be the only person among us, apart from poor Kate of course, who didn't know about the pair of them having an affair.'

'As you say, Philip, poor Kate.' shaking his head as he tried to absorb what he'd said and wondering whether Kate had been unaware of her husband's infidelities, but then perhaps it's true what they say about the wife or husband being the last to know.

'Good evening, Derek, you're looking very serious.'

'Ah, Sheila, good to see you. Obviously, you haven't heard.'

'Heard what?'

'About Steve Burrows – '

'Kate's husband; what about him?'

'He's been killed, Sheila. A car accident, out near the airport on the Ndola road, that's about all we know so far.'

'God! How awful. So, you've no idea how it happened?'

'No, we can only guess. Speeding I expect.'

'How's Kate bearing up; do you know?'

'Somewhat shell-shocked as you can imagine; she's with Peggy.'

'That's good. She shouldn't be on her own.'

'Sheila?'

'Yes.'

'Had you heard what I expect are no more than rumours that Steve and Valerie were having an affair.'

'Well, no I hadn't, Derek, but she has something of a reputation, and I'd often wondered why we didn't see much of Steve in here. Always felt a bit sorry for Kate actually.'

'Could be she knew what he was like.'

'Possibly. What was he doing out by the airport do you think?'

'I was talking to Philip just before you came in,' he said nodding over towards where Philip was now talking to Sally and her boyfriend, ' and he'd heard that Valerie was flying back to the UK today and would have had to take the domestic flight down to Lusaka – '

' – and Steve was driving her to the Ndola airport.' she finished for him, an unfathomable expression on her face, but having known Sheila for a number of years and being aware of her past links with the foreign office, knew better than to question her.

'Sheila, how remiss of me! You haven't a drink; what would you like, a G&T?'

'Thank you, Derek.' she smiled, but he could tell by her eyes, slightly unfocused, that she was miles away, which was all he needed as proof that her concern was more than one for someone she'd hardly known; it was as if her mind had moved away, somewhere beyond the accident. As he waited his turn at the bar he began for the first time since their comfortable everyday lives had taken such a dramatic dip, to attempt to make some sort of sense of the whys and wherefores. It had all begun with the break-in at the Lorimers' place and the subsequent disappearance of Alan, followed less than a week later by Steve Burrows' fatal crash. He supposed, ordering Sheila's drink and another lager for himself, those incidents, if he could describe them as such, could be thought to be isolated, but with what Philip had been saying, he wasn't so sure.

Derek had no illusions of how many of his fellow expats viewed him, but he may be a died in the wool colonial, more than a little outdated in his ways, but there was nothing wrong with his brain: Alan had been a victim of assault, his wife was in some sort of relationship with Kate's husband, and now he had been killed in a car crash, within a matter of days of each other. He would dearly like to discuss his observations with Sheila, but commonsense warned him he would be wasting his time. It was no secret that London's foreign office was synonymous with MI5, MI6, British Intelligence, or whatever, and the Official Secrets' Act all officers had to sign was for keeps.

Derek was spared the temptation of saying anything further to Sheila by Harry, along with Sally and Philip joining them, and while the conversation predictably revolved around Steve, the previous topic on the mystery of Alan's disappearance having presumably been shelved, none of them suggested a possible link and far be it for him to risk their indulgent comments by adding anything further to their speculations which in his opinion were way off beam. This was one of the times he was reluctant to bear the brunt of their ridicule, however kindly meant, with a good-natured chuckle. He was missing Peggy's comfortable presence but accepted his wife's role this evening was to be with Kate and in her inimitable and motherly way, help her to cope, not necessarily with the shock of Steve's death, but perhaps when she finally learned there was truth after all behind the rumours of which surely to goodness, she couldn't have failed to have been aware.

***

Christopher Musenge did not like coincidences. He didn't trust them. Even before he had broken the news of her husband's death, but when he had been told the name of the victim of the crash on the highway, his instincts had immediately alerted him to the possibility that this was no ordinary accident. He had nothing positive to base this suspicion on, other than the strained atmosphere emanating between the two people he had spoken to the evening before, also the fact that Valerie Lorimer had failed to turn up at the police station to sign her statement. This non-appearance of hers had only intensified his suspicions about the pair of them, resulting in him viewing the break-in and Alan Lorimer's disappearance in a totally different light.

Once he had made sure that Kate Burrows intended to take his advice and prevail upon one of her friends to help her get through what he knew were going to be a harrowing few days, he drove out of town to the crash site. He wanted to see for himself the exact spot where it happened. He had already heard from the officer leading the forensic team that the road was now clear and no doubt, apart from shreds of metal and glass at the side of the road, there would be little to show that only three hours ago there had been, by all accounts a horrific crash, and where a man had lost his life.

He had been right. There was virtually nothing to see: pieces of crumpled metal, lumps of burnt rubber and scatterings of glass, all as he expected. There were deep grooves on the tarmac, curving erratically in the direction of the bush and to where more than likely it may have merely ploughed into before becoming embedded in the foliage, and Steve Burrows would have emerged more or less unscathed, had it not been for the abandoned mammy wagon at the edge of the verge, another of the many smashed up vehicles, minus any re-usable parts, left to rot. It was quite clear to Christopher as he stood there, staring down at the resultant debris, what must have happened. Sheer bad luck had intervened when, presumably Steve having lost control of the vehicle, had hit the wagon broadside on, ricocheting off its already battered bodywork, and ending up in the middle of the highway, the outline of forensics' chalk marks still visible on the tarmac.

The initial report from forensic had confirmed that the pick-up truck had been facing away from the airport and back towards Ekabe. Presumably he had been returning to Ekabe and not driving further on to Kitwe, recalling Kate Lorimer mentioning work being done at the college there. Not that it was important. Steve Burrows had been driving from the airport. His wife could give him no reason why he should have been there, but he would find out, and climbing back into his car, pulled out from where he'd been parked on the grassy verge. He continued driving until he reached the main entrance to the airport and parked in one of the allocated spaces for police and airport officials.

Within minutes of stepping into the Arrivals Hall, the high ceilings echoing with the high-pitched announcements from the tanoys, merging with the general rise and fall of voices from the airport staff and the shuffling of passengers as they made their way towards the flashing lights above the departure gates, he was being escorted to a reception office. Scrolling down the passenger list for the Lusaka flight leaving earlier that morning, the young attendant swivelled the computer screen round to face him. Mrs. Valerie Lorimer had indeed checked in and boarded the ten-thirty Lusaka flight, arriving there thirty-three minutes later. A further enquiry, more tapping on the keyboard, and he had the information he had expected: Valerie Lorimer had reserved a seat on the Emirates' flight for London, Heathrow at thirteen hundred this afternoon. Christopher had no need to check his watch. He knew he was too late.

'The flight, Chief Inspector,' the young woman was saying, 'is now airborne.'

He thanked her and retraced his steps back to his car, cursing under his breath. Pointless of course. There was no way, given the sequence of events that morning, could he have pre-empted this moment. He should have done. Of course he should have. The woman hadn't turned up at the station to sign the statement. He should have followed up on that, or at least delegated such a straightforward task.

His mobile rang as he switched on the car engine and seeing Brian Phiri's name on the screen, switched it off again.

'Yes, Brian.'

'A report has just come through, sir from Vehicles, thought it important you should know.'

'Fire ahead.'

'They haven't completed the mechanical check on the pick-up, but so far they haven't found any fault with the mechanics and the electrics, but they believe they've worked out how the crash happened.'

'Yes.' prompting him, feeling the first stirrings of anticipation.

'There was an empty plastic water bottle wedged beneath the brake pedal.'

'Well, well, Brian, that is indeed very interesting.'

'It is, sir.'

'I'm at the airport, but about to leave, so should be with you within forty minutes or so. We can compare notes then; meanwhile, Brian, I want you to pay a visit to Ekabe Lodge.'

'Sir.'

'Valerie Lorimer is on her way back to the UK as we speak; I want a thorough print check carried out on her room, tell them not to re-book it until we give them clearance.'

'Is there anything particular you're expecting to find, sir.'

'The answer, I'm sorry to say, is I don't know, but if nothing else, take anything we can use later for DNA purposes. At present, Brian, it's very much a case of 'what if'.

# Chapter Fourteen

<u>Tuesday 24th October: London</u>

Beverly's mobile rang shortly before ten on Tuesday morning, then again fifteen minutes later; each time she ignored it, turning away from where she'd left it on the bedside table and burrowing her head under the duvet, but although whoever it was had stopped, the not so dulcet tones of Robbie Williams continued to reverberate, making further sleep impossible.

She had been on the last flight out of Edinburgh the night before and didn't get home until midnight and had every intention of indulging in the luxury of a lie-in, but in her tiredness had neglected to switch off the phone. It would be Andy checking up on her, demanding to know when he could expect the copy on her follow-up from Saturday's piece. Problem was, she groaned, flinging back the duvet, she didn't know. It wasn't often she was like this, almost at a loss for what she could add, or more to the point, get away with, but Calder Bay's latest murder was bugging her; she was missing something and at that precise moment as she turned on the shower, waiting for the water to warm up, she couldn't think what that elusive something could be.

*Think logically, Beverly. There has to be more. Why was John Milne murdered? Motive. Find the motive, Bev, and you will find the missing link.*

Automatically, she went through the motions: switching off the shower, towelling herself dry, pulling out underwear from the top drawer of the dresser, freshly washed jeans from the wardrobe and a royal blue cashmere sweater from another drawer, all the time thinking back to the last six days in Calder Bay, a long time for her to spend out of London and produce a mere three-column article, but she'd only stayed on because of the press conference. And what a waste of time that had turned out to be, but she should have realised there wouldn't be any likelihood of DCI Dale coming up with information they didn't know already, recalling the little he had proffered, and his measured responses to their questions. When she thought about it, there had not been many of those either. Mostly, they'd been about John Milne's girlfriend, whether there had been any damage to her property or if she had been in the house at the time of the break-in. His replies, brief and robotic, had been far from enlightening: no damage except to the back door lock; didn't know whether she'd been in the house or not at the time; the belief she must have left in a hurry and that only because her handbag and car keys were there, but no sign of her car. End of questions. But, realisation suddenly hitting her, it shouldn't have been. There was one question none of them had asked. That's what had been bothering her. Of course. How could she have allowed herself to become so blind-sided. Why had she neglected to question the reason behind the break-in? Okay. The obvious. Whoever it was had been looking for something. But what?

Ten minutes later, with the thermostat turned up in her study and a mug of freshly brewed coffee on the desk beside her, she had switched on her laptop and keyed in her password. Before taxing her brain in trying to fathom exactly why Laura Thomson's house, or even Laura herself, should have been a target, she had to find out all she could about her. So far, she had very little: her name, that she'd been employed by the bank in the High Street and had been renting a property in Beach Road. She had no idea what the woman looked like even; therefore, it was tantamount to starting with a clean canvas, aware she was actually holding her breath as she tapped into the social media platforms.

At first sight it was mind-boggling, but it didn't take long to whittle more than twenty women called Laura Thomson down to a possible three, a further five minutes and she was left with no doubt that none of them belonged to the person she was looking for. Could she be what must be a small minority among young women: someone with no interest in self-promotion so freely available on the internet? Who was she? Who actually knew her: her colleagues from the bank and John Milne, the boyfriend of only three months?

Not for the first time Beverly regretted her limited access to resources. Frustrating though this was, she knew from experience she'd get there in the end; she'd reach the core to what she needed to fit in the pieces for the full picture, but it all took time. With an exasperated sigh, she took her empty mug into the kitchen for a refill. There had to be a logical explanation for Laura Thomson's disappearance. She was finding it difficult to accept that she'd been abducted; even the chief inspector had been evasive when someone had raised that question at the press conference. Apparently, there had only been minimal damage to her property, going back to what had actually emerged the day before. Did this mean there had been no struggle? If there had been and she had tried to defend herself surely there would have been some noise, but no mention had been made of her neighbours reporting any disturbance. Not even from the old busybody immediately next door. So, what could she infer from that? That there was no noise, that Sarah had left the house of her own accord. She could of course have gone before the break-in, the intruder waiting until he had the house to himself, indicating no harm had been intended to Laura. What if the break-in had been a cover-up: an oblique explanation for her disappearance? But why; it just did not make any sense. No, that couldn't be right, she felt sure someone had broken into the property, although they likely had waited until she'd gone. There could only be one reason, and pretty obvious to her now as she remembered Joyce Myers' words: "*the flat's in a terrible state, even the furniture has been moved about*".

*Even the furniture has been moved about.* At the time she hadn't placed much importance on what the woman had said, not enough certainly to ask for any details, probably deciding how insensitive it would have sounded. Had the furniture in Laura Thomson's house been *moved about*, because if it had the inference must be that the person responsible was searching for something, and taking her newly formed theory a step further, if they had been unsuccessful with their first attempt in John Milne's flat, they were hoping to have better luck the second time.

What, she wondered, taking her coffee over to the window and staring down into the street below, had they been looking for? That was something else nobody had thought to mention yesterday. As theories went Beverly decided, taking a sip of coffee, it still didn't conjure up a motive for John Milne's death, although she was becoming more convinced than ever that "Lorimer Fruits" were involved. Could it be, turning the idea over in her mind, that John Milne had discovered some discrepancy which posed a threat. If that had been the case, he would have placed himself in a vulnerable position. So much so, the knowledge had put his life in danger?

Well, she sighed leaning her forehead against the window, it was a motive. And not so extreme. She had so little to go on, no-one to bounce ideas off and all the time feeling she was going round and round in ever-decreasing circles and getting absolutely nowhere. It was so frustrating! It was almost midday when her phone rang again and as soon as she heard Andy's voice she felt guilty for ignoring what must have been his earlier attempts.

'I was beginning to think you were still up there, in the wilds of bonnie Scotland.'

'Sorry, Andy; I was late getting home last night and decided to have a lie-in.' realising he probably didn't believe a word of what she'd said. Andy Walters knew her too well.

'Not flagging are you; stuck for that something special to rivet our readers.'

'Of course not.' Yes, he did know her too well.

'Liar!' he laughed, so loud she had to move the phone away from her ear.

'As you're in such a good mood, Andy I'm guessing you have something to help me on my tortuous path towards another scoop.'

'You guess right.'

'Don't keep me in suspense then. Please.'

'You sound desperate,' the laughter still present in his voice, 'so I will cease with all this banter.'

'I wish you would.'

'A message came through from Reuters earlier this morning of a fatal car crash in Zambia – '

'- in Ekabe?' interrupting him, her journalist antenna on full alert.

'Twenty odd miles away, on what's known as the Ndola/Kitwe highway to be more precise.'

'So who were involved, Andy?'

'Singular. A British guy; Steve Burrows he was called, employed as a site agent with Public Works, attached to Ekabe Technical College and a neighbour of Alan Lorimer.'

'Ah, I see, so you believe there's more to this accident?'

'It would seem it was no accident. An empty plastic water bottle was found below the brake pedal.'

'Wow! Are the police calling it murder then?'

'Of course.'

'What do you mean, of course; it could have rolled there.'

'No, Bev, it was well and truly wedged in.'

'You're not making sense; you've said this happened twenty-odd miles from Ekabe and I cannot believe he didn't have to use his brakes before then.'

'I'll enlighten you. He was actually returning to Ekabe; he'd been to Ndola airport having dropped off his lady passenger there.'

'Come on, Andy,' she urged, but curbing her impatience knowing it would only encourage him to prevaricate even more, 'who was the lady.'

'Valerie Lorimer.'

'Christ!'

'No, Bev, Valerie Lorimer, wife of – '

'- I know who she's married to, Andy, or I should say was married to.'

'Ah, yes, the case of the missing lecturer, presumed dead.'

'I don't get this. Were the pair of them an item do you know? Valerie and this Steve?'

'I would say from what I'm picking up from other comments coming through, that yes, they were having an affair.'

'The plot certainly thickens. Is she a suspect then?'

'The authorities are apparently covering themselves; she's being described as a person of interest.'

'But, presumably if this Steve Burrows was taking her to an airport, she was flying off somewhere.'

'You presume right. All I know is that she was seen about half an hour ago at Lusaka airport waiting to board the Emirates' flight to Heathrow, estimated time of arrival six-thirty tomorrow morning. Interested?'

'You bet, Andy. I'll be there; a small problem though.'

'Only one?'

'How will I recognize her?

'Can't help you there, but with your sleuthing skills I'm sure you'll find a way.'

'I'm sure I will.'

'Don't get carried away.'

'As if, Andy. I am the epitome of restraint; trust me.'

'That's what worries me.'

***

<u>Calder Bay</u>

For the second time in less than a week Dan was turning into the driveway of Ashburn House, driving slowly past the rowan trees bordering the lawn, their bright red berries a startling contrast to the greyness of the late autumn morning and, with the electric purring of a lawnmower somewhere in the distance accompanying him, he pulled up in front of the impressive bleached-stone annexe of "Lorimer Fruits".

He was not looking forward to this second meeting with Bruce Lorimer; there had been something about the man's manner which he'd found jarring, unpleasantly reminding him of the privileged types he used to come across at Glasgow uni. It had taken him a long time to shake off his inferiority complex, far too aware of his working-class background, when there had even been occasions when he had cause to regret the scholarship which had made it possible for him to be there.

Shrugging his shoulders and leaning over to pick up his file from the passenger seat, he stepped out on to the newly raked gravel and walked up the steps to the main entrance. The same girl was on reception, although this time she gave him a quick smile of recognition which was heartening, if nothing else.

'If you would like to take a seat, Inspector, I will let Bruce know you're here.'

He wasn't kept waiting long before Bruce Lorimer was striding towards him, hand outstretched in greeting.

'Good morning, Inspector.' he smiled, showing perfectly white teeth, 'I must admit I was rather surprised to hear from your office saying you wanted to talk to me again. I take it you haven't solved the case then.'

'We are still pursuing our enquiries, sir,' he answered, aware of how stiff and formal he must sound, but he was impatient to move forward, not wanting to waste time with an exchange of pleasantries which neither of them, he was certain, cared less about.

'Fire away, Inspector. It goes without saying I'll do all I can to help.' gesturing him over to the small seating area next to one of the windows. No offer of refreshments this time.

'I would like to discuss motive with you, Mr Lorimer.' he said sitting down and placing his file on the glass-topped table in front of him, pushing that day's "Scotsman" and "Country Life" to one side to make room.

'Motive?'

'Yes, the motive for John Milne's murder. He appears to have been a fairly normal sort of young man. He'd made a number of friends among the "Shipwreck's" regulars where he spent his evenings and weekends and here, at work. Nobody had a bad word to say about him; there had been no disagreements, no clash of personalities, nothing of that nature, and yet someone must have had a very strong reason for wanting to do what they did. Therefore, why was he murdered, and quite brutally, I might add?'

'Girlfriend problems?'

'Care to elaborate?'

'I'm only guessing, putting two and two together as one does, you understand?'

'Of course.'

'Mind you, I'm only assuming he had a girlfriend, but he probably did, good-looking chap like that: young, single, had his own place, good job, even if only on a short contract, but he would have had no difficulty in finding another one. How am I doing so far, Inspector?' *Cocky bastard! Centre stage, demanding attention. The last Bruce Lorimer needed was encouragement, but he just might come up with something useful.* 'What do you say that an ex-boyfriend of hers took exception to him. Quite feasible wouldn't you say?'

'Feasible, possibly, but unlikely.'

'What? You're dismissing it as a *crime passionelle*?'

'We have no evidence to support such a suggestion.'

'Well, you're the detective.'

'There is very strong evidence that his murder was carried out by professionals and if we are correct, it could indicate something quite different. For some, as yet unknown reason, he may have placed himself in such a situation that he had to be silenced.'

'Silenced?'

'Yes, silenced. As a motive for a murder of this nature, it isn't uncommon. Whether intentionally or not, he may have had some, shall we say, knowledge that he shouldn't have had.' choosing his words carefully, wary of saying too much, always with the restrictions from Interpol at the back of his mind.

'Can't think what that might be, especially to anyone as mediocre as the unfortunate chap.'

'You have to admit though, it is an interesting hypothesis.'

'I suppose.'

'Let's take this a step further, shall we?'

'If you must.' for the first time showing signs of, if not distress, certainly of discomfort.

'Humour me, sir. If John had acquired anything of such vital importance to cause him to be vulnerable, to even endanger his life, how do you think he could have come across this?'

'In the pub I expect.' he said immediately, obviously without thinking.

'Yes, that would make sense; it was where he spent a good part of his time –'

'Just a minute, I know what you're implying!' he interrupted, making a conscious effort to lower his voice. 'And you are quite wrong, Inspector; John's death had nothing to do with my family. Nothing.'

'I am not suggesting it did, sir. I was merely attempting to arrive at a credible explanation for the murder and we do have to look into every possible theory, because at this stage of our investigation that's all they are. Theories. And, whether you like it or not, your family if only because John Milne was employed by them, is involved and until we are satisfied otherwise, they will continue to be.'

'I think I've heard enough, Inspector. Time to bring this interview to an end I would say.' getting to his feet and making to move away.

'There are only a couple of points I'd like to clarify before I leave,' Dan said, ignoring his arrogant assumption to bring the interview to a close.

'Very well, but you will have to speed things up, Inspector, I have a meeting with clients shortly. his earlier display of cordiality now replaced by a coolness which he made no attempt to conceal.

'I'd like to go back to last Tuesday morning when a letter arrived from your brother in Zambia to say he was returning home earlier than expected.'

'What about it?'

'How did you all react when Callum broke the news?'

'It wasn't Callum who told us actually; he was still having breakfast and Myra told us when she came into the boardroom. As to our reaction, well none of us were too bothered, except father of course. He was delighted, but then Alan's his favourite son, always has been, and before you say anything, Inspector, it has never bothered me one little bit.'

'And Callum, what was his reaction?'

'Not happy.'

'Why do you think that was?'

'Disruption, mainly; the expense of having to sever John's contract because apparently he wouldn't be needed once Callum was back.'

'I see.'

'Is that it, Inspector?' once again eager to leave.

'When did you last see John Milne, sir?'

'You and your sergeant have already asked that.'

'Just answer the question, please.'

'As I said before, it must have been sometime on Tuesday morning.'

'You can't be more precise.'

'Not really. Days could go by when I didn't see him; our paths very seldom crossed in the normal working day, Inspector.'

'What about evenings?'

'What about them?'

'Did you go for a drink with him perhaps.'

'Very seldom; just now and again if we happened to finish work at the same time, this would be if on the rare occasion he was here after five o'clock and we might then bump into each other.'

'But not last Tuesday.'

'No, as I said it was during the morning when I saw him.'

'You say it was rare for him to work late; can you remember the last time you noticed?

'Last Monday well – ' hesitating, but only for a fraction of a second, barely perceptible, but long enough to pique his interest, '- the light was on when I passed the offices, but I only saw him through the window.'

'You didn't go in and have a chat with him?'

'No, I think I assumed he had some paperwork to catch up on and I didn't want to disturb him. John was very conscientious, you know.' he added.

'You mention offices; could you be more explicit perhaps. Was this the general office?'

'Oh, no, it was the one next to the stores.'

'I see. Could you draw up a plan of the office layout, it doesn't have to be accurate as far as dimensions go, just to give me some idea of where various members of staff were located.'

'Sure, I'll get one of the secretaries to do that and email it through to you later today.'

'Incidentally, sir,' Dan asked, standing up, 'did you happen to mention to anyone else about seeing him?'

'Only Callum.'

\*\*\*

Callum felt physically sick when he finally left the police station, almost tripping on the steps leading down to the pavement in his urgency to get away, the chief inspector's last word literally ringing in his ears, words that had formed themselves into the question of which he knew the answer. What the hell had he got himself into? Everything had been fine until Alan's letter arrived: the deal with Ben had proved a lucrative one, funds had been building up steadily in his offshore account, and apart from ensuring the consignments were scrupulously monitored by him from the moment Ben handed them over until, re-packaged and incorporated into the company's regular outgoings for distribution to their various European destinations, he had no further involvement. *But you are involved, Callum. You are a crucial link in a drug smuggling organization, so what are you going to do? Make a run for it like your so-called friend, Ben Maitland: jump aboard your luxury high-speed cruiser and sail out to the blue beyond?* The knowledge that there was no such option open to him, and one to which he hadn't exactly been blind to only increased his rising panic. He had to speak to Ben, impress on him that the pick-up couldn't go ahead on Thursday night.

Before driving back to the office, he sent him a text asking him to get in touch, relieved to see his phone's flickering green light as he was approaching Ashburn House, and pulling on to the grass verge at the side of the road, pressed the button.

*"All set for Thursday, twenty-one hundred hours. What's the panic? No need to meet before then."*

*"Crucial we meet soonest."*

*"Will have to be tomorrow; haven't got any spare time today."*

*"Sorry, Ben, important we talk today."*

A few minutes went by before another text arrived: *"Shipwreck. Midday."*

Tossing his mobile on top of the file on the passenger seat, he accelerated back on to the road, clods of earth scattering widely beneath the wheels and covered the remaining couple of miles in record time, impervious to exceeding the speed limit. *Bloody stupid to lose your temper, Callum. The guy's a controller, thought you knew that by now. Watch him; his priorities are nothing like yours.*

Callum didn't need his conscience to remind him, but he shouldn't allow Ben to get to him like this; it was definitely counter-productive. Over the months they had worked together there had been few disagreements, only because of his compliance; he had always been quick to back down and gone along with what Ben wanted, but this time he was determined to stand his ground, knowing he wasn't going to like it, but he had to convince him that to go ahead with Thursday's pick-up would be folly.

***

'So what with the attitude, Callum?' Ben's first words as he walked over to him, a pint of the "Shipwreck's" best bitter on the table in front of him.

'And good morning to you, too, Ben.'

'Look, I've no time for cordialities; I'm a busy man.'

'And I'm not.' noticing how his eyebrows rose in surprise; he hadn't expected that, but he'd been unable to restrain himself, realising it was more than Ben's manner which was bugging him: the time spent with the inspector continued to unsettle him, and without saying anything further he walked over to the bar and ordered a double whisky.

'Right, Callum,' Ben said to him when he returned, although waiting until he'd taken a sip of his drink, 'care to tell me what's wrong.'

'Thursday night.'

'What about Thursday night; you're not getting cold feet are you?'

'I've spent an hour this morning being interrogated by the chief Inspector which was not a pleasant experience.'

'Under caution?'

'What?'

'Were you interviewed under caution, Callum, was it recorded?'

'No, I was told I could leave at any time.'

'So, what are you so worried about?'

'It was the way in which he was leading the questions which was worrying; not so much about John's murder, motive, yes, but he was more interested in my reactions; about Alan's letter arriving last week, I mean.'

'Go on.'

'He asked me whether I'd told anyone, outside the family that is, about him coming back sooner than expected.'

'Which you denied.'

'Naturally, but he managed to wangle it from me that I came down to the "Crown" for a drink that lunchtime. He knew damn well I did, Ben. And I firmly believe he knew who I was with.'

'I expect you're right.'

'Are you telling me that you already know the way they're thinking.'

'Of course, Callum.' he grinned, 'Come on, don't be so naive, there's no doubt that the authorities are fully aware of my existence, also that they would have worked out that I'm one of the syndicate's leading lights.'

'Why the hell haven't they arrested you then and why the hell are you still here?'

'The answer is quite simple.'

'Is it?'

'They need evidence. Irrefutable and unbreakable. Circumstantial evidence is of little use.'

'My God!' he muttered, 'I'm beginning to understand.'

'Not before time.'

'To put it in a nutshell,' ignoring his sarcasm and taking a deep breath to give himself some time to assimilate everything, to understand the full implication of his situation, 'the police are waiting to catch us: the handover, the drop-off point and anything else they consider relevant to complete their big haul.'

'Correct.'

'All the more reason for cancelling Thursday night's drop-off.'

'I am not cancelling, Callum. No way, and that is final.'

'You have to.'

'I don't have to do anything.'

'You don't seem to realise,' attempting the rational approach, although knowing Ben as well as he did, with little hope of success, 'the police presence is still continuing, Ben. They appear no further in finding John Milne's killer; our company is under constant scrutiny and with me as their prime suspect. They won't give up, you know.'

'You're exaggerating.'

'I am not exaggerating. While I was being interrogated this morning, Bruce was receiving a visit from Inspector Aitken, his third interview by Calder Bay's police force, I might add. It is never ending, Ben. Bloody never ending and quite frankly, I'm sick of it. I quit.'

'Sorry, my friend, but that won't be possible.'

'You don't threaten me.'

'I just have.' he said, 'picking up his glass and finishing his whisky, 'We will meet at the usual place at nine on Thursday evening. I'll hand over the goods to you and from there it will be up to you how you arrange their ongoing transportation.'

'And if I don't turn up?'

'That, Callum,' he said quietly, 'would not be wise.'

***

'Let's recap for a moment, Dan;' Alistair suggested later in the day, 'to when Bruce Lorimer mentions about John Milne working late. This was the Monday evening, wasn't it?'

'That's right. It wasn't so much that Bruce saw him in the office, presumably after everybody else had gone home, which set me wondering; it was the way he hesitated, as though he suddenly regretted saying anything, but didn't know how to pull back, change direction if you like. I'm explaining it badly, probably making too much of it.'

'I wouldn't say that; as theories go, it sounds credible. You must admit none of us have come up with anything else which might provide us with a motive, therefore there's nothing to be lost in trying to expand on the possibility we may have found one. First of all, and as much as I dislike making assumptions, I'm inclined to make an exception for this exercise and say that John Milne may have already had his suspicions about some irregularities, perhaps only a gut feeling of something underhand going on, and had decided on Monday, when he would have had the place to himself, to have a close look at the company's records. Bruce notices him through the window, whether he considers this suspicious or not, we'll have to make another assumption. Anything you'd like to add at this point, Dan?'

'If we are working on the premise that Bruce is not involved along with his brother in the drug smuggling, when he sees John, he may well have been suspicious, nothing to do with the syndicate; he could have thought he was merely being inquisitive; an unhealthy interest in sections of the business which didn't concern him.'

'And mentioned this to Callum.'

'Which would understandably have made him nervous, and at the first opportunity he would have informed Ben Maitland.'

'And as we know, Callum was in the "Royal" the following lunchtime. If we are right so far, Dan, it wouldn't be stretching probability to say he did meet

Ben Maitland there, told him about John snooping around after hours and tragically for him he was murdered that night.'

'It's a neat hypothesis.'

'And credible?'

'I would say so, especially if we take into account that we never really ruled out that it wasn't carried out by professionals: the entry to his flat, the ruthless method of the killing, no prints and, apparently, a silent operation.'

'Exactly.'

'When all of this comes out, whether we're right or not about our alibi theory, it doesn't auger well for Callum, does it?'

'It certainly does not and judging by the nervous state he was in this morning, I would say he's close to panicking; it won't take much to push him over the edge and then it's anyone's guess how that will affect Interpol's investigation.'

Any further speculation came to an abrupt end with the ringing of Alistair's direct line and nodding to Dan as he left the office, picked up the receiver.

'DCI Dale.'

'Good afternoon, Alistair, Adrian Roberts here.'

'Good afternoon, sir; I was hoping you would call.'

'Any developments?'

'Nothing of a positive nature unfortunately, although we may have come up with a possible explanation for John Milne's murder. We've made no headway with tracing his girlfriend, although my team have suggested a couple of theories, but – '

' – but you've felt stymied because of the restrictions we've had to enforce, for which I apologise. And believe me, Alistair, it has been necessary.'

'How much longer will this situation continue, sir?'

'If you'd asked me that a few hours ago, my answer would have been until after the goods have been satisfactorily handed over, but there's been an unexpected turn of events which I'm sure you will be interested to hear, even although they will undoubtedly add to your workload.'

'I'm intrigued.' feeling the familiar surge of excitement, one that without fail pre-empted a surprise twist in any murder enquiry.

'News reached us earlier today of a fatal car crash on the outskirts of Ekabe; you won't know the victim, Alistair, but he was called Steve Burrows, attached to the same college as Alan Lorimer, also a neighbour of his. We've since received an up-date confirming that the vehicle had been tampered with shortly before the crash.'

'It was murder then?'

'Yes, fairly conclusively. No doubt you're wondering when I'm going to get to the point, but it has taken a fair bit of unravelling. Still intrigued?' he asked, and Alistair could tell he was smiling.

'Very. I'm sure there is a connection somewhere.'

'There is, but not what you might be thinking. However, to put you out of suspense, the authorities have a suspect.'

'Already?'

'Yes, although from what I've been told having since spoken to Lusaka's chief of police, it didn't take much working out. Steve had been on his way back to Ekabe from the airport in Ndola when his vehicle went out of control, ricocheted off the side of an abandoned truck killing him instantly. An empty plastic water bottle was discovered wedged beneath the brake pedal.'

'And they're saying they knew who was responsible?'

'Oh, yes; the woman he had driven to the airport. Security cameras there verified that he hadn't gone into the building with her, also his pick-up had not been out of his sight during the short time it had taken him to load her luggage onto a trolley, before setting off again back to Ekabe.'

'And the woman?'

'Valerie Lorimer.'

'My God! Alan Lorimer's wife! That *was* unexpected. Do they know anymore, why he should have been taking her there for instance?'

'It's unlikely.'

'Because they're not interested, having the proof they need?'

'No, not that. They want to pass the proverbial buck, Alistair.'

'To your people, you mean?'

'Not Interpol, no; the Met will be handling the investigation with your input of course.'

'Right. Who will be leading the enquiry, anyone I know I wonder.'

'I would say so; one of your own countrymen: Douglas Howe.'

'Dougie Howe; we were at Hendon together.'

'A small world, eh. Once he gets his team together you can expect to hear from him.'

'Fine, but this latest development concerning the Lorimer family is really going to upset them.' stifling a groan, already anticipating their reaction. 'You said Valerie Lorimer had been taken to the airport; presumably she's left the country?'

'Yes, she's actually on her way back to the UK as we speak and, with a brief stop-over at Heathrow for her connecting flight up to Edinburgh, she should be arriving there at eleven tomorrow morning.'

'That gives us plenty of time to arrange a reception party for her, but I can't help feeling slightly puzzled though; she must be aware she's going to be under suspicion.'

'I'm sure she is. I wouldn't underestimate the lady, Alistair; she's no fool. I don't want to say much more over the phone, but I've had some further information on the Ekabe break-in which I know you're going to find even more interesting, and hopefully will assist you and your team in getting to the bottom of all of this. We've already received copies of all the reports compiled by Ekabe's chief inspector of police, Christopher Musenge, including prints taken at the Lorimer bungalow and of the pick-up truck, and I'll be sending everything through to you within the next hour.'

'Before you ring off, sir, is there anything you can tell us about John Milne's girlfriend, Laura Thomson; we appear to have come up against the proverbial brick wall in trying to trace her.'

'I see no reason not to enlighten you now, Alistair and again our apologies for the time and resources incurred, but I trust you will appreciate how necessary it has been for you to remain in the dark about her.'

'I take it she was working for you.' unable to hold back an exasperated sigh, 'We were beginning to come round to that explanation, sir. It was either that or she was something to do with our Dutch friends.'

'Tactfully put,' he chuckled, 'hopefully your hard-working team will be as understanding.'

'All par for the course, sir.'

'Touché, Alistair.'

\*\*\*

## London

'My apologies for disturbing you so late, Joanne.'

'That's alright, sir.' she answered, struggling to an upright position from where she'd been stretched out on the sofa watching an old episode of "Minder", wondering as she always did, why the series had been so popular. She hadn't been expecting to hear from Adrian Roberts until she was back in the office at the end of the week, having earned herself a few days' leave following the completion of her assignment in Calder Bay. She'd been back in London since Thursday and, although looking forward to a break, she couldn't help feeling oddly adrift knowing that the part she played in Interpol's major drug case was over. It wasn't as though the months of working undercover could be described

179

as nail-bitingly stimulating, but at least she had felt involved, albeit on the periphery, of cracking wide open the syndicate which had plagued them all for so long.

Her brief had been clear from the start: find out what she could about the set-up at "Lorimer Fruits", or to give them their full title, "Lorimer Fruits & Distributors" who, according to their official profile, were one of Scotland's top international fruit growers: a family concern going back a couple of generations; well respected by their customers and competitors alike, distributing not only their own produce but a wide range of exotic fruits which they imported from Holland. They also had an unblemished reputation, a situation, Adrian Roberts had told her was in danger of becoming irretrievably tarnished with the growing belief emerging that they could be involved in receiving and distributing drugs. And this was where she had come in: establishing herself in Calder Bay by taking up a pre-arranged position as a banking clerk at the Royal Bank of Scotland in the centre of the town and the short-term tenancy on a house along the seafront and from there, left to her own devices. It hadn't taken long to find what she'd described to Adrian in one of her first reports as "Lorimer Fruits'" weakest link.

Getting to know John Milne had been ridiculously easy: he came into the "Shipwreck" every evening around six, always on his own and remaining at the bar. She was sure he had never realised how she always timed his arrival with her own, pulling out a bar stool close to where he was standing. She hadn't even had to make any overtures and affected surprise when he first spoke to her. There had been no side to him; he'd been ambitious, quite openly admitting he was using his time with "Lorimer Fruits" as a career stepping stone, of how he wanted to know every aspect of how the business functioned. He hadn't needed any prompting and within a few short weeks she had a clear picture of each member of the Lorimer family and those who worked for them. The only one he hadn't known was Alan Lorimer, the middle son, except from odd remarks he happened to overhear. It appeared there was no love lost between the two older brothers, a situation, according to John, acerbated by the father's preference for Alan.

He had been unable to hide his excitement about the discovery he'd made. He had been full of it: how the goods outwards' figures were being fudged and had been for well over a year. He had already told her that Callum Lorimer, in the absence of his brother, was solely responsible for the movement of stock, both coming in and out of the business, leaving no doubt in his mind that he was involved in something dishonest, but of course he had no inkling of just how dishonest.

"This sounds rather serious, John," she'd said to him when he'd paused to take a breath, also a sip of his lager which he'd been ignoring, "what are you going to do, forget about it perhaps."

"I can't, can I?"

"If you're thinking of reporting it to the police you'll need evidence."

"Oh, Laura," remembering the dramatic way he'd lowered his voice, "I've got that alright;" patting the top pocket of his leather jacket, "

"You mean you've taped all of what you've found?" feigning a mixture of shocked alarm, although it hadn't been too difficult, he had surprised her; she really didn't think he would have taken such a bold step.

"Yep; downloaded the lot, at least going back over a year and, this is the exciting part, Laura, 'there's a pattern."

"Really?"

"Every three weeks, there's a significant increase in the outgoing figures which don't tie in the way they should and, if I'm right, the next consignment should be on the twenty-second."

"That's a Sunday."

"I know."

It had been tantamount to taking candy from a baby; she could almost feel sorry for the guy, but that particular reaction was definitely off limits; she had a job to do and maintaining impartiality was one of the key attributes in which she had spent the last ten years perfecting, although when news reached her only two days later that he had paid the price for his over-zealousness did penetrate that wall of indifference. She hadn't expected that.

'It's to be hoped you haven't anything planned for the remainder of the week.' Adrian was saying, interrupting thoughts she couldn't afford to indulge in.

'Nothing, sir.'

'That's good.' recognizing the relief in his voice, 'Because there's been a further development in Ekabe, or to be more accurate, twenty miles north of the town, but with another, albeit slightly oblique, connection with the Lorimer family which requires looking into as a matter of some urgency.'

'To do with the current investigation?' she asked, only because she was sensing a slight hesitation; if she didn't know him better, she would think it was uncertainty.

'It could be. My apologies for sounding so vague, but it's too early to decide whether it is or not; it could be an offshoot. Even a coincidence, but you know my opinion on that. However,' he went on quickly, 'there is an indication that the early incident in Ekabe with the break-in and subsequent disappearance of Alan Lorimer may not be relevant to the drug smuggling after all.'

'But we were so certain that it was.'

'Yes, well, could be we were a trifle hasty in what, in hindsight, should have been more closely examined, but admittedly not easy when liaising with a foreign government and being dependent on their willingness to share. Not that is any excuse of course, but pointless to dwell on our shortcomings.'

'Will I be using my own name this time, sir?'

'Yes,' he answered, recognizing the smile in his voice, 'Laura Thomson won't be returning; it's unlikely she will be recognized outside Calder Bay, but if she is, Joanne, we'll deal with that if and when we have to. Although the person you'll be seeing tomorrow is one of the Lorimer family and has lived in Calder Bay for most of her life, it's unlikely either of you have ever met.'

'Sir?' mentally running through the various names John Milne had so freely, and unwittingly, given her.

'Valerie Lorimer.'

'Alan Lorimer's wife.'

'Correct. We've learned she's on her way back here from Zambia.'

'To London or back to Scotland, sir?'

'That, Joanne is questionable. 'She is actually booked through to Edinburgh, but with a two-hour stop-over at Heathrow. In the event she does take her connecting flight, arrangements are in hand for her to be intercepted at Turnhouse airport. However, if she doesn't, this is where I want you to step in. She's on the Emirates' flight arriving at Heathrow at six-thirty tomorrow morning; your brief, on this occasion, is only surveillance. I want you to be there when she arrives, follow her as best you can, but at least try to find out where she's headed once she leaves the airport, whether she meets anyone, that sort of thing. You know the score. We'll meet up later in the day and I'll bring you up to-date on the background; hopefully by then we will have had some positive feedback from Ekabe.'

# Chapter Fifteen

<u>Wednesday 25th October: London</u>

The Emirates' flight from Zambia landed punctually at Heathrow airport at six-thirty on Wednesday morning. It had been a long and tiring journey, made even more so with a two-hour stop-over in Dubai in the middle of the night and then having to endure a good thirty minutes being jostled at the carousel waiting for her luggage to make its appearance; her need for a coffee had become paramount. She spotted the Caffè Nero as soon as she emerged into the Arrivals Hall and weaving her loaded trolley between a constant stream of people, she walked towards the café's entrance.

Valerie had no intention of continuing her journey up north. She had deliberately booked the domestic flight to Edinburgh separately and to endorse the plan, one she'd had to hastily put-together only hours before she left Zambia, she intended to make her way over to terminal five as she would have done to check-in for the British Airways' ten o'clock flight, scheduled to arrive in Edinburgh at eleven-thirty but if anyone expected to see her among the passengers, they were going to be disappointed, this small triumph bringing a smile to her tired features as she pushed open the glass door of Nero's and stepped inside, the rich aroma of coffee assailing her nostrils.

It was good to be back. Already, the memory of the last eighteen months was beginning to fade, and she knew would soon be forgotten, but not yet; there was still much she had to do and provided she could remain focused and ward off the first signs of any panic, she would be okay. She only had herself to consider which suited her just fine. In the unlikely event that Alan was still alive, though God knows if by some miracle he had survived, it would be anyone's guess where he'd been for the last week. In any case, if he should suddenly reappear, their situation had not changed; new will or not, she was still his wife, a fact which brought her thoughts winging back to Cora Hamilton, but then wasn't she the reason for remaining in London and not returning to the family?

She ordered a large cappuccino and a *pain au chocolat,* carrying her tray over to one of the few remaining tables overlooking the concourse. As she sat there, scooping off the froth of chocolate from her coffee and savouring each spoonful, she was only partially aware of her surroundings: the hiss of steam from the espresso machine, the scrape of a chair along the tiled floor, the rise and fall of different accents from the straggling line of customers waiting to be served and the canned music from invisible speakers; her mind, tenacious and unrelenting, continued its hold, reminding her of the dangerous route she had taken, a swirling loop of images: Alan, stoney-faced, telling her he was divorcing her; Cora Hamilton, the *other* woman; DCI Chrisopher Musenge who clearly didn't trust her, and of course Steve: weak, ineffectual and, above all, a liar. She had given little or no thought to him since yesterday morning, not even to wonder if he'd made it back to Ekabe. She didn't regret what she had done; he only had himself to blame. He should never have moved Alan's body; there was no way she would ever believe him no matter how hard he tried to convince her that he hadn't. She knew why he had of course; he'd wanted to distance himself, and by doing so had well and truly messed everything up, making her situation even worse. She couldn't go to Inspector Musenge and tell him that Steve was responsible without implicating herself. She could still feel the pressure of his fingers digging into her shoulders as he had uttered those chilling words:

"But, my sweet," he'd hissed, his face so close she could smell the whisky on his breath, "you seem to have overlooked the fact that when the police arrived there was no body, therefore how do they know when the incident happened. Think about it." And, she had. At the precise moment she made her decision: he had left her with no alternative but to cut him right out of her life a little earlier and more drastically than she had intended.

Soon it would be time to head over to terminal five to complete the fiction in the unlikely event she had been seen arriving earlier; she would take a taxi into London from there, but first she wanted to check her phone in case there were any messages and, reaching into her bag, pulled out her phone.

There were the two she'd already read before boarding the plane in Lusaka; one from the Tavistock Hotel in Bloomsbury for the booking she'd made yesterday and the other from a firm of solicitors in Woburn Place, one she'd chosen at random from Google, confirming her meeting with one of their partners, James Hathaway, at four-thirty in the afternoon. This would give her plenty of time to work out a strategy, and one which must be foolproof, of how she was going to deal with the woman who, merely by her silent existence, was a threat; the plan had to be simple, possibly one that had been used many times. Tried and tested. She would have to be careful though: she couldn't afford to be seen by her; even out of context, Cora would recognize her.

There were no new messages and no missed calls, not that she expected anyone to contact her, but she couldn't help feeling a slight frisson of disappointment of being invisible. But wasn't that what she wanted, to be anonymous? And to achieve that she had to cut herself off from everyone she knew which included Alan's family, Callum especially, as he was more likely to want to know what her plans were as, presumably, they had all been informed of the outcome at Monday's inquest. *All in good time, Callum. Alan may no longer be the proverbial thorn in your flesh, but I am still here, and I will not be going quietly.* And, slipping the phone back in her bag, she left the café.

***

Bradley-Grant & Hathaway, Solicitors were on the first floor of one of the older buildings in Woburn Place, a short walk from her hotel and next door to a lively looking pub already beginning to fill up with late afternoon customers, some of them on the pavement outside the open doors with glasses of wine and beer making the most of the last rays of the autumn sun. She was shown into James Hathaway's office by a super-cool young woman whose smile made no effort to reach her kohl-lined eyes.

'Good afternoon, Mrs Lorimer; how was your flight;' James Hathaway asked walking towards her to shake hands, 'exhausting, I expect?' gesturing over towards an oval glass-topped table in the centre of the room and pulling out one of the softly upholstered chairs for her.

'Very.' she smiled, sitting down, and placing her bag on the floor beside her feet.

'I'm sure. I've asked my secretary to bring us in some coffee, or perhaps you would prefer tea?'

'No, coffee will be lovely, even though I've had more than my quota today.'

Polite, but inconsequential conversation, but not strained in any way. No doubt he was well versed in the art of sweet-talking his lady clients, the cynical thought slipping in from nowhere. He was certainly charming, good-looking as well: sun-tanned, blond hair worn slightly longer than the average London professional, appraising him as he took the seat opposite placing a slim folder on the table between them. How very different he was to the dried-up Jonathan Irvine tucked away in his crummy office in Ndola.

As if on cue, the door opened and a young woman, alarmingly like the receptionist, so much so, she wasn't entirely certain whether she was or not, came in with the coffee.

'Thank you, Belinda,' giving her one of his flashing smiles, 'just put the tray down here and we'll help ourselves.'

'I appreciate you being able to see me at such short notice.' Valerie said to him once he had poured their coffee.

'Not at all; I couldn't help but get the impression when you called us that you were in urgent need of advice, given the most unfortunate circumstances you've found yourself in.'

'They are certainly unfortunate, Mr Hathaway. You will have read the copy of the coroner's report I emailed you.'

'Indeed I have, and it does make grim reading, mysterious also. What are your thoughts, Mrs Lorimer; an open verdict must be extremely unsettling.'

'Which they only brought in because of lack of evidence. Of course I think they're wrong; it all happened more than a week ago, Mr Hathaway; if Alan had survived we would have known by now.'

'Meanwhile,' sounding sympathetic, 'you are in a kind of limbo, not knowing whether you still have a husband or not.'

'That's exactly how I feel. Also, and this is causing me considerable concern, I need to know exactly where I stand, financially I mean.'

'The case remains open?'

'Yes, and I have no idea how long I will have to wait until they decide otherwise.'

'From what I've read in the report and taking other aspects into account, not least that the incident occurred overseas in a country with different laws, it would be presumptuous of me to make any prediction. But, to return to what you've just said about your own situation, the law is quite clear in this country for British citizens: you are married to Alan Lorimer for as long as he lives; only divorce or his death can alter that. In other words, you continue to benefit, if I may use such a word, in the use of the marital home, access to available funds, et cetera.'

'That's clear enough.'

There must have been something in her reply, a slight change in her expression perhaps, which prompted his next question.

'Is there something else worrying you, Mrs Lorimer.'

'I don't want to waste your time and I'm probably being naive – '

'I would be very surprised if there wasn't anything else on your mind at what must be a harrowing time, and I can't help but feel you've been very much on your own when problems can so easily compound upon themselves.'

'I guess they have.' she answered, making up her mind what she was going to say next, to filter out the pieces no-one should hear, 'You see, Mr Hathaway, three days before my husband was attacked, he told me that he had instructed his lawyer to start divorce proceedings. This came right out of the blue; I had no idea.'

'Another woman?'

'I very much believe so, although he refused to admit it, or even to talk about why he was divorcing me. Of course I would have had to accept his decision eventually, once I had taken time to think things through; there would be a divorce settlement and I was confident he would act fairly, but – '

' – but he didn't?'

'No, he didn't. He'd made a new will, you see. I've talked to a solicitor out there; we'd lodged a copy of the original will with his firm shortly after we arrived in Zambia. I didn't have a copy and realising I would need one I made an appointment to see him and that's how I found out. Alan had cut me out of his new will, bequeathing his entire estate, in the event of anything happening to him, to the woman I'd guessed he was having an affair with.'

He took several minutes before replying, so long she had started to become fidgety worrying whether she'd made a mistake coming here. Perhaps she had already said too much, but she really wanted to find out how she stood. She had a damn good idea, but she needed to be sure.

'Well,' he said at last, moving his empty cup and saucer to one side and opening the folder, 'I do understand your concern, Mrs Lorimer; the situation you're in is, to say the least, an uncomfortable one, also from what you've told me, not one that's going to be resolved very quickly. But having said that, I can put your mind at rest on a couple of issues. As I've said, so long as your husband is not officially declared dead and you remain married to him, your status will not change.'

'What about the new will?'

'That will not come into effect while he remains alive, but presumably if you learn to the contrary, you will wish to contest it.'

'And how successful do you believe I would be, Mr Hathaway?'

'You could be successful, but it would depend on the provisions of the new will. Have you by any chance a copy?'

'Yes, I do; I have it here.' and leaning down to pick up her bag she pulled out the copy the Ndola lawyer had given her and passed it across the table to him. He didn't take long to read it, making notes in pencil in the margin of the coroner's report.

'Interesting in that he intended to bequeath, and I quote, "my entire estate to Cora Hamilton." Tell me, how does this particular wording compare with the original will, Mrs Lorimer?'

'Quite different, actually; there was mention of his estate, but he'd added a proviso that his shareholding of the company would revert to his father or if he should have died, to his two brothers.'

'And you were happy with that?'

'I was, yes, because I already knew that this proviso was one which had existed for the family since the company was first formed years ago, but Alan was already wealthy in his own right; he had investments, both here in the UK and overseas, also his late mother had left him a considerable part of her own personal fortune.'

'Therefore, if and when his family learned of this omission, what do you think their reaction would be?'

'They would not be at all happy, especially his older brother; there's always been a strong element of rivalry between them, more on Callum's side though.'

'Do you know the share ratio?'

'Alan and Callum have equal shares of twenty-five per cent, their younger brother, Bruce ten, leaving their father with the majority of forty per cent.'

'I see; again, interesting;' he paused for a moment, making more notes, this time on a sheet of A4 paper clipped to the inside of the folder, 'am I right in saying that "Lorimer Fruits" is a listed company.'

'Oh, yes.'

'And if twenty-five per cent of their shares should be held by a virtual outsider it could be a concern for them.'

'Even more so when eventually their father dies.'

'Really?'

'There's no love lost between Callum and his father, Mr Hathaway; I would be surprised if Callum is even mentioned in his will.'

'What about the other son, Bruce?'

'I don't think he would mind; his forte is marketing and selling and he's good at it, but he's not really family orientated. I'm quite surprised he hasn't moved away, come down south to work for instance.'

'Well, from the overall impression you've given me, Mrs Lorimer, I would say that the fact your husband excluded that all-important clause could, if it becomes necessary, place you in a fairly strong position to contest the will in its entirety based on its validity.'

'Sounds complicated.' *And it would all take time and at the end of the day there is no guarantee that Cora Hamilton would lose out.*

'I'm sorry I have been unable to give you more reassurance, Mrs Lorimer.'

'Perhaps not, but what you've explained has been helpful and has given me a lot to think about.' *More than you realise. Whatever you've said, informative or otherwise, the situation remains the same: Cora Hamilton continues to be a threat.*

Her resolve now strengthened, she was eager to leave and, perhaps intuitively reading her mind, he stood up, but before leading her to the door, gave her one of his cards. Hardly glancing at it she opened her bag, and taking out her wallet, slipped it in behind the hotel's key card, certain it would be unlikely she would be making another appointment.

***

Beverly very nearly missed her. She had arrived at Heathrow within minutes of the Emirates' plane landing at six-thirty and was waiting at the barrier well before the first stragglers came through. With only a remembered image in the photograph she had seen of who she had reckoned was Valerie Lorimer she realised she had to be quick in spotting her, a feat which was becoming more and more difficult as the passengers increased, many of them blocking her view, but almost on the point of giving up as the doors were closing, she saw her. She must have been caught up in a large family group, their trolleys piled high with a pile of luggage, because she was practically at the end of the barrier and had started to walk quickly across the concourse. It was definitely her alright: even with the lack of colour in the photograph, she still recognized her: the thick dark hair untidily tied back, the slanting eyes, cat-like, with finely drawn brows and the full, slightly pouting lips giving her a permanent discontented expression.

She wasn't heading towards the exit, but instead making a beeline for the Nero Café. Beverly followed her, not too closely although it's doubtful she would be noticed among those surging in all directions as though intent on impeding her progress. She had already ordered a coffee and moved to a table next to the window by the time Beverly reached the café, and keeping an eye on her in case she should suddenly get up and leave, she ordered an espresso and found a free table where she would be out of her line of vision; a necessary precaution to prevent her getting even the slightest hint of being followed.

Five, six minutes went by and apart from taking small sips of her coffee which must have grown cold, she made no other movement, not even to check on the time, but appeared to be lost in thought. She didn't seem to be waiting for anyone and Beverly could see no sign of nervousness, finding it hard to get her head round that the woman she was watching so closely could have, only a couple of days ago, caused the death of her lover. Dramatic stuff, Beverly thought, wondering what she was thinking. Did she regret what she had done, or did she feel justified? And what about her husband; the victim of an assault and presumed to have perished in a shark-infested river? Did she care? Beverly prided herself on being able to read people, but with Valerie Lorimer she was finding it virtually impossible; the outward signs were there and easy to interpret: the pale beige camel coat draped over the back of her chair, the dark navy designer jeans and the ice-blue cashmere sweater. They all made statements: expensive, implying she was accustomed to the best, money was no object kind of woman, and probably used to having whatever she wanted. But that was all Beverly could fathom out about the real person, of what made her tick. *And Beverly Grant you are only meters away from a suspected murderer and, yes Andy, I hear you: I will be circumspect at all times, and I promise to avoid any libel pitfalls!*

Valerie had now taken out her mobile from her bag; she wasn't making a call but appeared to be reading her messages. There had been no change in her expression, no hint of whether she was pleased or otherwise, watching as she put the phone back into the bag. And then, when Beverly was beginning to wonder how much longer she intended to remain there, she was getting ready to leave. She folded her coat, placing it on the top of her luggage and, pulling the trolley away from the table, walked out of the café.

Beverly fully expected her to make her way to the taxi rank, but instead she headed towards the ramp to the interterminal walkway. This was the way to the Heathrow Express. Why was she going that way?

It was less crowded here and Beverly kept well behind her, becoming more confused when she walked past the lifts and escalators for the station and continued until she reached the taxi rank. What the hell was the woman up to? Why hadn't she gone to the rank outside terminal three? She had to find out where she was going. She couldn't just assume she was taking a taxi into London. Could be anywhere.

Taxis were frequent and the queue moved quickly. When one drew up alongside her, Beverly managed to position herself as close to her as she could without her noticing, but she need not have worried: once Valerie had instructed the driver she was too preoccupied with dragging her luggage from the trolley and into the taxi.

For now, the pressure was off in keeping such a close eye on her. She knew where she was staying and that was all that concerned Beverly. It was going to take her at least an hour to get back to London, not by taxi: the cost would far exceed her expense limit, therefore it would have to be the underground.

She was impatient now to spend some time on this week's copy which, with the latest development, could provide a much-needed fillip to satisfy the insatiable appetite of her paper's readership, but first she needed to know whether anything else had come through from Reuters, anything she could expand upon and with luck, tweak out a hidden nuance or some obscure observation, to give it her own particular stamp, but always to exercise caution to prevent her copy rapidly winging its way back from Andy's desk.

***

Six o'clock and "The Queen & Sixpence" in Woburn Place was bustling with a steady influx from the nearby offices in Woburn Place. Beverly had been fortunate in finding a free table in one of the booths against the far wall and had taken an appreciative sip of a large glass of chilled Pinot Grigio she had been looking forward to all day, when Valerie Lorimer appeared in the open doorway. She had not really expected her to turn up here, although she had hoped as the pub was close to the Tavistock Hotel where she was staying. She seemed to hesitate for a moment as if trying to make up her mind to come in or not, but with an imperceptible shrug, she stepped inside and walked over to the bar. Beverly was amused at the way one of the bartenders. The younger one, tall, muscular, biceps taut under his tee-shirt and sporting a surfer's tan, bounded over to serve her. A wasted effort, Beverly thought almost feeling sorry for the guy; Valerie scarcely seemed to notice him, impervious to his boyish good looks and easy charm, her mind obviously elsewhere and it didn't take Beverly two guesses where that might be. She had talked to Andy earlier, but had chosen not to say anything about Valerie's odd behaviour at Heathrow: she had no wish to pre-empt his repetitive words of warning; they would only disrupt her thought process which was particularly fragile at the moment as she grappled with how she intended to wrap up her copy.

"Anything new, Andy since we last talked?" she'd asked him.

"There has been an interesting development actually "

"Yes?"

"It would seem that the Zambian authorities have literally washed their hands with the case, and it's now being handled by us."

"Wow!!

"Is that all you can say?"

"Give me a minute to take this in, Andy. Please. What you're saying, or I should say what the news agency is saying, is that Zambia is not interested in pursuing a murder, a murder which has taken place in their country."

"A British subject, Beverly, *ergo*, a British problem."

"How long will it be before this nugget reaches the streets, I wonder."

"Provided, if like us, the press are up to speed with the Lorimer connection to John Milne's murder, not long. So, on that note, your copy, Beverly. When can I expect it? Hmmph."

"Tomorrow afternoon."

"By four at the latest.'

"No problem, you know me."

"Why does that reassurance worry me."

"I don't think you realise, Andy, but I am way ahead of the pack; I didn't notice any of them panting around the barrier at terminal three this morning."

She had all she needed to put the finishing touches to her column, but the craving for that little bit more, that extra snippet of knowledge unknown to anyone else, was strong. Beverly was notorious amongst her peers for her unorthodox methods of sourcing information, the less charitable describing them as underhand, but no-one had ever accused her of fabricating, or even fudging the truth in order to spice up a story. She was a rare breed of journalist; without losing the competitive edge needed to survive in the newspaper world, she had held on to those first lessons she had learned as a cub reporter at the beck and call of sub-editors, editors, managing editors, even publishers, which was to pay close attention to detail, to check and double check facts and to be original.

But, as she sat in the warm familiarity of a typically London pub, she wished she wasn't so hidebound by an inbuilt correctness and could give in to a simmering compulsion to go over to Valerie Lorimer and give her some spiel about having met her before and use her inventiveness to really get to know her, to find out what made her tick and, more importantly, why she was in full public view when the news of her involvement in a murder investigation was on the point of exploding right in front of her. She wouldn't do it, of course. And, even if she did and submitted the copy to Andy, he would never authorize it. Also, and this would be the biggest blow, he would refuse to accept anything else from her. Her credibility would be in tatters.

Valerie had not moved away from the bar and continued to display little interest in her surroundings. She had placed her phone down next to her glass which could indicate she was expecting a call and, as if on cue, Robbie William's "*Candy*" wafted across to her. Valerie's reaction was instant: she glanced at the screen, frowned, but made no attempt to answer it. If she was waiting for a call, apparently this wasn't the one. A few minutes later it rang again, and as before she ignored it. When the phone rang for the third time Beverly fully expected a repeat performance, but no, she snatched up the mobile and with a flash of temper stabbed one of the buttons.

This was really too good an opportunity to miss she decided and taking her empty glass over to the bar with her, eased her way between a man in a dark navy pin-stripe suit impatiently trying to attract the barman's attention, and to where Valerie was elegantly perched on a high stool. Over the years Beverly had perfected the skill of eavesdropping: to blotting out extraneous noises until they became muted and less intrusive. Although Valerie had her head turned away from her, she was still able to hear what she was saying; even with only picking up part of the conversation, the gist of it made some sort of sense:

'How many times do I have to tell you, ……………… no, let me finish. Yes, I did have a flight booked up to Edinburgh this morning but I changed my mind ……………………………personal reasons, that's why ……………………………for personal, Callum, read confidential…………………………'

There was a long period of silence, Valerie making a number of attempts to interrupt until either her caller came to the end of what he was saying and was waiting for her response, or quite simply, he had run out of steam, she picked up from where she'd left off: 'You know, Callum, I do have a life and with Alan gone, it's more important than ever that I focus on that and, quite frankly, hearing you whingeing about a sudden influx of reporters turning up at Ashburn is tough! Anyway, you should be used to them by now……………………………no, I have not heard anything about a fatal car crash …………………………… and no, I hardly knew the man you say was killed; he was a neighbour of ours, that's all ………………'

Whatever was said to Valerie next must have further infuriated her, because she switched off her phone and, unzipping her bag, tossed it inside. One-sided, though the exchange had been, Beverly was not disappointed; she would enjoy selecting and extracting any fragments which would enhance the draft for her copy now almost complete. She was distracted by the waiter asking if she was ready for a refill, the guy in the suit now walking back to join his table with a full tray of drinks, a wide grin appearing as a loud appreciative cheer erupted from his fellow-workers.

*** 

James Hathaway selected a *Cabernet Sauvignon* from the stainless-steel wine rack in his state-of-the-art kitchen and expertly eased out the cork. His favourite time of the day when he could truly relax and be himself: not the city professional; the lawyer with the exemplary track record and the impeccable social manners, but the stranger he had left behind so many years ago. It was seldom he indulged in anything so melancholic but hearing the feint Scottish lilt in his client's voice that afternoon had struck a nostalgic chord in his memory, conjuring up almost forgotten times of growing up on Scotland's east coast. Valerie Lorimer. An intriguing woman, not for what she'd told him, but more what she hadn't: unexplained circumstances surrounding the attack and subsequent disappearance of her husband, culminating in the uncertainty of an open verdict, but very little else. Where had she been at the time, he wondered, taking a crystal glass from an overhead cupboard and pouring out a generous measure of wine; she hadn't said. That wasn't the only question he would have liked to have asked her, but that hadn't been his brief; she had specifically made the appointment to seek his advice on her personal legal standing in respect to the complications arising in a second will, in the event the husband's body was discovered. But then, he sighed, taking a long and satisfying sip, *how long is a piece of string.*

There was nothing he especially wanted to watch on television and once he'd caught up with the national news, all of it as repetitive and depressing as usual, he switched off. For a few moments he remained leaning against the work top appreciating the silence, idly contemplating whether to top up his glass or find something from the freezer to microwave while his thoughts kept drifting back to Valerie Lorimer and the vagaries of the British legal system which were unable to give her the answers she was looking for. She was going to have to exercise considerable patience in the weeks and possibly months ahead although she hadn't struck him as a woman to meekly accept that she had no choice but to wait. He couldn't quite make up his mind about her. She was attractive, stylish, certainly intelligent, although with a sharpness he hadn't found particularly appealing, but then she wasn't his type. And what did he mean by that? But, if he was honest, he knew why: it was her manner, the obvious way she had projected herself, the image she appeared to be trying that little bit too hard to portray. If he was going to be entirely objective and had met her for the first time, socially rather than professionally, he would have described her as cold and lacking in empathy. Certainly, when she'd told him about the recent attack on her husband and the mystery surrounding his whereabouts, she had shown no signs of grief, or pity for him; that she considered herself to be the victim came over to him loud and clear: her husband had suddenly announced his intentions to divorce her. He was leaving her for another woman and intended to disinherit her. *Don't you feel sorry for me,* had reached him loud and clear.

He knew he was being uncharitable; they were only his own private impressions of her, but she had intrigued him and he would love to know more if only to satisfy his curiosity, but where to start? She had been noticeably economical with any information about herself; apart from being married into what appeared to be a pretty traditional family, their company solidly established and listed on the stock market. She had only hours earlier returned from Zambia where, presumably, her husband had been working. And that was about the sum total of what he had gleaned. Strange though, he thought, taking out a steak from the freezer and putting it into the microwave to defrost, why had she decided to break her journey in London, why hadn't she taken a direct flight back to Scotland? But, perhaps not so strange: she didn't want her husband's family to know what she was doing, hence the one-off appointment with him. What was she hiding? *Now, where the hell did that come from? What could she be hiding: the truth behind what happened out in Zambia?*

Could he be right, James wondered; could his sub-conscience be trying to tell him something? It wouldn't be the first time and cynic though he was, he had learned to listen to his inner voice. His mobile ringing and coinciding with the ping of the microwave, immediately broke his train of thought which was probably just as well he decided, picking up the phone.

'Hello.'

'James; Pete here.'

'Pete, great to hear from you; how are you?'

''I'm fine, thanks. Are you free this evening?'

'You're in London!'

'Yep.'

'Fantastic; where are you staying?'

'The Strand Palace, but if we're meeting up I'd much prefer a decent pub.'

'Of course, how about the "The Coal Hole"; it's virtually across the road from you.'

'Good choice; it's years since I've been in there. We can catch up over a few beers and a bite to eat.'

'Suits me; I can be with you in about fifteen minutes.'

\*\*\*

James took a taxi to the Strand, his previous dreary mood having instantly evaporated at the prospect of seeing his old friend again. He had known Pete Small since their university days and over the last fifteen or sixteen years they had managed to keep in touch, although with Pete living and working up in Scotland it meant they could only meet when he had to be in London on business. As his taxi drew up in front of the pub the irony of Pete's unexpected call that evening hadn't escaped him: the Scottish connection, a continuation of his earlier preoccupations with Valerie Lorimer and his friend's fortuitous arrival? Perhaps it was true that life does move in mysterious ways.

Pete was already there, seated at one of the small tables along the length of the wall facing the bar, a large glass of what looked like a pint of Guiness in front of him.

'I didn't know what to get you.' he said standing up and shaking his hand vigorously.

'It's okay, I'll get myself a glass of red.'

'So,' James said, once they'd caught up with all the news on mutual friends and compared notes on ongoing professional gripes, 'how about your personal life; still with Amanda?'

'Yes, very much so,' he grinned, 'and you, my friend?'

'Nothing new to report.'

'Give it time, James; she was a great girl, Jill, but well - '

' – it wasn't to be.' finishing for him and not wanting to dwell of what might have been, 'anyway, anything exciting up there amongst all that mist and heather?'

'You may scoff,' finishing off his Guinness, 'but there has actually been a fair bit of excitement recently.'

'In what way, but first, how about another drink, Pete; another Guinness?' picking up his empty glass.

'Thanks, but I think I've had enough of the healthy brew; I'll have the same as you.'

He came back to the table with the drinks and a couple of menus which he pushed to one side.

'For later,' he said, raising his glass, 'Cheers.'

'Cheers and great to see you.'

'And you. You were saying?'

'Yes, and what I'm going to tell you will I'm sure set your little grey cells working.'

'Go on,' he laughed, 'I'm on full alert!'

'Well, 'taking a sip of his wine before explaining, 'a week ago we had a murder in our town. It was on the news, but only briefly and you may have missed it.'

'I must have, especially if Calder Bay was mentioned, but anyway, go on. Who was it, someone you knew?'

'I didn't actually know him; apparently, he was a relative newcomer to Calder Bay and was working for a local company: "Lorimer Fruit Growers & Distributors"; they're an old-established family business and pretty well-known internationally and I'm friendly with one of the sons, Bruce.'

'So, what happened to the poor chap?' James asked, his interest immediately piqued, not yet sure whether to dismiss the name Lorimer as a coincidence.

'Well, quite a brutal attack by all accounts but for some unexplained reason, apart from when everyone first heard about it, there has been very little else mentioned in the news although Bruce told me the other day that there was still a strong police presence in and around the town, with them paying frequent visits up to their offices; he's been interviewed twice by them.'

'Where was this guy killed then; at work?'

'No, it happened last Tuesday night, quite late the police believe. Whoever it was, broke into the guy's flat, killed him, ransacked the place, and made their escape and, of course, nobody heard or saw anything untoward.'

'So often the case though, isn't it?'

'Too true; nobody wants to get involved.'

'Are the police treating it as a random attack, a burglary gone wrong?'

'Hard to say, James; they seem to be playing their cards pretty damn close to their chests.'

'Why do you think they're paying so much attention to the Lorimer family?'

'God knows. I don't believe Bruce is all that perturbed, he's too laid back for that, but from what he was saying, his father is furious, especially as this business happened at the same as he's struggling with the disappearance of his son in Zambia. For a family, they are certainly going through it at the moment.'

'Who was it who said: 'coincidences hardly ever happen', Pete.'

'I think that's something of a misquote actually,' he grinned, picking up his glass and taking a long sip, 'anyway, what did you mean?'

'I don't believe I will be breaking any client confidentiality when I tell you that I had a client this afternoon called Valerie Lorimer.'

'Wow! Did you really; yes, surely that must be a coincidence. She's back in the UK then, well, all I can say is she hasn't wasted much time. Presumably, she will have told you about her husband: missing, but presumed dead, according to the consensus of opinion over there.'

'She didn't elaborate, except there's a divorce pending, or perhaps it is more accurate to say, was pending.'

'Whatever.'

'Why the cynical expression?'

'You may well ask, James,' another grin, finishing off his drink, 'because I couldn't help seeing a certain irony in the fact that it was Alan calling the shots, so to speak, in filing for a divorce and not Valerie I mean. I bet that came as a shock to her.'

'I take it, you don't like her.'

'Not particularly; she's what my mother would have called a gold-digger. Probably somewhat unkind, but with more than a grain of truth in it. I must admit I'm surprised to hear she's in London and not back re-asserting herself as the much-maligned little wife. She didn't enlighten you, I suppose?'

'No, I didn't ask, but no doubt she had her reasons.'

'You bet she did, James. Come on, enough of this gloomy talk, another drink?'.

## Chapter Sixteen

<u>Thursday 26th October: London</u>

Cora leaned over to the bedside table and switched off the alarm. For several minutes she lay there, quite still, waiting for the last shreds of a dream to dissolve, or go wherever played- out dreams went, not that this one had left any memory, merely tattered grey shadows skimming the edge of her conscience, undefined and without sound, but no less disconcerting. She had spent a restless night, waking often and taking an age to get back to sleep and hearing the rain slashing against the window, she was even more reluctant to make the effort.

The shower revived her, but only because she allowed the water to be as hot as she could bear, and it wasn't until she was dressed and waiting for the kettle to boil for the cafetière that she felt up to trying to fathom out when she had felt the first prickling of unease. It was only yesterday, shortly before midday: Paula from reception had called out to her to say she had taken a call from a woman asking for her contact details; although rare, this had not been the first time someone had phoned LSE explaining they wanted a tutor's advice on a thesis they were struggling with, the university's switchboard being their first point of contact, although yesterday's caller had declined to give her name. Cora, hurrying for a midday tutorial, hadn't given it a second's thought. Not until now.

She had left the LSE at four; the late October sun had been warm on her back as she'd walked along Houghton Street thinking about Alan as she found herself doing so often, and turning right into Aldwych, she had slowed down, knowing she would have several minutes to wait before her bus was due. There had been a few people at the stop: a couple of giggling teenagers taking selfies; a tall gangly guy grinning inanely into his phone; two middle-aged women, both wearing ankle-length Liberty print dresses and carrying theatre programmes, and as her bus drew up alongside the kerb, a dark-haired woman in an expensive camel coat and a Monsoon tasselled scarf in peacock blue, tagged on to the end of the queue.

She had moved along the bus until she came to an empty seat, the woman in the expensive coat walking past her and taking the one behind. Cora had barely glanced up as she went past but had immediately thought there was something vaguely familiar about her, but it had been no more than an impression. She hadn't liked to turn round to take a closer look but had spent the twenty-minute journey idly trying to remember if she had seen her before, trawling back through the years, even to her university days, but it was no use; whoever it was had remained tantalizingly elusive, finally giving up as they approached her stop.

She had been walking past "Gino's", the roar of traffic from the main road considerably less from there, even the sirens from the ambulances as they turned into Coram Street, when she heard the metallic click of heels on the pavement behind her. As she reached her apartment block and was keying in the security code, she glanced round to see the woman from the bus again, but she didn't place any importance on what was after all not all so unusual; there was no logical reason why someone should not board the same bus and take it to her stop in Woburn Place. No reason at all, she thought, stepping into the communal hall and closing the door behind her.

Her phone had been ringing when she let herself into the flat and in her haste to answer it, she completely forgot about her.

Graham Lorimer scarcely needed to introduce himself; he sounded so like Alan, it was uncanny.

"Mr Lorimer," she said, shrugging off her jacket and letting it fall over the arm of the sofa, "I'm sorry, but we keep missing each other; I did return your call, but - "

" – no, please, Miss Hamilton, there is no need to apologise. I wanted to talk to you about Alan."

"Have you any news; I feel so dreadfully cut off from what's been happening in Ekabe."

"I've heard nothing, not since Monday when I learned about the inquest's verdict which of course was totally unacceptable."

"So soon." realising he must be aware of how her voice was trembling, but what he'd just said had deepened her despair, as though the word inquest had brought Alan's fate closer somehow."

"They certainly didn't waste any time," hearing the bitterness in his voice, "and of course the coroner had no choice but to bring in an open verdict."

"I suppose so, but why didn't they wait?'

"Exactly! I question just how thorough they're being: asking the right questions, speaking to the right people, literally going over and over the same ground and, above all, not giving up."

"I think the same, but what can we do? I don't want to state the obvious, Mr Lorimer, but Zambia has its own laws and I can't see we have any choice but to abide by them. It is to be hoped," she added, "that their police haven't abandoned their search for Alan."

"I would say that's anyone's guess. However, I understand you spoke to my daughter-in-law on Saturday; she got the impression you had some strong views on this dreadful business."

"That's all they were, I'm afraid, Mr Lorimer and only because of my knowledge, not extensive I admit, of the terrain where Alan's pick-up was discovered. I cannot think of one single reason why it should have been there."

"Myra told me that you were refusing to believe Alan had – " he had faltered at that point, the anguish in his voice bringing tears to her eyes, " – forgive me, but I'm finding this difficult, but what I'm trying to say is, do you still feel the same way after almost a week and still no word?"

"I do feel the same, yes. There are too many unanswered questions, and even if it does seem pretty hopeless, I'm not going to give up hope. What about your family, do they feel the same as you?"

"Hmmph. There is a reluctance to talk about Alan and what may or may not have happened to him. Apart from Callum, my eldest son, I believe this could be in deference to my feelings."

"Callum thinks differently?"

"He believes his brother is dead, Miss Hamilton and refuses to discuss the matter."

"Oh, dear, but you know as far as I can make out and I have only spoken to my friend, Kate over there, but people are believing the worst, even the authorities."

"This is precisely what I've feared. How damned frustrating it all is!"

"I know." she sympathised, at a loss as to what she could say to him.

"Miss Hamiton?"

"Yes?"

"Would it be possible for you to come up here this weekend; I realise it is an imposition, but I feel if we could meet, you could describe to me what this place Ekabe is like, the people Alan knows and perhaps we could put something together which I could present to our police here. I'm on first name terms with the superintendent in Calder Bay and he isn't without influence. What do you think?"

"I think it might be a good idea, but I'm not sure, given my relationship with Alan, what sort of reception I will receive from your family. It could be unpleasant; for both of us, I mean."

"There won't be any unpleasantness, Miss Hamilton; I'll make sure of that. You will be my guest."

They had brought the call to a close with Cora agreeing to spend the weekend at Ashburn House, but despite his father's reassurances that her presence would not cause any resentment, she wasn't entirely convinced, but she wouldn't back down; she would go. Besides, she had liked Graham Lorimer, and it hadn't only been a deep understanding of sympathy of what the poor man was going through, she felt it was the very least she could do for Alan, and maybe, just maybe they could put something positive together which would help in some way to unravel what had happened in Ekabe. She was a long way to giving up, and long before then, she would fly out there and find out for herself what had happened.

With a decision of sorts decided, she felt a slight easing of the tension which had been building since Kate's call, and talking to Alan's father had helped. If nothing else, she'd had the chance to talk about him and despite any possible animosity from the family, she was looking forward to meeting them and hopefully share some of their memories of Alan. Of course there would be no change when she came back home: Alan would still be missing and she would still be as frantically worried about him, but with what his father had said about approaching someone in authority, perhaps there was a glimmer, a very slight glimmer, of what she might dare to call hope.

She spent the remainder of the evening flicking through the channels to find a programme she hadn't seen before, finally settling on one of Jane McDonald's cruises to the Caribbean and in a further attempt at escapism, she opened a bottle of *Pinot Grigio*.

It must have been well after midnight when she finally switched off the bedside lamp only to find she hadn't drawn the curtains properly: there'd been a slight gap where they should have met and, preferring the alarm at eight to wake her rather than the beams of flashing lights from early hour revellers taking a short-cut through to Bedford Place, she reluctantly climbed out of bed to close them. She didn't know why she looked across the road, but probably wouldn't have done if a car hadn't driven past at that moment, its headlights picking out the figure standing half-concealed by one of the trees bordering the Gardens. It must have been the way the light, only fleetingly, caught her full-face giving her no time to move further back or even to turn her head away, that Cora had recognized her. The realisation was so incredible, it was almost farcical. Why was Alan's wife outside her flat in the middle of the night? And why had she been stalking her, quite blatantly as though she wanted to be seen? Her behaviour was totally bizarre, but far too sinister to ignore.

But this morning she was no further forward in understanding what Valerie planned to do next. She must surely have a plan, but what was it? Did she intend to confront her, to openly threaten her with some unimaginable consequences if – ' but at that point, hovering on the brink of a place she didn't want to go, she stopped.

By the time she had to leave for work, relieved to find there was no sign of Valerie waiting for her to emerge from the building, she felt calmer It could be she had abandoned her stalking: she had after all found out where she lived, although what she intended to do next Cora was still loathe to speculate. She did feel vulnerable though, not exactly afraid, but nevertheless decidedly uncomfortable. But what could she do? She could contact the police; she had read somewhere that to stalk a person was a criminal offence, but she knew she would merely come over as too vague and she was reluctant to give them Valerie's name: the last she wanted was to cause Alan's family any more distress, therefore she was left with very little choice. Should she say nothing in the hope that Valerie would grow tired of whatever she was up to and give up, or should she confide in someone who could give her some impartial advice, but she couldn't think of anyone; her friends, even colleagues, were hardly likely to be objective. But she couldn't go on like this: she had to tell someone. But who?

She had almost reached the traffic lights at the end of her road, her brain continuing to search for a solution, scarcely aware of the dozen or so young students walking alongside her and chattering excitedly amongst themselves, eager to reach the lights in time, when one of them accidently nudged against her as he suddenly sprinted forward to the edge of the pavement quickly followed by the others, therefore she was slow to react to an increasing pressure in the centre of her back. Too late, she tried to keep her balance, even to grabbing hold of the pole of the metal barrier, but her outstretched hand missed, and she stumbled forward on to the road, the roar of the approaching traffic and the stench of diesel fumes accompanying her as the tarmac rushed up to meet her.

\*\*\*

Calder Bay

For the first time since word had reached him about Alan, Graham Lorimer woke up on Thursday morning, not exactly optimistic, but with a glimmer of hope. At last, he had found someone who shared his belief, however flimsy it might be, that Alan had survived. Cora Hamilton had intrigued him, and he looked forward to meeting her; perhaps they could work together in forming a plan, at least one which, given her knowledge of Ekabe and life among the expatriate community, would be sufficiently credible to persuade the authorities not to abandon their search for him.

Graham didn't anticipate any open hostility from the family, but why should they object to her coming here, except for Callum of course. By not telling him that Cora had returned his call was all the proof he needed that his eldest son wanted none of them to have anything to do with her. Callum's negative attitude, his refusal to discuss Alan, his abrupt decision before consulting the board to dispense with John Milne's services immediately Alan's letter had arrived, and his unexplained absences, had become a major problem, one that had to be resolved quickly before it escalated into something unmanageable. God knows, the fall-out from John Milne's murder had been damaging enough to the business' reputation without also losing the loyal support of the employees, many of whom had been with the company for years. How the hell, Graham muttered to himself as he made his way downstairs to the annexe, did the situation get to this stage?

'God morning, Alison;' pausing for a moment at her desk as he was passing,' everything alright?'

'Good morning, Mr Lorimer. Well, I'm not sure; I've taken a few calls from "The Scotsman" and the English national newspapers.'

'What did they want?'

'They didn't say, just that they wanted to speak to you or Mr Callum.'

She looked so uncomfortable; he didn't press her. Alison had been their receptionist for two or three years and during that time she had proved herself more than capable of being answerable to each of them without displaying any favouritism, no mean feat considering their diverse personalities.

'Persistent, aren't they? No doubt they will eventually give up.' he added, continuing towards his office, realising just how hollow his words must sound to her; theoretically though, the media would ultimately leave them alone, but when that was likely to be remained very much in the air: could be, when the current interest was superseded by something more sensational to whet the general public's insatiable appetite, or if, heaven forbid, there was a development which would further discredit his family.

Panic thinking. He was in danger of losing control of any rational thought, realising with a stab of apprehension that whatever transpired from the in-depth discussions he hoped to have with Cora Hamilton at the weekend could have an obverse affect: misdemeanours and indiscretions could surface. It would be like living in a glasshouse enabling the curious and the sanctimonious to speculate and pass judgement on the integrity of not only the business, but on his family. Was it worth the risk? But he already knew the answer: if it meant finding out why his son should have been the target for whatever happened over there, yes it was. He had to know the truth and he rather thought that Cora would feel the same.

Kirstie was already in his office and must have heard him coming, placing a steaming mug of coffee on his desk, alongside a couple of his favourite Abernethy biscuits.

'Thank you, Kirstie, that was thoughtful.' he said, exactly as he always did each morning, 'I understand the gentlemen of the press have been as zealous as ever. I would have thought they'd have realised by now that we have nothing further to give them; quite literally they have milked us dry!'

His phone ringing prevented the need for Kirstie to make any reply, although one glance at her expression told him what he knew already: what could she say? Kirstie was aware as much as he was that there was far more to the media's relentless harassing than the search for John Milne's killer: they wanted to know what the connection with his family was, sighing in exasperation as he picked up the receiver.

'I have DCI Dale on the line, Mr Lorimer; he's asked especially to speak to you.'

'Very well, Alison, put him through.'

'Chief Inspector, I trust you have some positive news for me this morning.'

'I'm afraid not, sir. I'm following up on the call I made yesterday and spoke to your son, Callum; I understood from him that you were unavailable at the time – '

' – if I could just stop you there for a moment; first of all, I was not informed of your call.'

'In that case, you won't have heard of the recent occurrence in Zambia involving the death of one of your son's neighbours out there.'

'I certainly have not, Chief Inspector! And unless this has something to do with Alan's disappearance, I cannot think of one reason why you should want to talk to me. It hasn't, has it?' To do with Alan, I mean?' realising how desperate he must sound, but the very mention of anyone connected to him, even as commonplace as a neighbour, had the alarming ability of bringing him out in a cold sweat and noticing the look of alarm on Kirstie's face only made him feel worse.

'As to whether there is a connection, sir, it is really too early to say, but suffice to say a certain anomaly has occurred which must be pursued as a matter of some urgency.'

'Good God, would you kindly get to the point! Whatever you have to say, just say it!'

'My apologies, Mr Lorimer; the last I wish to do is cause you any further distress. The victim was Steve Burrows, which of course won't mean anything to you, and his death is being treated as murder. The accident happened on Tuesday morning on the Ndola highway, twenty odd miles from Ekabe. He was on his way back from Ndola airport when he lost control of his vehicle, resulting in the fatal crash.'

'Yes?' Of course, there was more, instinctively, he knew he was not going to like what he was going to say next.

'Apparently, he had driven your son's wife to the airport; she was taking the domestic flight to Lusaka in order to connect with an Emirate's flight to Heathrow - '

' – if I can just stop you there; ' the implications of what he had just said hitting him with such force he immediately felt a quickening in his heartbeat, beads of perspiration forming between his shoulder blades, but with a presence of mind which surprised him, he took a deep breath, silently counting to six, before exhaling.

'Mr Lorimer,' the chief inspector's voice sounding inordinately loud, 'are you alright?'

'Yes, yes, I'm fine,' taking another measured breath before continuing, 'presumably, Chief Inspector, there was some relevance in you mentioning my daughter-in-law in a murder investigation. You did say the police were treating this man's death as murder, didn't you?'

'I did, yes; the evidence was found to be irrefutable.'

'And my daughter-in-law? Apart from being a passenger prior to the crash, where does she fit into all of this?'

'As in any murder investigation, it's crucial to speak to the last person to see or speak to the victim and this one is no exception.'

'Of course, I realise that, although I can't imagine she would have anything all that helpful to give them; he was only giving her a lift to the airport. It sounds to me she had a lucky escape, he could have crashed on the way there. How did it happen anyway, chief inspector, you haven't said.'

'Someone had lodged a plastic bottle beneath the brake pedal, Mr Lorimer, which could only have been done from the time he arrived at the airport, less than eight minutes or so, long enough for him to off-load Mrs Lorimer's luggage onto a trolley and make his way back to Ekabe. The crash site was only a mile away.' he added.

'Good God! And you suspect Valerie!'

'The Zambian government are no longer involved in the investigation; it's now with New Scotland Yard, with whom we'll be liaising. Contact still has to be made with Mrs Lorimer who, as far as we know is in London.'

'Hearing Valerie's name linked in any way, however innocent it may be, with a murder investigation is shocking. I believe I can speak for the other members of my family in telling you that we had no idea she was planning to return, especially when Alan's fate is very much in the balance and as far as I'm aware she hasn't been in touch with us; in fact, the last time she phoned home was to tell us there had been a break-in at their bungalow and his subsequent disappearance.'

'Yes, that's what Callum said when we spoke last evening.'

'Ah, Callum and his apparent poor memory, but why did you call him?'

'I really wanted to talk to you, sir, but he did promise to try and phone Valerie for us.'

'How exactly? Presumably, she would already have arrived in Britain by then and I don't believe either Alan or she owned a mobile phone.'

'According to Callum, she did have one; he was going to look for the number and try to get hold of her.'

'I see.' and he did see, all too damn well. *Was there no end to the deviousness of his oldest son? It would seem not.* 'And that is what you meant when you explained earlier about following up on your call yesterday. Hmm?'

'That's right. It is important to make contact with her, Mr Lorimer.'

'I am sure it is, Chief Inspector, but my main concern is for Alan, and I intend to go to any lengths to ensure every effort is made to find him. Quite frankly, callous though it may sound, I have no interest in the unfortunate murder of a man until only very recently I had never heard of.'

It was a relief when they brought the call to a close. As disturbing as the latest news had been, the way he was feeling as he replaced the receiver was nothing compared to his anger with Callum. Twice he had neglected to pass on phone messages; the first time he could in all fairness excuse as forgetfulness, but not the second time. Callum had deliberately taken it upon himself to withhold crucial information, information which could, once the media got their hands on it, rapidly reduce their credibility, not only in the home market, but internationally.

'Graham.'

Kirstie spoke so softly he had forgotten she was still in the office, her voice startling him for moment.

'I expect you got the gist of all that?' he asked her.

'Some of it.' she smiled sympathetically, reminding him for the hundredth time what an excellent secretary she was. In all the years she'd worked for him, he had never known her to flounder. Kirstie was loyal, and self-effacing to the point of shyness, but there had been times when she had surprised him by showing a genuine open concern towards a member of staff going through a bad patch, even on one occasion years ago patiently listening to Bruce in the wake of a broken romance.

'I'll organize some fresh coffee and then, if you feel up to filling in the gaps and, provided we don't have any interruptions, we can try to make some sort of sense from what sounds like another crisis.' she said.

\*\*\*

It was almost midday and Graham had still not seen Callum. The need to talk to him had become more urgent, unable to shrug off the impression that he was avoiding him, but perhaps he was being paranoid: Callum hadn't been in his office all morning, Myra hadn't seen him since breakfast and when he'd asked Alison if she knew where he was, all she could tell him was that he'd been in briefly around nine and then hurried out about an hour later saying he was late for an appointment in town. Conveniently not saying which town. More nails in his coffin, Graham muttered to himself, deciding instead to have an impromptu meeting with Bruce about a forthcoming visit of French horticulturists and eventually found him on the mezzanine floor with a selection of printer's proofs fanned out on the table in front of him.

'I take it these are for the winter brochure,' Graham said, picking up one of them and examining it closely, 'happy with them?'

'They're fine; should impress our friends from across the channel.'

'Good.'

'I was hoping to catch you earlier, Dad, but Alison said you were on an outside call, so I thought I'd get on with sorting these out and hopefully catch you before lunch.'

'Anything in particular, Bruce?'

'Well, yes; all a bit worrying actually, but thought you should know, that is if you don't already.'

'Yes?' *Why was he getting the distinct impression that this day was not going to improve?* metaphorically bracing himself for the next revelation.

'You've met my friend Peter Old, haven't you?'

'Yes, a couple of years ago; he's a lawyer, isn't he?'

'That's right, corporate law. Well, he was in London this week and met up with an old university friend of his, James Hathaway, he has a law practice there and – er, this is where it all sounds a bit, well, odd - '

' – go on, Bruce, I believe I know where you could be coming from.'

'It concerns Valerie.'

'I thought it might.'

'She arrived back in London yesterday morning and had an appointment to see James.'

'Presumably, he won't have told Peter the reason.'

'No, the confidentiality thing of course, but you don't appear to be all that surprised; did you know she was back?'

'Not until the chief inspector's call earlier this morning, but as for her wanting to consult with a lawyer, there could be two reasons for that.'

'Two?'

'With all this uncertainty over Alan, she could very well be wanting to establish how she stands; legally, I mean, especially as we knew there was a divorce pending.'

'Could be the case, a bit mercenary though, wouldn't you say?'

'Hmmph.'

'You mentioned two reasons, Dad.'

'Having listened to what the chief inspector had to say, Bruce, it sounds very much as if Valerie is in urgent need of some strong legal advice.' going on to tell him the seriousness of his daughter-in-law's situation. Bruce didn't interrupt, but Graham could tell by his shocked expression, how deeply he was affected.

'How absolutely awful! Does she not realise that the police in this country would want to speak to her; for God's sake, dad, what a bloody mess!'

'Did you know that Callum had her mobile number?'

'I wasn't even aware Valerie had a mobile; Alan certainly hasn't; I know that for sure. But who was this guy Steve Burrows? And how sure are they about what caused him to lose control of his vehicle.'

'I don't believe there's any doubt about that.'

'And they – ' stumbling over the words, ' – they're suggestion that Valerie – that she's responsible?'

'Not in so many words, Bruce, but the implication is there all the same - '

' – but they urgently want to get in touch with her.' finishing for him, 'And was Callum able to contact her I wonder.'

'As to that, Bruce, I have no idea. Callum has become very much a law unto himself recently. However, you may be interested to hear that I've invited Alan's friend, Cora Hamilton for the weekend.'

'Really?'

'You look surprised.'

'Well, I suppose I am; Myra told me that she'd been in touch; said she was finding it difficult to accept what everyone appears to be saying about Alan's disappearance.'

'What do you think, Bruce; I haven't asked you before?'

'Honestly, Dad, I don't know what to think. It's so damn far away, it isn't as if the investigation is being handled by our own police force.'

'Exactly and that's why I thought something could be achieved by talking to this young woman; she has just returned from spending three months in Ekabe; she's familiar with the life out there, the terrain and the general attitude of the people, not forgetting the expatriate community of course.'

'I believe I know where you're coming from; you're hoping to have a kind of brainstorming, perhaps gather any facts together, that sort of thing.'

'That's precisely what we're hoping to achieve; it would be another angle, Bruce and if we go about it the right way, tactfully I mean, someone in authority might be sufficiently interested in doing something more than they have done up to now in finding Alan.'

# Chapter Seventeen

Although she didn't lose consciousness, Cora's memory, from when she fell to being helped by a paramedic into the ambulance, was hazy and when she tried to remember, her head hurt. She had been reluctant to being taken to hospital but had meekly agreed realising it made sense and knowing that as her accident had resulted in an ambulance being called out she would be expected to explain how it had happened. There was no doubt in her mind that she had been pushed. Deliberately, and not by some young tourist rushing past her to reach the lights before they changed, but she had no proof.

By the time she had been attended to in A&E at the University College Hospital in Euston Road and having to wait for the results of the x-rays and blood tests, it was midday. She had managed to phone the LSE while she was waiting, and as she had started to explain to Paula, the full realisation of what might have happened suddenly hit her, Paula's genuine concern bringing her close to tears. Somehow, she managed to reassure her that she was fine, but intended to take it easy for the rest of the week and that she'd see her on Monday.

She hailed a black cab outside the hospital to take her home, but by then she had already made up her mind she had no intention of spending the night there; every instinct was telling her that Valerie was determined to get rid of her: crude, she knew, but could think of no other way of describing what the woman was up to. Valerie obviously considered her a threat, possibly a reaction to Alan's decision to start divorce proceedings. It was pure guesswork, also she had no way of knowing how her mind was working now that he was still missing. Of course she must have been outside her building earlier when she had left for work, probably hiding among the trees as she'd done the night before; when she'd seen the dozen or so students approaching she had merged with them as they hurried towards the lights, and once they'd reached the edge of the pavement, had moved forward and pushed her. Cora could still feel the pressure of her hand on her back.

There was no way, Cora decided, she was going to place herself in such a vulnerable position again. She would take an earlier train up north, spend the night in Edinburgh and as Alan's father had said he would arrange for someone to meet her, she could call him from the hotel in the morning. Once she was with him, she would tell him exactly what Valerie had been up to since she first spotted her the day before. Intuitively, she felt that he would know what to do.

She was reluctant to spend more time than was necessary in the flat. What had happened out there in the street in full view of everyone and being so certain in the knowledge of who had caused it, had frightened her, proving how desperate the woman must be, also to what lengths she was prepared to go.

There was a train leaving Euston for Edinburgh at two-thirty and after paying for it online, rang her local taxi firm asking to be picked up in fifteen minutes. She had intentionally only allowed herself such a short time to pack a bag with all she was likely to need for the weekend, but the certainty of Valerie Lorimer returning was too strong to ignore. At least, once she was in the station she would have the anonymity of being one of presumably hundreds of others milling around the concourse.

Danny, her usual driver, pulled up outside the building at exactly quarter past one, raising his eyebrows to find her already outside on the pavement waiting for him, but he didn't say anything, no doubt thinking she was leaving it fine to catch her train. If he but knew, Cora thought wryly, fastening her seat belt. How dramatically her life had changed in a matter of days: she'd had no premonition when she had returned home from Ekabe, buoyant with the plans she and Alan had been making, that those hopes would be so quickly dashed with the desperate worry over his safety and now her own life being threatened.

When Danny drew up at the lights at the end of the Gardens, she couldn't resist turning round and looking out of the rear window and then instantly wishing she hadn't. Valerie was walking past "Gino's", too far away to see her features, but the light-coloured coat and the brilliant blue scarf were enough to convince her. Had Valerie seen her? It had only taken them three or four minutes to reach the lights; she may have done. Cora had been so intent on climbing into the taxi she had forgotten to look out for her. How the hell could she be so remiss? *Admit it, Cora, you let your guard down. Only for minutes, but more than likely quite long enough!* By now, they were approaching another set of lights at the junction to Euston Road and would soon be at the station. Unless Valerie Lorimer was a mind-reader, she had no way of knowing where she was going. Even if she had spotted her travel bag, she could only make a guess, and that is all it would be; even if by some fluke she did take it into her head to assume she was heading for Euston, what could she do in a packed station? Could she really afford to show her hand? Up to now, apart from joining the bus queue yesterday, she hadn't drawn attention to herself.

The number of the platform for the Edinburgh train was already up on the display board and relieved she could go through the barrier to her train straight away, she pulled her mobile from her bag to show the ticket to the guard. In less than twenty minutes they would be on their way and as she settled into her seat, Cora reassured herself of the unlikelihood of Valerie being on the train, incongruously reminded of Agatha Christie's 'Death on the Nile' when against all probability the scheming Jackie de Bellefort made her surprise appearance at the pyramids, but Valerie Lorimer was no Jackie de Bellefort, and she refused to accept the role of the unfortunate Linnet Ridgeway. *All the more reason to keep out of her way then, Cora!* her inner voice needlessly reminded her.

∗∗∗

Adrian Roberts put a call through to Alistair Dale shortly before midday on Thursday which he hoped would kick-start the final stages of one of their most intricate drug investigations and which, to his frustration, had been proving sluggish for far too long.

'I can't help thinking, sir,' Alistair said, 'there's a certain irony in the fact that you have been able to access the information on Ben Maitland's intentions to terminate his leasing arrangements when it has been right on our doorstep. If you know what I mean.'

'I certainly do;' he chuckled, 'mind you, we wouldn't have been able to without another of our people being stuck in the harbour authorities' general office for these last few weeks, so there you have it, Alistair: Ben Maitland's berthing lease for his state of the art cabin cruiser expires at midnight, therefore we can safely say that the packages will be handed over sometime this evening prior to him clearing the harbour gates by then.'

'Do we have any part to play, sir?'

'Not especially, Alistair; this is Interpol's case; therefore the onus is on us to get it right, ergo, the buck stops with us! We will be employing two factions, one at the harbour to oversee the meeting between Maitland and his contact, namely Callum Lorimer, when the handover takes place. Once this has been done, he will be followed back to Ashburn House from where the second faction will pick up. We will already have officers in place in the grounds waiting until he emerges from his car and is witnessed with the package before they apprehend and charge him with the possession of drugs. Provided everything goes as planned, more comprehensive charges will be made once we have him safely in custody.'

'Do you envisage any problems, sir?'

'There will always be something unsuspecting turning up and for that reason we've kept our strategy relatively flexible. We're working on what we know, solid facts if you like, Alistair; Maitland has been holding that last consignment of drugs for well over a week now and he won't want that situation to continue for much longer. He will be aware that the only reason we haven't pulled him in is because our current priority is Lorimer and once that's accomplished at least we will have put a curb on the syndicate's link to Europe. As for any possible leakage of tonight's operation, I would say the risk, because of the short notice, is minimal. It's crucial that Callum Lorimer does not become aware he's being followed, but my officers are highly trained in surveillance; they're expert in being invisible.'

'Will you be intercepting Ben Maitland?'

'It's not on our agenda, but we're flexible. We will of course continue to monitor his movements. If he thinks once he's left the harbour unscathed, he may become careless and start to believe he really is untouchable, but again we remain open to any change which would bring him in sooner.'

'This news is going to be a blow to the Lorimer family.' Alistair said, 'especially the father; he's quite a fiery character and has made his views of how he believes the police are not doing enough to find Alan out in Zambia, I can well imagine how he's going to react when he hears about his other son.'

'And his daughter-in-law, Valerie Lorimer; has she turned up yet?'

'No, she hasn't. I've spoken to Callum Lorimer and he grudgingly admitted he had a mobile number for her somewhere; this was after I'd told him about the accident in Ekabe and that she was back in the UK. He promised to try and contact her, but I don't know whether he did; he didn't appear too concerned.'

'Families, eh.'

'Exactly.'

'She was traced to the Royal National hotel in Bloomsbury apparently, but I expect the met are keeping you informed, Alistair.'

'They are, yes, but I've since heard she's no longer there.'

'Obviously playing us.'

'I think so, but she's not going to find it easy to leave the country; not too bright of her to come back when she did; she must have realised she would be an obvious suspect for Steve Burrows' death. Incidentally, the Zambian authorities have released his body and it's being repatriated to London this week.'

'Whether the Lorimers like it or not,' Adrian pointed out, 'they are involved in what has metamorphosed into what has the makings of a unique octopus-like investigation.'

***

Valerie had just turned the corner into Taverstock Square when she saw Cora Hamilton emerge from her apartment building to the taxi waiting at the kerbside, not failing to notice the small travel bag she had with her. *Where the hell was she off to? By rights, she should not still be in the land of the living.* Valerie had been so certain she'd had the timing right: the lights had been mere seconds from changing to red at the exact moment when she had stepped nearer and given her the push which had instantly propelled her forward right in the path of the approaching traffic. She had seen her fall, accompanied by shrill screams from the group of youngsters at the edge of the pavement, but she hadn't waited; instead, she had turned round and walked back the way she had come, along Taverstock Square and, in what seemed only minutes, the frantic sounds of an ambulance could be heard, the pitch of the siren changing as it grew closer.

Valerie's knowledge of London beyond the West End and the Strand with Nelson's Column acting as a permanent tourist's compass point, she couldn't even make a guess to which hospital they would have taken her. And, as when she'd left Steve outside Ndola airport, she had accepted she would have to wait until news of the outcome reached her. There had been a certain irony that this had come from Callum, her brother-in-law. She had completely forgotten that he had her mobile number, and couldn't even remember when, or why, she had given it to him. All good reason, she decided, to dispose of the thing, having some vague idea that she could be traceable.

Her instincts were telling her it wasn't all that clever to remain in the same area, but she wasn't finished yet. She had set herself the task of dealing with Cora Henderson and she was determined to follow it through, but how she was going to do this she had no idea, watching now as the taxi pulled away from the traffic lights at the end of Taverstock Square. That bag she was carrying; did it mean she was going away somewhere? Perhaps her experience earlier had shaken her, made her nervous to be on her own in the flat, which it very well could have done if she suspected it was no accident. Also, late last night, Valerie had seen her at the window; whether she had recognised her was another thing, but she may have done. *Face facts, Val, the bird has flown. You haven't a damn clue where she's off to, so what do you do next, eh?'*

It was seldom Valerie was wrong-footed, but she had to accept, unpalatable though it was, that her plan had not worked; it had never occurred to her that Cora would take it into her head to leave. She couldn't stay away indefinitely, but there was no way she could hang around until she turned up. Also, there had been a flickering of unease with her since she arrived at the airport yesterday and one she knew she shouldn't continue to ignore. At first, it had only been a feeling of being watched as she had pushed her way through the crowd by the barrier in arrivals, but it had been impossible to pinpoint anyone who appeared to be looking directly at her and had decided it would be more likely to be her imagination: it had been a long flight and she had hardly slept, her over-active brain refusing to shut down and give her the respite she needed before she tackled the next hurdle she had set herself to achieve what she believed rightly belonged to her. The recuperative effect of the coffee and the sweetness of the *pain au chocolat* at the Nero café had been more or less instant, in that any notion she may have had that the Zambian authorities would have organized a reception party so soon for her, was extreme. She had allowed the mental images of being actively sought by a police force in a country more than seven thousand mils away to hallucinate. *How far-fetched can you get, Valerie? Who the hell do you think you are, a female James Bond!*

Valerie had been approaching the interterminal walkway when she realised her so-called pep talk was way off-beam. She *was* being followed. There was little consolation that her instinct for survival had been right; she had to think quickly and, stepping on to the walkway, she turned round slightly, casually, affecting an interest in her surroundings. There were several people behind her, the first two or three apparently anxious to get ahead, stepped out to the left to go past, leaving the man immediately behind her, a large leather-zipped travel bag slung over his shoulder and absorbed in flicking through his mobile phone and a couple of women further back, she didn't think they were together; neither of them had any luggage, one with a suede shoulder bag and the other what looked like a laptop case. It could be any of them, there was no way of knowing, but Valerie's sixth sense was telling her that she was being followed. By the time she had reached the taxi rank at the entrance to the other terminal for the Edinburgh flight, only the two women remained, not together as she had reckoned, but now quite close to her as she finally reached the head of the queue. Once inside the taxi, she leaned forward in her seat and asked the driver to take her instead to the Royal National Hotel.

The hotel lobby had been packed; a coachload of Italian tourists having arrived only seconds before had provided her with exactly what she wanted: a long wait before it would be her turn to check-in, reasoning that it was unlikely the woman with the suede handbag, who had that moment appeared in the open doorway surveying the mass of overseas visitors with their bags and cases taking up even more space on the lobby floor, would be prepared to wait. Presumably she had accomplished what she had intended, whether following instructions or for some other reason. Valerie hadn't been too bothered, confident that she would be able to give her the slip which she had; in less than ten minutes, having made sure there was no-one around showing her the slightest interest, certainly no-one with a suede handbag, she had stepped away from the queue, back to the door, and walking round the corner of Bedford Way checked-in at the Tavistock Hotel, taking the added precaution of using her maiden name.

Secure though she may feel for the present, this did not alter the fact that at this precise moment as she watched the taxi bearing Cora Henderson off to God knows where, she was stymied. But perhaps not. Why take a taxi? She lived and worked in London. Russell Square tube station was a five-minute walk away, the bus route even less, taxis were more expensive and given the density of the city's traffic, not necessarily quicker. *People take taxis to stations, Val, especially if they have luggage, less hassle. Alright, she only had one small bag. So, what!*

Could she be going to Euston; it was practically in a straight line from where the taxi had stopped at the lights at the end of Bedford Way? Pure guesswork, she admitted, but the more she thought about it, the more likely it seemed. Thursday afternoon, the weekend approaching, trains up north left from Euston and Cora Henderson was Scottish: at least with a surname like that she must be, therefore, what more likely she had family up there. By simple logic she had arrived at a very probable answer; her scare this morning had caused her to run home to them.

The question now was, how could she take advantage of this unexpected scenario, having convinced herself in a matter of minutes that she was right. Cora's flat would, presumably be empty. She had to find a way of gaining access. Provided there wasn't an alarm system, she didn't believe it would be impossible. Years ago, she had learned, through sheer necessity, how to pick a lock; chances were, the door to Cora's flat would have a simple one, the occupants relying on a more substantial locking system for the main door of the building. And, her mind racing ahead with possibilities, once she was inside, she could come up with a foolproof plan of how to deal with her for once and for all.

***

Cora emerged from Waverley Station at eight-fifteen in the evening, her train had been on time and she had surprised herself by sleeping for most of the journey north, deciding it must be the after-effects of, not only from the accident earlier that day, but the succession of incidents leading up to that almost fatal push. She found it difficult to believe that she could be the target of someone's hatred to such an extent. The very thought sent shivers down her spine. How she longed for this nightmare to end. In spite of the silence of hearing nothing further about Alan, she was still refusing to accept the worse: that he would never be found, that she would never know. She would phone Kate. It wasn't as if she expected her to tell her anything that she didn't know already, but merely to talk to someone who was actually there might, just might, give her some comfort, therefore she decided, as soon as she'd booked into the hotel she'd call her.

The Old Waverley Hotel, only a five-minute walk away in Princes Street was one she had often stayed in whenever she came to Edinburgh and as she had hoped, walking through the ancient double doors into the impressive reception area, they had a room for her on the second floor overlooking the gardens. Slipping off her jacket, she took her mobile from her bag and dialled Kate's number. Zambia was only one hour ahead, not too late she decided,

'Hello.'

'Kate! It's me, Cora – '

'Cora – Oh, you've heard then - '

She was positive that at that precise moment her heart skipped a beat, perhaps more than one, as hazy images flashed through her brain, robbing her of speech.

' – are you still there?'

'Yes,' she managed, scarcely recognizing her own voice, 'they've found Alan.'

'Oh, Cora, no, it's not Alan; it's Steve - '

'Steve?'

She listened without interrupting even if she had known what to say or how to express her sympathy, while Kate told her about Steve's accident and how the police were treating his death as suspicious, but when she mentioned Valerie's name and that she had been the last person to have been with him shortly before the crash, she felt her concentration going as she considered the implications. There was so much she wanted to ask her, but how could she? Kate was her friend, the least she could do was to show some genuine concern for what she must be going through and not bombard her with questions she very likely didn't know the answers.

'Kate,' she said at last, 'this is all so shocking, I don't know what to say.'

'There's nothing much anyone can say, actually,' sounding remarkably calm, but then Cora wondered, how did she expect her to sound. Presumably, the initial shock when she had first heard would have worn off by now and knowing

Kate as she did, she suspected she would be concentrating on practicalities.

'But how are you feeling, really?'

'I'm fine now; at first when I heard, I guess I was – well numb; I couldn't believe what I was being told.'

'Natural, I suppose. Will you be able to leave the country or do you have to be there for the inquest?

'I can leave at any time and because of the circumstances surrounding Steve's death, the inquest will be held in the UK, London actually.'

'I don't understand.'

'The Zambian authorities won't be handling the investigation, Cora; it's in the hands of the British police.'

'Isn't that unusual, not that I have any idea of how these matters are dealt with -'

'I don't either; they don't tell me much.'

'It all sounds so – '

' – sinister?'

'Well, yes. You are coping, aren't you; if there is any way I can help once you're back in London, you will keep in touch, won't you?'

'Of course I will and Cora, I realise you haven't liked to mention Alan, but there's been no news about him for days now. You won't lose hope will you?'

'No, I won't lose hope.' and with much remaining unsaid, they brought the call to a close. The room felt strangely silent, even with the window open slightly the only sounds were muted; with Princes Street now pedestrianised any traffic she could hear would be over towards Haymarket and the occasional voices drifting up from the pavements below in the street. She needed company, she decided, also a large gin and tonic with loads of ice, slipping her mobile back into her bag, and making sure she had her room pass, made her way down to the lounge bar.

There had been many changes to the hotel's Abbotsford Room bar and lounge over the years, wondering idly as she stepped on to the velvety royal blue carpet what the guests in Victorian times would have made of the pale greys and egg-shell blues of the contemporary décor, but it definitely met with her approval; the understated luxury and tranquillity of the overall effect was charming and exactly what she needed. The room was large, high-ceilinged with tall sash windows overlooking the castle, floodlit and looking as imposing as ever against the dark sky. Many of the leather sofas and chairs were occupied with presumably after dinner guests, reminding her she hadn't eaten for hours, but she wasn't hungry; all she wanted to do was to relax over the gin and tonic the waiter was bringing over to her table, and attempt to make some sense from what Kate had told her. And there had to be a logical explanation. Hadn't there? Taking a long and appreciative sip of her drink she trawled back in her memory, trying to tease anything out which may have been an indication of what was to happen, a sort of premonition perhaps, but there was nothing: the last few weeks before she left Zambia, talk in the club had been mostly about their forthcoming play; she and Alan had been making their own plans for their future and conducting their affair as discreetly as possible and then when he had told her Valerie's extreme reaction over the divorce. Could that have acted as some sort of trigger? Could Valerie have been so incensed learning that her marriage was going to end, especially if she knew about her, to do something to prevent the divorce. From there, Cora's attempt to rationalize a possible progression of what could come next faltered, but if she wanted to come up with any answers, however painful it would be to bring Alan into her reasoning, she had to continue, to delve deeper.

The main question, then; had the break-in, the attack on Alan and his disappearance been instigated by Valerie? There was no doubt in her mind that she could be quite capable, but she could not have acted alone. Steve would, Cora felt sure remembering the pair of them outside the rugby club on the night before she left. If he had been responsible, to even consider this, made her feel quite nauseous, he must have had the incentive which Cora reckoned forcing herself to push further ahead, but it wasn't too difficult to work out: widowed, Valerie would presumably be a wealthy woman and doubly attractive to Steve Burrows. From what Cora had seen and heard about her in Ekabe, also her behaviour since arriving back in Britain, she had no doubts whatsoever about her ruthlessness. And the sooner the police caught up with her, the better.

As she sat, enjoying her drink and the murmur of her fellow guests as a pleasantly unobtrusive background, she didn't know how she felt about Steve Burrows, although as she continued to believe that Alan was still alive, she was putting off that final moment to apportion blame.

\*\*\*

Callum drove back to Ashworth House in a state of mild euphoria. There had been no police presence, either on the road to the harbour or concealed between the buildings neighbouring the gates trigger happy and ready to reveal themselves and make an instant arrest as Ben had handed over the bulky package of the all-important drugs to him. As usual, Ben had been right in dismissing his doubts as being groundless, reminding him in that patronising manner he had everything under control.

Soon, Callum thought, changing down gear to leave the A92 for the approach to the quieter road down towards the coast, the intensifying suspense for more than a week, ever since that letter from Alan had arrived, would be over and he could start to formulate his own plans and they didn't include carrying the burden of Ben Maitland's machinations. Callum had yet to tell him that tonight's consignment would be their last, but his main aim was to complete the whole transaction as speedily as possible. They'd had a good innings, a lucrative one for him personally, which would have continued for a further six months if Alan hadn't decided to cut short his overseas contract. Callum seldom indulged in retrospection considering it to be a pointless effort, but there had been moments these last few days when he regretted telling Ben of Alan's early return, seriously wondering now why he had felt it to be necessary, but he had panicked. He had misjudged Ben's reaction; naively, he had believed he would have agreed with him and cancelled the scheduled consignment, not his out and out refusal, demanding instead that Alan should be prevented from returning and as the incident in Ekabe took place within a matter of days they had presumably not been idle threats. And, then perversely, when he'd mentioned his concern over John Milne's apparent interest, unquestionably a bigger threat to them all, Ben's response had been one of dismissal.

Of course! The realisation that he had been played was a physical thing, alarmed at the way his knuckles had turned white in the light from the dashboard as he gripped the steering wheel, steeling himself for the waves of anger which began to course through his body. He had been manipulated. Ben had wanted him to deal with the problem. He had been subtle alright, so damn subtle it had taken him over a week to realise he had been bloody set up! And he, gullible fool that he was, had fallen head-first into the trap.

Callum drove the remaining few miles as though he was on autopilot, his main concern to rein in his wayward emotions, to appear his normal self when he saw Myra, the most observant of women; her scrutiny being more acute recently when she'd asked him more than once whether something was worrying him. If only she knew!

Using his pass card to activate the double gates to Ashburn House, he drove off to the right from the main building towards the annexe, parking close to the main door. He picked up the package from the passenger seat and stepped out on to the gravel driveway. As he did so, a wide arc of floodlight pin-pointed him rigid in its broad beam, followed instantly by a disembodied voice piercing the night's stillness:

"STAND EXACTLY WHERE YOU ARE, SIR."

Even if he had wanted to, Callum was incapable of moving. His limbs were paralysed, his breathing sounded ragged and harsh in the sudden silence.

*So, Callum, you idiot, this is it, the end. Was it bloody worth it?*

# Chapter Eighteen

<u>Friday 27th October: London</u>

*Déjà vu!* Is it possible, Valerie cynically reflected, for time to pull you back but for everyone else to continue, earnestly pursuing that next stage in life which is weirdly being denied to you. This was exactly how she felt and had done as soon as she had walked into terminal three's arrival hall, half-expecting to find herself pushing the wayward luggage trolley towards "Nero's", the aromatic scents of their freshly brewed coffee drifting out from their open door only strengthening the illusion.

She shouldn't be here. The decision had seemed perfectly logical yesterday, but definitely not now. Was it her imagination, but was there more of a police presence this morning? She wasn't sure, there did seem to be quite a lot of them, two of them especially, standing with their backs to the stream of passengers emerging from Customs Control, closely scrutinizing, not so much the moving volume of people emerging on to the concourse, but anyone, like herself, who had a reason to remain where they were: waiting to meet someone, or for whatever reason. But they couldn't be interested in her, why should they be? Even if Callum, in his panicky way, had told her that Calder Bay's chief inspector was eager to talk to her, she refused to read too much into the reasons behind why the police in the north of Scotland should be so keen to know where she was. Steve's demise occurred in Zambia, a foreign country and thousands of miles away, therefore she reasoned the onus was on them to solve the case.

*Brave words, Valerie! And you believe you will emerge unscathed, eh?*

Perhaps she should listen to her conscience, it was persistent enough, but from the moment she read the message on Cora Hamilton's answering machine her brain had veered in one direction, recklessly dismissing the consequences.

The green light on the machine had been flashing when she had, with surprising ease, gained entry into the building, and apart from some minor scratch marks on the door to her apartment when, putting into practice an almost forgotten skill, she had picked the lock, there were no other signs of anyone having forced their way inside. As far as the main door was concerned, she had waited across the road by the trees she'd sheltered under the night before until one of the other residents appeared. It had been well after four before someone stopped in front of the door, a studiously looking character focused entirely on his mobile while, with a free hand, keyed in the security code. She had been ready; within seconds of the door closing behind him, she had stepped forward and eased herself through the gap into the hall, certain he hadn't even noticed her.

She'd had no plan of what she intended to do once she was inside, but confident something potentially lethal would come to her, but whatever she decided on must be simple, certainly not contrived and it must look like an accident. A faulty hairdryer? A slippery shower mat? An adjustment to the water thermostat? But, first, that flashing light. Whoever had left her a message could be useful Valerie thought as she had pressed the play button.

"Darling, it's me. I'm on my way back and should be arriving at Heathrow tomorrow morning at seven-twenty-five on the Qatar flight, that's Friday in case you didn't read this message earlier. I can't say too much on the phone, except that I love you."

My God!

The shock of hearing his voice was immense. He was still alive! Steve hadn't been lying after all! Not that it mattered; her problem remained. If anything, it had become more imminent, the only difference being she would now have to change her strategy; it would be risky but then if it worked, the end result could be even more effective. She had several hours of a head start, doing a quick mental calculation, reckoning he would be airborne for another fifteen hours or so before he arrived at Heathrow and she would be there, the plan already formulating on how she would tackle the situation, and one which would leave Alan in no doubt that his lady friend had finished with him, accepting it needed considerable fine tuning, but she would get it right. Of course she would.

Now she was here and about to check the arrival time of the Qatar flights from Lusaka she was beginning to have doubts. The two police officers who hadn't changed their position, bothered her. They bothered her a lot. Walking up closer to the monitors, scrolling down the list of that morning's early arrivals, she stifled a groan seeing that the Lusaka flight was delayed. That was all it said: delayed. *Damn! Damn!* She could try to find out more, but she didn't want to make herself conspicuous, uncomfortably aware she was doing just that, but unsure whether to move away, over to the café; she remembered there were mini monitors inside; at least she wouldn't have to remain in the centre of the concourse with the risk of drawing attention to herself, regretting once again coming here. Coffee, and a strong one, she decided, making to walk across to the café.

She had almost reached the glass door of Nero's when she felt rather than saw the two officers walking alongside her.

'Mrs Valerie Lorimer?' one of them asked her, placing a hand lightly on her forearm.

\*\*\*

'What you've just told me, Bruce is dreadful. How is your father taking the news?'

'He's surprisingly calm, actually,' Bruce Lorimer supressed a chuckle as he negotiated the roundabout before joining the M90, 'pretty mad with Callum of course, but then their relationship has always been a rocky one.'

'Once the news leaks out and the media get hold of it, he's going to find the situation difficult though, isn't he?'

'Probably,' giving his shoulders a shrug, 'but the old man's a pragmatic kind of guy, Cora, and it isn't as though he hasn't had a tasting of how they operate since Alan's disappearance.'

'I suppose,' but she was doubtful, 'but I would have thought this business with Callum has considerably more news value.'

'True, but at least we'll have a breathing space for a couple of days. I know one journalist who must be kicking her heels today.'

'You mean Beverly Gray?'

'Who else; the woman is ruthless. Have you read her column in today's "Times"?'

'No, I've intentionally kept away from the newspapers this morning; why, did she have anything significant to report?'

'Nothing that we didn't know already: Valerie's connection to this guy, Steve Burrows out in Zambia and that she was back here.'

'As you say, nothing we weren't aware of,' reluctant to discuss Valerie with him, wanting to wait until she was with the family, 'Are you sure your father is still okay about me being here; I don't want to intrude.' she asked in an attempt to change the subject, one that she still found upsetting.

'Don't worry, Cora, the old man was insistent.'

'Oh, well, then.' not knowing what to say, still reeling from the news about Callum and what it must mean to the family, also to their business; that one of their directors had been arrested for receiving and distributing drugs would without any doubt be viewed as a scandal and would inevitably damage their reputation.

'It's almost as if he half-expected something like this to happen.'

'Why do you say that?' turning slightly to look at him, noticing for the first time the similarity between his profile and Alan's: the same high forehead and the sculptured jawline. She was finding him easy to talk to; like Alan there was no side to him and she suspected, again like Alan, he had the same laid-back attitude towards life. She hoped he was right about his father still wanting to see her, but a bit late to start having doubts now; in less than an hour they would be arriving at Ashburn House, and presumably she would become immersed in another of this family's dramas.

'Hard to explain, but he's been acting strangely for a couple of weeks recently, around about the time Alan went missing, as though his mind was elsewhere; mind you, he is inclined to play his cards pretty close to his chest and no doubt he'll enlighten us when he's good and ready!'

'And not before.' she smiled, understanding what he meant. She had yet to meet their father, but the way Bruce described him, matched the impressions she had already gleaned from their brief conversation.

They had left the motorway and were now on the A9, signposted she was heartened to see for the coast when Bruce suggested they stop at the old spa town of Bridge of Allan. There was limited street parking outside the Allan Water Café but he managed to manoeuvre the Mazda Sports into the space immediately in front of the café.

'This place brings back happy memories,' Bruce said, opening the café door and gesturing for her to go in before him, 'my mother would always stop here on our way home from picking me up from school, my biggest decision being whether to have a strawberry milkshake or a raspberry one!'

'And that was a treat?'

'Very much so; milkshakes were definitely not on the school's menu.'

'Like me, it sounds as if you were also a boarder.'

'Yes, that's right, so you can probably sympathise then.'

Bruce was easy to talk to and for the first time in days she found herself relaxing, it wasn't that she was less worried about Alan, but being with his brother and the prospect of soon meeting the other members of his family, made her feel she wasn't on her own.

They took their time over their coffee, as if by some silent agreement they were prolonging that moment when talk wouldn't be an option and they would become embroiled in the aftermath of Callum's arrest becoming public property, which by now she reckoned, given the size of Calder Bay, would be the main topic of conversation. But, as they finally reached the gates to Ashburn House, she realised with dismay that the situation was far worse.

'Christ,' Bruce swore, 'the vultures have arrived!'

There must have been at least twenty of them: reporters and cameramen, the latter encumbered by their equipment, the trailing leads stretched across the narrow road to the television and film vehicles parked lopsidedly along the grass verge and all of them moving forward en masse as Bruce pulled up in front of the gates, but he was too quick for them; within seconds of keying in the code they were through and driving up the long driveway towards the house,

'So many of them,' Cora sighed, 'somewhat overwhelming.'

'I suppose it's to be expected,' pulling a face, 'but there's nothing we can do; just put up with them.'

'News is a big business now though, isn't it; not merely from the newspapers and the tv and radio announcements at regular times during the day, but the constant stuff being poured out on the internet.'

'I know, and most of them way off the bloody mark. Anyway, Cora, here we are, the family pile.'

'And quite an attractive pile it is, too.' she smiled encouragingly, sensing his buoyant mood up to now was on the wane.

Wide shallow stone steps led up to the main door, solid mahogany with a stained-glass fanlight and flanked by slender stone pillars, and as she stepped out of the car they were flung open.

'Cora,' a tall, slim woman in jeans and a light blue polo-necked sweater emerged from the dim interior and walked down the steps to greet her, 'welcome to Ashburn House. I'm Myra,' she added, linking her arm with hers, 'and I'm so glad you're here.'

'Myra. What a dreadful time this is for you and the family.'

'Tell me about it! But, come on in, there's some freshly brewed coffee, unless you'd like something stronger.'

'Coffee would be lovely.' following her up the steps and into a large square hall, wood-panelled with a sweeping staircase leading up to a minstrel's gallery. Myra pushed open a door on their left: high-ceilinged, more wood-panelling, but what would otherwise have been a somewhat oppressive and rather formal dining-room was instantly transformed by the exquisite view from the two sets of French windows opening out on to a tiled terrace: an immaculate lawn edged with late flowering rose bushes, their full blooms a fusion of peachy-pink through to deep orange; a hiatus of colour which she found quite lovely. Cups and saucers had already been laid outside on the rattan glass-topped table, together with a stoneware cafetière in a deep teel colour which she had only ever seen in France. The setting was so perfect it was hard to believe that here was a family who had only very recently received news which must have been devastating. And Myra? Either she was an excellent actress adept at hiding her emotions or the arrest of her husband hadn't been an entirely unexpected one. Time would tell she thought, taking a seat in one of the rattan chairs, and wondering when Mr Lorimer would be making his appearance. She couldn't help feeling nervous; it was all very well for Bruce trying to convince her that his father was insistent she should still come here this weekend, but she wasn't sure. Bruce, she had been quick to notice, hadn't joined them, making what sounded to her a trumped-up excuse of having a mound of paperwork to tackle.

'How is your father-in-law, Myra; I will quite understand if he doesn't feel up to meeting me just yet.' she asked her, waiting until they had almost finished their coffee, but wanting to know exactly how she stood, being virtually thrust into the centre of such a family drama.

'Oh, but he does, Cora, very much. We'll see him later this afternoon, I'm sure; he and Kirstie, that's his secretary, have been in his office since early this morning dealing with a mass of calls as I expect you can imagine. Also, the chief inspector was here again first thing, but to answer your question; he is fine and bearing up extremely well, but then not only is he a strong character, but he is extraordinarily resilient.'

'That's the impression I got when I spoke to him on the phone yesterday, especially concerning his very positive feelings about Alan.'

'I know, I just pray he's not heading for a dreadful disappointment – sorry, Cora, that was tactless of me.'

'You don't need to apologise, honestly; my optimism feels as though it's on a rollercoaster: one minute I'm full of hope and the next, well - '

' – and now with this latest news from Ekabe about the murder of one of his neighbours.'

'Steve Burrows, yes.'

'You would have known him, I expect.'

'Not really, but Kate, his wife, is a very good friend of mine; it was she who told me about his death actually. 'I'd phoned her last night in the hope she'd heard anything further about the search for Alan.'

'Oh, dear, that must have been a shock for you, did she say mention Valerie?'

'Only that according to the police, she had been the last person to see him before the crash, but from how Kate was speaking, it sounded as though they weren't being all that forthcoming, except that the case isn't being handled in Zambia, but by our police here.'

'We already knew that the police want to talk to Valerie, but so far they haven't been able to find her, although she is back in the UK.'

'I've actually seen her, Myra, but not to talk to.'

'Really! When was this?'

'The first time was on Wednesday afternoon; I realise this is all going to sound – well, odd really - ,' hesitating, not quite sure how much to tell her; Valerie was her sister-in-law after all and she had no idea how friendly the two women were, ' – but,' trying to pick up from where she left off, 'but, it was as if she had suddenly appeared,' and going on to explain the unease she had felt from when Valerie had got off the same bus in Bedford Place, right up to yesterday morning when she was certain she had pushed her into the road at the traffic lights.

'Oh, my God;' her hand instinctively going up to her mouth, 'she was stalking you! And then - ' stumbling as she attempted to put her words together, 'she – she tried – to kill you!'

'Fortunately, she didn't succeed; someone called for an ambulance and I must admit it was all a bit of a blur for a while, but they checked me out at the hospital and allowed me to go home.'

'Surely you must have been in shock, and on your own too, how awful. What can I say Cora?'

'There's nothing anyone can say really, but the incident frightened me, Myra, wondering if she was going to make another attempt.'

'Of course, so was that why you came up here a day earlier; I did wonder why you'd spent the night in Edinburgh.'

'I was panicking.'

'You should have called us, Cora.'

'I'm here now.' she said, attempting to lighten the mood, 'you all have enough to worry about and the last I want to do is bring you even more aggro.'

'Do you know,' she smiled ruefully, 'I'm too wound up in trying my damnedest to channel the anger I have towards Callum, so much so I am incapable of articulating the extent of the damage he has inflicted on the family, therefore I feel I can give myself *carte blanche* to call Valerie a few choice names!'

'Ah, you're out here;' Bruce called to them from the dining-room, 'is that coffee still drinkable or will I be forced into having a real drink?'

'It's probably cold by now,' testing the side of the cafetiere with the back of her hand, 'but I wouldn't say no to a *real* drink, what about you, Cora? We deserve something a bit stronger than Brazil's best!'

\*\*\*

London

It felt strange to be back; only eighteen months, but much had happened in those months and definitely not all of it good, the last ten days or so had been especially frustrating, also that moment which seemed a lifetime away, when he'd confronted Valerie about the divorce; her reaction, although not all that surprising, had been unpleasant, especially the way she had verbally abused Cora, thank God not to her face; Cora had been spared that. He was longing to see her again and couldn't begin to imagine what she must be thinking by now, hearing nothing about him, not knowing whether he was alive or not. As soon as the plane touched down at Heathrow and he'd collected his bags from the carousel and, following the steady stream of other passengers through customs and on into the main concourse, he'd switched on his mobile and dialled her number. He had been so sure he would catch her before she left for work; the disappointment, as when he'd tried to call her from Lusaka airport, getting only her answer phone, was acute, but he didn't leave any message this time, confident he would be catching up with her later in the day.

First, he decided making his way towards the exit and the taxi rank, he needed to off-load his luggage somewhere, the most obvious being to book into a hotel close to where Cora lived, and clicking on to Google, scrolled down those listed in the Bloomsbury area. He spotted the Taverstock Hotel, recalling that Cora had told him her apartment was across the road from Taverstock Gardens, and convinced he couldn't do better, dialled their number.

By ten o'clock he'd booked into the hotel, freshened up and, having bought a newspaper, was seated in a tiny Italian café across the road from the Gardens about to order a large cappuccino, when his mobile rang. It could only be Sheila Campbell; she had been with him at Lusaka Airport when he'd bought the phone and had asked him for the number which he hadn't wanted to give her, but as she had made all the arrangements for him to leave the country, he'd felt it would have been churlish to refuse.

He didn't want to talk to her. He had just spent a week as a reluctant guest in her house for God's sake! There was nothing further he wanted to say to her. Against his wishes he had agreed to do as her boss had asked: to feign his own death, to pretend he had perished at the hands of some imaginary thugs and even worse, to be denied contacting the woman he knew he could trust to remain silent if she was asked.

He didn't have to take the call; he could merely switch the thing off, throw it away and buy another one, but he didn't, pressing the button.

'Mr Lorimer, Alan Lorimer?'

'Ye – es?.'

'Sorry to bother you when you've just arrived back in the UK, Alan. I'm Adrian Roberts; I realise Sheila wouldn't have given you my name, but I'd like us to meet, sometime later today if that would be alright. There are a few points I would like to go over with you regarding our investigation, also I would like to thank you personally for your compliance.'

'Well, I've no doubt that you will have heard I haven't been too happy with the situation, but my concern now is for my life to return to normal, although learning about my brother's predicament, it's not going to be too easy.'

'I understand. You've been very patient and believe me when I say it has been much appreciated.'

'Good.' *That's right, Alan, don't give him an inch. Smooth bastard!*

'Perhaps we could meet for a drink later this afternoon; it will only be for a chat, Alan, nothing formal you understand.'

'Alright. Where do you suggest?'

'Somewhere convenient to where you're staying perhaps; either the hotel bar or the nearest pub.'

They agreed to meet at four in the hotel's "Woolf & Whistle" lounge bar and as he brought the call to a close Alan realised that nothing had been said about the outcome of the previous night's operation, that's if there was one, but it could be he was unaware that Sheila, possibly in a moment of weakness for what he'd had to put up with, had mentioned what had sounded to him as a make or break attempt to obtain the irrefutable evidence they needed to apprehend those directly involved at the same time as severing the link to the distribution of the drugs. Perhaps he would learn more from Adrian Roberts, not that he had any interest in the seedy underworld of drug smuggling, even if his brother had become entangled; as he had said to this Roberts guy, all he wanted was to get his life back and even before any demands from his family, his main concern was Cora.

'At last he had a perfect cappuccino topped with a decorative sprinkling of chocolate and once he had taken a couple of sips and allowed the restorative powers of the caffeine to take effect, he pulled the newspaper across the table towards him but without any real interest in what was happening in the world of politics and finance and one glance at the front page only confirmed what he expected: BREXIT debates continuing months after the referendum; an earthquake in the middle east and dire warnings of global warming from scientists on a recent visit to the North Pole. So very depressing he thought, turning to the next page.

## "FRIEND OF MISSING CALDER BAY MAN MURDERED

Readers of this newspaper will by now have become accustomed to reading about Calder Bay, once a small fishing village, placed as it is, nestling in a deep cove between Dundee and Arbroath on Scotland's north-east coast and facing the North Sea. The same readers will also recall the number of times Calder Bay has attracted media attention, but especially more recently with the murder of John Milne, a crime which has yet to be solved. Within a matter of days following the murder, interest in Calder Bay intensified as news reached our country of an incident in Central Africa where Alan Lorimer, a director of "Lorimer' Fruits", an old established family firm based in Calder Bay, was attacked in his bungalow although there was no sign of him at the scene. It is understood that the search for Alan Lorimer is continuing, but it has been generally accepted that he may not have survived.

As John Milne had been employed by "Lorimer Fruits", it is perhaps understandable that questions were being asked whether there was a connection between these incidents. At a press conference last Monday when DCI Alistair Dale was asked to corroborate this suggestion, he declined to answer.

The mystery surrounding the disappearance last Thursday of John Milne's girlfriend, Laura Thomson remains just that: a mystery.

As if all the above, the intrigue, the unanswered questions, the lack of communication from our police, was not enough to concern the people of Calder Bay, this Tuesday news came from the same town in Africa where Alan Lorimer had been living, of the murder of a British national. Steve Burrows was a neighbour of Alan Lorimer and his wife. Only a sceptic surely would insist that the death of this man had no connection with the abovementioned occurrences, that it was a coincidence. It is interesting perhaps to note that the Zambian police have handed this murder enquiry over to the British authorities.

It is to be hoped that these many loose ends can be tied up satisfactorily, and without any further delay, if only to put the minds of the long-suffering residents of Calder Bay at rest.

Beverly Grant

Investigative Journalist"


Steve Burrows is dead! Murdered! When the hell did this happen, he murmured under his breath, skimming through the article to see if it had been mentioned but only that the news of the murder reached the media on Tuesday; presumably via Reuters, therefore Alan reckoned he was killed sometime during that day. He hadn't left Ekabe until two days later therefore it would have already been common knowledge by then. Sheila would have known, but she had said nothing to him. Why hadn't she; but the answer was obvious. She had been told not to.

There was something very odd here he thought, and allowing his coffee to grow cold, he read the article again. He was familiar with Beverly Grant's columns, although it had been some time since he had last read one, English newspapers being in short supply in Ekabe, and had never known her to be so reticent. How was it, Alan wondered, she knew they were his neighbours but apparently didn't know how he was killed. Of course she knew. It was ridiculous to believe otherwise. There had to be a valid reason for what was tantamount to a wall of silence, but he wasn't sure whether he was ready to learn the reason. Not yet. And he made a conscious effort to put a firm hold on to the controlling way his mind was working; he would wait until he met up with Adrian Roberts later when he intended to insist on some answers.

His thoughts turned again to Cora and for the first time felt a niggle of unease that she hadn't been at home each time he phoned. He was likely worrying unnecessarily; his timing had been wrong: she had either been on her way to work or at work. *You are becoming a right old worryguts, Alan. Why shouldn't she be alright; she'll be home later in the afternoon; she will read your message, and know that you're back. And you'll see her this evening and then you can call your father, put the old man's mind at rest.* But he couldn't wait that long to hear her voice, to know she still loved him and picking up his mobile keyed into Google to find the number for the LSE and within a couple of minutes was being put through to their personnel department:

'Good afternoon; how may I help you?'

'I hope you can and I'm sorry to bother you, but I've just arrived back from overseas, and I wondered whether it was possible to speak to Cora Hamilton.'

'You're Alan, aren't you'.

'Well, yes,' taken aback, 'that's right.'

'I'm Paula,' she said, surprising and alarming him at the same time recognizing an edge of concern in her voice, 'Cora should be at home, Alan. Er – she had an accident yesterday morning on her way in - '

' - Is she alright?'

'Yes, she's fine; she phoned from the hospital to say she was waiting for some tests; you know, blood pressure, that sort of thing they always do when you arrive in A&E, and then she intended taking a taxi home.'

'And you really think she's alright, not merely putting on a brave face.'

'No, honestly, Alan; she only sounded a bit shaky, that's all.'

'How did it happen; did she say?'

'Not really; she had a fall, I think it was at the traffic lights near where she lives, but I didn't like to bother her with questions.'

'Of course not. Anyway, Paula, thanks and I'll give her a call now.' and switched off the connection, dismayed to find his hand was shaking. *Get a grip, Alan. She's alright*, but as he dialled her number, he wasn't convinced and as once again the answering machine kicked in, he knew his instincts had been right. His brain, the logical part, failed to convince him. Paula had said the accident happened at the traffic lights, the same ones no doubt he could see from where he was sitting by the window of the café, wondering whether anyone from here had noticed anything. If Cora had been calling Paula from the hospital, there would probably have been an ambulance and, taking his empty cup with him, he went over to the counter.

'Ah, signore, un'altre cappuccino?'

'Please. I understand there was an accident yesterday morning, at the traffic lights – '

' – Si, si! C'era un ambulance – at the lights – many people, students, you know, from altre country!'

'Did any of your customers,' Alan asked him, hoping there had been, 'see when it happened?'

'Si, il signore,' he said lowering his voice and nodding discreetly in the direction of an elderly gentleman seated at a table further along from them, 'he saw signora fall.'

'You are Gino?'

'Si, I am Gino.'

'The lady who had the accident, Gino, was my friend and I want to know what happened.'

'Naturalmente, signore.' passing his coffee to him, 'Your cappuccino is 'on the house'.'

Thanking him, Alan stopped at the table occupied by the man who must have been one of the café's oldest customers.

'She was extremely fortunate you know; that could have turned out to be a very bad accident, fatal even.' he said without any prompting when Alan asked him whether he had witnessed what happened. 'I come into "Gino's" often during the day, the best coffee for miles and I always sit at the same table. I see the young lady every morning.'

'Did she appear to be in a hurry, perhaps not wanting to be late for work.' Alan prompted him.

'No, not at all; walking briskly, you know and there was no reason as far as I could see why she should suddenly fall. Mind you,' he went on, 'there were a load of these foreign students and they were running, trying to get to the end of the road I expect before the lights changed. Young people are extremely impatient.'

'Perhaps they bumped into her.'

'No, nothing like that although one of them did get a little too close to her, right outside this window as a matter of fact, nudged her arm, but he was very polite, and I think he apologised to her.'

'She may have just tripped.'

'Mmm, she could have done I suppose, but she seemed to fall very heavily.'

'And someone called an ambulance?'

'That's right, a young man; he was already at the crossing at the time. Decent of him.'

'Yes, it was. Especially as you say they were mainly young people around.'

'That's true; there was one other adult though, but she didn't stop. To be honest I thought it a bit thoughtless, but then perhaps she was in a rush because she turned round and walked quickly back along the pavement towards the park gates.'

It was as though someone had tightened a chord in his chest, a numbness which for a couple of seconds rendered him speechless. He hated the way his mind was working but was totally incapable of reigning in the horror of his suspicions. He had to find out more. *Ask him only one question, Alan. Don't torture yourself like this. Remember what the old man used to say when you were a kid? Truth will out; once it shows its face, the rest will follow.*

'Had you ever seen her before?' Alan could tell by his bemused expression that it wasn't the question he'd been expecting; he had even surprised himself by asking it, but nevertheless he was eager to hear his reply.

'Now you come to mention it,' he said, 'I had. Twice in fact. The first time was on Wednesday afternoon; she walked past the window, this would have been about half-past five and then again much later. I don't know what time it was, but it was pitch black and I was taking Pixie for her last walk of the day, and she was by the gates to the Gardens; they were closed of course, but she was just standing there. I didn't see her at first almost hidden by the trees; it was Pixie who spotted her, but she didn't seem to notice us. Odd, wouldn't you say.'

'Very.'

# Chapter Nineteen

The call from New Scotland Yard came through to Alistair's office at five-thirty on Friday afternoon as he was on the point of going along to the incident room for the end of the week briefing with the team. He had last spoken to DCI Douglas Howe on Wednesday when Valerie hadn't turned up at Turnhouse airport that morning, a fact which had been no surprise to either of them, resulting in the search for her being intensified, at the same time trying not to attract the media's attention.

'Well, Alistair, playing it low key has played off,' Dougie said, unable to suppress the excitement in his voice, 'Valerie Lorimer literally fell into our laps this morning.'

'Go on.'

'Somehow, she found out that her husband was arriving back today and actually turned up at Heathrow where she was spotted by a couple of uniforms and duly escorted to New Scotland Yard; protesting quite volubly I might add.' he chuckled.

'What did she expect; she must have realised she couldn't continue to remain invisible indefinitely. Incidentally, we weren't aware that Alan Lorimer's ordeal was over and that he was now free to return.'

'We don't know the ins and outs of what happened over there, but it sounds to me that he'd had enough.'

'As simple as that.'

'Possibly, but it could have been that Sheila McIntrye let slip, intentionally or otherwise, about Thursday night being the last chance for the syndicate's handover he decided Interpol's reasons for him remaining were no longer valid, and as we know, all went as planned: Ben Maitland, one of their key operators, and Callum Lorimer, both under arrest and awaiting trial at some time in the unforeseeable future. However, Alistair, back to the wife; she's been questioned under caution and, to give us some time to unravel this mess, is being held in custody for the requisite twenty-four hours, although we have already applied for this to be extended to the thirty-six, and believe me, it is *some* mess!'

'Apart from her being the last person to have been seen with Steve Burrows, presumably there is some evidence which is not circumstantial to substantiate holding her?'

'You and I both know, Alistair what a grey area we're talking about here. There was only one set of prints on the plastic bottle, and they're hers. Also,' he added, 'some silk threads were caught up in the jagged edge at the top of the bottle, possibly from a scarf, and are being DNA tested. I've requested a priority result, but I think we're still talking about Monday at the earliest.'

'How did the interview go then; any ideas of why she would have wanted him dead?'

'None yet. I can't make the woman out, whether she is exceptionally clever or mentally unbalanced. She was giving nothing away, the 'no comment' being her standard response.'

'Television crime series have a lot to answer for, Dougie.'

'You're not wrong, but there's something else which, in retrospect, I'm finding quite ominous.'

'Yes?'

'I had a call from Adrian Roberts a short while ago; he'd just had a meeting with Alan Lorimer, nothing formal, just to make sure there were no hard feelings about him having to lie low for this past week. However, Alan told him about his growing concern for Cora Hamilton - presumably you know about her?'

'Yes, she's not long back from Zambia herself; apparently they met when she was out there on secondment from the LSE.'

'That's right. Well, he's being trying to contact her, but without any success, then, as a sort of last resort, not knowing who else to ask, he phoned LSE and was told that she'd had an accident on her way to work yesterday morning.'

'What sort of accident?'

'Nothing serious apparently, although it could have been a lot worse. She had a bad fall at the traffic lights in Tavistock Square, quite close to where she lives. Someone called for an ambulance, and she was taken to hospital, but she'd phoned into work while she was there and told them that she was fine and would be going home for the rest of the day. Sounds as though she was quite shaken. However, Alan tried her home number again, but continued to get the answering machine and then, thinking he might hear something about what had happened, he went to the little Italian café in the same street and spoke to the owner and a few of his regular customers but, apart from the ambulance, that was all they saw, although there was one of them, an elderly gent; he had been sitting by the window and recalled seeing a woman near to where Cora had fallen and instead of trying to help she had quickly turned away and walked off.'

'Didn't want to get involved I expect.'

'Possibly, but our witness had seen the same woman twice the day before, once walking past the café in the afternoon and the second time much later. It had been dark, and he'd been taking his dog for a walk, and she'd been standing by the gates of Taverstock Gardens directly opposite to Cora Henderson's apartment building.'

'And this woman was Valerie Lorimer.'

'From how he described her, it certainly sounds like her. He was in the café again this afternoon; they were just about to close, but my officer managed to have a chat with him, and he says he would be agreeable to attending an identity parade.'

'How did this accident happen, do you know.'

'Not in any detail, but from putting the bits and pieces together, it appears she fell as she approached the main road at the traffic lights. She was surrounded by a group of students, probably all eager to get across the road before the lights changed, so she could have become caught up in them and lost her balance or - '

' – or she was pushed.'

'Quite.'

'And if this witness does identify the woman as Valerie Lorimer no doubt she'll deny being anywhere near there.'

'I know she will, but then it would only be her word against his.'

'She'll become complacent, Alistair; they always do, sooner or later. Meanwhile, she can spend tonight in the cells, and we will pick up from where we left off tomorrow, hopefully, with a line-up of look-alike Valerie Lorimers for our witness.'

'If it does turn out that she is Valerie Lorimer, while it may suggest that she's been stalking Cora, that's about all it is. Unless someone saw her being pushed, deliberately I mean, any evidence of the intent to harm remains insubstantial, wouldn't you agree'

'Of course I agree, Alistair. And doesn't she know it!'

'I've been wondering.'

'Yes?'

'How did she know that Alan Lorimer would be arriving back today?'

'That's a damn good question; how the hell did she?'

'Would he have told her do you think; phoned her before he left Zambia?'

'I would say that was very unlikely; they were in the process of divorcing, and I get the impression it's not going to be an amicable one. From how Adrian Roberts described him, he was solely intent in contacting his girlfriend, even before calling his family.'

'He would then have tried to phone her, but you said he'd tried several times.'

'And always got the answering machine.'

'So, in that case if she hadn't been at home that message wouldn't have been read.'

'I'm thinking out loud here,' Dougie said, 'just say that the woman our witness saw was Valerie Lorimer and when she'd been hanging about outside Cora's flat, she found out that it was empty – '

' – and broke in; the water bottle under the brake pedal indicates how resourceful the woman is, and once she was inside the apartment she read the message on the answering machine.'

'Highly hypothetical of course.'

'But credible.'

'I can't come up with any other explanation of how she knew, not that it's all that relevant now and unfortunately doesn't bring us any closer to finding more evidence to strengthen the Steve Burrows case.'

'We may very well have reached stalemate, and it will be left for the lawyers to thrash it out between them in court.'

Alistair was thoughtful as they finally brought the call to a close and he headed towards the incident room. Dougie had been right in saying there was something ominous in the way Valerie Lorimer had been acting. Stalking a woman with apparently one aim: to harm her. Details of yesterday's accident remained unclear, also the intent, whether fatal or otherwise. Either way, they needed to find out. Knowing where to start was the problem: the reasons behind both Steve Burrows' death and the attempted murder of Cora Hamilton. There was so much more they needed to know, not only about those involved, but the background of their lives leading up to the situation as it stands right at this moment, but as they were picking up the investigation second-hand this was going to be no easy task. It was very much like being in two places at once: in central Africa, over five thousand miles away, a country with a different culture and government rules, and here, in Britain with the security of familiarity, but somehow, they had to make everything come together and as he'd said to Dougie to ultimately let the courts decide. And he was confident they would.

\*\*\*

The whiteboard in the incident room was a stark reminder of the lack of progress in the John Milne murder enquiry. Only a quick glance was needed to trace the early stages: the door-to-door questioning, the numerous interviews, including repeat interviews, of those who had known him, either at work or socially, diagrams showing where and how they connected, but after the first flurry of police activity there was a significant decline in any new information. The possibility of Superintendent Bob Williams deciding to make an unprecedented appearance almost brought Alistair out in a cold sweat. And, although his inevitable outburst would have been deserved, any protests of the mitigating circumstances he came up with would be dismissed. "Breezy Bob" was well aware of how they had been over-ruled by Interpol, but he wouldn't want to be reminded. He was answerable to the Chief Constable and that was the way things were.

'Right, we've a lot to cover before we finish today.' Alistair said, walking up the room to face the team, 'As you're aware, we are now working in conjunction with New Scotland Yard in the Steve Burrows investigation. Up to now, this has not made any noticeable impact here, but from what I've learned today, this is likely to change. I'll cover those points in a moment, but first I want to stress that we must continue to focus our energies in bringing the John Milne enquiry to a satisfactory conclusion.

'There is no doubt that his murder isn't 'Operation Gemma' related, but Interpol want us to continue, at least for the present, with our own line of enquiry. I realise we have made little progress, but we have covered considerable ground. Dead ends most of them, I know, but at least we've been able to narrow the field as far as possible suspects are concerned.'

'Are you ruling out any of Ben Maitland's mob, sir?'

'Colin!'

'It's alright, Lilian,' Alistair grinned, 'I think we can excuse Colin's venture into gangland jargon, but to answer your question,' he said turning to Colin, 'no, I'm not ruling them out, but I believe it's unlikely. I'm harping back to motive again; whoever broke into John Milne's flat that night knew where he lived and possibly that there was something incriminating inside, perhaps a tape proving "Lorimer Fruits'" involvement, but how did they know? If, for instance, it was a tape, how did they learn of it in the first place? I would say it's fairly safe to say that John only confided in Laura Thomson, even to entrusting her with some form of evidence in the event of anything happening to him. Sweet irony, eh? So, who else knew about this? The rest is all supposition; Bruce Lorimer saw him in the office on the Monday evening after everyone else had gone and he mentioned this to Callum. And Callum, as we have already discussed, passed this on to Ben Maitland. Perhaps we should pause at this point and consider who had the most to lose with the possibility, probably a strong one, of the syndicate's link to "Lorimer Fruits" being revealed?'

'I would say "Lorimer Fruits".' Dan suggested, making a note on the pad in front of him.

'Maitland wouldn't give a damn, once he'd offloaded that last consignment.'

'You're right, Colin,' Lilian put in, 'especially as he had his cruiser for a quick getaway whenever he needed it.'

'Fat lot of good it did him though.' Colin muttered.

'What do you think, sir,' Dan asked Alistair, 'now that, once again, we've arrived back to presumably our first suspect?'

'The picture has become clearer,' he answered, shaking his head wearily, 'in that we may now have a motive, but we still require more in the way of solid evidence. We may suspect Callum Lorimer of murdering his employee, but we have nothing to substantiate it. Nothing. We need to take a closer look at alibis; there could be a link, an overlap which doesn't quite fit, anything in fact which doesn't feel right. Lilian,' he said, 'were you able to neaten up Kirstie's alibi?'

'I spoke to her again, sir and she still says that she left her friend's house at ten o'clock, although too insistent I thought. I didn't go back to speak to Mary Struthers; she was so vague before I think she would quite likely have agreed that it had been ten o'clock and not later. However, I did ask Kirstie where she parked her car that night and that's when she became evasive, saying she always parked in the council's car park.'

'Did you mention about the chap Colin spoke to?'

'I did; that flustered her a bit, but then after a couple of seconds she said there were no free spaces, so she had to find somewhere else.'

'That's surprising; if it had been a Friday or a Saturday night, yes, it probably does get full, but it was a weeknight.'

'I think she realised I didn't believe her; she's not a good liar.'

'So, where did she park?'

'At the back of the "Kinloch Hotel".'

'There's only room for two or three vehicles; it's an apology for a car park.'

'So it might be, Colin,' Lilian reminded him, 'but the "Kinloch's" customers mainly live locally, some of them are quite elderly and don't even drive.'

'I know. I know. Anway, if Kirstie did park there it meant she would have had to do a U-turn and drive back along the High Street.'

'What are you getting at?'

'What I'm getting at *Sergeant* Lilian Woods,' flashing her one of his boyish grins, 'is that she probably noticed John Milne and his girlfriend either leaving the "Shipwreck" or she passed them as they walked along the pavement towards Beach Road.'

'And, yet,' Alaister said, picking up from where he was coming from, 'when first questioned she said she hadn't seen anyone. Strange. There could be another reason for her not parking in the council car park, because I'm finding it difficult to believe it was full. Also, why didn't she find a spot in Beach Road; that's a lot closer than the "Kinloch"?'

'She could have seen someone she knew and wanted to avoid them.'

'That's an interesting point, Lilian. Let us assume for the moment,' he went on thoughtfully, 'that she did leave her friend's place at half-past ten; it would only take minutes to reach the bottom of Green Lane, she may or may not have been held up at the traffic lights, but in either event if John Milne's killer was leaving his flat around that time, she would have seen him.'

'And recognized him.' suggested Dan.

'Alright, disregard for the moment we are only theorizing, and taking into account that for some reason her normal routine that night was different, why hasn't she spoken up.'

'I have an idea.' Lilian tentatively suggested, 'it's no more than guesswork, sir, but Kirstie McKenzie has worked for Graham Lorimer for a long time; she's never married as far as we are aware, therefore if she did recognize the person leaving John's flat as being Callum, I think that out of loyalty towards her boss might have prevented her.'

'Makes sense, sir,' Colin put in quickly, 'it sounds as though she is a creature of habit, therefore it's possible she saw something to make her park somewhere else, or I should I say, someone, why else all the confusion over the time she left her friend's place?'

'Mmm. The theory is a plausible one and worth following up on, and given that Callum Lorimer is currently in custody, she may not feel the same obligation, but - ' pausing for a moment, anticipating his team's reaction. He appreciated their eagerness in taking advantage of their first credible lead, but he had to be cautious: to consider the consequences that if by putting any pressure on Kirstie to admit seeing Callum near John Milne's flat that night, it was questionable whether it would be considered any more than circumstantial evidence, 'I believe we should consider very carefully how we proceed here. I'm not suggesting we shouldn't question her again, even more aggressively this time, but if we are wrong and there is a perfectly reasonable explanation for her movements on the night of the murder, this could have a negative affect on police/public relations.'

'You're right, sir,' Dan agreed, 'and it's unlikely Callum Lorimer will be going anywhere very soon.'

'Which gives us a slight breathing space, although I don't need to remind you that as he is now under arrest for his part in the smuggling offences, we will require new evidence in order to question him, either that or court approval. I suggest therefore we review the situation at our briefing tomorrow. Meanwhile, there have been further developments in the Steve Burrows case which are going to further involve the Lorimer family, although the good news is that Alan Lorimer is now back in Britain.'

'You say Britain,' Colin put in, 'does that mean he hasn't returned here, to his family?'

'Not yet,' Alistair answered, 'he's still in London which brings me to the further developments I mentioned. Valerie Lorimer, his estranged wife, was arrested early this morning, at Heathrow.' he added.

'Was she trying to leave the country then?' Dan asked him.

'Actually, no,' smiling despite the seriousness of it all, 'according to what she told the officer she was there to meet her husband.'

'Why?'

'Exactly, Colin, why? However, thanks to Alan Lorimer doing his bit of detecting we have a fairly clear idea of what she'd been doing in London since she arrived on Wednesday, but not why she would have wanted to meet up with him. The lady declined to elaborate.'

'So, what had she been doing?' Colin asked.

'Stalking Cora Henderson.'

'The girlfriend?' a look of astonishment on Colin's face.

'What strange behaviour.'

'It becomes even more strange, Lilian; if our witness is to be believed, she made an attempt to push Cora on to the main road near where she lives in Bloomsbury. Fortunately, the attempt failed.'

'Is she likely to be charged with attempted murder then?' Colin asked.

'I would say that was debatable. Although the Met will be arranging an identity parade, at the end of the day it wouldn't necessarily be absolute proof. However,' he went on, 'the way evidence is piling up against Valerie Lorimer for Steve Burrow's murder, her future is looking bleak.'

'What a can of worms,' Colin whistled under his breath, 'I wonder how the Lorimer family are faring with this latest blow.'

'In a state of shock, I would say.' Dan put in.

'At least with the return of his son, Graham Lorimer will be much relieved.'

'Of course,' Colin put in, 'the prodigal son – *he was lost, and he is found!*'

\*\*\*

It was a lovely autumn morning: the mist of earlier now a diminishing silver-grey film over the North Sea as Alan changed down gear at the approach to the Tay Road Bridge. Mid-morning, and traffic was light, allowing him a clear run for the remainder of his journey along the coast road north. His hire car from the airport, a Peugeot 2008, was easy to drive and had responded well to the demands on the motorway from the airport, so different to the dun-coloured roads of Zambia's Copperbelt and which he had been so used to for what seemed to him much longer than eighteen months. So much had happened since he and Valerie had first arrived there; he had been looking forward to the new experience: living and working in a country whose culture was so different to his own. He had no idea what Valerie's thoughts had been, but now? Even to think about her filled him with such an anger, the intensity of which shocked him. That the woman he had been married to for fifteen years could have been capable of committing a crime of any kind was abhorrent to him, but what really enraged him, feeling his hands tightening on the steering wheel, was her attempt to harm Cora. The fact that she didn't succeed made no difference. She could have.

Soon, in less than an hour, he would be arriving at Ashburn House and Cora would be waiting for him. The relief when he'd heard her voice the night before was indescribable, even although when he had finally decided to phone his father, he had not begun to seriously worry about not being able to get hold of her, but perhaps, subconsciously after hearing about how close he could have been to losing her, he was believing the worse. He would never have imagined that while he had been trying to call her, she had been on her way to Ashburn House to spend the weekend with his family, and when she had explained, it all sounded so likely, so logical.

"I'd been so desperately worried about you," she'd said, 'and there was no-one I could talk to, not even Kate when she phoned me had sounded positive, but I think she was just echoing what everyone else in Ekabe was saying, and then I spoke to Myra and then to your father. He felt so strongly that you were still alive," she'd gone on, and he could tell in the way her voice trembled that she was close to tears, "he didn't hesitate, you know, Alan, and told me to come here."

"And thank God you did, my love. I'll have another word with the old man before we ring off."

"Okay, and Alan?"

"Yes?"

"I love you." she whispered.

"I love you too, my darling Cora, and I'm so sorry for what you've been going through - '

"Ssh, we're safe now." and she had passed the phone over to him. His father had sounded different, older in the way his voice wavered slightly and if he didn't know him better, he would say that the man who had brought him up to be as fearless as himself, was crying. *And is it any bloody wonder? He's been in mental limbo for almost two weeks being told by the authorities that his son had perished in Central Africa, and then less than twenty-four hours ago, learned that his other son was in police custody with a charge of drug dealing hanging over his stupid head.*

He had mixed feelings about his brother. They were polar opposites but that was no reason why they had never been close, not even in the early days before Callum had gone off to boarding school. Callum, the eldest, always ready to pick a fight and then in later years, equally quick to find fault. He had hoped when Myra came along and after a surprisingly short time – for hesitant, stick-in-the-mud Callum that is - he had married her. For a few years, they rubbed along alright, but then the old Callum re-emerged and this time a stream of bitterness had appeared distorting his edgy personality. No amount of analysing his brother's psyche and to understanding why he should have fallen foul of the law in the dramatic way he had, gave him an answer.

He was now almost home and driving past the familiar sights: the ancient Norman church with its neat lines of deeply engraved headstones in the cemetery and shielded from the road by hedges thick with dark purple brambles; the grey-stoned primary school, those hedges now replaced by black wrought-iron railings along the whole length of the building to the start of the high street with its shops and cafés. He caught brief glimpses of the sea from each road on his right leading down to Beach Road, and as he turned left before the road curved to sweep around the bay, he soon left the town behind, and he was on the last stretch which would take him to Ashburn House. The gates were open, and he swept through, tyres crunching on the gravel drive as he finally pulled up in front of the house, and there she was: Cora, looking as lovely as ever, her blonde hair tied loosely back from her face. He wanted to hold on to this moment, prevent it from escaping, and for a fraction of time he remained, motionless, his hand half-raised to open the car door. And then, as if in slow motion, the illusion cleared, and he was running up the steps to take her in his arms.

'Hello, son.' his father, waiting in the shadows of the hall, greeted him solemnly, 'it's good to have you back home.'

'It's good to be back, dad,' he answered, 'I'm sorry for all the worry and stress this has all caused you.'

'Not your fault, Alan, not your fault; you're home now and that's all that matters.' his voice gruff as he ushered them both inside and across the hall to the lounge where the log fire had been lit, flickering orange flames transforming the dark-panelling and high ceilings of the room the family rarely used, preferring the west-facing dining room on the other side of the building. Drinks and a selection of savoury bites he noticed had been laid out on the sideboard, a little taken aback that such an effort had been made for his return.

'Alan,' Myra moved away from where she had been standing by the window and walked towards him, her arms outstretched in welcome, 'we have been so very worried about you. Are you alright; no ill-effects from your ordeal?'

'I'm fine, Myra.' kissing her on the cheek.

'Really?'

'Really.' he reassured her, at the same looking at his sister-in-law closely, but apart from appearing paler than usual, she wasn't showing any signs of the turmoil she must be going through, but decided it might be best not to mention Callum. He would leave that for one of the others.

'Alan! Old boy, I thought I could hear your dulcet tones,' Bruce, grinning widely, strode into the room and flung his arms round his shoulders.

'Whoa! Steady on, you're strangling me!'

'Great to see you; expect you have loads to tell us about your adventure in the wilds of the African jungle!'

'You don't change, do you?'

'I sincerely hope not.'

'Come on, Bruce,' Myra interrupted, 'perhaps you can dispense the drinks. What would you like, Cora?'

'A gin and tonic would be lovely.'

'Right, madam,' Bruce moved quickly across to the sideboard, 'a G&T coming up. Dad, a whisky?'

'Please, Bruce. If you'll excuse me for a moment, I'm just going to make sure Kirstie is intending to finish up in the office; she's been working non-stop all morning.'

To an onlooker, Alan thought fifteen or twenty minutes later having had their drinks topped-up and his father had rejoined them, and to someone who didn't know his family, there would be nothing in the scene unfolding in front of him to give any indication of how the very substance of what his father, and grandfather, had spent their working lives creating "Lorimer Fruits", was in danger of becoming eroded through the irresponsible and selfish actions of Callum. It was, he reckoned, too early to tell what the actual outcome would be. There would be two factors, both reflective of the other: a tarnished reputation would trigger lack of confidence in the marketplace where, in a snowball effect, share prices would drop. Like a pack of bloody cards.

But there they were: his family, whether intentionally or not, valiantly giving the appearance of normality, exchanging small talk over pre-luncheon drinks. Cora had said little as they'd come into the room, and he could sense her unease; the bemused expression on her face as she appeared to only half-listen to what they were saying. Was his father really interested in the price difference of petrol at the garage in Calder Bay from Sainsbury's: a good five miles out of town? And he was damn sure Myra couldn't possibly be concerning herself whether everyone would remember to put all the clocks back next morning. A poorly scripted stage play and Cora and he reluctant members of an invisible audience. How long, he wondered, feeling his tension building-up, did they intend to continue with this farce, because that's what it was. What the hell was the matter with them? Cora, slipping her hand into his and squeezing it gently, calmed him. She understood. He had recognised how naturally she could empathize with a person finding themself in an awkward situation from almost when they had first met. He could even recall exactly when it was:

There had been a crowd of them in the club; a Saturday night, and the recent casting for Noel Coward's "Blithe Spirit" was being discussed when Peggy Bovington had scathingly remarked that Sally's northern twang was totally wrong for the part; whether she had been aware that Sally was standing right behind her, was he had thought at the time, debatable but to his surprise, Cora had immediately jumped to Sally's defence. "Really, Peggy," she had said to her, "as a *girl* from Essex, are you really qualified to denigrate a person's accent." Apart from a brief silence during which Peggy made a noticeable effort to recover from her injured pride, conversation around the bar soon resumed. He had been impressed by the way Cora had reacted to Peggy's rudeness, noticing the watery smile on Sally's face as she silently mouthed a thank-you.

Recalling those days in Ekabe and the easy camaraderie among the fellow expats where invariably all they had in common was the fact that they were expatriates: transient people who had chosen to live outside the confines of family life and who, now looking back, made him aware that he shouldn't ignore the comfort of continuity among people he had known all his life where there was always time to make amends, mend a fractured friendship and not among the indifference of the expatriate community when their time together was too short to hold grudges. They really didn't have much of a choice: they had to get on with each other. Even Peggy, after a large G&T had humbled herself by apologising to Sally. Perhaps, therefore, he should not be so judgemental towards his family. *Too right, Alan. What do you expect them to say? They've already made it clear to you that they're relieved you're back home. What the hell more can they say? They are already now aware of the reason why you were prevented in leaving Ekabe. As far as mentioning Valerie, it could be they are merely too embarrassed.*

'I know about Valerie being a prime suspect for Steve Burrow's murder.' he said breaking a lull in the conversation, 'Also,' he added, aware of his lips tightening with the return of the anger, 'her attempt on Cora's life.'

'I won't be pressing charges, Alan.'

'I didn't think you would be, but I felt it should be mentioned.'

'I'm not sure I agree with you, remaining silent, I mean.' Bruce surprising him. 'One more nail in her coffin once they find her.'

'They already have, Bruce.' he answered, 'Yesterday morning in fact; she was arrested at Heathrow and is currently in custody.'

'Good God,' his father gasped, 'she's been charged?'

'Yes, Dad.'

'With this chap Steve's murder?'

'Yes.'

'The disgrace of it all.' Myra murmured, her voice barely audible. 'Another one - how is the family going to survive all of this scandal?'

'My dear, Myra,' his father moved quickly towards her, placing an arm around her shoulders which were rigid with despair, and knowing the stoicism of his sister-in-law realised she was doing her utmost not to lose control, 'we will get through this, trust me.'

'How can you be so sure?' her voice little more than a whisper as she leaned against him, her head turned away from the others.

'Because I've been around long enough to believe the family will pull through. I'm not under-estimating the seriousness of the situation, but that's the situation today, Myra, not necessarily tomorrow.'

'Some will find it extremely difficult to forget, Dad.'

'Well, Bruce, that's their prerogative; we have a family business to run, and I have no intention of being intimidated by a bunch of damned pessimists.'

Graham meant every reassuring word he had said to Myra. Certainly, Valerie now under arrest for murder with every likelihood of finally being convicted, added more smoke to the proverbial fire, but her crime had no connection with the company; the murder of the poor fellow had taken place thousands of miles away, and apart from the possibility of her name being linked by marriage, while it might add the bit of spice apparently required by the media to sell their newspapers, he didn't seriously consider her offence all that damaging to them. It might even gain them sympathy.

The focus, when the news of Callum's arrest hits the national press, was going to be the real issue. Inspector Alistair Dale had for once when they'd spoken earlier, had been more informative when he had been outlining the charges. "I'm not going to downplay the gravity of the charges brought against your son, Mr Lorimer;" he'd said, "being in possession of Grade A drugs with intent to distribute, also falsifying corporate records, carry heavy fines and frequently long-term prison sentences."

"I fully understand, Chief Inspector."

And he did understand. He also knew that Callum was guilty of much worse. The shame of those charges as described by the officer was far less devastating than the one of murder. He didn't know why Callum had so brutally taken that young man's life. He had no wish to know. The knowledge, although with no proof was, as far as he was concerned, enough. John Milne had been murdered by his son. As for the reason, again he wished to remain in ignorance. He'd had his suspicions from the beginning: Callum's surliness, his negative attitude and reluctance to delegate even the most mundanc of tasks and the secretive way he moved away when taking calls on his mobile, but the most telling were what appeared to be an inordinate number of times the police were visiting, even on one occasion, according to Myra, when he'd been interviewed down at the police station. That had been on Tuesday, the same day their Inspector Aitken was here interviewing Bruce, and that was the last any of them had heard any mention of John Milne. Alistair Dale hadn't mentioned the case yesterday; their conversation had only been concerned with Callum's involvement with some drug smuggling syndicate. He'd said nothing about a return visit from any of his officers; this time there had been two of them, not to speak to Bruce again, but to further question Kirstie.

He had seen the blue and yellow markings of the police car disappearing at the end of the drive from the landing window. Alan had arrived only minutes later, and he had reached the hall to greet him as he was pulling up outside the front door. Ill at ease and wanting to know the outcome of yet another visit from the police he had made his excuses to have a quick word with Kirstie before she went home.

She hadn't been in her office, the smaller one adjoining his own, but standing at the open window of the hospitality lounge on the mezzanine floor; she must have heard his approach, noticing the way she slowly pulled her shoulders back before turning round.

"I saw the police car, Kirstie," he'd said, walking over to join her, "what did they want?"

She had taken so long to reply, he was beginning to think she wasn't going to, but with a deep sigh, she lifted her head and looked at him steadily before she spoke: "There were two officers this time," she said, "the same woman as before, DS Wood, and the inspector."

"DI Aitken." helping her.

"Yes, DI Aitken," she repeated, "I found him quite aggressive."

"In what way?"

"He kept asking me if there was anything I wanted to change in the statement I gave them earlier."

"This is about your alibi, I presume?"

"Yes; about the time I left my friend's house. I'd already told Sergeant Wood that I'd left at ten, but he persisted that I could have been mistaken, that it was nearer to half-past."

"Why should he think that?" puzzled, unable to come up with one possible reason, but there was something in Kirstie's manner which told him she knew why.

"I'm not sure," giving her shoulders a slight shrug, "he didn't say. And then he went on and on about me saying I hadn't seen anyone on my way home that night. I kept telling him that I'd already confirmed that when I was questioned by the sergeant."

"And had you seen someone?" he had asked her quitely.

Although she didn't look away, she remained silent.

"Kirstie?"

"Mmm."

"Did you see someone?" he repeated, lowering his voice even more although none of the others would have been able to hear them. It was at that precise moment that any doubts he may have still been harbouring evaporated, and he answered his own question, "You saw Callum, didn't you?"

She had nodded, her expression troubled as she had looked at him, "I didn't change my statement, Graham. It was very dark that night, and foggy in patches; I needed all my concentration on driving which meant of course I had to keep my eyes on the road."

There was so much he could have said to her, but he couldn't think of any words which would adequately express his gratitude. That she had perjured herself didn't sit well with his conscience, but Kirstie knew him too well; she knew that for the family to become publicly tainted with murder would destroy him. Now, he had the strength to continue, take more of a back seat perhaps; it was something he had wanted to do for some time, but the growing unease and doubts over Callum had held him back.

He hadn't said any more to her, except to tell her to go home and not to worry. They would talk again on Monday if she wanted to.

\*\*\*

Saturday night. Only half-way through the evening and already the "Shipwreck" bar was packed. Even with a couple of extra staff, Ken Morris was struggling to cope with an inordinate number of thirsty customers clamouring to be served. Beverly, coming into the bar from the hotel's reception, recognized a few familiar faces: Jenny and Patsy from the bank, the couple from the newsagents, Joyce giving her a cheerful wave, and in their usual place at the end of the bar, the three regulars, full tankards of beer arranged in a neat line in front of them, their attention momentarily distracted when they spotted her. In all the times she had seen them they had never exchanged words, not even a nod of recognition. Beverly, by this time, knew her place: she was a visitor to Calder Bay, albeit a fairly regular one, but in their eyes, she was a stranger, a fact she used to her advantage, and she didn't think she was going to be disappointed this evening judging by their animated conversation and for once their beers remaining untouched.

'I heard he was back.'

'Who?'

'Do I have to spell it out,' Ed, 'they might not want it to be common knowledge yet.'

'I suppose you mean the Lorimer boy.'

'Aye, that's right,' the one she remembered was called Bill answered.

'Strange business.'

'Aye.'

'At least he's back home safe and sound.'

'That's more than can be said about his wife.'

'What about her?'

'She's been arrested.'

'Where did you hear that?'

'On the news, at six o'clock.'

'That's bad,' Ed put in, shaking his head, 'so what they've been saying in the papers was right then, about her being wanted for questioning for the murder of that man in Africa I mean.'

'Funny that?'

'Can't say that there's anything funny about murder, Jack.' Bill frowned at him over the rim of his now half-empty tankard.

'I don't mean it like that; I was thinking it odd that they've printed all that about a murder which happened thousands of miles away and they haven't said a word about Alan Lorimer coming back or what happened to him over there.'

'All hush hush, I expect.' wiping the froth of beer from the ends of his moustache and gesturing over to Ken Morris for a refill.

'You mean MI6?' making a poor attempt to keep his voice down, not that he needed to worry, Beverly thought looking around: no-one was taking any notice of them, concerned only with enjoying Saturday night in their local.

'Come to think of it,' Jack put in, aligning his empty glass next to Bill's, 'you could be right; his disappearance could be what the police call sensitive information.'

'You mean like drug smuggling?'

'Ssh; keep your voice down, man.'

'Nobody's listening.'

'Maybe not, but you can't be too careful coming out with remarks like that.'

Beverly, about to take the first sip of her vodka and tonic, paused as realisation dawned. Of course! It had taken three old codgers to penetrate the fog she had been struggling with right from the beginning of this investigation; there was a big picture here, much more than the break-in at Alan Lorimer's bungalow and his disappearance, both of which the police had refused to admit there was any connecting link with the murder of John Milne. And then, with the murder of a man with no apparent connection with "Lorimer Fruits", she had allowed herself to become sidetracked. She might be none the wiser, but she was somewhat gratified that she had listened to her instincts and decided to make yet another visit to Calder Bay. The Metropolitan Police may well be handling the Steve Burrows' case, but Beverly was convinced that this was where it all started: a parochial little town on Scotland's east coast and was where it would end.

The pensioners had now moved their deliberations on to the unsolved murder of John Milne when her mobile rang. Seeing Andy's name come up on the screen, her inclination was to ignore it, but knowing how persistent he was, she moved away from the bar towards the door to reception before answering.

'Andy.'

'What a noise; are you at a party or something, Bev?'

'Good evening to you, Andy, and no, I'm not partying. I'm in a pub.'

'Oh, well, can you go somewhere quieter?'

Back in reception, apart from a couple booking in, she had the place to herself and now that the communicating door was closed, only the muffled sounds of raised voices and laughter could be heard coming from the bar.

'That better?' she asked him.

'News filtered through from Reuters about half an hour ago which will no doubt surprise you;' he began in his characteristic direct way, 'Callum Lorimer is under arrest.'

'Since when?'

'To be precise, Bev, twenty-one hundred hours on Thursday.'

'Why on earth has it taken so long to filter through?' her mind instantly latching on to what she'd been thinking only minutes ago, 'What are the charges, Andy; drug offences?'

'What are you, psychic!'

'No, not psychic exactly,' unable to keep the smile from her voice, 'just something I happened to overhear.'

'When?'

'About ten minutes ago.'

'Beverly, what the hell are you playing at – and where the hell are you?'

'Andy, for goodness sake, calm down. I'm in Calder Bay for the weekend.'

'What!'

'Andy,' she warned him, 'I am a free agent remember; I don't need your approval.'

'Okay. Okay. Point taken, but why, I thought you'd finished up there, especially now with the arrest of Valerie Lorimer.'

'As to why, well I'm not quite sure. Call it a gut feeling. And now, with what you've just told me, it sounds as if I was right. What exactly has Callum Lorimer been charged with?'

'With possessing and distributing Class A drugs, also the falsification of company records. He's also suspected of being part of an internationally operated drug smuggling syndicate and one which has been under investigation by Interpol for the last year and a half.'

'He can expect a heavy sentence. Another blow for the Lorimer family.'

'Ah, well,' Andy chucked, 'there's always one, isn't there?'

'One what?'

'Bad apple.'

'Very droll, Andy. Anyway, more to the point, what's the situation with regard to us; is there likely to be restrictions in our reporting?'

'They haven't issued a media blackout as such,' Andy went on to explain, and sounding much calmer now, 'but those restrictions mean we can only report facts as seen and heard; in other words, no investigating, Bev.'

'I see, it's to be expected I suppose, but what about the unsolved murder of John Milne? Has any mention been made of him, I wonder.'

'Not as far as I'm aware. Could have been swept under the carpet, in a manner of speaking of course.'

'Of course. And you think that's acceptable, Andy?'

'Politics.'

'One word, eh. Forget about it. Just like that.'

'I wouldn't have you down as a moralist, Bev.' his voice half-mocking, making it impossible for her to read him.

'I'm a realist. I believe in justice.'

'Let the punishment fit the crime?'

'I'm serious.'

'I know you are.'

'There's a story there, Andy and it's waiting to be told - '

' - leave it, Bev.'

'Why should I; don't you care that the murder of an innocent young man is being ignored, abandoned to some shelf in police archives, a file marked *Cold Case*, to be opened every eighteen months or so, an obligatory read-through, check facts and figures collected at the time, only to be put back on that shelf.'

'You're not a detective.'

'I know. I am an investigative journalist, and I have the freedom to investigate as I feel fit; that's what I'm good at, Andy.'

'There's nothing I can say which will persuade you to change your mind, is there?'

'No, there isn't. I have a damn good idea who killed John Milne, and I will do my utmost to prove it and ultimately expose him.'

Other titles by Margaret Alty:

*Tangled Web*

*Search for the Lion*
A sequel to *Tangled Web*

*Jenny*

*Camouflage*

*The Last Orange*

*A Reflective Image*

*Chasing Shadows*

*The Infinity Juggler*

A Meadowbank Mystery

*Murder in Meadowbank*

*Double Act*

*Murder After Hours*

*A Gathering of Crows*

*The Circus Comes To Meadowbank*

*A Disturbing Element*

A Calder Bay Mystery

*Carbisdale*

*Pass the Parcel*
A sequel to *Carbisdale*

All published by arima Publishing.